2023

The Fall of an Empire

by

Abel Cain

2023: The Fall of an Empire
© 1999-2008 by Abel Cain

Visit www.2023TheFallofanEmpire.com

ISBN: 978-0-615-26277-2

2023

The Fall of an Empire

by

Abel Cain

Your feedback, comments, notes and thoughts are welcomed:
abelcain@2023thefallofanempire.com
or on Lulu.com at
http://www.lulu.com/content/4756095

For the woman that taught me not only the power of words, but how to discern the difference between when a man's silence is demonstrating consent, contempt or respect for the people and world around him.

My Mother, Carol

Chapters

I.	The Unholy Trinity	8
II.	Viva Los Derechos	35
III.	When In Rome	56
IV.	Enter the Northwest	75
V.	Queen's Pawn to E4	128
VI.	On the Island of Misfit Toys	147
VII.	The Art of War	170
VIII.	Surrender Your King	186
IX.	Ink and Paper	224
X.	The Sword and The Shield	241
XI.	It Takes a Village	267
XII.	The Guff Is Empty	281
XIII.	The End of Love	302
XIV.	Wormwood	321
XV.	When Iron Birds Fly	336
XVI.	Trail of Tears	405
XVII.	Mate In Three	425
Epilogue		440

The Unholy Trinity

"We were at war for a long time... we just didn't know it."

"How can a whole country be at war, and not know it, George? Are *we* at war?"

"It's not that simple any more."

For a moment the two men sat quietly, making their own observations of the space and people around them, each, completely unaware of what the other was thinking. Ronald stared down at the small wooden table in front of him. It was their regular seat. Third table from the back left corner of the small local bar they had frequented since college. He pushed his bar nap around discovering, as if for the first time, the carvings scarred in the wood. "VIVA EL INITIATIVO. DERECHOS! NW 4-EVER. GO HOME, MOJADO! UNITE... and more." He sipped his bourbon and watched the amber liquid swirl in the glass, slowly melting the ice, as it formed the calming liquid he had come to rely on for comfort.   Leaning back into his barstool, avoiding eye contact with his friend, he concentrated on the deep scrawlings. Each etching offering a small glimpse into the minds of those who had, on some occasion, taken the time to widdle their hatreds. As his body began to accept the familiar numbing he allowed the alcohol to speak for him. "I just can't believe you're going to pack up everything, and take Caroline and the kids up to live with those damn nuts in the Northwest? You're really gonna pack it all up and walk away so you can be around a bunch of crazy white people?"

"I don't think they're crazy."

"For Christ sake, George, they've declared war against your own country and you don't think that's nuts?"

"I need the work, and it's not a 'war.' They're just against *The Initiative*. Can't you see? It's not *our* country anymore!"

"Yeah, that's the whole problem with you people isn't it?"
An uncomfortable silence.

"Right now all I want to do is make sure my family is safe. Caroline is so damn scared living here that she never leaves the apartment. Alli can't even go to school anymore. It's too dangerous for her." George furled his brow as he swirled his drink in his hand and concentrated on the ice, as though he was expecting answers to magically appear in the cubes. "Hell, Ronald, I have to look over my shoulder walking up to the apartment to make sure I don't get swarmed and beat down by a bunch of little punks that have nothing better to do than beat up the only white boy in the neighborhood. I'm a freakin' trophy, and I know it. I can't make a living off of what I earn here. We barely get by. "
George signaled the waitress for another round.

Ronald shook his head at what he felt was an exaggeration of circumstances. "I'll tell you what it is... it's super sized *'white flight.'* Do you even hear what you're saying? Man, I thought I knew you." Ronald, still shaking his head in disbelief, was unsure of what else to say.

Suddenly, George challenged "Have you even *read* The Initiative?"

"I've heard about it. Who hasn't? I've also heard that for the first time in history Canada's manned her borders... to keep you people out. The goddamn British Air Force is flying with orders to shoot on sight and you think the same herd of militia groups that

Canada's worried about can keep you and your family safe? Get you a job? Make everything alright for you? "

"There's work in Portland. I don't have a choice. Besides, Canada's manned her borders to keep *everyone* out, not just the Command. They don't want to end up like this."

George was decided.

"We're a melting pot. We always have been. It's gonna take little while for all of this to settle, but it will... eventually. *We've* dealt with it for a hell of a lot longer than you have. " Ronald countered, trying to appeal to reason.

George ignored Ronald's comment as the waitress dropped off two fresh drinks. Eyeing lipstick on the rim of his glass he paused for a moment then gently smudged it clean with his thumb and wiped the hot pink smear on his pants, too tired to complain. Looking into the eyes of his friend, now showing signs of the years that had passed, George pleaded.

"I can't take that chance. I'm taking my family the hell out of the south and I'm heading north where I know we'll be safe."

Ronald smirked, laughing under his breath, as he raised his glass towards George, as if to toast his sentiment. George glared, momentarily failing to realize the implication.

"As the old saying goes, my friend: *It's a black thing. You wouldn't understand.*"

George took a moment to digest the comment. Maybe it was the alcohol, or the impending move; his mind began to race as issues, normally carefully avoided, entered the conversation and his tone grew increasingly sarcastic. "You know, it's all of those little jabs that brought us where we are today. It doesn't matter what *we* do everything has to be an issue doesn't it? You know, slavery ended 175 years ago! But no one would let it die! You think life in Africa would be so great? It's not like you'd be living it up over there right now. Eighty percent of the continent's dead or dying. Hell, they've stopped burying the dead, 'cause the living are too weak to do it! "

Ronald took a deep breath trying to process the sudden, unexpected assault. Regaining his composure, he glanced over at George's tense expression and argued, in a stern, quiet tone. "Because the *white owned* pharmaceutical companies wouldn't give them the medicine. They let little babies die, because they wanted to not only kill us off, but they wanted to profit off it, too."

George rolled his eyes. "Yeah. *Give* them the medicine. God forbid anyone get a job and work for the money, like I have to!"

"Like *you* have to? You have no idea what its like to be black in this country... or anywhere else, for that matter. You know it was easy for white people to sit there and judge when *their* neighborhoods weren't being flooded with drugs and alcohol. When the government's not creating diseases to kill off *your* people. Look at yourself! You're moving your family in with a bunch of racist crackers that have armed themselves to the teeth and told everyone darker than a peanut to stay the hell out! You're putting your kids in the middle of a war zone run by a bunch of trigger happy militia groups that would sooner shoot me than sit here. What would you call it?"

"It's not about color, it's about The Initiative."

"You keep telling yourself that, man. It's a war and it's just as much about color as anything else! It's *always* been about color. You think this company in Portland would hire *me*, George? Answer *that*... no, wait! *You* don't *have* to, the answer is no. They'd take one look at me and the answer would be no. You *know* it!"

George's face begged for empathy, but the lines between them were clear. "I'm *living* in a war zone, now! Half my check goes to pay taxes to help support people that are too lazy or too cracked up to work and now they want more. And they'll want more still! I'm tired of it, Ronald! *I want out!* I can't get ahead! It's not a war, it's... it's... civil disobedience. Listen, just because Oregon and Montana refused to disarm that doesn't make them *wrong*! *Their* streets are safe. *They're* not going to let the gangs run their cities."

"No, civil disobedience isn't penning yourself in a prison where a bunch of gun nuts roam the streets enforcing their own version of the law. Civil disobedience is about freedom and equality and fighting for your rights. You're fighting for segregation. What *my* people fought *against*! It's what we *died* for! You don't run away from that! You stand and you fight, and eventually everything will work itself out." Ronald's voice grew with his frustration.

George stared down at his hand flexing his fist then turned to Ronald with almost no expression, demanding understanding. "How far has *it* gotten *you*? Look at this country. Look at us."

"What?" Ronald asked knowing their conversation was about to reach the point of no return.

"Civil rights." George paused for a second, almost hesitant about the words that had just fallen from his lips and unable pick them up from the table. He tried to explain,

"What difference did it really make? It's not *equal* when one group has more privileges than another, Ronnie."

"Now, wait just a damn minute! You have the nerve to sit there and talk about all these *grand* concessions that you've made as a *white* man, and you call yourself my friend, but you have *no* idea what it's like to live in this skin! White people take credit for granting us civil rights, like your sitting at the right hand of God or something.... but then you always have that to hold over us. *Don't you*? That self doubt that sits in the center of every black man's mind. Like we weren't good enough to get a job or an education on our own. Let me tell you something, I *earned* my education and I *earned* my career and there isn't *anyone* that's gonna sit there and tell me different. Not even you."

"Where the hell did *that* come from?" George looked over to his friend, stunned by his reaction and unable to understand his motive.

Ronald stared back, frustrated. "I'm not telling you to deal with it, I'm telling you the way you're going about it is wrong. You're helping someone else's agenda and you're going to end up on the losing side. And at what cost? You're fighting the friggin' United States of America, for God's Sake! Can't you see you *can't* win?"

"You're right! I *can't* win! I can't win, *here*!"

The angered tone of their conversation had drawn the attention of the faces around them. Suddenly aware of their surroundings, the men fell silent hoping the room would lose interest.

George rubbed his eyes, looking up toward the lights of the dimly lit tavern, as if he was searching for guidance in the dirty ceiling fixtures. A trapped roach crawled around, frantically pondering escape from the small dusty globe that hung above them. He watched it flounder, struggling with death, unable to escape the heat.

Ronald looked down at his glass and then turned his attention back to George. Trying to remember a time when they both saw the world through less clouded eyes, but he couldn't get away from the feeling that he was looking into the eyes of a stranger.

"Are *you* gonna pick up a gun, George? Who are you going to kill to further someone else's cause?"

"That's not funny! No one's being killed!"

"Really? Leticia's cousin? The Banker in Seattle? No one's heard from him in three months! *Three* months! What happened to *him*, George?! I'll tell you, even if the media won't. Your damn 'gun nut' buddies is what happened!"

"I don't believe that for one second. For all you know he's sittin' in some gutter somewhere with a crack pipe. Or maybe he just wanted to get away from that psycho wife of his or those obnoxious little ingrate kids of theirs? There's a million scenarios! *You don't know*!"

Ronald's voice grew increasingly defensive, "Oh, I see. Because he's *black* it has to be drugs, or infidelity, or..."

"That's *not* what I said! Oh my God!"

"It's what you were thinking!"

"You have no idea what I'm *thinking*."

Ronald paused and stared for a brief moment. His resentment grew equally in proportion with his agreement with George's assessment. "You're right. I *don't* know what you're thinking. I don't even know who you *are* anymore! You're just as racist as the rest of those crackers out west. I'm sure you'll fit in just fine."

Ronald stood up as George sat in his chair trying to figure out where their conversation had fallen apart. George began to get up from his barstool as Ronald snatched up the bill then reached for his wallet. Speaking in a tone he had never before used to address his friends, he quipped "No, no... don't get up! I'm just gonna go home. Maybe eat some fried chicken, a few slices of watermelon, get drunk on some malt liquor, and beat my wife for a while... does that about sum up all of your little stereotypes?"

"Ronny, wait..." George tried to appeal to reason, but there was no hope and the alcohol prevented him from finding the right words.

Ronald defiantly slapped a $50.00 bill on the table. He looked George straight in the eye then started to turn away. He took a step and stopped, not looking back, as he posed one more question to the door before walking out."

"Let's say it *is* a war, George. Standing with all of those white boys, would you see past the color of my skin before you pulled the trigger? Or, would you rather see me dead, then have to admit that your best friend was a black man?"

George looked over to Ronald unsure of the right answer to his question. His eyes fell to the floor for a second as he struggled for a verbal escape. Ronald shook his head, not allowing time for a response, "That's what I thought!"

Ronald pushed open the door, pausing for a split second before crossing the threshold, as if he was hoping George would have something else to say. Those few unknown words that could salvage their friendship.

But there was nothing.

George looked over at the empty glass across from him. He had noticed when Ronald stopped at the door, but either his pride or lack of words kept him from chasing after another man like some heartbroken schoolgirl.

Past mistakes and decades of unanswered questions had left people of different races unable to speak to one another, on too many levels. In their minds it was simply easier to avoid those topics, just as the generations before them had. And both Ronald and George had done just that, very successfully, for over twenty years. But, even a peek into the modern political Pandora's Box was enough to break the strongest bonds.

The modern divisions that America was facing were far more complicated than just race alone. Politics, religion, legal issues and language had all but torn the country in pieces. Close friendships, even marriages, were no exception.

An obvious process of self segregation.

Of course, looking back, that had been going on for over half a century but no one seemed to pay it much attention. Perhaps the politicians of yesteryear couldn't foresee the ripple effect that would eventually pass on from the more subtle divisions of small town America, to the total division of many states, and finally, the United States as a whole. Conceivably, other countries did, and were just waiting to reap the spoils.

Hostilities stretched far beyond the North American Continent.

In the words of long gone great warrior, "All war is deception." Americans could not possibly have known that the self imposed destruction of their country, was nothing more than another nation's carefully crafted plot that they had unknowingly participated in carrying out. Ultimately, it would result in not only the loss of The United States but it would change the political landscape of the world forever. And, eventually, a new standard would fly high on the flagpoles where the Stars and Stripes once proudly waved.

As the years marched on the country found itself suffering huge economic losses. Crime and drug use were on a steady rise, as jobs became more and more scarce and the middle class slowly dwindled away; drawing clear divisions between rich and poor America and leaving many devastated with their own side of the fence. Noveou riche families of the late twentieth century now found they could no longer afford to maintain their high mortgage payments or the luxury lifestyle to which they had become accustomed. Repossessions and foreclosures were rampant. Banks closed, unable to find buyers for the paper mansion properties on which they, themselves, had once placed such high values.

The price of gasoline soared to over $8.50 per gallon and in 2016 the Federal Government was bombarded with cries for action, as the average American was now burdened with paying over $800 per month, just to commute to work. Many simply left their careers unable to justify the cost. The price of food and basic goods rose through the roof, and long established businesses failed at an alarming rate.

Major employers, including the nation's largest retailer, began closing stores and laying off workers by the tens of thousands in an attempt to stay afloat. Automotive companies followed suit, along with the country's two largest soft drink manufacturers. Unions crumbled, unable to represent the workers that faithfully paid their dues. It was no longer about fair pay. There simply was not enough work.

In the same year, the US toyed with the idea of revaluing the Dollar but feared an unfavorable ranking in the international market. They then tossed around the idea of joining in on the Euro system, as Canada had in 2011 but nervously abandoned that idea when neither the Republican or Democratic parties could agree. Americans were sentimental about the Dollar. Religious groups began to cry that the apocalypse was nearing as they prophesized that the Euro seemed to be rising as the one world currency predicted in ancient texts to be a foreshadowing of end times. In an effort to calm the superstitious beliefs and ever growing fears of the Religious Right the concept of America participating in furthering the Euro's efforts were abandoned. Since deserting the gold standard though, the dirtiest little secret was that the Dollar had no more value than the paper it was printed on.

With little financial stability left, many Americans found themselves moving into the poorer neighborhoods they once looked down upon. Now, it was all they could afford. Upon their arrival, they found that although guns had been removed from the homes and the hands of the law abiding, gangs and criminals still seemed to have free access to them. As seasons passed, many lived in constant fear within their own walls.

This was the place George Anderson had found himself. Although, many individuals had labeled it as "white flight" he had slowly convinced himself that his decision to move to the Northwest wasn't based on race. Living in a modest apartment complex in the suburbs of Atlanta, he was uncomfortable with the people around him. A mix of cultures, languages and beliefs he couldn't relate to or understand. He argued he wasn't leaving because of their skin tones, but rather because his new neighbors didn't 'think' like him. Truth be told, he had never taken the time to speak with any of them.

Upstairs from his unit, quietly living out her few remaining years, Mattie Henson often watched George as he hurried from his car, to his second story flat. Clinging tightly to his briefcase, and always looking behind his shoulder as he pulled his keys from his pocket. She swore she could hear his heart pounding when one of her three grandsons occasionally passed him on the stairwell. Sitting in her chair, on a small porch that came out from her living room, she admired the dark wrinkled skin on the back of her hand. Then, turning to her palm, she compared her lighter side to George's face and smiled to herself.

So similar.

George had never noticed the old woman that seemed to pay him so much distant attention. Instead he focused on the tagged signs and dumpsters around the complex. Gangs marking their territory like dogs pissing on fence posts.

His most inner fear, that those gangs would get hold of his children and pull them into a life that required being beaten up or "sexed in" to be considered part of the group. And, although he wasn't entirely sure what being "sexed in" meant, he wasn't going to give the Latin Kings or People's Nation the opportunity to teach Alli the definition.

He shuddered off the thought of staying in this depraved complex and making a life in the once beautiful DeKalb County neighborhood: now adamant to make a new life in a place that would take him miles from his home State of Georgia.

As he entered their small hovel, he found his life now packed away in cardboard and neatly stacked around the room. He reached out to hug his wife, Caroline, as she walked to the door. The bounding of little feet echoed from the hall, as Georgie and Allison ran down to show off their latest creation.

"Daddy, Daddy! Look! I drew a flag! It can be our new flag!"

"Alli, I am pretty sure Oregon already has a State Flag." George remarked, dryly, showing little interest.

"Yeah, but Georgia's always changing theirs, so maybe in Oregon they'll like mine better and use this one." She shrugged her shoulders and handed George the picture, "Well, you know, this can be the new one! They can change it. Mine's better." The child stated with naïve determination in her voice.

On a piece of neon yellow construction paper she had brilliantly designed her most recent masterpiece: a colorful flag filled with flowers and smiley faces and something that resembled an airplane or a bird. Alli stood in front of her father and beamed with pride, as she anxiously awaited his response, rocking back and forth from her heels to her toes, in anticipation of compliments and her father's praise.

"That's real pretty, Alli." George glanced at the paper for a split second, then handed it back to his daughter.

"See, I'm just like Martha Washington!"

"Martha Washington?" her father questioned.

"Yeah! She made flags! Everybody knows that!"

"No. You mean Betsy Ross."

"Besty... who?" Allison looked at her father, puzzled.

"Betsy Ross, Alli." George shook his head, annoyed at the idea he would have to explain anything to the child. He turned to Caroline, as he slapped the paper. "You see, *that's* why this country is failing. We can't even teach our kids *basic* history. They're all bunch of incompetent little morons!"

Hurt by her father's remark Alli looked up at her mother, feeling belittled, as she shyly reached for her picture. She didn't want her father to have it, anymore.

Caroline looked down sympathetically apologizing for her husband's comment with her eyes. George could be so callous and insensitive sometimes.

"I'm going to call Ty' and say goodbye." Alli said in a quiet voice that hinted tears were not far from the surface.

"Come on, Alli. That's a great idea. I need to call Tyrone's mommy anyway, and after *we're* done talking, *you* can say goodbye to Tyrone. " Caroline embraced the change of subject and tried to seem enthusiastic, despite her exhaustion from packing.

"That could take hours!" Alli exclaimed, throwing her hands in the air in true diva fashion and turning around. She started back down the hall, her blonde ringlets, still damp from a recent bath, bounced with every stomp. Her little brother, Georgie, toddled in tow. Their mother shook her head, watching them walk away, and smiled as she headed for the phone.

Caroline called out to George as she started to dial, "Did you and Ronald enjoy yourselves?"

Not wanting to have a conversation, George simply replied, "Yeah. It was fine."

In the adjoining room, he opened a recently packed box of liquor and took a long sip from the first bottle that found his hand. Cautiously, he eyed around the corner, replaced the cap and repacked the bottle, thinking no one would be the wiser.

From the living room, he could over hear Caroline and Leticia, Ronald's wife, chatting away while the children played a game of make believe in the small bedroom that the two of them shared. Walking toward the window of their small upstairs unit

George could see an older man in a beat up Dodge picking up a young girl that lived a down the street. Although she looked young, he thought to himself that she must have been a prostitute. His mind flashed, and a chill ran down his back, at the thought of raising Alli in such a horrible place. But, it was the same everywhere now. Gangs all but controlled all of the major cities, anymore. Atlanta, Miami, New York, Detroit, Chicago, Los Angeles and D.C. were little more than wastelands for the damned. Returning to his seat, he remembered his childhood. How different things in "the city too busy to hate" once were, he thought to himself.

It wasn't that long ago.

George checked for his wife as he reached for the bottle again, but after a few swigs, he found himself resting the bottle on his knee, no longer hiding it from view. As the sounds of chatter and giggles swirled around the room, George's thoughts returned to the restaurant, and back to the words of his friend. He confused himself with the thought that he could know a man so well, yet not know him at all. He began to wonder if they were really friends. After a moment of reflection, he reached the conclusion that they must have been, but was still unable to answer his own question.

They had been through so much together.

A bond that seemed unbreakable.

The old soundtrack in his mind began to play.

May 2012

Roswell High School

Roswell, Georgia

He remembered a hazy blend of shooters laughing and chanting, as they fired at random, into one room after another. The haunting screams of terror from the living, moans from the dying, and the long sound of the air as it made its final escape from the mouths of the dead.

The dreary song that was carried through the vent ducts.

At any moment George could recall those glimpses that seemed endless. Those moments he lived that would eventually play a role in changing the nation forever. The final catalyst. He had no memory of the aftermath, just the one memory that played eternal, frozen in the few minutes of time that he was most terrified. He relived the feeling of the hot salty trail on his cheek, the panicked breath of his friend rushing past his right ear, the noise, the cold tile below, and the expressions of death on the faces around the room.

He remembered the fear.

It all came rushing back, but he allowed the liquor to push it away. As the whiskey flowed through his veins, he found himself in a more philosophical frame of mind. Maybe he really *didn't* know Ronald. Maybe Ronald really didn't know him. But, until tonight he had no doubt.

Easing into his chair, he remembered someone else. A scrawny boy, for his eighteen years, by the name of Robby Benton. A smart kid, but a loner. Still, George and Ronald had called him a friend.

At least when no one else was around they did.

High School was such a superficial place. It wasn't real life, but it so seemed that way to an eighteen year old.

In Mr. Sanders' Honors Senior Biology Class, Ronald and George worked on their final project. While dissecting a fetal pig, they joked about a senior prank that the class of 2012 had planned to pull the coming weekend and hoped that the rain pouring down outside would break by the weekend. It felt like it had been raining for a month, which was unusual for springtime in Georgia.

Robby worked alone on the other side of the room. Sanders, occasionally walking over to him, nodding with approval, but feeling sorry for him, "Son, you've got the hands of surgeon. I think you may have found your calling." Over the years he had seen so many kids like this pass through these halls. Every class had one.

The misfit.

Sanders patted the young man on the back. Robby half smiled, as he looked down at the dead piglet, carefully carving and labeling its innards as he cut them out. Just within earshot, giggling, two of the school cheerleaders at a nearby table made comments about his less than sophisticated dress.

Normally Robby would cringe, feeling the heat rush up the back of his neck as he tried to pretend he had not heard the comment and knowing that everyone else around him had.

But, today would be different.

Robby smiled knowingly at the two girls. They sneered back in unison and continued on with conversation, now making plans to run up charges daddy's credit card at Lenox mall.

Noticing the response, and assuming that Robby was finally learning how to handle the constant barrage of insults he was subjected to, Ronald nudged George and gestured in Robby's direction.

"Hey, Robby! Are you *in*?", Ronald shouted across the room and looked at Robby as if he should know what he meant.

Robby glanced up at the clock.

It was 1:11 p.m.

Turning back to Ronald and George, looking confused, he questioned, "Yeah... Are *you*?"

"*Hell* yeah! We can take my car!" George called back expecting Robby to be thankful for the invitation.

"Take it... take it... where?" Robby responded with a confounded expression.

"Friday. Friday *night*! Class of 1-2! This is going to best Senior prank ever!"

"Uh... Umm... Yeah, yeah." Robby looked back at the clock, the second hand pounding.

Ronald shrugged his shoulders and returned to the project and his conversation with George. Even though they weren't the best friends in the world at least they gave this kid the time of day and he lived in the neighborhood. Besides, Robby's parents spent more time traveling than they did at home and Robby was always good for grabbing a bottle of liquor from their stash.

Even Robby, in his quieter moments, knew it was pity or usury but it was still someone to talk to.

Then suddenly, joking and laughter was broken by the sound of a hail of bullets as they flew across the room. George and Ronald dove under their table sheltering each other and scared out of their minds.

The sound of the gun repeating fire. Glass shattering. Uncontrolled ricochets hitting unintended targets.

It was Robby.

But the echoes from the hall told everyone he wasn't alone.

Before leaving the room, the boy turned back once to look at his former classmates and take account of the room. Mr. Sanders fought to remove a scalpel that had accidentally been flung forward by a bullet on ricochet and had lodged itself in his throat. The blood gurgled out, as he struggled to remove the blade, but nothing could be done. As they stared back in horror, unsure of what he intended, Robby gave a sympathetic smile, looking down at the teacher that had tried to help him so often. The man that had tried to build him up and show him there was a life outside those walls. Sanders' death was an accident. Robby's expression was almost apologetic, before starting out the door to join his counterparts.

A singular decision.

The little boy that felt bullied by the world, had sold his soul for a brief moment of revenge and camaraderie. At last, he was part of something. He knew it was wrong, but for once he was on the inside, instead of just looking in. Robby Benton smiled at the two cheerleaders, now slumped over. He skipped down the halls, laughing. He fired off his final shots, but kept one bullet aside, which he had planned to use to take his own life.

Another teen would save him the trouble, when he reached the stairwell leading to the second floor of the building.

When they found Robby Benton, his eyes were wide open. A single bullet clenched in his fist.

George often wondered what it was that could bring a person to such a point. The three boys had grown up together on a small street in the Land of Lakes subdivision, only a few miles from the school. A quiet middle class neighborhood that was framed around a singular and seemingly misplaced mansion on a lake that all of the smaller, more average homes seemed to be constructed around: almost as if they were forming a ring of envy.

That was Robby's house.

A perfectly landscaped and seemingly peaceful abode whose residents were as distant and lonely as the earth's poles.

Robby's family would rather have spent money than time. He always had the best games and technological gadgets to play with. Robby didn't really care about most of it, but it bought him friends.

At least for a short while.

But, really he just wanted someone to talk to or, even more, someone to listen. Eventually, he would find those friends. But, even they would come at a price.

On the internet, he wasn't the weak and unattractive boy that everyone around him saw.

He had another identity.

Another image.

He had his own space.

Inside, though, he was still the same frightened and misunderstood child.

But, The Unholy Trinity understood him. U.T. was a cyber gang that had formed sometime over the summer of 2009 and somehow had escaped detection from law enforcement, due to their complicated system of code speak and communication. With the internet and text messaging having been reduced to acronymic communication, most parents couldn't decipher the difference between ROLF, A/S/L or POS, never mind the more sinister abbreviations that UT taught.

On that dark, spring day. At exactly 1:13 p.m., 254 schools across the nation would experience similar devastation.

College campuses.

High schools.

Middle schools.

Even elementary schools were no exception.

There was no escape. The media would not allow the country to grieve with so much fodder for their 5:00 programming. Images of kindergarten children, bloodied and dying was too much for them to resist. Democrats took center stage and demanded the nation disarm.

Americans wept and frantically searched for answers, as mothers packed their worries in little boxes lined with satin and buried them six feet in the ground.

Alcoholism and divorce rates soared in the months that followed.

There was no one common denominator that linked all of the group. No single background, education, home life, race or upbringing. But, there was a common drug - Concetrin.

Doctors labeled Robby as "hyperactive" when he turned eight. He wasn't really. He was just a happy, active little boy. But, with two careers to handle, and little time for their child, his parents pumped him full of Concetrin to keep him calm and make him focus on schoolwork. No one realized that the combination of the drugs, and the simulation games he played, only pulled Robby's impressionable mind deeper into a fantasy world that, eventually, he would bring to life.

The lives of the children he killed were no more significant than blips on a television screen. Massive lawsuits were brought against the drug's manufacturer, which also happened to be the largest supplier of antidepressants and penicillin in the nation, forcing the company into bankruptcy and causing a national panic over mental health drugs and antibiotic supplies.

When Robby's parents brought themselves to open the door to their teenage son's room, for what seemed like the first time in years, they had no words. Robby's room had been neatly organized the morning before he committed those acts. Things, once important to a teenage boy, discarded in the trash. His parents would later search his computer for answers. What they found would leave them stunned at the sadistic insanity which resided within their own walls.

Three weeks later, after much finger pointing, they filed for divorce.

For all these years, George had wondered what could bring a seemingly normal kid from his own neighborhood to do what he did. What made Robby so different from Ronald, or himself?

Thinking back to their childhood, George recalled the name calling. All of the rhymes and insults that Robby was forced to face. The time he was locked in a janitor's closet by a group of giggling twelve year old girls. The football team lining the front of his athletic cup with muscle rub. They laughed and pointed as Robby ran to the nurse's office in tears, pulling the crotch of his shorts away from his skin.

The names.

Surely, it couldn't have just been the words. George had been called names, too.

George thought through the list of words, wondering. He pondered all of the words of hatred and pain that he had in his vocabulary. The slurs, the offensive words. He debated the English language itself.

There were so many words to express anger, and hatred, but only one to truly express love.

He questioned that.

He began to wonder if man had discovered a need to express this rage against one another since the time he had found his own voice. Maybe it was simple the nature of the beast, but to admit that would be to admit the beast within, and that was something he was not ready to face.

He dismissed himself from his alcohol hazed analysis leaving the bottle on the floor. From the kitchen Caroline called out breaking his concentration, asking him if he wanted to say goodbye to Leticia.

He waived her off, still wondering how his long term friendship with Ronald could fall apart over the course of one simple drink.

They had been friends since they were second graders.

Alli appeared in the hall, wide eyed, and with one arm on each hip. "I'm never gonna get to talk to Ty'!", she exclaimed, throwing her arms in the air and storming back into her room. After quickly wrapping up her conversation with Leticia, Caroline called her back over and gave her the phone. Alli reached up for the handset, annoyed by the wait. She glared at her mother, asking for privacy with irritation in her small eyes, then turned around to tell Ty' about her latest masterpiece. Caroline called out to Georgie informing him it was time for his bath.

"Aowwwah! Maaaamaaaaaaa!"

Caroline walked over and found a seat on top of one of the boxes in front of George's chair. Running her fingers over the top of her head, tired from the day, she looked up at him with question in her eyes, but working to keep that doubt from appearing on any other part of her face, and trying to sound upbeat despite her exhaustion.

"Ronny and Tish are thinking about moving up to Philly."

"He didn't say anything to me about that tonight." George said dryly, disinterested in Caroline's news.

"Yeah. Well, you know Tish, she'll get her way if it's what she really wants. Says she has a sister up there. They might go stay with her for a while."

"Really?" George yawned.

"Yeah... She's a preacher's wife. Her husband has his own church, or he runs it or something. I don't exactly know how that works, but that's what she said." Caroline's voice softened, as she searched her husband's face for eye contact. "She said it's just too hard to find work here. Ronny hasn't had any luck finding a better job, either."

"I know."

Caroline paused, half lost in thought, and half wondering if Georgie was getting ready for his bath. "Are we doing the right thing, George?"

George nodded softly.

"I think so, too. I mean, I hope we are... I really hope we are."

"What? Did Tish say something? Is she trying to convince you this is a bad idea? It's not." Frustration grew in George's voice. "We have gone over this too many times. Dammit! Caroline, we're packed and I am..."

Smiling sweetly, but cutting him off as her tears welled, Caroline reached over and took George's hand, keeping one ear on her daughter's conversation, and speaking in her most calming tone, "No, no, no. Tish was sweet. She thinks we're doing the right thing. Really, she does. I do, too. God, I'm gonna miss her though. She's like my sister, George. She was the first friend I made when we moved down here in seventh grade. She was the first person that ever spoke to me here, it seemed like. I felt like such an outcast before her. And when I got pregnant with Alli, she was right there, even when no one else was. She's always been there. She's my best friend. How do you say goodbye to a friend like that?" Caroline tried to convince him she was optimistic.

George cleared his throat, as he stood up and turned away from her, "I don't know...." Done with conversation, George started walking towards their bedroom and called back to his wife, as though she was a waitress. "I'm going to hit the shower. Fix me a drink. Bourbon. Two shots, 3 cubes."

George headed to the shower, as Alli continued to babble with Ty'. As Caroline watched him walk away, she questioned his distance, but reverted to duty, "Georgie needs to take a bath, hon."

George called back from the hall, "He can wait. I'm taking a shower."

A gleeful, shreekish, small cheer followed from the children's bedroom as Georgie realized he had been given a fifteen minute reprieve. Caroline sighed, knowing that she would not be able to find her bed for at least another hour, now. She flipped open the top of one of the boxes, taking her annoyance out on the cardboard, and pulled out the bourbon.

She noticed the other bottle on the floor, but was too tired to care. She forcefully shoved it back in the box without saying a word and looked over at the dingy blinds that she had worked so hard to clean that day.

They still looked dirty.

After getting Alli off of the phone, Caroline poured the drink she knew he did not need, and contemplated taking a shot, herself. She mixed the drink, and annoyed with her husband, she simply left it on the nightstand and occupied her time cleaning up after the kids as she waited for George to finish in the shower.

In mild rebellion she tossed in four cubes and shorted the liquor.

When she heard the water stop running she purposefully made her way over to Georgie and started talking to him about nothing, as she helped him undress. Secretly hoping to avoid conversation with the man she had married. When she heard the bedroom door close, mother and son headed to the bathroom.

George sat down on the edge of the bed in his towel, his hair still wet and dripping on the comforter. He tried to collect his thoughts as he took a sip of his drink and then made his way to over to a clean pair of underwear that Caroline had left out for him. Slipping on his boxers, he then found the covers. In the distance, shots were fired, but they were far enough away that they didn't worry him. He had gotten used to the sound over the years. He laid down on the mattress, listening to Georgie's splashing and Caroline's laughter. The flashing and buzzing of a neon sign creeped in through the window, and he rolled over: the room intermittently lighting up with a pinkish glow.

"What had happened to the world, in the past eight years?" he wondered.

Drifting into sleep, George dreamt of a better life. That shadowed place where the American Dream, or at least part of it, still existed.

Viva Los Derechos

Although not perfect, the initial ideals were right.

So much division in a nation that was founded on such utopian ambitions. The concept that 'all men are created equal.' In the end, the founding beliefs would be the ones that would tear them apart.

Although the notion looked nice on paper, it neglected to take the most important thing into account: man, himself.

Man didn't want to see himself as equal to his neighbor. He didn't know, or relate to, his neighbor. In truth, he didn't even really like his neighbor. Although, he would rarely admit it.

No matter how pretty the parchment, a document can never dicate what lies within the heart of a man. There was always a division he could find to separate himself from the next person.

Segregating by color was only the first step.

It was the simplest separation, since it didn't require any form of communication. It wasn't really racist, not by its truest definition, it was just easy.

And everyone was guilty.

Split the nation on the color line and start fresh from there.

Although outside nations dubbed it a "race war", it was about much more than that. True, groups gravitated toward or away from one another based on their skin tones, but that was only the first fracture on the surface of an unstable nation.

America had lost her faith.

There was no commonality that bound one American to another. No common religion, heritage, beliefs, language, friends, enemies or history. Effectively, there was no common culture. There was no stable ground for one individual when he dealt with the next and the nation had litigated itself to the point that people were afraid to even inquire about their differences. There were no safe topics, no safe havens, no safe places and no security.

The land of opportunity was left with nothing, but the right to divide.

In the process of trying to force unity, it would be separation that would prevail. Over the 250 years that America had her glory as a financial and military power she had tried to tell the world how to live. She policed other nations, forcing her thumb on the moral pulse of humanity. Yet, she never found peace within her own borders. There were always disagreements and hatred.

She just chose to ignore them.

Wandering like an innocent lost in the valley of the damned, preaching unity, but unable to realize that even those born into Eden found reason to hate their brother. Hate was as old as man himself. It was his one true possession.

That singular emotion: his purest creation.

Logic came second to instinct.

Of course, if the final divider hadn't been race it would have been religion, or party. Diversity unchecked made it impossible to find any similarity. No one could even come up with a definition for an "American" which would satisfy every group.

In 2013, in response to the UT tragedy and the growing gang problems and street violence that plagued the nation, cries to disarm the country went out. In the autumn of

2014 a series of unbelievable laws were passed and the US constitution was amended. Oregon and Montana openly refused to comply, and those that refused to give up their right to bear arms flooded into what were referred to, at first, as the "Maverick States."

Militia groups began to unite and thrive in the Northwest.

As for the rest of the nation, divisions within divisions made it impossible for any faction to have a unified identity or cause. Well before the year 2000, even the political parties were noticing serious rifts in their own infrastructures.

Hindsight is... *it's an old adage.*

As Americans nightmared about terrorists from the Middle East, they neglected to dream about the threats that were brewing from within their own, increasingly vulnerable, borders.

America had lost this war years before it began.

It was just a matter of time.

Until the new millennium there had never been a true threat to the two party system to which Americans had attributed their success. The notion of a new party, of a group of independents grabbing for the brass ring of the Presidency, it was almost laughable. No third party had ever been able to unite a large enough voting block.

In the months preceding the Y2K elections, though, a third party *was* rising. They wouldn't even be realized until the elections in 2016.

As Republicans and Democrats alike prepared for the campaign trail cries of "unity" had echoed from both sides.

A selfish and unrealistic demand, really.

It wasn't so much the unity of a nation they were seeking, but rather order within their own groups and the naïve hope that a new century would grant that New Year's Wish. The first threads had been pulled years ago, but the fraying of the fabric was only now becoming apparent.

The year 2000.

Once again, America was asked to choose sides.

But, America was uninterested in the voting booth. The economy, then still reaping the benefits of a bull market like had never been seen in previous history, seemed stable. Americans could have cared less who took over the Presidency, as long as their pockets weren't affected.

But, winning an election required votes.

At the time, the Hispanic vote was one that both the Republicans and Democrats had marketed hard to obtain. As the black population was losing their majority minority status, they found their voices falling on deaf ears, of both parties, as groups tried to swoon the Hispanics to one side or the other.

It was a two party system. They *had* to choose. Both parties knew their survival hung in the balance as the Hispanic population continued to grow at an astounding rate.

Historically, Hispanic voters had favored the Democrats. It was a vote that Democrats were counting on in order to maintain power into the new millenium.

Then, at the most unfortunate time, a war broke out.

On the US/ Mexico border hoards of Mexican rebels opened fire on US Border Patrol Agents, with automatic weapons, escorting illegals by the thousands into America on a daily basis. It was briefly reported in the media that Border Patrol Agents, armed

only with 9mm hand guns, were on a fast retreat.

But, that story was soon dropped.

It didn't serve the parties.

Both Democrats and Republicans knew it was a threat with the elections closing

in. If the white majority, and the then official majority minority black community,

realized the borders were compromised there would be an uprising. Anti-immigrant

sentiments could flare and the parties would be forced to decide between the majority

vote or the Hispanic vote. They couldn't have it both ways, and the Hispanic population

was growing too fast to ignore.

Even if they weren't key to this election, they would be in the next, or the one

after that… and everyone knew it.

They needed to strike a balance.

Fast.

Illegals were no secret in America. Economically, they were necessary. They

took the jobs that white and black America refused to work, or would have demanded

much higher pay for. Many even attributed the recent financial boom in the US economy

to the Hispanic labor force. It was critical to divert America's attention from the truth.

Little Miguel couldn't have arrived at a better time.

For weeks it was "All Miguel, All the Time" television. America argued over the

fate of a young Cuban boy as he was paraded around like a show dog for all the world to

see. The nation should have realized that with so much attention being blitzed on a trivial story, complications being forced into it, something wasn't kosher. There was larger story that was being avoided.

But, America continued on with their normal routine of water cooler gossip and quasi-legal debate.

Not only did Miguel serve to divert America's attentions from her own borders, he created a sentiment of sympathy for illegal aliens which would help both parties over the next year.

At least, that was the hope.

Both delegations knew that they needed to show a sympathetic stand towards illegals in order to gain Hispanic voters and they chose their political positions carefully.

However, Miguel's INS status couldn't have been clearer. He was an "unaccompanied minor." That is, until his father was found.

It was cut and dry.

According to the laws of the land, he should have been returned home the moment his father claimed him. Where he was born was no factor in the eyes of the law. Although they tried to stall it, his unavoidable return caused an unforgivable rift.

In the key Electoral State of Florida, the Cuban population quickly grew bitter. Having floated on makeshift rafts to a better life, themselves, many of them identified with the little boy's plight. Feeling betrayed by the Democrats in power, they took their revenge in the voting booths.

The war on the southern borders continued without attention from the media.

Miguel was returned, not long after the battles on the border subsided.

As the gunfire quieted, over half a million illegals were beginning new lives in the US. Among them, were at least three of the terrorists which would eventually be linked to orchestrating the attacks on September 11th, 2001.

Americans went back to their daily routine of microwave dinners, internet chat rooms and television. Content to live in blissful ignorance.

They knew no other way.

Then came November.

Even a simple head count had become too much for the nation to handle.

America had exposed her Achilles heel.

While the struggle between the parties continued a new group, with unified beliefs, was rising in California.

The *Derechos*.

At the turn of the century, they were loosely organized, but that would soon change. They understood their growing position even if the rest of the nation did not.

Legal or not, Hispanics were the growing majority minority. They were predicted to be the majority by the year 2050: an estimate which would prove to be off by a full 30 years. They were out-breeding white America by a ratio of more than 3:1, and with an organized criminal group of Puerto Ricans, New Yorkers, Californians, Floridians and Texans, called the *Papelitos*, selling their birth certificates on the internet for a few hundred Dollars each, there was no true way to separate real immigrants, from US citizens or illegals.

Democrats rallied to give voting rights and Social Security benefits to border crossers that had found their way into the country in the hope that it would buy their devotion, but with the Papelitos in the background it opened up a can of worms that no one could have imagined. Years after the laws passed, the elections of 2020 would be won by a landslide margin that outnumbered the Hispanic population itself. With multiple ID's and multiple voting cards, many Hispanics voted as many as ten times in the Presidential Election: all under pseudonyms that were backed up by the papers that the Papelitos had helped them obtain. The Democrats had handed the Hispanic population the very sword that would soon slit open the great elephant's throat and leave Republicans crying foul, but with no way to intervene without being accused of racism.

Congress selectively battled issues, turning their backs on the more basic concerns of the people. States soon found they were struggling with the issues that the Feds choose to ignore. A war of words began in two languages: English and Spanish. Even though English was the international language of business, America couldn't establish it as the official national language within her own borders. Counties in Texas began declaring Spanish the official language of the County and demanding English speakers bring translators to traffic court.

Other groups took notice and soon towns and counties, across the nation, found attempts to make Pakistani, Italian and even Arabic the "county language" were rising as major topics of local political discussion. When those efforts were squashed, or simply ignored, the groups bringing forth the action cried discrimination.

Lawsuits arose.

In other areas, businesses, and States, poured out money to please unsatisfied members of the Spanish speaking community who felt English dominance was discriminatory. They then found themselves facing similar arguments from other cultures.

Naturally, this led to more litigation.

The EEOC was overwhelmed with requests and simply began rubber stamping "right to sue" letters, just to move the paperwork through their offices and meet their own self imposed deadlines.

As the Hispanic population was growing, Spanish speakers stood at the helm of the massive bilingual movement and demanded equal rights. In their version this meant equal access to information, education, television, legal services, and representation.

That meant translation.

And lots of it.

But there was a problem with interpreters. They were just that. Individuals put in place to give an *interpretation* of what was either written or said. It was impossible to be perfectly accurate. Spanish didn't have the legal-eeze that English had developed for itself. Furthermore, Spanish was not universal. Guatemalans spoke Mayan dialects. Mexican Spanish used different vocabulary than that of Columbia or Argentina. Portuguese, spoken by Brazilians, was a language of its own.

As a result, when laws were translated white and black America found themselves being held to a different standard of the law than that which was imposed on those who spoke Spanish. Furthermore, if language couldn't be argued, culture was. The "Cultural Defense" allowed lawyers another loophole.

For many Latina girls, their quinceñera, or fifteenth birthday celebration, was marked by a great deal of pomp and circumstance. Parents would spend thousands on festivities to commemorate their daughter's symbolic transition into womanhood. As a result, this offered a great defense for Hispanic pedophiles that fancied young girls in the 13-16 year old age group. In 2017 a man by the name of Pedro Vega Rodriguez successfully beat 47 counts of statutory rape against white, black and Hispanic children by arguing that in his culture his young victims would be considered women, or close to being women, therefore their had been nothing wrong with his actions.

The youngest was only 11.

The families of the victims were outraged and the decision opened the door for thousands of imprisoned sex offenders to appeal their cases based on the precedent that had been established. America had created one nation, divided into two legal systems, and two languages.

The black community saw their voices being heard by smaller and smaller audiences, with no real power, and the white majority saw their numbers slipping fast to the Hispanics.

More lawsuits were prompted.

Reverse discrimination suits soared, but rarely prevailed in court.

With the economy failing, and work becoming harder and harder to find, many immigrants from the farthest corners of the globe began to see a new opportunity for financial security. If they couldn't earn a living in the land of milk and honey they would sue for it. With a legal system built not on law, but on precedent, their cases flooded the courts using antiquated decisions to their advantage.

Individuals that spoke even the rarest earthly dialects began to demand information in their own language. With no national language, and fearful of discrimination suits, companies began to cave in to the demands, screaming for action from the federal level. With the nation in an uproar, the Feds were forced to act. As seats in the House and Senate were slowly falling to Hispanic representatives, they knew time was running out.

In 2011 English was passed as the national language, but it didn't come without compromise. It was vigorously fought by the powerful Spanish speaking communities, but a deal was struck to ease the blow.

In 2013, all immigrants within US borders were naturalized. The feds believed that if the threat of deportation was removed, states would be able to recoup some of their losses through tax revenue. A mass rush of immigration flooded up from the southern borders, as those hungry for a better life, raced to meet the September 1st deadline.

People smuggling was a booming industry that year.

Coyotes prowled the borders preying on those desperate to make it across the fine line that divided them from their new homes and access to a laundry list of social services. Unfortunately however, it wasn't just the labor force that was attracted. Elderly individuals flooded the country, too. Under the Aged Statute for Social Security, they were guaranteed a monthly wage far greater than they could ever hope to earn in their home countries, just because they were over 65. Many individuals, with no proof of age, simply lied to INS. Men and women as young as forty claimed SSI checks, based on the fact that their papers now said they were entitled. A separate set of papers, purchased through the Papelitos, would allow them to work under another name.

Children lied, too.

Wanting the rights and privileges of an adult, they adjusted the age on their applications, as well. The handicapped and disease ravaged made their way to the US, too. Free healthcare, and medicine were also part of the package. It was a simple matter of paperwork.

Civil liberties groups worked hard to import the burdens of other nations into the full care facilities that the US had to offer. A lottery system was put into place for nursing home admissions, and many drug rehab centers converted to full care facilities for the elderly, leaving addicts to wander the streets.

In the winter, hundreds of old elderly men and women died in the street, unable to find shelter amidst the competition. Their bodies, unceremoniously tossed into paupers graves with no attention from the media and little or no effort to find their next of kin.

Crime grew at an alarming rate.

As those born outside of US borders were learning more and more about how to work the system, many citizens began to panic and anti-immigrant rAllys formed across the nation. For those who had purchased multiple birth certificates, there was an added bonus of being able to collect additional checks. Since the INS didn't require fingerprints, there was no way to prove who was who.

In a bold move, Oregon and Montana, now joined by Wyoming and the Dakotas, passed strict laws, cutting off all State services to immigrants including public school and healthcare. They furthered tightened control of their regions demanding that citizens be required to produce State issued ID cards, separate from driver's licenses and all other identification, which were issued to all residents, including children enrolled in State schools. Under the new laws, a five year old would be required to produce identification, on demand, if requested by law enforcement. Immigrants fled the stringent Maverick States, moving into more lenient communities.

In other areas, identity theft was rampant to the point that long cherished credit scoring systems were tossed to the wayside and labeled completely ineffective, forcing three major US credit companies into total financial ruin by the year 2019. The Social Security system, completely bastardized by the Papelitos, was no longer an effective method of uniquely identifying individuals. Traditional methods of credit scoring would become a thing of the past by 2022.

Diseases long wiped clean from American soil found a new, fertile breeding ground. Vaccine production couldn't keep up with the demand. Measles outbreaks, rubella, yellow fever and even leprosy reentered US hospitals. New strains of drug and vaccine resistant hepatitis, meningitis and tuberculosis were rampant.

Unable to support expensive research and tracking of these illnesses, the doors of the CDC closed permanently in 2021.

With more and more US employees either out of work, or working for companies that had cut insurance benefits in an attempt to save money, families clogged emergency rooms and fights for treatment became almost commonplace. Hospitals demanded full payment, up front, before administering vaccines, but due to the immense shortages, prices had soared out of reach of most Americans. Scam pharmaceutical companies pimped their snake oil on the internet, resulting in hundreds of deaths nationwide before the media could effectively communicate the threat.

In 2018, a fierce strain of the rubella virus claimed over 137,000 lives.

Most were children.

The healthcare and pharmaceutical industries were overwhelmed with the onslaught and hospitals, already suffering from staffing shortages, had trouble maintaining workers in the diseased and violent environments.

Pregnant immigrants, determined to give birth in a US hospital, piled in the ER rooms of the country. Smothered by their own admissions, hospitals began outsourcing their birthing centers.

Quality of care dropped so significantly that many US hospitals began to resemble third world clinics when it came to standards of cleanliness.

Doctors raced to chase the almighty Dollar in the midst of a storm.

Individuals, once diagnosed as terminal with cancer or lupus, suddenly found themselves "in remission" as more profitable, and less time consuming, illnesses entered the market. Malpractice suits inundated hospital administrators in every city.

Violent crime shot off the charts and random murder victims, neatly filed, sat on the desks of homicide detectives patiently awaiting justice. Officers, forced to deal with an uncooperative public, were unable to even decide where to begin, and were uncertain if anyone even cared anymore. Having dedicated their lives to protecting and serving an ungrateful and disinterested public, many began to question their choice of career and failed to see a future behind their badges.

Gangs controlled most cities, and people were afraid to speak out.

With almost no competition or fear of interference from the police, once rival gangs dropped their oppositions and united on racial lines, seeing opportunities for total dominance in many cities. Sur 13, Sur 14 and the Latin Kings formed a new united gang which became known as "Sur Latinos". The Bloods, Crypts and Peoples Nation merged under the latter name. The Sur Latino and Peoples Nation gangs became household names, no longer hiding their presence or immense power.

They were everywhere.

Jews protested as the Peoples Nation took their Star of David as their gang's symbol. Fearful of marking their children as targets for assault by other gangs, synagogues tearfully denounced Jews wearing the Star.

Israel put a call out to her children telling them to come home, and thousands did, but the increasing violence and bloodshed in the Middle East forced many Jews to look in other directions. Huge Jewish populations sprung up, seemingly overnight, in Argentina and Brazil and those countries slowly began to rise as economic forces over the next decade.

Veterans of the police force, unable to deal with the number of cases, the long hours, or angry and disrespectful citizens took early retirement, or simply quit under pressure. There was no respect left for the law, or those who had dedicated their lives to trying to enforce it. By 2016, large portions of the east coast's police force marched towards the Northwest, weapons in hand, attracted by politics, as more and more surrounding States, including; Idaho, Colorado, Arkansas, Nevada and Washington State now joined in the same line of thinking. Slowly, they were forming the borders of what would eventually become known as the Northwest Territory.

Saddled with other burdens, Washington D.C. chose to ignore the political rebellion and sentiments on the other side of the country. Although average citizens had disarmed, guns still found their way to the streets and cities slowly became dominated by one gang or another. Afraid to put their children in public schools, parents hesitantly kept them home as they headed off to earn a living. Gang memberships soared, and the practice of sexing in young girls led to a sharp rise in HIV and other venereal diseases. Those that were lucky, would simply find themselves infertile in their twenties. The less fortunate died; unable to afford the recently developed, and extremely expensive, AIDS vaccine.

Gen X'ers , now on the brink of entitlement, watched their Social Security money fall into the hands of people that had never worked one day's labor in the United States, and became infuriated. In 2015 Social Security announced the new age for filing claims would be raised to 75, but the kitty was completely depleted over the next seven years.

White America lost their long standing majority status in 2021.

Although, on paper, English was the official language, it didn't carry over into the Spanish speaking communities and law fell to the wayside. Courtroom trials were still held in Spanish. Schools taught in Spanish. Communication broke down within communities and corporations split themselves by tongues. For those who only spoke English work became hard, if not impossible to find.

The Tower of Babel.

The basic need to be understood forced groups to one side or another. Hispanic populations gathered together where job markets were still strong, forming tight knit unions among those that spoke their language. Forcing whites and blacks out, due not only to language barriers, but differences in culture.

For all of their past problems, white and black America had become codependent.

They united, for a brief period, in 2019. Standing together, only long enough to realize they had too many of their own issues to attack, before moving forward. Then, they simply returned to their original divisions, accusations and finger pointing.

The English language, alone, was not enough to hold them together.

Unable to resolve a century's worth of problems, the attentions of White America were drawn to the Northwest. The need to fit in, and to feel protected, led whites to be among themselves. Living under the laws defined by the newly formed Northwest Command, a highly organized group that exerted control across lines of the Maverick States, maintaining peace and order and enforcing new laws regarding identifications many were simply content to feel secure. Work was plentiful in the Territory, and white America tolerated life in what was, effectively, becoming a police state environment in exchange for safety and financial security.

In their own efforts to demand attention from the White House, black America rAllyd behind a man that called himself Elijah Drew. Drew was a Muslim leader that emphatically preached that black Muslims should be immune from the ten percent Catholic Initiative tax that had been passed in 2020 by the new, predominately Hispanic, Derechos government and gained a huge following of converts. The Islamic Nation, the group that Drew led, quickly grew in both membership and power.

Stadiums filled with black Americans that came to listen to Drew's powerful and charismatic speeches, convincing them to convert to their "true" religion. Large conversion ceremonies marked the close of his events, where Bibles were burned and exchanged for copies of the Koran. Fervor spilled out into the streets following his gatherings and cities argued with venture capitalists that were determined to profit and bring Elijah Drew's hate mongering to their doorsteps. They begged to keep him out, unable to contain the overzealous crowds, with their dwindling police forces.

But, these were the cities Drew most loved to target.

Hispanics in power soon began to question what to do, as both white and black America leered with angry eyes at Washington, each group plotting their own form of revenge for what the Derechos had taken from them. Unfamiliar with how the group was able to rise so quickly to power and infuriated by their politics and strong alliance with the Catholic Church, white and black America, along with the world, now sought to study the well organized all Hispanic Party and dethrone them from their seats of power.

But, that would be no easy task.

Their own divides, running so deep, whites and blacks could not unite, not even for a common, mutually beneficial, cause.

The Derechos were incredibly powerful.

They were a strong, well structured political group, founded at the turn of the millennium by Hector Luis Gonzales. Gonzales was a handsome man, born in California to the parents of migrant workers and would be later alleged to have strong ties to the Tiajuana drug cartels.

Early on the cartels had solidified their continued success by funding the Gonzales campaign.

In the summer of 2003 the first meeting of the Derechos was held. Led by Gonzales, and a small group of his followers, they gathered in a church to speak to a sympathetic group of supporters that had seen his simple ad in a local Los Angeles Spanish newspaper.

```
"Viva Los Derechos:   Primera reunion, el 7 de Augosto,
2003.   La Iglesia de la Virgin. 7:00 de la noche.
¡Saber es Poder! ¡Juntos Podemos!"
```

His ad was small, adorned only by a small photo of the Virgin Mary posing like

Lady Liberty, but it attracted the attention of two hundred plus believers in his cause.

Soon word of mouth began to spread throughout the Spanish speaking neighborhoods and

meetings began to grow exponentially.

The plan was in motion.

There was no way to stop the population growth in the Hispanic communities, and

Gonzales was smart enough to realize that if he established himself early, he would be

guaranteed the Presidency.

He had a plan.

Their first meeting was well choreographed. He entered the room with all of the

fanfare that would be deserving of a man in the position he so desperately desired. He

shook hands as he walked in the door, smiling and waving to the crowd. He was careful

to craft himself, not along national lines, but to the Hispanic community as one unified

group.

As the meetings progressed, he showed census statistics, and encouraged his

followers to move into key electoral states and form their unions. The power before the

Hispanic population was revealed and his political stance was appealing to the group. In

his plan, the United States could become little more than an extension of Mexico.

And with the cartel's funding, it would be.

Groups of Derechos Party Members migrated into all of the key electoral states

and began to spread the message to the Hispanic population, recruiting hundreds of new party members each day and encouraging Hispanic owned businesses to hire other party members. Membership in the Derechos became synonymous with job security and the hope for a better life, permanently, in the United States.

White and Black America were oblivious.

Over the next fifteen years, Gonzales' following grew to the tens of thousands, and eventually millions, but was kept away from the English speaking media. Recruiting Offices were established in major cities, including; New York, Miami, Los Angeles, Houston and Newark. His following remained faithful to their cause, as he visited the offices, quietly campaigning to a group that would, in the end, carry him to power.

In 2016, English speakers furled their brow in confusion at the dark stranger that came so close winning the Presidential Election as an independent, but soon forgot his name and moved on with their daily routines, arguing over Republican and Democratic party lines.

Spanish speakers didn't forget Gonzales though. They were *so* close. Just as he had promised. Their salivary glands were wet with the taste of impending success.

Black and White Americans were stunned when the elections of 2020 placed a man in power that spoke only Spanish on the campaign trail and in his national addresses. In their dismay, they searched for answers and realized the one great unifier that was so overlooked within the Hispanic community.

The one thing they had ignored.

The unbreakable bond.

The Hispanic people were more American than any of them.

One nation.

Under God.

Indivisible.

When in Rome

While Hispanics were known to bicker over nationality, or World Cup favorites, there was a strong tie they shared. It was not language, nor nation, nor political ambition that united the Hispanic population in the United States. Almost without exception, Hispanics bowed before a voice heard from halfway around the world. A voice which spoke with more authority, which commanded more territory, than any politician had ever dreamed.

The Catholic Church.

Over previous years the Catholic community had faded in America and around the world. Even their strongholds in countries such as Ireland had leaned away from their ancient agendas. But the Hispanic community was an exception. Hispanic faith in the Catholic Church was always strong and the Vatican realized the opportunity that existed for an alliance with the Derechos Party and the cartels.

Hispanics could have easily turned away from the leaders of the drug world, had the truth behind the Derechos funding been exposed, but the word of God was another issue.

And the Vatican seized the chance.

Even though the economy was weak, the world still relied on the United States for so much that, internationally, there had been a domino effect.

Save the Middle East, whose oil market kept her strong.

But, with the Vatican involved, America could rise again.

It was an opening they couldn't pass up. In 2008, the Catholic Church began quietly pouring funds into the Derechos cause and, from behind the scenes, controlled much of their actions. An odd alliance of drug money and church contributions paved the road to the White House for the Derechos.

The Church maintained the stronghold, though.

Even power hungry Hispanics feared and respected the Pope.

Every Sunday, figureheads in the church encouraged Hispanics to fight for the Derechos and support their efforts for the betterment of the Hispanic community. A misunderstanding of the translation led bilinguals, early on, to believe Derechos was a reference to 'equal rights', and not a political party. Their cause persisted with little attention from media.

In 2016, when The Derechos made their first attempt for the coveted seat of power, a few voices were raised, but the nation soon refocused on ways to repair the economy. In their arrogance Republicans and Democrats, alike, refused to acknowledge they were only a few moves away from checkmate with no available escape on the board.

In 2020, Hector Gonzales took over the Presidency of the United States, and was sworn in by the Pope, himself. Separation of Church and State was never even argued.

The State now belonged to the Church.

They had paid for it in cash.

As Gonzales stood before the nation, his hand on an aged bible, he swore allegiance not only to the country, but to the Catholic Church . A sea of Spanish speakers filled the Capitol, waiving flags from around the Americas, and chanting in unison:

> *"Viva Derechos! Viva Gonzales!*
>
> *Viva Derechos! Viva Gonzales!"*

The new leader of the United States smiled down at the crowd. Charismatic, and with a powerful voice, he courted the masses with devilish charm. His wife, Ana, stood in the background, watching the spectacle with restrained glee.

La Primera Dama.

Throughout the ceremony white and black Americans stared on, in shock. Watching from their televisions and internet broadcasts many seemed unable to fathom the implications of the church's involvement in the politics of United States as they watched the English subtitles of Gonzales' speech float across the bottoms of their screens. Other nations, some former allies, were left unsure of how to deal with America's new religious alliance.

At the close of the ceremony, the Pope blessed the crowd, then disappeared into the White House with Presidente Gonzales. While some saw it at a partnership, or a marriage of powers, the fact of the matter was it was a silent overthrow of the United States government. So gentle, neither Republicans nor Democrats felt the sword pierce their bellies.

It was the easiest battle the Catholic Church had ever fought. A small group of powerful Hispanics had risen to office, and poorer Hispanic laborers, led by the Church, were simply used to make their mark in the voting arena. Hispanics were told that it was their duty as a good Catholic to support the Derechos, since the Derechos supported the Church.

White and Black Americans were depicted and unholy and unrighteous.

Anyone, who was not Catholic, was publicly denounced from the Oval Office.

Slowly the Constitution fell to the wayside, as the Church infiltrated and demanded control of a nation with no moral backbone. Once long time Allies of the United States sat back, awaiting the inevitable, as rumors that Gonzales intended to turn over control of US Military powers to the church swirled.

The next two years would send America spinning, as Hispanic Congressmen and Senators stepped into the ring, winning elections by record margins. Many, already holding seats, simply announced a change in their political association. It was impossible to defeat any bill they presented. They voted in a solid block.

Catholic influence in the schools brought back corporal punishment, Roe v. Wade was overturned, and the church began to have a major influence over the passing of new laws. In one of his first acts as President, Gonzales proposed a 10% national sales tax that would be implemented to support the Church and their efforts to manage military forces. It shouldn't have been a surprise, though. It was all neatly detailed in "The Initiave."

The *Catholic* Initiative.

It was, in the mind of the church, payback. Simple reimbursement on the investment that they had made to carry Gonzales this far.

Gonzales yielded to Papa's every request.

He was a puppet for the Papacy.

As Americans were debating the significance of hanging chads in the post 2000 elections, a younger version Hector Gonzales was promoting a beautiful young Latina singer, named Ana Cristancho, on the Latin music circuit in Los Angeles. Sitting in the VIP section of one of LA's most popular Mexican nightclubs, he ranted on about his ideas for the formation of the Derechos Party as he kept one eye on the woman he would one day make his wife. Her hips snapping from side to side in perfect rhythm to the intoxicating meringue beats, she captivated the crowd, while Hector knocked back shots of Petron with the club's owner and reputed shot caller for LA's notorious Sur 13 gang, Pablo Cortez. Sucking bits of lime pulp from between his teeth, after just having finished his eighth shot of tequila, Cortez reached for the salt shaker and poured another heavy handed round as a four hundred pound bouncer walked over with Hector's take from the door money. The imposing young man handed Hector the envelope stuffed with cash and Hector quickly put it in the vest pocket of his coat, not bothering to count it.

Even if the money was off, there was no arguing with Cortez.

Hector's clean cut and almost boyish appearance made him seem out of place in the sea of thugs and gang bangers that frequented the establishments that he made his living off of as a promoter. Behind his back, Cortez and others like him often joked about Hector's seeming desire to align himself to corporate appearance. Still, no one could argue that he knew how to pack the house and he was popular with the club owners that used him for special events and bookings. He represented about fifteen bands and a few individual singers, some of which moved on to recording careers after having gotten their start with him. None got as much individual attention, though, as Ana.

Ana was a gorgeous girl with long dark hair and sultry eyes that were accented by thick, long eyelashes that perfectly framed her light chestnut eyes. She was smart and she worked her good looks to her advantage to ensure regular bookings through Gonzales, but she never crossed the line to flirtation and, to Gonzales. However, to him, that only made her that much more attractive. Her caramel skin was so perfect and creamy it almost seemed as if it had been painted on in one continuous smooth coat. The clothes she chose to wear on stage showed off as much of God's flawless design as she could legally get away with in public. Men loved her and other women hated her, especially those that were trying to break into singing in the same circles where she dominated. In reality, though, Ana never had big dreams of stardom. Instead, she used her voice to make her life easy as she put her way through college. The money she earned was far better than what she was making as a waitress and the hours allowed her more time to study and Gonzales' infatuation with her assured that she would get top billing at the best clubs in town.

And she knew it.

Occasionally, she would throw just enough of a look in his direction, from the stage, to make him wonder if she had any interest. But, just as quickly as she exited stage left she would return to business as usual and get ready to go home without staying for as much as one cocktail, despite the many offers that presented nightly.

Gonzales glanced over as she entered into her final set and continued his sales pitch to the heavyset, tattooed Mexican that sat before him. *"Oye!* We win on the numbers alone! Think about it, Pablo! If we organize now, in a few years we will see a Mexican in the Oval Office! *Nuestro pais!* It's all promotion! I *know* how to do promotion! In a few years our numbers will make us the majority! Why should we have to choose between Republican or Democrat? *Please!* Vote to help the white man that worked us in their fields and exposed us to pesticides? The same white man that would work us for minimum wage to increase their profits then deny us citizenship? Or the Democrats that would serve to give what our people have worked for to the whites and blacks that didn't even want the jobs in the first place! Those that were too lazy to do the work we broke our backs for at minimum wage? The whole reason we are here! The whole reason we struggled? Why help their cause when we can have our own!"

Cortez licked the salt from the cradle between his index finger and thumb and knocked back another shot before signaling his bouncer to bring another bottle of the top shelf tequila to his table, then shook his head as he smiled and ran his hand over his shaved head as he often did when he was thinking.

"Promotion? I think you'd be better off sticking to putting asses through the doors than worrying about Presidential Campaigning. Besides, who ya' gonna get to run? *You?*"

Puzzled, as if the answer was obvious, Gonzales nodded. "Yes, *me!* Why not? I have my degree, my family grew up here, I'm in touch with the community, I can speak in public… *Mi madre se murió del cancer* from working in the orchards out here so some rich gringo could get richer and save a few bucks! Every night she came home with her fingers bleeding and choking from the pesticides they sprayed over those fields. It's the story of our people. Whites used us just like the slaves. That campeñero knew she was illegal, but working her for two Dollars an hour, seven days a week was acceptable to him. She left behind nine kids and no life insurance! *We* are *her* legacy. They made us citizens and *now we will make them pay!*" His eyes were tainted with anger as he reflected on the memory of his mother.

Cutting him off, Cortez quipped. "Por favor, chingero, you're not even old enough to run!" Smacking his shot of Petron on the table.

Unfettered, Gonzales went on, still passionate about his plan. "No. But, in a few years I will be! I'm thinking long term, Cortez! Ten... maybe, twelve years. But, if we get started now we are sure to win! I can feel it! I just know! *Juntos podemos!* But, we don't need any white man to tell us that! This country is ours. All we have to do is take it!"

For a while, Cortez dismissed the idea of participating in political nonsense. But, one afternoon while mocking Gonzales in a conversation with his father, Cortez was surprised at his father's interest. Back in Tiajuana, Manuel Cortez did not find Gonzales' idea so laughable and he quickly convinced his son to get on board with the idea. Unable to travel to the United States due to legal complications, Manuel wired $25,000 US to his son, Pablo, with instructions on exactly what he wanted him to do. He then instructed Pablo to have Gonzales come to Tiajuana to meet with him and some of his associates.

The following week, Gonzales traveled across the Mexican border and met with Cortez' father and some of his associates in a small cantina on the outskirts of Tiajuana. In Hector's mind they were investors, but to the cartel Hector was a simple pawn. Manuel could read the naiveté in Hector's expressions, but his group played along. They were happy to have such a handsome, yet controllable young man as the spokesperson for their cause.

Upon Hector's return to Los Angeles, the Derechos Party was born.

Over the next decade things would go much according to the plans that Hector had laid out to one day gain the Presidency. For years, the cartels would even pay to move large numbers of Hispanics into key Electoral States and help them gain the required paperwork they would need to become registered voters. It was a good deal for most. Charmed by his initiative and enchanted by his new found, powerful circle, in 2009, Ana Cristancho became his wife and a perfect arm piece for photo ops. Over the next ten years, they would reach almost iconic status within the Latino community, yet they somehow managed to escape the English speaking media's coverage.

But, Hector had failed to plan beyond Election Day and now found himself the focal point of international concerns. Staring into a crowd that cheered with fury as they fed his ego, Hector was drunk with power. Waving to his supporters and smiling for the camera was easy, but behind closed doors, Hector felt lost as phone call after phone call poured in from all corners of the earth. Other nations demanding to know his position on the issues that concerned them and every one pressuring for information on the rumored Civil War that was about to break out in America.

That was the problem.

He had no positions on the issues.

Looking around the room at his first Cabinet meeting he realized he was in trouble. His Cabinet had no answers, either. These men had no experience in dealing with other nations, they were simply appointed at the Cartel's request. His brother-in-law / Secretary of Defense riled the group as he passed out shots of tequila and another ranted on about the fifteen whores that the Cartel would be sending over that evening as a "White House Warming Gift" for the men. Each, touting their own power and position and joking over who would get to use the Lincoln Bedroom for their debaucheries first.

The sloppiest and most unkempt member of the group, and also the highest ranking in the Cartels, leaned back in his chair, laughing as he pulled an over chewed and half smoked cigar from his mouth. Turning to another member of the group, whose eyes were already getting bloodshot from the tequila, he claimed his position. "Ain't no way no mutha fuckin' way no Secretary of Agriculture gonna be up in no mutha fuckin' Lincoln Bedroom before the Secretary of Interior!"

And then, the men turned to another classless topic, as thoughts raced through Gonzales' mind. He sat quietly, almost oblivious to the chaos and consumption that sat right in front of him as his mind rambled with questions in an almost nonsensical manner. "Why do they want to know my position on ethanol? Am I *supposed* to have a position on ethanol? What *is* my position on ethanol? Ethanol's good, *right*? *Why* is it bad to like it? Why do *they* care? *What* trade agreement were they talking about? They all sounded different. There must be more than one. I *don't know* how many nukes we've got. *They* know how many nukes we've got. It's like some game with them! Why are *they* asking *me* when *I* know *they* know the number. I'm not in this office *a week* and they expect me to know *everything* about this damn country? I wish Britain would *tell* me the number. Thought they we're supposed to friendly! *Yeah!* How hard *is* it to pick up the phone, '*Top o' the mornin' Gonzales, ol' chap! Your country has 232 nukes!*' Is *that* hard? It's *not* hard! *Wait!* That sounds high? Is 232 a lot? Maybe it's low? I wish China would *stop calling* in the middle of the night. Like they're so special they can call *me* at three in the morning and expect to chit chat! At least India's polite enough to wait 'til eight! Well, they should know our normal business hours. It's not like they haven't been answering phones for half the businesses here, for decades. I'm *hungry*. I wish we had some chorizos. *Wait!* I'm the President. I can *make* someone go get me chorizos *and* cook them and bring them to me!"

He was slowly losing it, and he knew it.

Gonzales placed his snack order with one of the members of the White House Staff that had remained. Several of them quit, or simply stopped coming in, only about a week into his Presidency when they suddenly realized that his friends and so called Cabinet Members had decided to turn the once respectable home into little more than a frat house. He then turned his attention the activities in the room and allowed his mind to blather on to itself in silent contempt for their debauchery as the mocking tone of his own voice echoed in his head. "*Look* at them. They're all a bunch of *morons*! *Who* wears flip flops to a meeting like this? *Who* brings a case of tequila to a meeting like this? Can someone tell me *that*? *Okay, calm down!* He's Ana's brother and he's family. Either the baby batter was a little old or the oven wasn't quite working right by the time they got around to making him, but he's family. Oh, *but God*, he's an *idiot*! Look at him! *Better to ignore him.* Just ignore them all. I don't even know half these people. Who let them in? How am I going to answer all these questions about the Northwest? Everything's fine. Why does every one think we're at war? We're not. *Right?* No, *I* would know if we were. *I'm* the President. *Nice. Oh, that's nice!* My Secretary of Health and Human Services *is pissing* on my peace lily plant. *Please tell me* the Secretary of Health and Human Services is *not pissing* on my peace lily plant. *No.* He *is.* And *they* think it's funny. *Of, course! Why not?* Not *one* of them has a clue! I am *so* screwed. And, Euclides there! The only thing he knows about being Secretary of Agriculture is that the title's gonna help him get laid! I doubt he's even stepped foot on farm! I'm *fucked*! I am *so* fucked! *Oooh! Wait!* China had questions about agriculture stuff! I'll give them *his* number. We'll see how much action he's getting after fielding fifteen phone calls from the Pacific Rim in the middle of the night!" Gonzales smiled to himself, his mind continuing to converse with itself, as he watched his soon to be victim of three in the morning phone calls mingle with the other men as two more made use of the new bathroom.

For all of his charm and charisma, Gonzales was not a politician, nor a Commander in Chief. Although he was power hungry, he did not know how to respond to the world's demands to understand America's new political agenda. To ease fears, he proposed a bill in 2022 to share control of US military forces with the United Nations, but the church was not willing to share, and the bill died in Congress.

Oregon, Montana, Colorado, Wyoming and Nevada began to seriously debate secession as other States around them were whispering the same sentiments in back rooms unready to go public with their thoughts.

Already heavily populated with current and former members of the US Military and law enforcement, the Northwest Command began taking control of bases and dutifully documenting the inventory of weapons stockpiles within the Territory knowing that Gonzales was ignorant of most high level secrets. Surreptitiously, many officers and military officials in the Pentagon, CIA and FBI began to collaborate with the Command, and fed information about some of the nation's best guarded secrets through the Territory's back door.

With the help of a super hacker, known only as "Tommy", a link inside the military controls of the US was established and the Command soon had the ability to access even those weapons that were outside of their borders. General Stahl patted the young computer programmer prodigy on the back and smiled to himself as he wondered what Gonzales' reaction might be if he had been aware of the Trojan Horse that was working inside of his own camp or how his own men might seek to betray him as the new leader of the free world.

General Ivan Stahl, the highest ranking member of the Northwest Command, who was credited with helping them quickly organize across state lines, was an amazing military strategist. In 1984 he had defected from Russia and served several years in the US Military, where he had earned among many commendations, the Silver Star and the Medal of Honor. He maintained a close, but clandestine relationship with many Officers stationed up and down the east coast from the Command's Headquarters in Cheyenne.

The Territory was fast becoming one of the safest, although most rapidly changing, places in the US. Sitting in the war room of what once was NORAD Headquarters, Ivan Stahl carefully monitored the multitude of screens before him, managing to keep up simultaneously with the information and the stories that each monitor told, as if he was individually focused on each one. Suddenly, something on a screen on the far left caught his attention, but without changing focus on the center monitors, the white haired General demanded a Commander to dial his contact in the Port of Savannah. His voice heavy and baritone, and with a still significant Russian accent, spoke with his back to the speakerphone in the center of the conference table, as Commander Rick Thomas looked at the satellite images of the Georgia Coast and tried to determine the threat.

The General responded to the voice that answered the line. "Lt. Commander, Zealy. Is Santa's sleigh what I see approaching the Intra-Coastal?"

"Yessir, General. The reindeer are on the roof. The elves are in position. We will have Coast Guard escorts until the package reaches the Port of Savannah."

"You please me. My men are to meet you at border to make delivery in eight hours. You do good work, Lt. Commander."

"Thank you, Sir."

"So you will to be to join us, Lt. Commander? Life is good in the Territory."

"I will be personally escorting the package, Sir. I would like to cross over, at that time, with your permission, Sir."

"Permission granted. I will notify troops assigned to meet you."

"Thank you, Sir."

"We see you in Cheyenne."

Stahl nodded to Commander Thomas, signaling for him to disconnect the phone, as Thomas questioned, "So our new weapons have arrived?"

General Stahl, in his traditionally stoic manner, simply nodded his response.

"Gonzales has no idea what he is in for!" Commander Thomas commented hoping to engage Stahl in conversation. When Thomas had first arrived, it seemed as if Stahl was more communicative, but now he seemed focused and distant. Thomas wrote it off to the ever changing events around them as he watched the General analyze the monitors before them, and waited patiently for his next instruction. Commander Thomas had an incredible amount of respect for the General, who seemed to fall into military poses as if his muscles had memorized their exact placement for each one: every ligament falling into perfect alignment. The long scar that ran over his left cheek, seemed less like a disfigurement and more like a badge of honor that he wore with silent pride, though not one of his men had the nerve to question its origin. He was clean shaven and seemed younger than his 76 years, easily commanding the respect of any room which he entered with nothing more than his presence. Thomas, a handsome young pilot with strong German features, admired him and served Stahl loyally.

"Call the border. Tell them to expect Lt. Commander Zealy. He is to be flown here. I do not wish for him to travel by car. He will have papers I am in need to review."

"Papers?"

"Are documents from dear friend in Russia. Should we have need. They are to come to me directly."

Thomas nodded as he took note of some of the screens before them and understood what it was that the General would wish to have a newcomer avoid. Thomas could tell from the General's tone of voice that Zealy would be welcomed straight into Headquarters: an incredible privilege in the Command. Zealy had served in the Coast Guard and earned the General's respect when they had worked together on a top secret mission following 9-11. Over the years, they stayed in contact and for the past twenty four months Zealy had been feeding information to Stahl regarding national security readiness planning. Stahl always acted impressed by the plans, but secretly he was searching for the gaps in the plans that Zealy had developed.

He only found a few.

Despite urban legends detailing stories of detainment camps, and of former prisoners and those opposing the Command meeting with horrific and unimaginable deaths, people fled to what they saw as "the new land of opportunity". As their ancestors before them, many whites began to hear the cry, "Go west, young man." And the populations in the Northwest, through to Nebraska and down to Oklahoma, began to swell. Eventually, the Mississippi River would become the dividing line of an area known as the Northwest Territory.

The nation continued to divide itself. With the Catholic Church at the wheel, there were no safe havens for agnostics, or atheists. Not that all of America was so lacking religiously, but the message was clear. In Gonzales' America, there was no right religion, but the Catholic religion. Slaughter over religious beliefs began in the streets. Those remaining Jews, that had not already fled west or moved out of the country, and fearing a second Holocaust, hung Catholic crosses around their necks, as they marched themselves, in shame, toward the Northwest, or simply fled to South America, as so many of their 1940's religious counterparts before them.

By spring, of 2021 over 235,000 white and black Americans had headed north to Canada, in an attempt to vie for Canadian citizenship, all the while complaining about the "damn immigrants that ruined their country." They never even realized the irony in their words. But Canada, seeking council from her big sister, Great Britain, refused to sit back and allow recent history to repeat itself on her own soil.

Canada turned them away.

A great many by force.

Watching the chaos below and fearing involvement, Canada manned her borders for the first time in history with assistance from the British Air Force. They were given orders to shoot on sight, without question. China and Russia, still economically devastated, salivated as they cast their eyes on Alaska. But, both decided to not to act, with the Brits so close by.

Those Americans that had already set up homes within Canada's borders, years prior, were once again rounded up and asked to prove their financial ability to support themselves. Canada kept many of the well educated and financially secure professionals that sought citizenship, but now required them to prove their financial stability on an annual basis. The rest, were simply deported back to the United States. House to house sweeps, searching for Americans living illegally on Canadian soil became commonplace and drew harsh criticism from international media.

Canada didn't care.

Even those who were privileged enough to be allowed to stay, found life in the great north very different than what they have left. They were told, in no uncertain terms, the laws of the new land in which they were confined. Here, there would be no uprisings, no civil rights movements, no changes to the current establishment. Canada was happy the way it was, and had no intention of yielding to any newcomer's beliefs. *"This is our way. You will learn it, or you will leave."*

Considering the images below them, many Americans living in Canada, found new words entering their vocabulary.

Patience.

Tolerance.

Adaptation.

In the end, Canada gained 42,368 new citizens.

They kept a *very* accurate count.

Back in the US, the divides were growing clearer. With gunfire in the streets, most heavily on the east coast where gangs struggled for control over one neighborhood or another, white Americans continued migrating west feeling secure in the knowledge that the Northwest Command (an odd mix of militia groups, former military and police officers now residing in the Northwest Territory) was armed. Gang violence and uprising was not tolerated in the regions where the Command had control.

It was a Police State, but it was peaceful.

On January 1st, 2023, the Northwest Territory, heavily armed, and with much of the former United State's military intelligence residing within her borders, officially declared war on the United States of America. The actions of the all white territory caused an anti-white sentiment across the rest of the nation.

The aged fingers of the Catholic Church pointed to the Territory in disgrace.

Black America, divided among both Muslim and Christian lines, could find no common ground with the Catholic majority. They agreed, to stand united, and fight for their own rights and rebelled against the establishment, feeling betrayed by their Hispanic counterparts and refusing to pay the 10% tax that the church sought from them.

A new movement began.

With the Northwest cocooning in her own shell, Black America analyzed the Hispanic rise to power. Leaders in the northeast, still trying to turn chaos into order, called upon their black brothers and sisters to see this as, not as a separation, but a celebration.

In the winter of 2022, there was a gathering of black religious leaders which was held in Harlem, New York. Together, they convinced themselves, that this was not the end of the United States, but the beginning of a new and stronger nation which would be able to start fresh. More cautious followers glanced west of the Mississippi, unable to comprehend the full implications of the Territory's declaration. With the highest levels of military power still heavily guarded inside the Territory, some worried about how far the Territory would go to reclaim a broken nation.

With the national economy in ruins, international investors pulled back their monies, as rumors of a civil war were broadcast around the world. The Vatican worked hard to squash such discussions within the US, and tried to keep all such coverage off of the airwaves. The underground media soon jumped on the story, though, and whispers in the streets slowly grew into battle cries.

Untrusting of the whites in the Northwest Territory, Blacks and Hispanics began to distance themselves from their self declared and rapidly expanding borders. Even those who had no interest in marches, or politics, felt uncomfortable sitting so close to the unpredictable group. Slowly, as more Blacks moved into the Northeast, rallying behind Elijah Drew's group which was centered in Harlem, Hispanic groups made their way further south.

The lines were drawn.

Borders defined.

America was lost.

Enter the Northwest

George and his family had packed themselves, and their worldly possessions, into their car and a small hauling trailer. There wasn't room for everything, so they packed what they could and began making their way over from the Georgia border to the edge of the Northwest Territory. At the time, no one really knew where the borders were, or would be, but they were Portland bound. A few hours into their journey, they stopped off to grab a bite to eat.

Along the way George had noticed the same scenes of abandoned homes and 'for sale' signs lining the streets, repeating themselves, as they made their way from town to town. Once beloved pets guarded the doors of the empty houses that no one was coming home to, as they struggled to keep their skeletons in their skin.

Hungry, they found themselves inside a small restaurant. Alli raced to the bathroom, little brother not far behind. She ran in, and when she emerged, she found Georgie outside the women's room door hopping from one leg to another, trying to stop his bladder from exploding.

"Didn't you go?" Alli thrust her hands on her hips, impatiently.

"Noooooooo. Dir'y.", the toddler whined looking for her help.

Georgie made a face as he looked back at the men's room. Now, jumping up and down his eyes implored his sister to move out of the way, as he looked passed her to the clean floor of the women's bathroom, still trying to hold off. Adamantly, Alli affirmed the sign above her, "Well, you *can't* use this one. It's for girls. See the *lady* on the door?" Alli pointed to the sign indignantly, then ran off, leaving her little brother to contemplate the exclusivity of a restroom. Sign or no sign, he quickly concluded that if it was unguarded, it was fair game.

Georgie returned to the table and the family ordered. The waitress seemed annoyed that she even had to deal with the pale faced group. George and Caroline had grown used to attitudes such as hers and tried not to let it bother them. Caroline looked around the room, noticing how much their faces stood out in the crowd. Whispers circulated around the room. Although she tried to ignore it, she knew that Alli didn't, and she wondered what effect the treatment they were being subjected to would have on the children.

Maybe she had just come to accept it.

As they ate, the eyes upon them felt hot on the back of their necks and certain comments made way to their ears. It was best to ignore it. Caroline, in her own mind, tired to examine what it was that would make an adult behave that way towards a child, though.

If only God had given us the gift to see ourselves, through a stranger's eyes.

She looked over at Alli, watching her as she carefully ate her peas, one by one, in her usual fashion. She remembered the day she was born and the innocence of new life. Caroline was only a child, herself, the day Alli came into this world. She thought of the hopes she had for her new daughter and George's smile as he held her. He was so afraid she would break. As she looked through the room, and noticed the hate in the eyes of people that surrounded her, she realized, at some point, someone must have seen the same innocence in their eyes.

Even if only for a brief moment.

Searching for answers in her scrambled eggs, she picked through the pieces that were burned black.

She had asked for them over easy.

George quietly ate, his mind drifting to a far away place, as Caroline tried to force conversation with the kids, just to avoid having silence at the table. Georgie smiled and laughed, as he pounded a small pile of mashed potatoes with his spoon. He wasn't a great eater. Alli, now discontent with her food, and disgusted with both her brother's table manners and her mother's unwillingness to make him stop, sat back and listened to the room.

"*Chinga los gringos y todo el pais.*" a voice carried, as the man's dark eyes glared over, gesturing to the small group.

It didn't matter how much Caroline had told Alli that people that acted this way were 'just mean.' She knew that Alli had seen it so many times, that she must have thought the whole world was 'just mean', by now.

Alli looked to her mother, but didn't say a word. They both knew what it meant.

If someone wants to hate their neighbor, it's easier to do if he never gets to know him. If they communicated, they might actually have found common ground, but it was too late for that now.

Maybe it was too late fifty years, ago.

Then again, if it hadn't been race or language or religion, it would have been another issue. Another line drawn to separate one group from the next. America had suffered from "check-a-box" syndrome for far too long.

As they finished their meal, Caroline wiped the potatoes from Georgie's face. He was wearing more than he ate. He clapped his hands, smashing bits of the mushy root onto himself and all over the table. Caroline smiled, as George signaled for the check. Alli neatly folded her napkin and carefully placed it on the table, aggravated by the mess her brother was making.

George glanced at the bill, and put it back on the table. $32.84. Concerned about money and the gas it would take to carry them to the other side of the country he left thirty three on the table. Noticing the numbers, Caroline whispered, "Aren't you going to leave a tip?"

"For what?"

"For the waitress."

"*They* don't tip. Why should *we*? Let's go." George stood up abruptly.

Embarrassed, Caroline avoided eye contact with their young server, as she picked Georgie up, adjusting his outfit, and searching for the one shoe he had tossed off. Reaching in her pocket she found two Dollars and some change. It wasn't much, but it was all she had. When George wasn't looking, she threw it on the table and quickly made her way to the door. With Georgie in her arms, she stuffed the small shoe in her pocket and headed to the parking lot.

Back in the car, they settled in for the next leg of their long journey. The drive seemed an endless repetition of dreams abandoned as the days passed on their approach to Portland. It had taken them over four full days, already. Both their money and their gas supplies were running low.

George, anxious to get to his new job, had driven through the night refusing Caroline's pleas to stop and rest, or to let her take over the wheel, for a while. It had been 17 hours since they last really stopped and rested, and with money so low, he refused to pay for another hotel room. To avoid argument, she let herself sleep, knowing that the worst that could happen would be that he would run off the road and she would no longer have to deal with his obstinance.

She awoke to his not so gently nudging of her leg and rain pounding on the windshield as they approached a sign welcoming them to Portland, Oregon.

"Do you think you can wake up and fix your face so you look semi-decent when you meet my new boss?" George scoffed, as Caroline struggled to awake from a coma like sleep.

Although her mind raced with a million insults she could fire back with, she ignored his comment and quietly responded, "My purse is in the trunk."

"Why the hell did you put it there?"

"Well, just pull over, I'll get it."

"I don't want to stop. We're almost there."

Caroline paused for a second, gathering a lie. "Well, I need to use the bathroom. I'm sure the kids do, too. I'll get it then."

Really, she just wanted to wash her face and have an excuse to put a door between George and herself. A few miles later, they stopped off at a Burger King and she headed into the restaurant's bathroom with the children following behind. George made his way to the counter to search for the cheapest items on the menu board.

Inside the restroom, Caroline splashed warm water on her face, bracing her arms on the sink, and took a moment to stare at herself in the mirror. She wished she still had her mother to give her advice, even though she had always chosen to ignore the counsel she had been given years ago. "What else could I have done?" the voice in her head questioned as she looked over at one of the stalls and saw Alli's little pink sneakers, suddenly rise up and disappear behind the metal door. Now, eight years later, she realized she wasn't happy and she wondered what kind of example that was setting for the daughter she had changed her life for when she, herself, was just a girl. George was all she had known.

She had settled.

And that was a miserable realization.

Although she loved her children dearly, she wondered for a brief moment how her life would have been without them. *What would her life be like, if she had followed Leticia to college and lived out their girlhood dream of being college roommates and terrorizing men on campus? If she had gone ahead with the abortion, like her mother suggested? What if she had never married George? She looked in the mirror and remembered a young girl, with long flowing hair, now reduced to more practical, short locks and wondered. What would life have been like had she lived her own?*

As tears of frustration quietly rolled off her bottom lid, she heard the flush of a toilet and quickly splashed her face again and pretended to be drying water away from her eyes as her daughter emerged. In her true, intuitive fashion Alli inquired, "Mommy, are you alright?" as she looked up trying to read her mother's expression.

Faking a big smile, Caroline looked down at her, "*Me?* Oh, sweetie, I am better than fine. Daddy's going to get a new job and we are all going to be very happy here, now come here and wash your hands." Over the years Caroline had become an expert at faking emotion, yet she neglected to realize the accidental gift she had passed to her daughter: intuition. Alli knew better than to believe her mother, but was an equally talented actress. So, she just smiled back.

While Alli washed up, Caroline started to fix her makeup, smiling at the child in the mirror. "Why don't you check on your brother and help him clean up. Tell daddy I'll be out in a minute."

As Alli led Georgie out the door, Caroline continued with her make up routine, and returned to her emotions, but refused to let herself cry while her mascara was drying. Not wanting to keep George waiting, she quickly ran a brush through her hair and looked for satisfaction in her reflection. "Good enough.", she thought to herself.

She exited, still arranging things back in her purse, only to find George waiting impatiently at the door holding two bags of fast food. She sighed to herself, noting his expression. She decided a pre-emptive strike would be the best approach.

"I'm sorry, honey, the kids needed to use the bathroom, and I needed to make myself pretty.", she said, trying to invoke a slight hint of coyness in her voice as she smiled at him, taking the bags of food from his hand.

"And *that's* the best you could do? After 15 minutes?"

For a moment, part of her hated him. Truly hated him. She wanted to cry, but refused to give him the satisfaction, or to shed tears in front of the children. As George headed to the bathroom, she simply countered, "I'll take the kids to the car. And it wasn't even 5 minutes... not *even* 5 minutes." Her voice trailed off as she whispered "asshole" in her mind.

Caroline walked out to the car, one arm to her forehead, not wanting to let the rain ruin her newly applied face. As the rain dripped on her back, she leaned in the car and made sure Georgie was buckled in to his seat, then found her own. She turned around to Alli, as she rummaged through the high calorie sack and asked her what she wanted, then dolled out the rations, accordingly. George had barely gotten enough food for the children and, given his own appetite, Caroline did without satisfied to let her anger nourish her. He didn't even seem to notice she hadn't anything to eat.

Suddenly the driver's side door flew open, and George planted himself at the wheel and reached for his own meal. Without a word, he started the engine and started the family on their way to his new job, and their new home. About 35 minutes later they arrived at the offices of a small construction company. George took a minute to finger comb his hair in the rear view mirror and pick slivers of lettuce from his teeth, before he made his way to the entrance, continuing his silent streak.

He hadn't said a word since the restaurant.

A few minutes later, without warning, he appeared back in the doorway; feverishly waving Caroline in, as though she should have known she was expected to enter. She unbuckled her seatbelt and grabbed the car keys, telling Alli to watch Georgie for a minute while she went inside the building.

"Well, this must be your lovely wife, George! You're a lucky man! Lucky, indeed." A tall, frail man, that must have been eighty if he was a day, with deep green eyes and salt and pepper hair. He stood up from behind the desk in the office to which

George had led her, putting out his hand to shake hers. His hands were bony, but soft and his eyes were gentle.

"Hello. I'm Caroline Anderson." she said softly, still trying to put earlier conversations out of her mind, but feeling self conscious as she pushed her hair back off to the side.

"Mort. Mort Epstein. Lead Architect and one helluva golfer, but I think that's just because most of my employees are afraid to let me lose to them. It's a pleasure to meet you, dear." Turning away from them for a moment, he coughed up another ball of phlegm into his handkerchief: over sixty years of working in dusty construction environments had taken its toll on his lungs. After clearing them out for another few minutes, he turned back George and Caroline and continued, "Really. You're a lucky man! So, are you kids ready to head off to your new apartment? Long way from, Atlanta, huh? Well, we're excited to have George joining the team. We made your housing arrangements, and the plan was to give you a few days to settle in, then George, here, could start once you're settled. I suppose Monday, the seventeenth, would be fine. I'd love to run you out there, myself, but it isn't far. We are on deadline for a bid and I don't think you'll have any trouble. Utilities are on. You should be all set."

Caroline listened as her husband's tone changed to suck up mode, but Mort didn't catch most of what he said as it was time to evacuate his bronchi again and his loud coughing covered up most of George's words. "Oh, no sir, we'll be fine. Caroline, here, well, she's just great about getting the house set up, and she's quick, too. If you need me sooner, I'm happy to come in. I'm just really excited about the opportunity. Caroline, too. We've been looking forward to this for weeks."

Mort nodded, looking down as he tried to discreetly check for signs of blood in the mucous that had cleared from inside him. He smiled, but it was obvious he wanted to keep the conversation and formalities as brief as possible. Always a gentleman, he didn't want to admit that he could feel the crackling inside his lungs as the fluids built nor his desire to strongly force it to the surface and out of his body. After the usual goodbyes, and handshakes, the two made their way to the front secretary and picked up a package with a map to their new apartment, along with all of the typical new hire paperwork that would be imposed on an employee. From behind the closed door to Mr. Epstein's office they could hear the old man hacking so strongly it was almost un-nerving, but the secretary seemed un-phased by the noises.

With a whispered voice, she passed a package to them, saying. "I told him he should've given up all those cigars years ago, but you know how it is with stubborn fathers." She shook her head sympathetically at his office door as Caroline nodded empathetically at the young woman.

In silence, they drove out about another five miles and found the apartment complex to which they had been assigned. Caroline's eyes grew wide with surprise as they drove through the gates.

"Oh, George. This is nice." Caroline was impressed by the idea that her husband had seemingly made a sound decision. His first in years.

"See. I told you we were doing the right thing. This *is* nice. What did I tell you?" George pretended he had been confident in his decision since they had left Atlanta.

For a brief moment, Caroline questioned her own hesitation. As they snaked their way through the complex, they finally made their way to the little piece of this town they would be calling home. Relieved that the long adventure was over, Caroline looked at the building and smiled.

They were home.

Once inside, she found herself growing even happier as she took in her bright new surroundings. The apartment was furnished and that shortened her workload tremendously, although she didn't remember that from the initial offer letter that had been sent out, now, three weeks earlier.

"I didn't know the apartment would be furnished, George? This is great!"

"I didn't either. There's a number on the paperwork here that we need to call to have stuff removed that we aren't going to use. Hmmm. That makes things easy."

Caroline wandered into the kitchen and began to assess her new domain. "George, look! There's even food in the fridge!"

At first she questioned the expiration dates, but quickly noticed everything was fresh. "Huh? I guess the old tenants must have left in a hurry." George called back.

"No. Everything's new? I don't understand. I've never heard of a company doing this?" Caroline was made almost nervous by the perfection of it all.

"I told you. This was a good decision. It was exactly how I expec..."

Suddenly a shrill scream broke their discovery time.

"Oh my God, Alli, what is it!" Caroline raced toward her daughter's voice, panicked and angry with herself that she had momentarily lost track of her own children in the midst of her own exploration. She quickly found Alli in the side bedroom, off the kitchen, the little girl was waving her hands in a desperate attempt to gain her mother's attention.

"The pool! There's a pool! Can I have this room, mommy? The pool is right down there! Look! It's right there under my window!" Alli pointed out the window with determination.

Caroline breathed a heavy sigh of relief, pausing, then walking over to see what had caused her daughter to have such a reaction. As she looked out the window and realized there was no threat, the adrenaline slowly subsided. Thirty feet below, the kidney shaped attraction, surrounded by lounge chairs, dominated the scenery. "Yes, Alli. This can be your room. If you promise to *never ever* scream like that, unless it is an emergency. Do you promise?" Caroline's nerves were still frazzled, but she calmed herself by quickly hugging her daughter tightly.

Still excited by the thought of a junior swimmer's paradise within eyeshot, Alli pulled back. Wide eyed and clapping, as she jumped up and down, Alli nodded in fervent agreement with her mother's request to not express herself at such a decibel level. Caroline shook her head, sighing deeply with relief, then made her way through the rest of the house, waiting for the other shoe to drop, expecting something to be horribly wrong, but she could find nothing.

It was perfect.

It was home.

For the next several hours, the family unloaded the essential boxes from their small trailer, and for the first time in years, Caroline felt safe. The neighborhood was quiet, and peaceful. There was no threat of swarming, no gang tags, no gunfire, no prostitution, no evidence of troubles. As she worked to unpack the same boxes she had carefully packaged only the week before, she smiled to herself as she found new homes for all of their little cherished belongings, and, for the first time in ages, George volunteered to get the kids ready for bed. She desperately wanted to call Leticia, but, given the time difference, she figured it would be too late, so she decided she would put that one task off until morning.

A knock at the door interrupted her debate and she opened it to find an elderly couple that introduced themselves as neighbors.

Muriel and Alfred Goldstein.

Holding a blueberry pie that was more of a tool to gain access to the home than a gift, Muriel stretched her neck to see around Caroline and gain access to a glimpse of the Anderson family's worldly possessions. Not waiting for an invitation, Muriel stepped over the threshold and began to make her way into their home. Her accent, quickly giving away her Long Island heritage. "No need to tell me where the kitchen is, dear, all these units are laid out the same. I'll just set this delicious pastry right in there so you all can enjoy it when you like! I hope you like blueberry! It's my favorite! Alfred doesn't care for it much, but a new neighbor is a perfect reason for me to fire up the oven and get at my baking!" Muriel scoped the apartment, taking her own mental notes, as she found a place to put the pie.

Caroline nodded politely as she pushed her hair from her face and checked it in the mirror and remembered Georgie's violent allergy to the berry. She was not expecting visitors and was embarrassed by her appearance as she hoped the elderly woman would simply drop the pie and leave. Muriel quickly made it obvious that they weren't going anywhere as she sat down then invited Caroline to sit on her own couch. Alfred, a little man that appeared to be in his early eighties, with a thinning layer of silver hair, followed in quietly, showing all of the indicators of a man that was used to being dominated in conversation for many years. He sat down, politely removing his cap as he leaned on his cane and allowed his wife to continue her attempts to engage Caroline in conversation.

"Here, sit, dear! You look exhausted! Moving is tough on us all! So I see you have the three bedroom unit? Nice! Alfred and I just have the two. One for us and one for our grandbabies for those rare occasions when that witch of an ex-wife will allow our son's precious offspring to come visit. I told Keith not to marry that money grubbing little wench! Ah, but what can you do? Love is blind! Right, Alfred?... *Alfred!* Right?"

The old man simply nodded, smiling, as if he had no interest in the conversation. Caroline, still trying to deal with the sudden invasion, fussed with her hair trying to think of a polite way to ask them to leave. Drawn in by the sound of the new voices, the children found their way to the room, although all Caroline could focus on was that it was past their bedtime.

"Well, my word! Aren't you two *muffins*! You *are*! You are just *muffins*, you are! And what are your names?" Muriel asked in a voice reserved exclusively for little ones.

"My name is Alli and *that's* Georgie." Alli looked down at her baby brother, still annoyed by his recent decision to watch her favorite doll go swimming in the toilet.

"Alli be nice. I'll take care of the doll." Caroline interrupted.

"Well, you can call me Miss Muriel and this is my husband, Mr. Alfred. Okay?" Alli nodded then bounded off to see what else of hers had been subjected to Georgie's curiosities.

"Is it just the two wee ones, then?" Muriel questioned and Caroline affirmed with a smile.

"Well, dear, I would not be surprised if number three comes along in the near future. These Portland winters have a way of drawing folks to the bedroom! A cold and foggy night, a little wine… next thing you know, you're coming home from the hospital with a little bundle in your arms!"

"I… We're not planning…"

"Of course, you're not planning! Who *plans*? Alfred and me, we just had the one boy, Keith, but we lived on Long Island most of our lives. Too expensive if you want to school them properly! We did. Our son graduated with honors from Harvard. Smart boy, always was. Still, ends up marrying that bimbo! One day, he tells me he's got a date with a khatikha from Jersey… three months later we're standing there watching our only child under the hoopah breaking crystal and throwing away half his money! Pretty girl, they had two beautiful children, still he should have thought it through and been asking the Rabbi *'Kamah Zeh O'leh?'* before saying 'I do'! *Right, Alfred?*" She whipped out a photo of two adorable little chubby cheeked tikes and passed it to Caroline, smiling proudly, as she continued. "Anyway, dear, enough about us. Tell us about your husband. What does he do? I assume the man that was with you is your husband, right?"

Suddenly feeling like she was in an interrogation, Caroline tried to keep her answers short. "Um, yes. That was George. He's going to work for Mort Epstein, here in Portland." Caroline tried to not seem as frustrated as she truly was about the sudden overthrow of her new living room in an attempt to not seem impolite.

"Oh, sure! Mort! We know Mort! Nice man! Really nice man! Alfred plays golf with him sometimes, when he is not in Denver. My husband works with the Command, so he is gone a lot." Muriel spoke as though Alfred was not even in the room, which did not seem to bother her companion of over fifty years who simply took casual note of his surroundings and lost himself in his own thoughts. Noticing the surprise on Caroline's face, though, as she looked at the man whose back was beginning to slump over with age, Muriel continued. "Oh, no, dear! Alfred doesn't actually serve on the front line. He works at the Denver Mint. For almost thirty years we had a wonderful printing business in the city! It thrived until the economy went down the pooper! So, the Command employs Alfred at the Mint. Actually it's the Northwest Command Commerce Division. Pays good money, but he's gone an awful lot. You're lucky to catch him! He ships out in two days." Caroline imagined that Alfred didn't mind the time away from home as much as Muriel suspected as she continued to ramble on. "It's real good that Mort is employing your husband. His business is NWCCD compliant, so you'll be fine."

Caroline looked puzzled as she asked, "NCWD compliant? What's that?"

"NWCCD, dear. Northwest Command Commerce Division Compliant. Long story short, before you go into any businesses you need to look for the NWCCD seal on the door. Basically, it means they take Dollars and not Euros. Most of the businesses around here do, but with Canada being so close some of them thought they would switch to the Euro since the Dollar became so unstable. But, you're fine! Those businesses are dropping like flies around here as the Command is gaining more and more control. We're taking this country back, dear! At any rate, be glad your husband works for Mort. He's a supporter of the Command, so his business will be fine and your husband can cash his check at any of the NWCCD businesses here. We don't have much use for banks, but don't worry. The Command has control of the Mint. Unfortunately, they also have control of my Alfred, here. Poor thing! I know how much he misses me when he's gone!"

Alfred smiled at the wall and patted Muriel's hand as his mind wandered back to a cozy bar in Denver where he could smoke cigars and have a nightcap far away from Muriel's criticisms. He relaxed himself with the thought that he would be returning there soon.

For a moment Caroline could not understand how a Dollar could have value on the east coast, and a Euro on the west, and she couldn't contemplate the idea of Euros being used as currency in the US. Had the truth been known, having control of the Denver Mint was a key part of the Northwest Command's control and also one of their most heavily guarded secrets. In reality, the Command had no real money inside the US Borders, but with the Denver Mint under their control they were able to print and circulate all that they needed within the Territory. As no one ever left the Territory, those inside of the Territory had no idea that the familiar bills they used to buy and exchange goods were, on the international market, quickly becoming worthless as the Euro replaced them.

A few years earlier, businesses in Portland and throughout the Northwest had begun accepting Euros to stay afloat. Their prediction that the Dollar was on a fast track to failure would be correct, but the Command needed to convince people otherwise. Early on, they began planting employees within the Mint and soon almost everyone employed was with the Command. To the outside world, it looked like business as usual. Inside however, truckloads of bills were being diverted to the Command. Those within the now tightly secured Territory received checks, just like they had in the past, and most didn't question the bank closings as the mortgage crisis had put many out of business. Business owners associated with the NWCCD received a 1% cash bonus from the Command for all checks they cashed from the Command and Command Friendly companies. The Command knew that with money in their hands, white America was content to live in a police state, oblivious to the truth. But, unaware of any of that she questioned, "Why would we not use banks? I've always used a bank? What is this whole NWCCD thing again?"

"Oh, you'll figure it out, Caroline! That's the trouble with being in your age group! Smart enough to know you now know more than you did at seventeen and too dumb to realize that us old farts might just save your brain from worrying about a thing or two. Set your mind at rest, child! You are going to do just fine, here. It's a very simple system. So tell me what do you do for a living, Caroline? Oh, wait! Let me guess, I'm good at this! Hmmm... give me a second... I have it! You're a teacher? Right? I'm right, aren't I? You might want to talk to Mrs. Campbell, just down the hall. I understand they are hiring a few teachers at the elementary school. Her first name is Ann. Lovely woman."

Caroline's eyes fell and she shook her head, almost flattered that Muriel would mistake her for a college graduate. "No, Muriel. I haven't got a degree in teaching... I... well... I haven't got a degree in anything. I just take care of the house and the kids."

Muriel waved her hand in dismissal, laughing. "Caroline! You don't need a degree! You need the ability to teach! You're a mother! You're qualified! Oregon passed a law, years back, when they were hit with a massive shortage of teachers. You can teach up to the fourth grade level without one. Well, except math. They cut that off at second grade, but still. Don't worry about it. I know they need the help. And, why... you'd probably get Alli in class."

"I couldn't. Georgie's too young and we can't afford…"

"What? A babysitter? You're looking at her! *I don't even charge!* Oh, I have plenty of references I could give you, but you're better off just getting to know your neighbors. I sit for all of their children when they're away. Work, shopping, hair appointments and even when they just need a break for a few hours. I don't mind at all! Especially, when Alfred is gone, which is most of the time. I love having the house filled with life! They keep me young! *And!* We have lots of fun baking sweets and all kinds of fun treats, so I can send them back to you all plumped up and smiling! Well, it is my right as a grandparent to do those kinds of things, you know? It is. And, well, for free babysitting most of the mothers don't mind." Muriel smiled as she looked at her next client, trying to cover up the fact that babysitting was nothing more than an attempt to fill the void left in her own heart in the absence of her grandchildren.

"I don't know what to say. Thank you for the offer." Caroline, as any young mother would, seemed stunned by the offer of pro-bono child care but, in the moment, she was certain she would never have reason to take advantage of the kindly offer.

"No need for thanks, dear! I am happy to do it! The apartment seems so quiet when Alfred is gone. I enjoy the company!"

Caroline smiled shyly to the man that had not said a word and, seeing an opportunity to dismiss her company, she faked a long yawn and said, "Well, it has been a long day and I really do need to get the children tucked in, but thank you so much for the pie and the offer to sit them. I really appreciate it."

Muriel stood up. "Oh, any time, dear! I know we are going to become great friends! We're just two doors down. I go to the market, nightly. I like all the treats for the wee ones to be fresh, so I go everyday. If you are ever in need of a gallon of milk, or some eggs, just let me know. I usually make my run between 4:00 and 6:00 pm. Don't hesitate to ask. All the mothers do!"

Looking for a graceful way to end conversation, Caroline stood up and reached out to shake their hands, but was taken back by a sudden and unexpected hug from Muriel. She stuttered through a rushed goodbye as she attempted to hide her uneasiness. "Thank you, really… for making us feel so welcome. I'm sorry you didn't meet George. He must already be sleeping, which is what our children should be doing right now! You'll meet him another time. My goodness, I can't believe it is 8:30 already? No wonder I am exhausted! I think I am still on Atlanta time. And, thank you again for the pie!"

Alfred stood, leaning heavily on his cane for stability. Ready to acknowledge Caroline's desire to settle in, he reached for his wife's hand gesturing for her to join him in his return to their own home as Muriel, as always, made effort to have the last word. "We will be seeing a lot of each other, I am sure!" With that, Muriel and Alfred made their exit and Caroline walked to transfer Georgie's little blueberry lined anaphylactic attack into the trash. She would later tell Muriel that George gobbled it whole, but would gently break the news that such behavior was good, considering she vaguely remembered the doctor saying that Georgie was highly allergic to blueberry. Just in case she ever did babysit.

Once the children had been tucked away, Caroline found the shower and then bed. Drying her hair with one towel, and wrapped in another, she made her way into the bedroom. When she entered, she found George, already sleeping, so she quietly slipped into a T-shirt and crawled, gently, into bed. Her mind racing with a million thoughts, she

listened to the rain and smiled as she slowly entered a dream, and for the first time in

what felt like decades, she slept the entire night through.

In the morning, Caroline called Leticia and rambled on about how wonderful life

was in their new found home State. If Leticia had been honest, she would have admitted

a certain pang of jealously, but she was content to revel in the idea that her best friend

was, for the first time, in so long, seemingly happy.

Surrounded by a war zone of looting and chaos Leticia found her thoughts, more

and more, in Pennsylvania. Life was becoming ever more threatening by the day and

Ronald began to consider Leticia's proposal to head north. Even though he didn't care

for Leticia's sister, he was starting to worry about how his bullheadedness would affect

Ty' in the long run. Riots were breaking out in the towns that surrounded them and calls

to join Elijah Drew's cause were growing louder.

This week, on Riker's Island Elijah Drew was spreading his message of hope and

hate to the masses.

And they listened.

At first, Elijah Drew was not a household name to most Americans. He had

gotten his start as a Muslim preacher and founded the Islamic Nation after failing to make

a career as a concert cellist. Overly impressed by his own talents, he was certain the only

reason he was turned down by the London Symphony Orchestra had been because of his

race. He wanted desperately to be a musical success, but as those hopes faded he turned

his talents to the Islamic Nation and used his public speaking skills to gain the notoriety he so desperately desired. His hatred of society, of the Whites and Jewish, festered as his popularity grew among a new found and captive audience: prisoners.

Donations poured in, supporting the Islamic Nation and their cause to spread the word of Muslim teachings to the black community. No one seemed to question that much of the monies that were dumped in the laps of Drew and his followers seemed to come from a variety of Muslim nations outside of the United States. Drew, in turn, took much of the funding and used it to start a "charity" to help free those he felt were falsely imprisoned by and unjust and racist, white majority legal system. After a few court victories with cases that were hand picked by Drew to be flaunted in front of the media, Drew, and the Islamic Nation, soon became synonymous with hope inside the prison walls of the United States. After his latest court victory, Drew would stand before a sea of photographers and camera men as he recanted how the Islamic Nation had freed yet another falsely accused young, black man.

The Islamic Nation gained international attention.

His round face and deep eyes, accented by thick and wiry salt and pepper brows, stared out into the crowd as he stood with his arm around a young black man, too thin for the suit that hung off his shoulders. In a deep voice, Drew bellowed. "And, today, justice is served! Not as is it was on September 3rd of 2013, when a jury *not of his peers* convicted this fine man! But, today, we have justice! Today, Marcus Keenan Washington is a free man! Today, we have made the courts see the truth and this fine young man's innocence has prevailed!"

The crowd thundered with enthusiasm.

Drew embraced the young man then passed him to his mother, who was already crying for the cameras, as Drew continued to field questions from the press. His organization now credited with freeing yet another wrongly accused, as prosecutors simply shook their heads at the spectacle in abhorrence at their failure to see the truth. Although it was true that of 18 cases that the Islamic Nation had worked on, 16 of the accused offenders had, in fact, been innocent, in the case of Marcus Washington, he was among the two that were not.

He had served only 6 years of a sentence that should have landed him the death penalty in only a few months, for the rape and murder of an eleven year old girl in North Carolina. He was now set to have a second chance as a free man. Marcus Washington would use that chance to brutally abduct, violate, torture and kill another child less than two years later but, in the moment, no one could know such information.

In the courtroom, attorneys for the Islamic Nation argued that the prosecution never bothered to run DNA evidence in the case. That was true. The murder weapon, bloody fingerprints and boot prints at the scene, were enough for the first jury. But, to the shock of the prosecution, when DNA was run, it was not a match. Marcus Washington walked away a free man.

No one had questioned if he had a partner.

It would take them almost twenty three months to reconnect.

And less than sixteen days after their reunion, little Lakreshia Tonkin would be found in a dumpster behind the apartment complex where her family lived. Her throat slit, her pelvis broken and her body set on fire in a vain attempt to cover up the evidence that might have convicted them both this time around.

Her family would have no justice.

They both fled and, presumably, they continued to walk among the masses of innocents they would turn into their next victims, given opportunity. By 2021, a total of sixty three children went missing before Marcus was gunned down by an uncle with a hunch.

At the time none of that mattered, though. The Islamic Nation continued to gain national celebrity as they worked on one case after another with increasing success. Requests from inmates poured in daily, and Drew struggled to keep up with the fast paced schedule of lectures and preaching that were beginning to make his a household name.

Even Ronald and Leticia were beginning to admire his work.

Truth was never a priority unless it served the Islamic Nation's cause.

Soon, Ronald and Leticia made plans to head to Pennsylvania. Much of their conversation on the way would be dominated by Drew's work and the frightening implications that the nation had inherited under Gonzales. Leticia shared her most private conversations with Caroline, but questioned how much of the information Caroline had provided was propaganda, given the negative attention the media had focused on the Northwest.

They made their way north to Philadelphia. Ronald had decided to drive straight through, and Leticia had prepared them well for the journey. Plenty of food and drinks were stored in a cooler in the backseat, with Ty' acting as guard of the goody jar. Behind them, they towed their lives in a large trailer. Pushing further up the coast, careful not to exceed any posted speed limits, they only stopped to use bathrooms when they refueled their car. Ty' found his bladder filling up faster than the gas tank was emptying and it took him a couple of stops to get his timing down.

When they arrived, at Leticia's sisters' house, all three could feel the blood rushing back from their lower back to upper thighs as they stood up, stretching the drive off of them. Leticia checked her makeup in a small mirror. The long drive had taken its toll on her. She licked her index finger, and pushed a rebellious lock back down into place, just in time to hear her sisters' voice echoing out from inside a modest two story brownstone.

Leticia's sister, Kenya, looked like a chocolate female version of the Pillsbury Dough Boy, a sharp contrast to Leticia's slim and elegant build. They had different fathers, which would explain most of their outward differences, but they were just as opposed on the inside as well. Growing up, Leticia had always been both the pretty one, and the smart one. She succeeded, seemingly without effort, much to Kenya's frustration and, at a young age, Kenya sought to define her own identity through the Baptist church. If she couldn't get anyone's attention through her physical attributes, or accomplishments, she would at least opt for moral superiority over her other relatives. God, in many respects, was the only person she felt comfortable talking to. She did have one great talent of which Leticia was always a little envious: her voice was no less than truly angelic.

At the age of 17, Kenya left school and married a 38 year old preacher by the name of Clyve Samuels, much to her mother's anguish. Leticia went on to college at GSU in Atlanta. By the time Leticia graduated, she had four nieces and nephews and Clyve had taken over a ministry of his own.

Ty' exited the car and braced himself for the inevitable attack, as he watched his oversized aunt's heavy feet pounding toward him. Her breasts reached him, a full foot before her body did. He tossed his head, seeking air, between the great hilly forms, struggling for freedom with his arms forced back behind him. It was just as well, he wouldn't have known what to do with his hands anyway. She kissed Ty' all over his head, leaving his hair feeling slightly dampened in a couple of spots. His bladder full, and unable to breath, Ty' thought the torturous shower of affection to be hellish. Ronald look on sympathetic, but quickly filled up his arms with the cooler and a few small toys, figuring that it would prevent similar assault. When she finally released him, Ty' could smell the lingering odor of Jasmine perfume which had seemingly worked its way into the fabric of his own clothing. He raced straight passed his Uncle Clyve and ran into the bathroom.

"Where is my baby sister! Ooooh! Look at you! Come over here, right now!" Leticia walked over to her sister, finding herself in the same position as the one her son had just escaped from. Ronald snuck off, his arms loaded down, and met up with Clyve on the front porch. Clyve nodded approvingly at his clever escape and pointed in the direction of the guest bedroom

After their hellos were done, Kenya showed Leticia and the family to their room. It was a small bedroom with a queen size bed, a dresser, and a closet that was too full to put anything else in; stuffed with choir robes, prayer books, and an odd collection of paperwork, including old family albums. There was more under the bed, as well. Leticia and Ronald crammed what they could in the little room, and exchanged glances to express their dissatisfaction with the surroundings. The tenement was so small they would surely have been heard if they said anything, but it didn't matter. They had perfected their own form of silent communication.

From the kitchen, the clanking of pots and a stir of conversation could be heard. As she cooked, Kenya broke in to a soft version of Amazing Grace. Leticia rolled her eyes at Ronald. She had never been much for religion and the cantation came across as a haunting reminder of why the families had always separated themselves by so many miles. They were just as far apart spiritually as they had kept themselves physically.

All of a sudden, Leticia caught a sense of a horrible scent on the musty air that floated through the room. As she made her way into the hall, it grew stronger and her nose furled as her mind wished it was just her imagination. But the odor was unmistakable. She walked through into the kitchen, her nose leading her past the sickeningly sweet jasmine perfume that Kenya was bathed in, and ignoring the rest of the dishes in progress, Leticia focused on a boiling pot on the stove. A large pot of green beans tainted with the stringy pink flesh she so despised. Kenya smiled, and continued basting several racks of ribs that would soon be taking their place in the oven.

"Mmmmm. Pork?" Leticia said faking interest as she watched bits of pig guts swimming around in the water, infecting every green legume with the vile flavor.

"Oh, yes, baby. Not just pork, my very best patented BBQ pork ribs. Nothin's too good for my baby sister!"

"Hmm. You even put it in with the *green beans*?" Leticia questioned, gently.

Kenya edged over to the stove to stir the pot, barely squeezing by a small table, and cornering Leticia right next to the pot, as the steam carried the stench to her nostrils.

"Gotta have that ham hock, baby. Clyve's from southern Alabama. He likes a ham hock in just about everythin'. He'd put one in his Corn Flakes if he could. Here, taste!" Kenya held up a spoonful of beans, fresh from the pot, just inches from Leticia's face. Her eyes immediately focused on a misshapen, clear piece of fat that jiggled on the spoon.

Leticia forced her way out, politely kissing her sister on the cheek, "No, no. Don't want.... to... spoil my appetite. You just... just work your.... magic!" she pushed out of the kitchen and back to find Ronald. She grabbed him by the arm, and pulled him into the bathroom, closing the door and turning the faucet on full blast so no one could hear.

"I don't believe her! Do you know what she *did*!" Leticia fussed in a hushed and angry whisper.

"She's cooking *pork*! She *knows* I hate pork! I always have! She did this on purpose!" Ronald looked away, afraid to confront his wife's adamancy, and remembering this same argument from a family reunion years ago.

"Just... calm down. Maybe she forgot."

"Forgot? *Forgot!* We grew *up* together! She even put it in the green beans! Who the hell dumps a chunk of hog fat in a pot of *vegetables*!?"

"Well, my moth..."

"*Ooooooh!* I don't want to hear about your *mother*!"

Leticia clenched her fists as she looked at her husband, her blood beginning to boil with frustration. An unexpected pounding on the door interrupted them. Clyve's voice bellowed from the other side.

"The Lord ain't providin' this household with free water, ya' know!"

Leticia's eyes flared at the wooden barrier between them, as she reached over to slowly turn off the faucet. Her fingers choking the metal handle as if it were Clyve's neck. She kept her one hand tightly around the faucet, her knuckles turning pale, as she looked over her shoulder at Ronald. He pushed the air below his hands down, signaling Leticia to relax.

Their first evening in Kenya's home set the mood for the weeks to follow. Soon the cramped conditions and differences of opinion would take their toll on the household, and Ronald realized he would have to make other arrangements.

Living in a preacher's home, with a preacher's family, was difficult for the small group that claimed no official association with any organized religion. Ty' was the only one that seemed comfortable with his surroundings. He was more than happy to sit in Sunday school listening to old Mrs. Guthries as she told stories of a Jewish carpenter with an excitement that made it seem like she had known the man, personally. Wednesdays were his favorite day, though. He spent long hours in the kitchen with Kenya, as she prepared treats for Mrs. Guthrie's' class, and Ty' assigned himself the duty of licking bowls of brownie mix lined with a sweet drug, new to his taste buds.

Sugar.

Aunt Kenya dealt the crystal white powder with criminal skill, and had found an excellent customer in Ty'. She frequently exchanged his help with chores for treats snuck into his system under Leticia's radar.

Ty' possessed an innocence that had eluded most of his generation. In his short life he never met a stranger. Partially due to his parents' sheltering, but then again, it was

103

just the child's nature. He could stare into the eyes of Lucifer, himself, and not see evil. Looking, instead, for the qualities that once placed such a creature at the right hand of God, and wondering how such a fall from grace could occur in the company of angels.

Kenya cherished this.

While Ty' was enjoying the time with his new playmate, and Leticia was focused on escape, Ronald spent his afternoons sitting at a table in a small local coffee shop looking for work. But, even here, jobs were scarce and he had no luck. He felt himself a failure, as their savings dwindled away a little more each day. He had always made his own way, and been able to support his family, but things were getting tough. His only comfort being that the rest of the nation had similar stories.

But, he wished things were different.

Sitting in the diner, he made one last pass through the want ads, hoping that the one grand opportunity to change his life had somehow eluded him the first two or three times around. Certain he had read every line of newsprint, twice, he concluded there was nothing. Not ready to return to Kenya's, he ordered another free refill of coffee and began thumbing through the paper for an article that would capture his attention or at least block his mind from the discouragement that was drowning it in the moment.

Most of the paper boasted about Gonzales and tried to sell the message that America was on the brink of a complete economic turnaround. As he read the articles he shook his head in disgust at the propaganda and wondered exactly how many people in the country were reading the same information and believing what was written. Every page he turned seemed to speak of nothing more than the positive impacts of Gonzales'

Presidency, but as he looked around him and reflected on the past ten years of his life he couldn't find reason to agree.

His mind wandered to thoughts of George and his family. Images of happier times, of birthday parties, of nights on the town, flashed in his mind like some a brief series of video clips. Happy little images that were burned in his memory. Why his mind had chosen, of all of the moments of his life, to keep these specific ones so close to the surface, he didn't know. A laugh, a certain expression, a smile: they were all right there whenever he chose to call them back.

He wondered, if faced with certain death, if these would be the same images that would flash before him in the final seconds of life, or if there was some special reel that his mind was saving for that occasion. And if so, how would they be different?

Staring into the space across the table from him, with no specific point of focus, he realized he missed his friend. He had forgiven George, but not himself, for their conversation. Now, he didn't even know how to get in contact with him or what he would say, if he could. As he continued making his way through the paper, he came upon an article on Elijah Drew.

This he could relate to.

Instead of the Vatican influenced stories that now dominated the media, this was an article that spoke to him. Elijah Drew was established as a very prominent leader of a large group of black Muslims, based in Harlem, NY. His organization, the Islamic Nation, had become a force to be reckoned with especially in the past few years. An unsuccessful attempt to assassinate Drew in 2018, only helped to rocket him to pop idol status and further the goals of his organization as more and more top rappers and musicians began composing music about Elijah.

The main goal of the Islamic Nation was to convert black America away from Christianity, preaching that the Muslim religion was the one true religion of the black man. As the Catholic Church's influence grew stronger in the US, so did membership in the Islamic Nation. The black community felt more and more isolated by uncompromising Christian ideals being dictated from Rome and odd mixes of the Baptist and Muslim religions began to spring up in major cities, including Chicago, New York and Atlanta. Although, Baptists still prayed to "God", the ideals of "Allah" became more and more prevalent in the weekly sermons that echoed down from the pulpit. Sermons, which were fed to churches by the Islamic Nation. It was a gentle conversion that left many not even realizing they were slowly changing religions.

In an ingenious move, they released *The True African Bible*. A bastardized version of the Koran that was easy for Black Christians to accept and an invaluable tool in their attempt to convert the masses. The Islamic Nation had many agendas, but those that were most public were not the ones that were their greatest concern.

However, the article before Ronald did not deal with religious rights or wrongs, or conversion or conspiracy: it simply dealt with opportunity and hope. The Islamic Nation was excellent at selling this message. For years they had practiced in America's prisons marketing their promises to those who would seem to have the least amount of hope at all: those serving life sentences. Over the years, America's prisons had become violent extensions of the war zones that existed on the streets and the same gang leaders that once roamed the alleys of America's cities still held power to control masses from behind bars. Confining them in their concrete rooms did little to effect change on the problems that still existed in the streets, but somehow it seemed to comfort the American people's psyche to know they were locked away.

A countrified notion.

With all hope of ever seeing the world outside their prison cells removed, shot callers had little motivation to step away from the only lifestyle they had ever known. There was no desire to better themselves, to educate themselves, or for maintaining good behavior. They, better than anyone, knew that after so many years behind bars had passed, even if there was a chance for life outside those walls, they would no longer know how to function. They were institutional men.

Bloodshed bought more respect than brownie points with the warden ever could.

The Islamic Nation injected hope into the system, though. As prisons segregated themselves based on gang affiliation and race, as much as the rest of the country was doing beyond the razor wire fences, whispers in the prison system promised a life beyond the metal that twinkled in the sun. Hope of escape to a better life that was guided by Elijah Drew's hand.

In 2014, a huge prison break at the Atlanta Federal Penitentiary placed no less than 36 men serving life without parole back onto city streets. They disappeared into the night and were never heard from, again. Citizens in Atlanta screamed for tighter security as prison officials scrambled to explain how such an escape could have been coordinated.

Although the Islamic Nation never claimed official credit for orchestrating the escape, or the riot that preceded it, prisoners knew the truth and began to equate conversion to the Muslim religion with freedom. Elijah Drew was hailed a hero. In the minds of those living life behind bars, Elijah Drew had given back hope to every prisoner in the country.

Although the real truth was never revealed, and the Islamic Nation was never proven to have been involved, rumors circulated quickly that after their escape the men were rushed to a local mosque where they were all provided with new passports, bearing Muslim names, and then taken to Newark, New Jersey. After their trip to Newark, they were ferried out into international waters to rendezvous with a cargo ship that carried them to the Middle East, where they eventually would end up in a Pakistani training camp.

It was easy to convert their loyalties against a nation that intended to watch them die in a stony room, cut off from their families and the world. The devil found a rich market for converting souls in the prison halls that peppered America's landscape, as politicians made promises to work harder to keep evil penned away from society. By 2017, six similar prison breaks had been successful in removing a total of 126 hardened inmates from their cinderblock caves.

When the media began to scandal that which was common knowledge in certain criminal circles, the Islamic Nation rebelled and simply accused the US government of trying to slander their religious beliefs and Elijah Drew. Blacks, regardless of their religious affiliation, protested the government's accusations openly in marches across the country. White politicians, fearful of being labeled with a Scarlet "R", immediately backed off from the conflict.

On September 8th, 2018, while leaving a local rally in Chicago, Illinois, a sniper's bullet found its way into Drew's skull. After 15 hours of surgery, he miraculously survived and his quick recovery only helped to fuel the belief that he was larger than life itself. A war of words broke out in the media between the US government and the Islamic Nation, who accused the CIA of the assault. The US Government countered by accusing the Islamic Nation of associating with, and receiving funding, from known terrorist groups in the Middle East.

Untrusting of the US Government's agenda, black America turned a deaf ear to their accusations and instead began to hail Drew as a visionary. The next Martin Luther King. A voice for the people.

Soon, the rooms of black youth and prison cells alike were adorned with posters of Elijah Drew that likened him to Moses. The words "Let my people go!" emblazoned in red ink. Responsible for the escapes, or not, the people had rendered their verdict and Elijah Drew was their hero.

As Ronald read through the article, paid for by the Islamic Nation, he, himself, found inspiration. The article spoke nothing of the Islamic Nation's politics, but it did speak about job opportunities and growth in Harlem. As he thought about the cramped conditions that he and his family were sharing with his sister-in-law, he began to wonder if the grass just may be greener on the other side of the Pennsylvania border. What could he possibly have to lose?

His reading was interrupted by the waitress, as she topped off his coffee and took note of what he was reading. "*Oooh!* Elijah *Drew!* What a *great* man! I mean a *great man!* They's gonna *save* our people! I got *no* doubt! *No doubt!* Just like they's saved my cousin!" The thin woman with a dark complexion and a neatly tied scarf, testified to Ronald.

"You *really* think so?" He questioned as he looked around the room for another opinion.

"Baby, I *know!* Elijah Drew's the only good thing the black man has going for him in this country. You think them honkies was racist? Honey, take a look at them Mexicans! You think things gonna be any better when we all gots to report to the peoples that trained us to be enslaved gots control of the whole damn country?"

"I don't recall Mexico having anything to do with slavery." Ronald quietly argued as he sipped his coffee and focused his attention on the paper.

"Course, you don't! 'Cause them Mexicans don't want you to know! But, Elijah Drew he gonna tell you the truth, baby! He gonna tell you 'bout them sugar fields in Cuba where they done 'trained' us to be slaves. He gonna tell you 'bout how we was whipped when we prayed to our true African Gods and so we had to rename them and pray to our Gods by the names of white Saints. He gonna tell you 'bout how the white man done us, but he gonna tell you 'bout them Mexicans, too. How you think Santeria got born? It was how we gots some connection to our roots! The white man didn't want that and he hired them Mexicans to enforce them rules and break us so we'd work them fields. Didn't keep us from prayin', though! *No, Sir!* We *still* prayin'! I pray *every day* that a man like *Elijah Drew* make his way to the White House and do the right thing by us."

"That wasn't Mexico. It was Cuba. Cuba was the holding ground. That's where Santeria was born. They aren't Mexican. It's a different country. You're mixing religions, here."

"Cuba… Mexico… all the same to me! We's all the same to them, too. All I know is that Drew is fightin' to change that! Now they's got the White House, who knows what gonna happen? All I need is to feed my babies, but there ain't no Mexican gonna care 'bout me. They *all* mixed religion to keep us from Allah. And that's the *damn* truth!"

"I don't know that you can say that. The whole country is a mess, but it's not their fault. You can't blame one group."

"I ain't sayin' its they's fault, I'm sayin' Drew is the only thing standin' between us and a future Black Holocaust. Brother, you need to hear him speak! He gonna make you think! He's done saved two of my own relatives and provided for good jobs and they's doin' good! If I could, I'd be on the next bus to Harlem."

"So why aren't you there, already? You have family there, you said?"

"True… true… I'm gonna be honest, I was raised in the church. I *love* Jesus! But, Elijah Drew has explained how Jesus is the God of the white man and that Allah is our God. The God the white man *took away*. I struggle with that, but I's tryin'. I's tryin' to do right by my ancestors." She adjusted the headscarf that she had seemingly, only recently, become accustomed to wearing.

"Why can't you love both? *Accept* both?" Ronald questioned as he reflected on the concept that he had posed the question of the ages to a simple waitress, yet held out hope that perhaps she would have the answer that all the leaders of great nations did not.

For a moment she pondered, giving serious thought to his question, then she answered. "Cause somebody got to think they's right. It's like math. Can't be, but one right answer to who God be."

And there it was; simple, yet honest.

And for an hour they spoke of Harlem and hope.

Walking back to the overcrowded brownstone that was his temporary home, Ronald's thoughts meandered across state lines. He made his way to the front steps of the dwelling and from the sidewalk he could smell dinner cooking and he knew his wife would not be in a pleasant mood, again, this evening. He was almost in agreement with Leticia that Kenya had chosen to torture her by serving her most hated foods, although he couldn't admit it to his wife. As the scent of fried chicken livers carried its way out to the street, he hung his head, and before he turned the doorknob, his decision was made.

Now, all he had to do was convince Leticia.

That evening, after the normal chaos of their evening meal, Ronald and Leticia settled into bed. She nestled into his shoulder, one leg tossed over his, comforted by his arm pulling her close. Her stomach's only comfort, yet again: a piece of cornbread and some unsweetened iced tea. On the floor, resting quietly on a small air mattress, Ty' was beginning to dream about his secret affair with chocolate cakes and cookies that Aunt Kenya was happy to enable. Rolling over on one side, and propping his head up in one hand, Ronald gently stroked the side of Leticia's face with one finger and gazed into her eyes. The lights from the street provided just enough illumination to allow him to see her face clearly. She was so beautiful, and he loved her more than he could have imagined loving any other person or thing on the face of this earth.

"Tish, are you happy here?" he whispered.

She smiled shyly and took her eyes from his, not wanting to respond, knowing he already knew the answer to his own question.

"You're not. I know. And, I'm sorry." Ronald's voice echoed defeat.

Her eyes darted to his, and with an almost sympathetic gaze, she pulled herself up, half over his chest. "Sorry? What on earth would *you* ever have to be sorry for?"

A million small infractions raced through his mind at once, but he settled on the one thought that was hardest for him to admit, "I'm sorry... for not making you happy."

"Oh, Ronny, as long as I have you, and Ty'... I'll always be happy. I'm the one that should be sorry. This was my idea. This pork lined, cramped, religious zealot's paradise of a mess was all my idea, not yours, I suppose I should have put more thought in..."

"Stop, Tish! Really! Stop! I love you! I have loved you since the first moment I saw you and wished those long legs accented by, what I must say was and extremely short red mini skirt, were wrapped around me. I never stopped loving you, but in this place I can't provide for us. You know that." He winked, knowing he didn't need to elaborate on their misery as she simpered back.

"Ronny, we're fine." Leticia said in her typical, reassuring fashion.

"Tish, we're cramped on a queen bed in a bedroom that used to be used as back up storage for the choir, as our son is trying to sleep on an air mattress on the floor, that I continually trip over, and you think that's fine?"

Leticia simply stroked the side of his face, uncertain of words, and not wanting to bruise his ego, though he saw the truth in her eyes. So, he proposed. "Harlem? What do *you* think?"

"I think we don't know *anyone* in Harlem." She said softly, discontented by her surroundings, but thankful that they were familiar.

"I could get a good job there, 'Tish. I spoke with a waitress at the coffee shop and..."

"Please *do not* tell me that coffee shop waitresses are now guiding my future?" Leticia seemed to immediately lose interest in the conversation.

"Listen, please. I spoke with a waitress at the coffee shop and she gave me the numbers of a couple of people that can get me work and get us a place to stay. Our accounts are running pretty low, you know. Besides, you're miserable, here, 'Tish... please *consider* it."

"Okay. For you... anything, my love! Anything for you. We will *consider* it." Leticia spoke gently, knowing the wrong words, or too quick a response, would emasculate him. In truth, though, she was ready to pack and leave in that moment.

Suddenly, loud commotion in the living room drew the couple from their bed to investigate. There, being helped onto the sofa, was Clyve. His face bloodied and his left eye so swollen, it appeared as though his eyelid would burst open at any second under the pressure of the fluid that was building. Kenya hurried to the kitchen to grab a bag of peas from the freezer as Clyve grasped his chin, moving his jaw bone from side to side, in an attempt to assess the damage.

"What the hell happened?!" Leticia questioned anxiously, horrified by the scene.

"It's nothin', baby, go back to bed." Kenya tried to reassure her, waving her away from the situation.

"*Nothing?* Kenya, I am looking at your husband's face! Don't tell me *that* is nothing!" Leticia approached cautiously, noting the trail of blood that had dripped from the front door to the recliner where her brother-in-law now sat with his head tossed back.

"He'll be fine. This is nothin'. It's been worse." Kenya pressed the cold plastic against the swelling, and Clyve nodded a thank you to her.

"*Been* worse? This has happened *before*? When did this happen before?! What happened to him?!" Leticia nervously begged answers from her sister.

"A few of the kids from the buildin' over. They just wanted them some money from the church collection plates, they don't mean no harm."

Leticia looked at her sister in disbelief, "*This* isn't harm to you? My God, Kenya, *look* at him!"

"Hurt or not, ain't no one takin' the Lord's name in vain in my house! Just go to bed. I'm fine." Clyve interrupted as he waved his finger at the ceiling and fired an angry look towards Leticia in an attempt to regain his manhood.

"Like *hell*, I will! This is crazy and you *know* who did it? I'm calling the Police." Leticia countered as she walked towards the phone. She almost seemed proud to emphasize the swear and make her point in front of Clyve as he scowled in her direction.

Kenya rushed over, their hands reaching the phone simultaneously as Kenya kept her hand firmly wrapped around Leticia's, not so gently pushing her nails into her sister's flesh, preventing her from dialing. "Leticia, ain't gonna do no good. You'll get us *killed* if you try that. Besides the po-po don't pay no mind to what goes on in this neighborhood. If you want to help, pray for the poor boys that lost their way thinkin' this was their only answer. They just tryin' to make ends meet, too, baby girl."

Leticia looked at her sister unable to decide if she was certifiably crazy or overly forgiving. The two women were at a crossroads mentally, but Leticia knew her sister was sincere in her belief, and given the circumstances, she did not want to do anything to make the situation worse. She released her grip on the phone, and Kenya smiled and nodded as she placed it back on the cradle, patting the top of Leticia's hand.

The creaking of a floorboard down the hallway, signaled that Ty' had been awoken by the conversation and Ronald immediately moved to run defense and keep Ty' from seeing his uncle in this condition. He walked down the hall and scooped the sleepy little guy up in his arms, cradling his small back to his chest and forming a swing with his arms, Ronald carried Ty' back to their room, making sure he kept him facing away from the troubles in the other room.

"*Whoopsie!* Here, we go! Back to bed, little man!" Ronald whispered, trying to convince the boy that nothing was wrong. Speaking in a tone that was reserved specifically for those top secret father-son conversations, Ronald tried to keep his only child from suspecting anything was less than perfect in the room behind them. "That's just your mommy and Aunt Kenya getting into it, again! Aunt Kenya sure is silly, isn't she? She makes good cookies, though! Yeah, you like those chocolate chips! *You're a little chocolate chip!*" Ty''s little eyes fell shut as he gave a little smile and a nod. "I know she gives you all that sugary food! You and I need to keep that a secret from your mommy. *Ooh, your Aunt Kenya and mommy don't need any more reason to argue, do they?* Let me go straighten this out and you stay in here and I'll make sure I keep your mommy busy while Aunt Kenya is baking all those goodies tomorrow." Before Ronald even pulled his favorite blanket up over him, Ty' was already dreaming he was in the kitchen licking cookie dough from the bowl and sneaking handfuls of chocolate chips from the bag when his mother wasn't looking.

Leticia came in and shrugged her shoulders, satisfied there was nothing she could do to help and having decided that help unwanted was nothing more than interference. Back in bed, Ronald felt the timing was right to revisit the notion of moving on to Harlem and told Leticia about the article he had read, earlier, that afternoon.

"I don't understand. You want to work for the Islamic Nation? We're not Muslim, Ronny." Leticia looked at him, almost bewildered by his proposal.

"No, I don't want to work for them. They run a job center in Harlem. Starting pay looked pretty good, too." he sighed, "We've gotta do something, Tish. I'm gonna call this guy that the girl at the diner told me about."

"Okay. I suppose it can't hurt. Honestly, it might be better. I can't believe what just happened. What if those guys try to break in the house? What if they follow Clyve home? If he's carrying around the collection money, they might think there's more here?"

Leticia and Ronald debated only briefly before deciding to go. It seemed the lesser of two evils and given the events of the evening, Philly was seeming no safer than the life they had left in Atlanta. At least, in Harlem, they would have the opportunity to be in their own space. They had both grown to feel like they were squatters in Clyve and Kenya's home, which was already filled with members of their own brood that all seemed to keep different sets of hours. Ty' was a heavy sleeper, a trait he inherited from his father, but Leticia was not so lucky. Every creak from the floorboards upstairs, every twig that tapped their window on a windy night, every car that drove by: they all woke her at the most inconvenient hours. She often found herself lying in bed in the morning, still exhausted, and it showed at the breakfast table. As a result, she often found herself taking naps in the daytime when Ronald went for his daily walks and most of the rest of the house was either working or sleeping, too. Kenya kept Ty' occupied and enjoyed sharing her soap operas and sweets with the small boy that seemed so fascinated by the gossip from the daytime programming. He still hadn't quite figured out that the stories weren't real and would often look shocked as Kenya described the horrible betrayals of one character against another, tilting his small head to the side like a sheepish Labrador trying to understand.

And they bonded over scripted drama.

Moving day was a relief for Ronald and Leticia, but for Ty' it was a painful separation. He had grown very close to his Auntie Ya-ya in the time that they had spent in her overcrowded home that held more dusty knick knacks than their church had bibles. Kenya wiped away his tears, as his lower lip pushed forward wrinkling his small chin, promising to visit soon, knowing she was lying. In a final attempt, she had begged them to let Ty' stay, and the youngster's eyes filled with momentary hope, but his parents would hear nothing of it. Ty' pressed his small hand against the auto glass from the back seat, as Kenya mirrored with her own on the outside, now wiping away the warm waters that were flowing down her own cheeks, as Ronald threw the car into drive and they were both forced to let go waving.

Ty' sobbed quietly the whole way to Harlem. Unable to find the courage to ask, Leticia wondered what it was that her young son saw in her sister that she had failed to.

Upon arriving in Harlem Leticia and Ronald bore witness to the excitement promised. A renewed faith and spirit engulfed the city, and was inescapable. They had waited over two hours in traffic as Ronald carefully made his way through the hectic city streets and, as the ad had promised, he encountered the Islamic Nation's headquarters in Harlem. The center bustled with those seeking opportunity for work.

They entered the small community center and announced their presence to a man named Mohammed, who handed Ronald a package of paperwork to complete. A couple worked at another table which had made arrangements to provide temporary housing in local hotels at discounted rates. Leticia took notice of the plain young woman, who quietly focused on arranging paperwork, as the man, assumingly her husband, welcomed newcomers and helped arrange for their shelter. The woman, garbed in a loose fitting grey outfit which covered her from head to toe, avoided eye contact with those that approached and didn't say a word the entire time that Leticia was watching her. As Leticia looked around, she noticed almost all of the women were dressed like this and she suddenly felt a little self conscious about how short her skirt was, as she pulled it down to its most modest, but still very above the knee, level.

It took about an hour and forty five minutes to complete all of the paperwork required to receive assistance from the Islamic Nation, but Ronald was happy to encounter the list of open positions. He gladly handed over his resume and chatted away with one of the recruiters, while Leticia sat quietly with Ty', who was growing restless for sleep, waiting for him to finish. They then found a suitable hotel, and Leticia, Ronald and Ty' wandered back into the street. All of a sudden, Leticia felt a stinging in the back of her neck. She instinctively reached to feel for broken skin and examine the source of her pain. She turned around only to find a small group of boys, of mostly nine or ten year olds, throwing rocks at them.

"What the hell do you think you're doing!", she screamed over to the group calling attention to herself.

"Whore!" a child, no more than twelve, cried back from the group.

Leticia reached down picking up the rock that had assaulted her. Tossing it in the air, like a baseball, she snatched it back from the air, as it was falling, and quipped, "You could have really hurt someone you little jerk!"

"I was hoping to!" the pitcher called back.

"Well, then! *Me, too!*" Leticia rubbed her neck then fired the small chunk of granite back at the group, careful not to hit anyone, but close enough to scare a few of them.

Leticia, in her younger days, was a star athlete for GSU's Softball Team.

"You really should get your wife under control." A passerby commented quietly to Ronald. Glaring at Leticia's behavior, as if she was a misbehaving child, he continued on, shaking his head as he walked away. Suddenly Ronald began to realize he had spent the past few months moving his family from one war zone only to enter another. He noticed how Leticia's long legs and short skirt must have stood out in this sea of grey gowns and, for the first time in his life, he felt embarrassed by her appearance.

This was the foothold of the Muslim community. It was growing stronger and larger by the day. The black community, which had fought so hard for minority rights, now found that since they had lost their majority-minority status to whites, under a, now, Hispanic majority they had no real clout. They were grouped down with the voices of Asian, Indian, and other smaller minority communities. That, to the masses, was unacceptable. But, with the white population sealing themselves away from the rest of the nation, there was an opportunity for an alliance with Washington. At least that was the message the Islamic Nation was pimping.

The Islamic Nation was organizing, not only themselves, but the black community as a whole. Regardless of the average black person's religious or political affiliation, they were united under the Islamic Nation when it came to the idea of the "Permanent March on Washington." Black leaders rAllyd the public, as plans for the march were being made and protests were being planned. Thousands were converting to the Muslim religion in the hopes that Drew's promise to exempt Muslims from paying the national 10% sales tax that was being paid to the Catholic Church would come to fruition.

It was, in the minds of the black community, an attempt at recapturing their own version of the "American Dream". But, for the moment, for the many, it was just that: a dream. Yet, more and more that dream was becoming no different than one that passed in the night, and could not be completely remembered. Most could agree that there were bits and pieces of it that were wonderful, but, no one could remember all of the details.

But, they could plan.

And planning, they were.

Ronald picked Ty' up, and sped up his pace, in an effort to hurry their way to their car and find their hotel. Leticia noticed her husband's rushing, but wrote it off in her mind to his being anxious to get to their room. A few blocks away, they settled into their new temporary home on the eleventh floor, relieved to have a little privacy for the first time in what seemed like ages. Leticia hopped in the shower, as Ronald helped a sleepy little boy into bed. As she emerged from the bathroom amidst a cloud of steam,

Ronald raised a finger to his lips, then pointed to Ty', signaling that he was crashed out, asleep.

Leticia smiled, knowing he was out cold and she had missed her chance to say goodnight. She then made her way over to Ronald, whispering in his ear, in an almost seductive voice, "You know the thing I missed the most, when we were stuck at my sister's house?"

Ronald answered playing along, with the hope that her answer would arouse more than his curiosity. "No. What's that?"

"Thirty minute hot showers. I was getting ready to stick that egg timer up my brother-in-law's backside. You just can't get clean with a four minute shower! I don't know how Kenya has put up with him all these years!"

Shaking his head, Ronald almost laughed, at her sarcastic tone, "Oh, is *that* what you missed most?"

"Well, there may be one other thing that I kind of missed." Leticia gently pulled Ronald to the bed, batting her eyes flirtatiously.

"Oh really, now? What might *that* be?"

"*You'll see.*" She taunted him with a coquettish grin.

Ronald smiled as he moved into kiss his wife and looked over with one eye to his son making certain he was still fast asleep, as they quietly fell to the bed and pulled the covers up over themselves, shielding their passions from little eyes. They then entered into what was, prior to their stay at Kenya's, their normal, private nighttime routine. Holding each other close, they fell asleep, both hoping that this time they had made the right decision. Their most valuable possession, lying in the bed next to them, was dreaming of a kitchen in Pennsylvania and quietly suffering through a case of sugar withdrawals. Leticia smiled to herself, as she broke with the conscious world, knowing that as long as she had her little family together, she truly had everything.

As she allowed sleep to overcome her, she found herself on a boat in the middle of open waters. At the stern, she could see her sister and brother-in-law and nieces and nephews, quietly enjoying the journey and facing out over the seas they had traveled together. At the bow, Ronald's dark, impeccably trimmed fade sparkled in the sun as their most prized creation looked over the port side pointing out at some dolphins in the distance, not far from Leticia. His small, bright eyes twinkling even more in her dream than they did in true life, but that would be expected from a mother. She found lucidity within her dream, as she often did, and marched towards the bow, happy to assist in the steering while her husband retreated to the deck below. Now aware and determined to sail them to the version of Aruba that her mind had imagined for itself. Suddenly, a painful yelp broke her desire for finding a southern heading.

Turning back, in the space that Ty' once stood, was nothing but a tangled rod caught between the boat and the sea and as she looked out over the now choppy ocean, all of a sudden they seemed dark and the playful dolphins in the distance had been replaced by sharks swimming in ominous waters. She was no longer lucid and fought to gain control of the dream. Ty' was gone and she screamed for Ronald's assistance, as they turned back to look for him.

Ty' was gone.

Then, without notice, she saw a small hand in the water and she reached for it in desperation and felt it yank her overboard. The next thing she knew, she was pulled under, but she could hear her husband's voice calling her name in a frantic, muffled tone.

And she sat straight up in bed, soaked in own cold sweat as if she had, indeed, just emerged from the murky waters that she could now only vaguely remember. The sensation of fear was all that lingered as she tried to force her mind to recount the details.

Something about a boat and being unable to find Ty' was all her mind would give her.

She looked over and found her son sleeping peacefully and wrote off her paranoia to new surroundings. Leticia was a creature of habits and all of the recent changes and moves had left her mind nervous and uneasy, though she would never dare share those emotions with Ronald. She knew he was doing his best to keep things together for their family and she didn't question his decisions. Right or wrong, she knew they were made with their best interests in mind. Still, it broke with her comfortable routine in Atlanta.

6:00 am:	Wake up.
6:15 am:	Shower, brush teeth, make coffee.
6:30 am:	Start breakfast and get dressed.
6:45 am:	Wake Ty', as Ronald showers.
7:00 am:	Family breakfast and morning conversation.
7:15 am:	Kiss Ronald goodbye and get Ty' dressed.
7:30 am:	Feed the stray cats, abandoned by neighbor, and clean kitchen.
8:00 am:	Go for walk with Ty'.
9:00 am:	Call friends and work on internet home business.

11:00 am:	Meet Caroline, Alli and Georgie for playtime & gossip.
1:00 pm:	Run errands.
2:00 pm:	Call Ronald to say "I love you" and take dinner requests.
2:15 pm:	Go to the grocery store.
3:00 pm:	Clean the house.
5:00 pm:	Start dinner.
6:30 pm:	Family dinner and conversation.
7:00 pm:	Do dishes, while Ronald gives Ty' his bath.
7:15 pm:	Get Ty' ready for bed.
7:30 pm:	Bedtime stories.
8:00 pm:	Wine and conversation on the sofa.
9:00 pm:	Make love.
9:30 pm:	Shower together.
10:00 pm:	Layout clothing for next day and go to bed.

And for years, this had been her routine. She never saw reason to break with it. It was structured and organized and comfortable. It worked for them.

Then Ronald, like so many, was laid off.

As they watched their savings slowly slip away, she began to urge Ronald to head north as talk of a stronger job market in the northeast began drawing people by the thousands. Her home was her sanctuary and her peace of mind and a far cry from the clutter and chaos that her sister's reflected and she hated to leave it, but saw no other way. And, although they were not that close, she knew Kenya would not turn them away.

Growing up, their childhood home had been kept much like Kenya's and it always drove Leticia nuts. Her half of the room that she shared with Kenya as a child always dusted and with everything in its proper place, while Kenya's dirty clothes and schoolbooks decorated the floor in a haphazard manner. Perhaps Leticia turned to neatness and organization as a method to control some small part of her life where she would have otherwise had no control. Wiping the sweat from her brow, she gently pulled herself out from under the covers, careful to not wake Ronald, as she made her way over to the window and looked out over the street far below. Still left with a troubled sensation, but unable to remember why, she glanced over their hotel room and longed for the day when she would be able to return to that comfortable pace in their own home.

On the drive from Philly, Ronald had spoken with such hope in his voice. In the back of her mind she wondered how it had come to pass that some waitress seemed to be dictating her destiny, but she would not share those hesitations with Ronald given his enthusiasm and faith in the opportunity that he would find work in Harlem. Scoping the city lights Harlem was bustling, even at two thirty in the morning, and it did give her some splinter of optimism as she looked over the many businesses that still seemed to be holding their own in these strained economic times. It was far cry from the streets of Atlanta, where liquor stores and pawn shops were regularly found next to rows of boarded up businesses and foreclosure signs had become common yard ornaments. She looked as far down the street as she could see from the 17th floor of the hotel and was unable to see even one plank of plywood covering the windows of any of the buildings.

Maybe the waitress was right.

Maybe there was opportunity, here.

She smiled and then suddenly wondered why she was out of bed. All memory of the dream that had woken her was now gone and she was happy to return to her pillow and curl up at Ronald's back with the hope that better days would be ahead of them.

She drifted off only to realize the sharks had found her, once again.

Queen's Pawn to e4

Thousands of miles away, Caroline was settling happily into her new life on the western side of the country. Comfortable enough with her neighbors that she would allow Alli and Georgie to go out and play under their own supervision and, for the first time in her life, feeling valued.

She was teaching.

Due to the incredible shortage of educators in Oregon public schools, laws had been passed years ago that allowed her to teach at the elementary level. Patience and understanding were valued more than a degree: and with Ann Campbell's glowing reference and Muriel's free daycare she landed the position easily. All of the curriculum had already been dictated, outlined and neatly prepackaged for presentation to a roomful of second graders, leaving her with the not so simple task of making multiplication tables sound exciting to a group of eight year olds. She taught art, too, and there she shined. Her enthusiasm for finger painting with the children made it easier for them to tolerate the less thrilling task of solving word problems. They loved her class. She was popular and Alli beamed in the lunchroom, bragging that her mother, Mrs. Anderson, was a teacher. For most children, taking math lessons from mommy would have seemed a horrible punishment, but for Alli, life was perfect.

Her mother was happy.

Meriwether Lewis Elementary was Caroline's new and treasured domain.

Sitting at her desk, she worked through a stack of quizzes, carefully grading each one, and leaving short, but encouraging, notes for each child, regardless of their score. Suddenly, just as she was taking a bite from her sandwich, the doorknob to her classroom turned, causing her to drop a large glob of grape jelly on little Vivian Ashley's test. She quickly rushed to chew, embarrassed by her spill, as she looked up and saw the man in the doorway. He noticed her blushing, as she wiped the purple mess from the paper with a napkin, trying to quickly choke down her bite.

"You know. A woman as pretty as you, should not be left to eat alone."

And there it was, again.

"Well..." she mustered, smiling, her hand over her mouth, rocking her head from side to side with each clench of her jaw, and wishing she had not used so much peanut butter.

"I am serious."

It was Vladimir Stahl.

He stood about six foot three, with light brown hair that was always groomed to the standard of conservative perfection, and a toned physique that perfectly filled out the sweats that were his daily uniform. His buttocks had been the topic of conversation more than once in the teacher's lounge and he knew that more than one of his coworkers had had a crush on him for quite some time. His eyes were magnetic and, more than most, Caroline found her own inexplicably drawn to them, but she could never interpret his expressions. Vladimir was an unknown to most. In true Russian form, he had no time for silly games and he came across as almost overly formal with the woman in the school that had a strict policy of separating boys and girls in the classroom.

But with Caroline, things seemed different.

Maybe it was all in her own head, but she noticed a marked difference between the way he interacted with the other women and the way he spoke to her. Although he was only that way when he was certain that others couldn't see him, so she suspected that perhaps that was how he was with all of the other women when she was not around, or when he found himself alone with female companionship. For months she had interpreted his occasional winks and sly grins as a distant flirtation, but Caroline was never sure if he was truly flirting, or if was just his way. There were moments, though, when she looked into his ice blue eyes, that she found her own so drawn to them that she didn't want to look away: those brief, intermittent moments when they both allowed the connection. His thick Russian accent was seductive and she sometimes secretly fantasized about how words from his lips would feel rushing past her ear in the throws of passion.

And, there he was.

In *her* classroom.

Unannounced.

He had sought her company out and that was something he never did. He never went to the teacher's classrooms, instead preferring to stay with his students in the gym or on the track. Without fail, rain or shine, during his free period, he would run laps and classrooms that faced that big burnt sienna oval were considered prime real estate.

Caroline's did.

Even though she was new, her classroom had traditionally been the art room and it was the only one equipped with enough storage for the supplies. As he stood there, smiling, she quickly swallowed and checked her teeth with her tongue making sure no unattractive remnants of jelly were there. *Maybe this was it? Maybe he was about to finally let her know he was interested in her? But, then again, what could she do? She was married. She knew that. Still, it would be nice to be flattered.* Her heart began to beat a little faster as she took a sip of milk and looked into his amazing eyes.

"So, husband? He is to attend play tomorrow?"

And, she was crushed. Though, her expression would give no indication. Wishing he would avoid George as a topic of conversation, but wanting to play the role of the good wife, she nodded slightly, remembering her place and wishing she could find another. "I... well, George isn't much into... I... I don't know. Maybe. We'll see." Caroline nervously stumbled through conversation as she shrugged one shoulder, indifferent about George's participation. Vladimir always made her feel a little nervous. In truth, she was somewhat afraid of watch she might do if the opportunity presented. She sat, watching Vladimir, as he made his way to the window to observe a group of young boys making their way around the school track, in his mind grading each boy's individual performance and preparing the appropriate lectures. Carefully, he removed the label from a tube of unflavored lip balm. Caroline had witnessed the ritual at least fifty times. He pressed the moisturizing stick to his lips and she could not help, but wonder how soft they must be, as he asked. "He would miss daughter in play as Dorothy? She is star, no? And, lovely wife who has put so much talent and effort into painting such colorful "munchkin land"? He is silly man to pass up opportunity to be in your company."

And there it was, again.

His eyes glanced over from the window to hers, flashing deep. He gave her a half smile, winked and then refocused on the track.

Caroline cleared her throat, looking for something to say. Class would begin in another ten minutes and now she was determined to get to the bottom of things. The man who half of the women in the school pictured in their minds while they were making love to their husbands was interested in her. He *had* to be, she was certain! *Why else would he say such things?* There were so many things she wanted to do with Vladimir, and when she allowed her mind to wander, she always found him in those daydreams. Maybe, if she could keep him alone long enough she could figure out if this was truly flirtation. It had been so long since she had flirted with anyone, she seemed to have forgotten how, but she had to say something. "So... how is life in the P.E. department? Are the boys behaving themselves?" She asked in a lilting and attempted casual tone but, immediately after she heard her own words, she felt like an idiot.

Vladimir, grunted gently, smirking, then turned to her. "No. Today, they make me mad. So... they run laps. Many, *many* laps." He winked at her, almost enjoying the power to impose misery.

"But, it's raining?" she questioned, feeling sorry for the little ones.

"Da. And, they need to learn. Life does not stop because of rain." He watched the group, seemingly disinterested in their discomfort or the approaching lightening. "They all rally behind this 'Pate' boy. He cause problems for entire class, yet, they laugh at jokes, not work, not complete tasks. Perhaps now he is not so much a funny man? You know this child?"

His eyes engaged hers again and, shyly, she stuttered a response.

"No. I only ever see the girls. I might have his sister, though. I have a Julie Pate in second period."

Vladimir turned from the window and headed for the door, pausing in front of Caroline's desk, momentarily tapping the corner as if he was giving a serious instruction.

"This 'Pate' in your class. Keep eye on her." He smiled and winked, pointing his finger at her coyly, he then continued his march.

Not wanting him to leave, Caroline tried to stop his exit, hating the words as soon as they fell from her tongue, and now certain she had no idea what she was doing in the flirting arena. "Vladimir. I have half a PB&J, if you are hungry? You could join me? We still have a few minutes before next period?"

She could only hope she didn't sound too obvious. At the door, Vladimir paused, and smiled back at her. Her behavior had been transparent, but Vladimir was flattered by the confirmation of his own suspicions and he turned to her.

There were the eyes, once more.

Those amazingly intense azure eyes.

"No. Thank you. I must get boys ready for next class." He smiled, knowingly. In truth, he wanted to gently push things himself and he knew the time was approaching when he would. Then, noticing a shelf of board games, he ran over the edge of one box with his finger. "You play?"

As Caroline tried to quickly remember exactly how many spaces a knight jumped on the board and whether the bishop moved diagonally or in straight lines she, without hesitation, she beamed with seeming confidence, "Yes!"

"Really?" Vladimir questioned suspiciously as he challenged her to a match. "Good! Tomorrow we play. You are too pretty to lunch alone."

With that, Vladimir made his exit leaving Caroline in the same state of confusion she had struggled with for so many months now. She couldn't decide what this man wanted from her, if anything, although she had her own ideas. Was it his eyes, the

Russian accent, or the fact that he seemed so unattainable, given her marital chains, that made him so appealing? She had spent hours fantasizing and daydreaming about this man and she wondered, secretly, if he knew. More so, she wondered if he did the same.

That night Caroline returned home to find George in his normal, after work state of drunken avoidance of duties. She didn't care, though, and instead ran around their apartment like a woman possessed.

"Alli! Is your costume ready? Do you have the ruby slippers? Where is that stuffed dog I bought, I can't find it anywhere! *Alli!* Did you take my lip gloss?!"

Alli appeared in doorway of her parent's room, only to find her mother rummaging through the closet in an attempt to find something to wear the next day. "*What?!*" Her mother snapped as she continued the hurried quest for the perfect outfit and Alli furled her brow at Caroline's odd behavior.

"Nothing. The slippers, Toto, my dress and the wand you made for Glenda are all in the basket, in my room. I'm ready. *And!* I have been studying my lines!"

"Good, sweetie, that's good!"

"Mommy, *what* are you doing?"

"Mommy needs to find a nice outfit for tomorrow. I have nothing to wear! *Nothing* to wear!"

Alli looked at the strange woman that had seemingly taken form in her mother's skin, but wrote off her actions. She knew how much work her mother had put into the play and that it was important for her to make a good impression. As for Alli, she couldn't wait to show off her acting talents and so she inquired about, what was for her, the most important member of the audience. "Is daddy going?"

Caroline called out to George, speaking in a rushed voice, hoping he would say no and purposefully playing his mind with her words, "George, are you planning to go the play, tomorrow night? If so, plan on being home by ten or eleven, I need to help clean up so it will be a late night! I promised Principal Schelhammer that we would leave the auditorium spic and span! Or, if you would rather, I can take Alli and you can go out with the boys! Muriel can watch Georgie! I am sure she won't mind!"

"Eleven?! Caroline, you know I need to get up by 5:00 a.m.! By the time we get home and get the kids to bed... "

Caroline rushed from the bedroom and hurriedly kissed George on the cheek, then headed directly for the phone, not giving him time to change his mind. "No worries, Muriel won't mind, she loves Georgie. We'll take plenty of pictures. It'll be just like you were there." She started to dial.

"But, mommy, I *want* daddy..." Alli followed her.

"Daddy is a busy man, Alli, don't be such a pest!... Hi!... *Muriel?*... Hi, it's Caroline!" she, nervously, cut of her daughter's thoughts, uncharacteristically glaring at her small face, filled with questions, as she shoed Alli away and concentrated on her telephone conversation with the neighbor down the hall. Alli retreated to her corner of the world, confused by her mother's conduct and a little hurt that her own father would not take the time to come see her. She pictured him sitting in some bar, getting drunk with his friends, as she was doing battle with kindergarteners in flying monkey suits and it angered her. Still, she was the star. And she certainly was not giving up that position to her snotty little understudy, Becky Bagley. Becky had been trying to get every kid with a cold to sneeze on Alli's lunches for the past week in the pathetic hope that she would be too sick to perform on opening night, leaving Becky with the starring role.

Her elementary school version of bio-terrorism would fail, come opening night.

The next day Caroline awoke, a full hour early, to get dressed in anticipation of her lunch time rendezvous with Vladimir. She felt like a schoolgirl and embarrassed herself with the thought of what it would be like to draw in closer to his eyes.

So seductively deep and blue.

In the shower, as the hot water and soapy bubbles combined to form a slick mixture over her skin, she allowed her hands to explore the parts of her body, so long neglected by George. Steam rising, she inhaled deeply, keeping quiet, but determined to find release as she fantasized about Vladimir's touch, as she had so often before. Her pulse quickened as her body responded to her mind's desires, pulling her closer to the relaxing flood she desperately desired and wishing that it had been Vladimir's body, pressed to hers, that brought her to this end.

The thought of George, only a couple of rooms away and getting ready to leave for work, left her with a twinge of guilt.

However, now satiated and with her tensions relieved, she turned off the water, taking a moment to gather her senses, before grabbing a towel and flipping her hair up, turban style and finding her robe. Making her way to the kitchen and calling the children to breakfast, she avoided eye contact with George, feeling somewhat ashamed that all of her sexual fantasies revolved around another man. She focused her attention on the Cheerios, pouring maple syrup over them, just like Alli liked them and tried to justify her thoughts by telling herself that since George had neglected her needs for so long, it was only natural that she would have such desires, not that she ever had any intentions of acting on them. Her fantasies were no more harmful than those of an imaginary, and very sexual, friend.

As the children made their way to the table, Caroline headed to the bathroom and started to towel off her hair. It was growing out, now. She had stopped cutting it three months earlier, but now, with her locks falling gently to her shoulders, it was really starting to change her appearance. She smiled at herself as she admired her own profile in the mirror, happy that the signs of her once boyish haircut were fading and that her reflection was beginning to look softer and more like it had when she was younger. She rummaged through the lower cabinet and rediscovered her makeup bag. Carefully blending earthy tones across her eyelids, her mind started to focus on lunch with a certain P.E. Coach.

For the first time in ages, she plugged in her curling iron then rushed out to get Alli ready for school and prepped Georgie for his now usual daytime routine with Muriel. After readying the children, and packing their lunches, she returned to her primping like a teenager getting dressed for the prom.

At 11:30, she dismissed her third period class and took a second to check herself over in the mirror as she anxiously awaited her date and contemplated what she should be doing when Vladimir arrived. She wanted to seem casual, so for fifteen minutes she paced and wondered, changing positions, moving about the classroom, looking out the window to the field and wondering why her lunch date was so delayed.

She began to grow impatient.

As she stood looking out the window, wondering if he had forgotten her and taken to the track, the doorknob to her classroom turned announcing Vladimir's arrival. Startled, and with a half smitten expression, she pushed her hair back from the side of her face and Vladimir entered, smiling at her. He turned to the shelf of games by the door raising his eyebrows, as if to challenge her and giving her one last opportunity to back out before certain defeat. Carefully, he removed the chess set from the middle of the stack and walked over towards her.

"You are certain you are to be ready for me?" he questioned, almost implying more than a game.

"You're late." Caroline countered, gently.

Putting the chess board on her desk, he walked over and took her hand, and in true gentleman fashion, he kissed it, holding eye contact so deep that her heart started to pound so hard she was sure he could hear it. *If he only knew what she was thinking.* "I'm sorry. You will forgive delay? I must to deal with a student. I did not mean to make you wait."

"It was no trouble... I... I don't mind waiting. I had some papers to grade, anyway so it worked out well. I just got done." she lied and he knew. "Mr. Pate, again?"

Vladimir nodded reassuringly, smiling, his eyes locked in on hers. "So, we begin?"

Caroline accepted the change of subject, walking towards the desk, her body slightly flush from his kiss and her mind wishing that his mouth had found more interesting places to venture than the top of her right hand.

But, she refocused, as usual.

She often found herself consciously refocusing her mind in his presence. He dumped the box open, and turned over the board, then quickly began to set up his side of the battlefield. Not quite remembering the details of the game, like an American seated at a banquet table and unfamiliar with the proper fork to use, she simply decided to follow his setup, copying what he did, and creating a mirror image on her side. Vladimir smirked, sensing victory, as she moved her final pawn to the front line.

"Your queen?"

Caroline quickly checked the board, certain she had copied him exactly, then questioned, "What about her?"

Still grinning, he answered. "She is not on her color. Queen always must to start on her own color."

Playing it off as an innocent mistake, Caroline quickly swapped her king and queen's positions then looked to him, smiling and trying to hide her embarrassment.

"Your move." Vladimir gestured to the board.

"No, that's alright. You can go first." Her plan had been to just copy him long enough to make it through lunch and not make too much of a fool of herself.

Shaking his head, smiling to himself, but knowing better than to hurt her feelings, he countered, citing custom. "You are white. White always to move first. It is... how do you say... *tradition*?"

Again, stumbling to cover her lack of familiarity, but certain she was exposed as a novice, she nodded, as she studied the 64 squares in front of her and tried to remember the right opening move. She had played this game as a child. There was a move. A standard opening. She visualized a memory from her twelfth year of life, and, almost without thought, she moved her queen's pawn forward two spaces on the board.

Vladimir nodded, pursing his lips, and wondered, momentarily, if her overdone ignorance was nothing more than a strategy to throw him off. "So we play Sicilian defense? This is your move?"

Caroline hesitated for second before nodding, faking confidence in her strategy and intoxicated by his voice and accent.

He mated her in four moves.

Her head in her hands she stared at the board, stunned by the sudden defeat. Her sad little king pinned with no escape, and his queen unable to come to his rescue as Vladimir casually flipped her over and over the fingers of his right hand, proud of how quickly he had captured her most valuable piece. Vladimir chuckled, and after two more games, with similar results, he decided to lay down his arms and leave her with her dignity. "You know, is hard, when you not play in long time. And, I am... well... you know, not so bad at this game."

Caroline nodded, helping him to pack up the board, beginning to feel just slightly humiliated, as Vladimir smiled in his heart, knowing she had only wanted to spend time with him. Noticing her downcast expression, Vladimir rose to return the game to its usual position and then walked back over to the desk, sitting down in front of her, one hand resting against his chin as he gazed over, almost sympathetic for her losses. She glanced up with the same, almost apologetic, expression that Alli would have on her face when she broke a dish. "I'm sorry. I guess I just haven't played in a while. I guess that wasn't much fun for you." Then her expression quickly changed, determined to pull her mind from its forlorn thoughts, she smiled, and reached in her drawer to offer him the full

spoils of war. "One thing I can do, is bake! And I have cookies! Care for a truce?"

Caroline held forward a large, misshapen baked treat, dangling it in front of him as if she

was waving a white flag under his nose.

"Chocolate chip? Well... since, is my favorite! I must accept this offer of peace."

He said, jokingly, as he gently ran his index finger through the middle of her palm,

retrieving his trophy from her hand, and with just enough seduction to make her really

question if there was something there. Gazing at the cookie, he posed a question, not

looking up at her. "So, Caroline... You are lovely... you are sweet... and, now, I see you

cook. Not such a chess player, but few Americans are... *Tell, me*... does husband know

he is so lucky?" His eyes then flew to hers, and hers found the floor. Her mind racing

with a million indiscretions and unable to admit the truth about her marriage to even

herself, she simply nodded, but couldn't look him in the eye while she did. Her eyes

returned to his, and he tried to read the sadness behind the glinting green mirrors before

him.

He allowed her to lie, again, but saw the truth.

And she knew. To some degree.

"I now must go. I must to return to gym and prepare for next class. Thank you,

for... delicious cookie."

Caroline watched as he took a bite and nodded with satisfaction, getting up to

leave. She didn't want him to go. To delay him, if only for a few seconds, she blurted

out, "Vladimir! Wait! Um... are you coming to the play, tonight?"

"I am. I would not miss lovely Alli as star for world. And... well, Mr. Pate and little friend, Mr. Matthew, are to be well punished by to clean all of Emerald City."

Caroline smiled, not knowing what to say, but thankful for the help that had been so unexpectedly offered. "I... I didn't expect any help... I mean, a couple of teachers were planning to help, but, I... I don't know what to..."

He cut her off. "I know."

She looked away, smiling with gratitude and entertained by the notion that he would be around later that evening.

"Caroline, tell me... George... you are certain he is not to come this evening?"

And there it was again.

She shook her head, still avoiding eye contact, but not a bit unhappy with her husband's failure to attend. To admit the truth, she didn't want him there and wondered what Vladimir would say if he knew how much she thought of him and the effort she had gone to keep George away tonight. She looked up as Vladimir was at the door, now approaching the hallway, he had intended to leave. But he stopped and, leaning back in across the threshold, he had to tell her one more thing.

"By the way, you look very pretty in that dress today."

"No." she looked down at the green dress she had chosen to wear and wished she had gone with the red one. She had not been accustomed to compliments and became uncomfortable when she had to answer to Vladimir's, but he enjoyed watching her reactions.

"Caroline, there are two things you must to remember about me." He smiled, as he awaited her interest. "First, I will not ever lie to you. Second, much like in game, I am always to be eight moves ahead. So, when I tell you dress is pretty, is truth! And, so is

woman that wears it, da?" And with that he took another bite, and gestured a thank you,

holding up the cookie, as he winked and closed the door.

And she missed his company immediately and began to analyze his words.

She still couldn't decide if he was flirting.

Suddenly, the bell rang, startling her and signaling a large group of children were

coming to visit her.

Caroline tried to put aside her fantasies and focus on the class, but her desire to

daydream brought her to pop a quiz, allowing her a few minutes to look out the window,

gazing toward the track. Her mind wandered out there and into his arms, but she

reminded herself of her vows. At one point, she swore he looked right at her. Even from

a distance, their eyes were like magnets, drawn to each other, but she still questioned if

he really saw her, standing in the window. With a sly grin, he turned away, turning his

attentions to his pupils and she did the same with her own, wondering.

She allowed herself to occasionally daydream through seventh period until the

giggling and bounding feet of little Alli interrupted her thoughts. Basket and stuffed dog

in hand, she anxiously sought her mother's help with makeup and preparation for the

stage.

"Alli, it's three hours before anyone will be here."

Alli, with the Scarecrow and Tin Man, following like her entourage, begged her

mother's attention. "*Mommmm!* My hair needs to braided, and Nikki and Jimmy have *a*

lot of makeup to do if we are going to look good up there and Jimmy's mom won't be here until six and we need to get ready and we need to eat *and* we need to practice our lines so that everything is...." she pressed incessantly in a hurried voice.

"Alright, alright! We'll get ready. We can't eat until later, though, sweetie. The parents from the kindergarten class won't be here with food until 5:00. I have some cookies, though, if you're hungry?" Caroline tried to end the assault.

"No! *We aren't hungry now*!" Alli spoke like a true diva, "We *need* makeup!"

"Fine, *fine*! We'll do your makeup. Will *that* make you happy?" Caroline begged.

"No, start with Jimmy! He has the most to do. I have his silver makeup in my basket, *and he needs to get ready*!" Alli chastised her co-star like he was Georgie.

"Alli, there's only enough here for one application? I think we should wait and do Jimmy's makeup closer to the curtain call, don't you?"

"Yeah! That stuff itches! I can wait. Do me last! It'll rub off anyway." The small boy tried to put off the face painting, but Alli cut him off. "No! You're the art teacher, mom! You have more paint! Geesh!" Alli firmly demanded and Caroline was somewhat surprised, but amused, by her daughter's new found passion for the stage. As Caroline began braiding, little Becky Bagley, with her own click of second graders, walked passed the open door of the classroom in her own blue and white checkered dress, seemingly annoyed that Alli had survived her attempts at sabotage. When Caroline wasn't looking, Alli stuck her tongue out at the small group and gave a snooty grin as she got ready with the other stars. Becky having had a crush on the boy that was playing the scarecrow was irritated that Alli would be the one planting a kiss on the raven haired boy's cheek right before her triumphant return to the farmhouse.

Two hours later, after having prepped three of the main characters for their performance, Caroline found herself backstage checking for imperfections in the yellow brick road and secretly thinking about Vladimir.

Satisfied that every munchkin in munchkin land was properly floraled and fauna-ed, and with the set ready for display, Caroline took her position and gave the nod to Alli to begin the scene, as she raised the curtain. Alli nodded confidently and gave such a performance that her mother's eyes never left the stage, unable to turn away and amazed at her own daughter's previously unknown talent. And, an hour and a half later, when the children returned to Kansas, greeted by roaring applause, they rushed into the audience to receive the accolades of their peers and those that had shared the evening with them. After pulling the curtain closed, Caroline then turned around, surprised to find Vladimir right behind her and she was a little startled by him. She had been so engrossed by the performance she never thought to look back. He smiled, in a way that was different. His expression was softer and with a hint of question in his eyes. She wondered how long he had been standing there.

And there they were, alone in the shadows, but his eyes still seemed to sparkle.

And she realized, for the first time, the situation had pushed past flirtation.

Somehow, it had happened.

She didn't know when, or how, but at that moment, she felt it. Again, she shied away from her own emotions, complications racing through her mind as her eyes fell down to the wooden floors that desperately needed to be stripped and refinished.

He wouldn't allow it, though.

Not tonight.

His hand found her face, gently lifting her chin. His gaze more intense than it had ever been. He pushed her hair aside, knowing they shared the same desires. He had known for some time, now. Her heart raced as a million fears simultaneously flooded her mind. She knew what he was about to do would change their relationship and her marriage forever, but if she pulled away now she might never get the opportunity and she so desperately wanted to feel his lips to hers and see if the reality was as intense as the daydreams she so often had. Even before the act, she began to wonder how she would feel afterwards and tried to decide if she would feel guilty for allowing another man to kiss her when she had already promised herself to George. She realized, she wouldn't and for *that*, she did feel a little guilty as she realized how easy it was for her to set aside the words she had spoken before God and their families. But, none of that mattered now as she found herself closer to Vladimir's eyes than ever before. Gently, she moistened her lips and that answered all of his questions, despite her obvious nervousness.

And, there, somewhere on the other side of the rainbow, he kissed her.

On The Island of Misfit Toys

As life in the Territory was growing more and more into a Police State environment, and with tensions rising between the Command and the part of the Northeast controlled by Elijah Drew's Islamic Nation, many former Americans found themselves with no place to call home. Unable to decide where to move, and terrified of the rumors of hate crimes and murder that seemed commonplace inside the Territory's borders, huge blocks of Americans settled into living the lives of gypsies.

Mixed race individuals, homosexuals, interracial couples, pacifists and the politically undecided, formed small villages mostly throughout the southeastern United States where the year round temperatures were warmer and the farms were plentiful. Many had applied for Canadian citizenship, but were turned down; others simply wanted to avoid the violence of the gang controlled cities. They came from all walks of life and income levels, but they shared a desire to live peacefully among those that shared similar ideals. Some villages aligned based on religion, others on political ideals, and, a few, based on lifestyle or language. Still, there were many that were simply a hodge podge of those that got along well with the existing group.

The basic need for food and shelter caused most of these townships to spring up centering around once active farms. Previous owners, now either living inside the Territory, or having moved on to other places, the industrious inherited their earth and worked hard to either recover or plant new crops. It was common for people to wander through several villages, before finding a place to call home.

America nicknamed this place "The Island of Misfit Toys."

They were the people that did not fit in anywhere else, but together they forged a life. Arguably, it was the most peaceful place in the country. Cooperation was critical for survival.

"Well, darlings, I do believe our own little version of stone soup has reached a boil! Dang! This is gonna be tastier than black eyed peas on New Year's Day!" Miss Edee announced, with a strong Tennessee drawl, stirring the boiling pot of chicken and vegetables and waving everyone to gather round and partake in the feast. "Come on, come on, let the little ones through, first! And much thanks to our dear friend, Alfonso, who was nice enough to take care of the not so nice task of getting the chickens into the pot! I am sure we are all quite thankful to have a little meat in our diet, this evening!" she cheerfully exclaimed, as she dolled out bowls of soup, rich with broth, carrots, celery and egg noodles. "Thanks, also, to the kind gentlemen from Opelika, who was kind enough to trade us that cow for our surplus tomatoes and peaches. She's a little old, but her milk is good and I am sure she'll be rewardin' us seein' how we've saved her from the butcher's knife." The crowd applauded their trade as glasses of warm milk made their way through the crowd and into everyone's hands.

Bending over, and gesturing enthusiastically to two of the littlest new arrivals, Miss Edee encouraged them to jump ahead in line and come get their dinner. Young brothers, Perry and Tony raced ahead of their parents, anxious for their warm meal. Carefully, Miss Edee portioned out their bowls, ensuring the tykes got extra helpings of chicken and cautioning them to be extra careful with the hot liquid. "Now this stuff's hotter than me in my red thigh high boots, so you two let it cool before you go off burnin' yourselves!" Their tired mother smiled as she looked on at the almost seventy year old that was providing them with the first hot meal they had seen in almost a week. She

instructed the boys to take a seat on the large yellow picnic blanket their family had laid

out, while their father, Will, tried to figure out how it was that he had reached a place in

his life where a man in a dress was serving their up his supper. Noticing her husband's

critical eye and, more than obvious, silent denigration and critique Heather elbowed his

side and looked to him with an expression she normally saved for their children when

they forgot to say "thank you" for something.

"We're hungry. Be thankful." Heather smiled at the "drag queen impersonator" as

she spoke softly to her questioning husband.

Miss Edee King.

She was not shy in discussing that, although straight and a father herself, she lived

life as a woman. Perhaps, this is what had brought her, or him, depending on the day, to

live among the other 'misfits', as they happily referred to themselves. From the way she

carried herself and the way the other villagers responded, it was obvious that Edee and

Alfonso seemed to be in charge of this particular camp. As Will accepted his bowl,

without saying a word and only nodding his acknowledgement of thanks, he quickly

decided that his family would only be passing through this odd village where these

geniuses seemed to think it was fine to allow their children to take their evening meals

with an elderly cross dresser. He tried to wrap his head around the concept as Edee was

engaging in a conversation with his far less judgmental and more accepting wife,

Heather. Still, he quietly wished she would just take her soup and stop talking to the man

he had already decided must be completely insane. Out of earshot of the conversation between Heather and Edee, Will, a straight laced and conservative man who was staunchly homophobic, was making plans to pack up and head to the next village.

They had gypsied through six, and not yet found a home.

While Heather indulged herself in conversation with this perfectly coordinated man, her husband leered on trying to decipher the riddle before them. Edee was wearing a shade of lipstick that was perhaps one too bright for her complexion, and wore a scarf, strategically positioned to cover up her Adam's apple. Heather's husband sat with the boys, simply observing what he saw as an obvious accident of nature. He ate his soup, watching Edee, and trying to figure out what terrible tragedy or mental debility must have led someone to live such a life.

And Edee noticed his glances.

She had seen such looks before and she amused herself with the different psychological reasons that each of them must have had to be fascinated enough to stare, yet unwilling to speak about what made them so curious. Being on the Island of Misfit Toys seemed appropriate to her and she smiled at the idea that there were so many misfits, of one kind or another, out there and she welcomed them all with open arms though only a few had chosen to stay. She had seen a good many men like Will pass in and out of the village, and she had become so accustomed to being judged that it no longer had any effect on her. All her life, Edee had felt like a misfit. Even before her fifth birthday, as a young boy that was too young to understand his own sexuality, he was certain that God had made some terrible mistake. Orphaned by the tender age of ten, Edee was sent to live with relatives where he guarded a dark secret as a child. He had no interest in men, he just didn't care for their wardrobe, so when no one was around he cast aside the overalls that society had assigned his gender and slipped into the high heels and taffeta that he felt better became him.

Edee tried to conform, but it just wasn't in the cards.

While other boys were off playing with their army men, Edee would spend time in the attic playing dress up while his adoptive family was under the impression he was out climbing trees. Later in life, he would become a father and a successful engineer. But, in quieter moments he would return to his secret indulgences until one day he decided that life was too short to only indulge yourself in what others would allow you. So, one day he packed up the life of a man once known to the world as Edward and Edee was a secret no more.

And, like a true Tennessean, it was to hell with those that wouldn't accept her.

Now, happy living as a women, but aware that others knew she was a man, she enjoyed her own psychoanalysis of the people she encountered and was secretly amused by their reactions and behaviors, especially of those like Will. They had no idea. There was nothing more obscure than the obvious. What people couldn't discern on the surface was that Edee was brilliant. She had worked for NASA with some of the most brilliant minds of the time, and she read quantum physics for fun. She had published theories, given lectures, and in academic circles was highly respected. But, no one would have known that from her outward appearance and she wouldn't volunteer such information in conversation.

No.

People had to ask for it.

And she had become so good at reading people, she could almost immediately decide if they would get the whole story, or the casual version that was easy to cut off. Still, she knew that those in the village talked and would often share the truth about her with the occasional new comer that judged her too quickly. And she would chuckle to herself imagining their expressions: picturing them as if they were trying to divide 236 by the square root of yellow.

And, even for those who knew her well, Edee was truly that complicated.

Edee walked over to Will, her hips swaying gently, from side to side and walking more elegantly in high heels than most born women could. She sat down, gracefully crossing them at the knee and unfolding a napkin in her lap. Will's posture spoke to his discomfort with Edee's choice of seats and he focused his attentions ahead, trying not to make eye contact. And Edee saw an opportunity to have a little fun.

"Now, I saw you starin' at my gams from over there, young man. And, now that I am over here, I must admit, they're not too bad lookin' considering they've been dragging this ol' body around for the past sixty eight years. But, I must tell, you, I am straight, so don't go getting' any inappropriate notions." Edee smiled and awaited the inevitable awkward reaction as she pretended to admire her shoes.

Not knowing where to look, or what to say, Will simply rolled his eyes, a string of words ran through his mind, but he didn't say a word. Edee could almost psychically sense when the word "freak" had entered someone's thoughts and it was, in the case of people like Will, the moment she waited for. Edee thought for a moment and decided to change her approach, after taking a delicate swallow of a teaspoon of soup, she asked. "So the two little red haired ones are yours? They're cute. Mine are grown, now. All have kids of their own. Yep, I have six grandchildren and one great grandchild on the way. One of the families moved into the Territory, but the others are here, in this… well, whatever this place is. I think we are still calling it L.A…. *Lower Alabama*, that is. I suppose it don't matter much about the ones that moved off. They haven't spoken to me in almost fifteen years. Couldn't handle the idea of dad showin' up for Christmas Dinner in a skirt. Can you imagine how closed minded some people can be? Oh, well. I still love 'em all." She smiled, pretending for sport that Will was among the unprejudiced, as she reached into her purse and pulled out a man's wallet, opening it to reveal several pictures of young faces that still reflected a family resemblance, even through his makeup.

Disinterested, Will nodded politely and glanced at the photos, giving a slight smile, but Edee pressed on determined to engage him. "So what did you do for a living, Will? You know, when the world still seemed real?"

"Sales." He answered, trying to be as brief as possible.

"Really? That can be a hard way to make a living, you need to have a real knack for it. You know, the gift of gab?" Edee raised an eyebrow in an attempt to provoke a response from her sarcasm.

Will shrugged his shoulders, almost defensive. "I did fine. I'm sure I did better than you." Will glanced over to Edee fully expecting him to respond by telling him he had worked in a circus, or as a designer or that he had owned a flower shop. Something that would fit a comfortable stereotype he had already boxed Edee into, despite their limited conversation. But, instead of starting in with her work history, she simply commented, "You know, Heather said it was Will, right? You know, Will, you bear an awful strong resemblance to a professor I once met from Georgia Tech."

In truth, Will looked nothing like the professor that Edee was referring to but the line gave her an opening to make a point and she so enjoyed these little psychological experiments. Will slightly shrugged his shoulders and looked at Edee as if to say "Who cares?" but Edee continued on, not missing a beat in conversation and unphased by Will's apparent lack of vocal cords. "Oh, yes. This professor from Georgia Tech, just thinkin' about him makes me smile. You see, one day I'm sittin' in this little restaurant, famished, I do mean, just famished from the day. And, I'm in my grungies, you know a gal can't run around cleanin' gay bars in stilettos. That's what I did, I took care of the cleanin' at this little place called The Heretic. Nice place, good people. Real good people. Your wife, Heather? She would have appreciated it. Fun place for the straight gals with the balls to accept constructive criticism on their hair and makeup. Safe, though. After all, it's not like any of those young men are interested in what's in a *woman's* pants, but they're still willin' to buy a drink for a lady with good conversation skills and a little heart. Don't quite still know where I fit in, but they took care of me." And, with that Will was confident his assessment was correct and he began wrapping Edee in the nice little preconceived box he had created for her in his mind, and she knew it. But, this was the exact point where things got fun for her. "Anyway, here I am an' I'm just as filthy as a coal miner with a dirty mind and I see him sittin' there with his little Georgia Tech ID and his Georgia Tech Shirt and a pair of slacks with a crease so sharp it could've cut the steak he was eatin'… oh, yes, and his ten Dollar haircut. You know the type, Will? Makin' sure the whole world knows what an important professor he is just from the way he dresses. Anyway, here I am with my little sandwich and my Coca-Cola and I notice he's reading a book and from his ID, I can see he's with the Physics

Department. And, I don't know if I mentioned, Will, but just so happens I have a good friend that works in that department, so I ask the man what he's reading. Well, I *did* mention I wasn't exactly wearin' my Sunday best, but still there was no need for the man to be rude and he quite pretentiously informs me that I would not understand the contents of his little book. But, I ask him for the title and he quite sarcastically tells me then throws in that the subject matter was theoretical quantum physics and snidely asks me if I had read it. Well, no doubt I was not expectin' that kind of response to my simple little question, but I suppose he was not expectin' me to answer back that I had in fact read the book and, while I found parts to be interestin', I disagreed with Gurthe's theory on Spontaneous Quantum Ignition. I then also recommended that, if he had not yet, he might try reading Green's *The Elegant Universe*. Goes on a little too much about String Theory, but still it's a good book. Well, you can imagine he turned redder than Georgia clay when his colleagues started laughin' at him. Hell, *I* thought it was funny!" Edee smirked, satisfied, and awaited the inevitable challenge.

"A gay janitor? And you expect me to believe you know quantum physics?" Will commented with disdain as Heather walked over and took a seat next to her husband.

"Now, Will, stop flirtin' in front of your wife. I was very clear in tellin' you I'm straight." Heather chuckled, but Will found no amusement as Edee continued on. "Heck no! My little cleanin' business was just somethin' to do when I figured out that I was happier doin' nothin' than I was all those years workin' for NASA and the government. Yes, I know what you're thinking… how is it that a pacifist ends up designing rockets and weapons for the government? Well, let's just say I was good at it." Edee smiled with a knowing glint in her eye, hoping he would continue to test her.

"*You* worked for NASA?" Will countered with doubt and sarcasm.

"What? The dress? Oh, honey, I didn't dress like this at the office. Well, not most days. Didn't you know that all us folks that worked for NASA, well, we were all a bunch of freaks on some level. I firmly believe that everyone with an IQ higher than the speedometer on most sports cars has to be at least a little insane. Dressin' up? Hell, that's nothin' compared to some of the things I saw. That's what made it so much fun." Edee's eyes seemed to gleam with fond memories.

At first, Will had trouble trying to believe that the man in the dress before him had intelligence and degrees that dwarfed his sad little masters from Duke. After about an hour of conversation, though, Will found himself so engrossed in the stories that the drag queen impersonator was telling him, he couldn't help but want to hear what this fascinating individual had to share. The three shared and enjoyed conversation, until finally they were interrupted by a tall, bald Cuban with a look of innocence that had somehow managed to stay with him, in spite of his years.

"Hey, Edee, you think we're gonna to have this many tomorrow? I'm thinking we need more than five birds, if we're gonna serve more than thirty five?"

Edee introduced the family to the young man that had designated himself as the town butcher, and who went by the name Alfonso, then went on to tell them about him. "Yes, Alfonso here handles all of the animals for us. There were a couple of abandoned farms, up the road, and he takes care of our need for meat. And when the good lookin' single gals pass through, he takes care of their need for meat, too!" Edee winked as Alfonso blushed, then continued. "Most people have trouble with the slaughter part, so we just ask everyone else 'round here to help out with growin' the veggies and herbs.

Whatever you grow, you share. That is pretty much the rule around here. 'Course if you've truly got a black thumb, we'll put you on collectin' eggs, and if you're clumsy *and* you've got a black thumb, will throw you on the spit and tell anyone that comes a lookin' for you that you headed down to Opelika." Edee smiled again as Heather just shook her head at Edee's wit. "All jokin' aside, the meat, Alfonso is kind enough to help out with. His place is also the first place you want to run in the event of any trouble. He's the only one around here with any weapons, far as I know, but he has about eighty guns, so we jokin'ly call him our 'little army of one', don't we? Just don't feed him any alcohol, or you'll hear him shootin' squirrels at three in the morning, drunk as skunk!"

Alfonso grinned, blushing guilt as he countered. "Yeah, but I've also got all the good weed, so they put up with me." And, Heather's eyes lit up with interest.

The Cuban smiled with incorrigible mischief and then returned to his questions about food supplies for the next day. Finally, the group reached the decision that they would try to get by with just six chickens for the evening soup the next day. They had to be careful with their resources, and conserve some eggs for hatching to ensure future supplies. Alfonso kept up with all of the math and dolled out supplies, as needed to the group. He also told Will and his family that there was an abandoned house just a few blocks away, if they were interested in getting out of their car for the evening.

"Oh, yes, good ol' 5650! It's our own little Chelsea Hotel 'round here. I reckon 'bout 70 families have passed through. Only thing we ask is that you leave it like you found it, eventually it'll be home to a new neighbor and we are runnin' short on houses. And, if you decide to stay you can lay claim to it." Edee stood up, then leaned down placing a hand on Heather's shoulder and whispered in a soft and inviting tone. "And I hope you will. You seem like a nice family and we've got a lot of real good people here."

Heather looked up, her heart already at home.

Suddenly, Alfonso clapped his hands together and questioned Edee. "So, what'll be tonight? Baby, Francis or Mercedes?" Edee had a habit of naming all things that she treasured on this earthly plane. Cars, guitars, and even precious stones were no exception.

"I reckon it feels like a Mercedes night." Edee answered then explained he would be playing guitar that evening and invited the family to join. "If either of you play, I'm happy to let you pick on Baby or Francis. Francis is a cantankerous curmudgeon sometimes, but Baby, well… her name suits her. She's sweet as orange blossom honey!"

Heather shook her head, admitting that neither of them bore any musical talent. Edee held out her hands, as if to say "Oh, well." Alfonso took off to retrieve a single guitar. So, accompanied by those that would become their new neighbors the group set off and took position around the firewood and Edee prepared to play for the masses. In a perfectly coordinated leopard print skirt suit, she sat down immediately adjusting her bobbed auburn wig and gently lifted Mercedes, her favorite guitar, from its case. Will found himself, as the rest of the men in the group had previously, suddenly forgetting her gender and simply amused by her openness as she asked for requests from the crowd. In the firelight, her deep set eyes and sharp Romanesque features softened and the signs of her age faded to the point she seemed to drop almost twenty years in an instant.

And she began to play.

She loved to play.

It showed in her smile.

And for those that had not heard her before, if her intelligence had not been impressive, her talent certainly was. She strummed and the group laughed and sang along for nearly two hours, until she suddenly announced. "Well, my fingers are tired and my drink's gone weak, so I reckon it's time we all found our beds. Sleep well, darlins!"

And she left her audience.

Will was still not certain that this was the place to call home, but Heather had made up her mind. She was tired of the traveling and was happily enchanted by Edee and Alfonso's kindness. It was unusual to find such a welcoming and they were more used to moving on than moving in. The little house at 5650 Clairwood wasn't big, but it was homey. It was filled with mismatched furniture that had obviously made its way there from a variety of owners, but Heather was sold on the big yard, the large kitchen and a vase of freshly picked wildflowers with a simple note that was most likely left by either Edee or Alfonso:

"Stay a day... Stay forever... Stay in touch, and pray for better!"

Living on the road had taken its toll on Heather and she was determined to convince Will that this would be their new home. The idea of the family sleeping in an actual bed was so amazing to her that she fell asleep almost instantly. Her last thoughts being those of what they could do to contribute, not understanding they were already welcome. It was a common routine that was repeated throughout the The Island of Misfit Toys. An odd mix of the least, the lost and the left out, blended with those that did not fit in anywhere else, or who simply refused to take sides. Running through the abandoned farmlands that stretched through Alabama, South Georgia, along the Northern Florida

Coast and into Mississippi, these were the areas that no one else wanted. Open spaces filled with pig and chicken farms that required work to maintain. Each camp was different. Little villages established based on the resources in the particular area. Some areas ran fishing operations to feed their groups, but here, poultry was their resource.

Will and his family had been driving through, stopping off in various villages on their journey to find somewhere to settle. His wife, Heather, was afraid of the Northwest Territory and the cities to the north were far to dangerous to enter, so they lived much like vagabonds out of the Mercedes SUV they had been calling home. It was obvious from their behaviors and mannerisms that they had once known a far better life: yet, still, Heather was not afraid of work and was more than willing to roll up her sleeves and carry their weight for the privilege of living amongst the group. Of all of the camps they had seen, this one seemed friendlier and more peaceful than any other. It was obvious that Edee and Alfonso seemed to control the activities that went on amidst the thirty five or so seemingly permanent residents, but they were always prepared for a few more as people made their way through these various areas. Some staying a night or two, and others up to a week, while they tried to get their bearings.

For others, though, this would be home, at least until things in the troubled nation settled down. They were all hopeful, although most were cut off from communications with the world that surrounded them. Between the little villages, there was some barter and trade. Edee had a friend in south Georgia that would come in to trade peaches and onions in exchange for eggs and chickens and other crops that had been established. In one of the barns, Edee, a true scientist, had established a hydroponics lab which was kept secret from everyone except the most highly trusted members of the group. Even seeds were collected at the end of meals, or during food preparation and kept so they could be used to grow a continuous supply of food. Some questioned why, but didn't argue, assuming they were being saved for planting. The lab had only been in operation for a few months, but several of the crops were approaching time for harvest.

Heather, a one time socialite housewife, had been used to the routine of filling her afternoons with play dates and shopping. Still, she feared her mind would turn to mush if she didn't do more to occupy her brain, so she would constantly sign up to take one class or another at the local community college or participate in various programs that were advertised in her neighborhood paper. From art programs to wine making, she had done it all, and some of the programs peaked Edee's interest: specifically canning.

Soon, Heather would spend her days exchanging fashion and beauty secrets with the scientist cross dresser, and sharing her canning and wine making skills with a few of the other women in the village, while the children took care of the light duty work of collecting eggs, providing fresh grain to the chickens and feeding hay to the town dairy cow they had affectionately named Miss Moo-Moo. After having lost her mother to cancer, Heather had often felt alone. Oddly enough, in Edee, she found a motherly role model and Edee happily accepted.

There had been a time in life where she had been a wonderful father, though her own children had sometimes failed to see beyond the stockings and glitter.

For hours, each night, regardless of the physical labors at hand, they talked their way through the events of the day and even the harder work seemed to pass with ease. "We lost her several years back. Cancer." Heather said, fighting to hold back the tears that she had cried too often before. She prided herself on strength and didn't often discuss her mother's passing, knowing it would bring such emotion to the surface. "She fought hard. She played tennis, right to the end. The last six weeks were hard, though. We tried to joke about it. She had accepted it. We thought we had, too, but I think she knew better. She was a teacher, Edee. People *really* liked her. And, before she left us, she had one last lesson. Of course, we all knew her time was drawing close. She was in the living room, in the hospital bed that they had sent over from hospice when they gave up on the chemo and basically told us she was down to days. Well, as we did everyday, we asked her what she wanted; you know, what could we do to make her happy? We couldn't make her better, but we could make her happy?" Tears streamed down Heather's faced as Edee, in true fatherly form, reached over to wipe them. "And, do you know what she said? It was so her revenge!" Heather laughed, as she cried. "She says she wants Thanksgiving Dinner! Thanksgiving Dinner in *February*! And she was *serious*! Can you believe that!? *That* was *my* mother! So, we call the family and pretty much everybody agrees and so I head out to Kroger to find a turkey and we had it all! Turkey and dressing and cranberry sauce and vegetables and everything you can imagine. I could hear her humming while we cooked and updated her as she corrected our recipes, but when it came down to the time to eat she wasn't hungry. That wasn't unusual. She was so sick. But, she reassured us that the smells and the sounds of everyone eating together were all that she needed to feel included and occasionally we would call back. And, towards the end of the meal, she stopped answering. At first, we thought she had just fallen asleep. We found her, smiling. Ambulance said she had been gone for about ten minutes."

Empathetic and able to see that this was a tale that Heather did not often share, Edee simply encouraged her new friend with the words that came to mind for a Tennessee native that was fast approaching seventy. "You did her proud, kiddo!"

And she watched Heather's expression as she questioned herself.

"Naaaahhhh! Come on, now! You *did*! You did good, kid! *Real* good!"

Heather laughed through her tears, and explained how she had tried to find forgiveness in charity. "Every year, we donate to the American Cancer Society in her name. Hopefully, one day they'll find the cure." Heather wiped her face.

"Oh, child! Donating to them is a waste! They're about as useful as an impotent man with a ten inch dick! Sure, the package is pretty but what the hell good is it? We've had a bunch of cures. Cancer's not a disease, baby, it's an industry. If doctors cared about curing it they'd have implored their patients to try alternative cures. There's no money to be made in curing a disease, but treating it was an industry. FDA, my ass! I have a much better use for that acronym: Fucking Dirty Assholes, every one of them! Whole damn system was fucked up! They were all for sale at our expense. Why'd you think they tried to ban Pau d'Arco, dear? It worked. It fuckin' worked and they banned the real shit they could profit. Cancer is not a disease, hon. It's a fuckin' industry."

Heather looked at Edee, not wanting to believe him but equally wishing she had met him ten years earlier, when her mother might have had a chance. Edee never promised she had a cure, but something Heather that she would have searched heaven and earth for something that may have bought her mother even two more weeks if they had been friends then. Even a few more hours would have been enough. There was so much she never had a chance to say.

Heather, a true believer in the America that once was, had a hard time accepting the idea that her country would choose to allow so many people to die. With her mother long gone, and this new information, she felt a bit of a failure, when Edee said something that really made her think

"Remember Aqua-dots, dear?" Heather nodded.

"Don't you think it's odd that the FDA would allow a 'toy' known to turn into the date rape drug GHB, when swallowed, to freely flow into this country, yet they would ban the import of some tree scratchin's 'cause it might give a dyin' person hope? Oh yes! Let's give children access to GHB and keep Pau d' Arco a secret from the people. Think about it."

It was more than Heather's mind could handle, in the moment, and she politely dismissed herself to get Tony and Perry ready for school. She would spend the rest of the day thinking about her mother: and wondering… and feeling a little guilty.

Heather sobbed, openly, for what seemed like the first time in years.

But, life moved on.

In the afternoons, Mrs. Murphy would gather the children for basic English and Math lessons and allow various members of the small village to speak to their own areas of expertise. Today, Michael Cole, an inventor that lived among the group, would be addressing the topic of magnets and had prepared some interesting experiments for the little ones which they richly enjoyed. Heather looked on, as she often did, still unable to get Edee's words out of her head, despite the roaring applause from the children. She gave her mind enough attention that the thoughts became overwhelming enough that she simply had to refocus to save sanity. So she did: on her canning classes which were scheduled to start tomorrow. Heather had never taught in front of a group before, and the idea made her a little nervous, still she figured all she had to do was to regurgitate that which had been taught to her.

This, she could do.

As crops were harvested from the hydroponics lab, they were immediately canned and distributed evenly among the group, with the rest being stored in a barn cellar, so the items could later be used for trade. When goods arrived from other areas this became the standard procedure for processing and slowly the small village found that their food supplies were expanding far beyond chicken soup for dinner.

Their growing supplies began to make Edee and Alfonso nervous, however.

Fearful that other villages may become jealous, or simply try to steal their resources, they moved most of their supplies to a secret area that would be easier to guard and allowed those that would wish to trade to enter the cellar and see only a small amount of what they truly had available. To outsiders, it would appear they were suffering as much as those around them.

Over time, visitors would be less welcome in the little village and the evening "community style" dinners would cease. The original group of thirty five having grown to fifty some, Edee and Alfonso decided that was a manageable number, but they were not interested in expansion or drawing any attention to themselves. With food supplies choked by the Northwest Command's dominance of the Mississippi River, they were wise enough to know that, eventually, hunger could lead others to move in and take over and, despite Alfonso's large stockpile of weapons, they knew they did not have enough bullets to take on a full scale onslaught.

The hydroponics lab was their most heavily guarded secret.

Edee was good at keeping secrets, though.

She had kept a good many in her life.

Everyone residing in the small village, they would eventually name Cambuslang, knew the cost of violence. They had seen it on a larger scale throughout the country and they knew, through stories exchanged with other towns, that things in the United States were only growing worse. The northeast was a war zone, dominated by Elijah Drew's men and rumors carried the message that his intent was to eventually take over the country. His funding, allegedly coming from Muslim nations that strongly supported his plans to destroy what was left of America, as Washington D.C. was struggling to hold the pieces together. Hispanics, now able to find work and opportunity back in their home countries, were slowly making their way back across the newly defined southern borders of the US.

South Florida had all but declared itself independent as the struggle for political power raged on with the Cuban population. It was difficult to decide who to vote for, though, as frontrunners often ended up either being found shot dead in the streets, or simply disappearing.

Leaders of various Indian Tribes, now having been forcibly evicted from their Reservations inside the Northwest Territory, gathered in northern Florida and debated the prophecies of their ancestors, convinced that the end of the world was coming soon. Between philosophical debates, once warring Tribes now focused on the simple concept of survival. They had all suffered, and decided it was now best to work together in an attempt to figure out what to do next.

But in Cambuslang, Heather was settled and she busied herself with preparing dinner, while her two impetuous sons looked for ways to misbehave in the living room. She opened a can of peaches that she, herself, had prepared only a couple of months earlier, and dumped them into the pastry lined tin pie plate and hoped that the recipe would turn out correctly. She thought to herself how much easier it was when she could just pop a Mrs. Smith's in the oven and call it a day. As she heard the boys getting louder and louder, she decided to occupy their little hands and keep them out of trouble, so she put them to the task of setting the table.

Soon after, Edee and Alfonso arrived and the family sat down with their guests for dinner. Heather apologizing, at the end, for the far less than perfect dessert that had made its way to the table, though Edee and Alfonso would not allow such regrets. Always polite, Edee would assure her that it was nothing less than delicious and excuse the only half eaten portion by explaining she was stuffed and needed to maintain her "girlish" figure. Heather knew better, but simply smiled shyly and cleared the table, telling the children to get ready for bed. She was anxious to get them away, as she had been watching Alfonso's uncharacteristically quiet demeanor all evening and she wondered what it was that was on his mind.

Tucking Perry into bed, she noticed how short his pajama pants had become on him, and while they would fit her youngest, Tony, in a few months, she worried about the clothing needs of her first born. Surly the stores around her had all been raided of goods in the riots and violence that had taken place over the past year. She wondered if Mrs. Murphy might trade her some of her son, Tanner's, hand me downs and thought about what she might exchange as she looked around the little home filled with the unwanted left overs of others that they had inherited. After going through her nightly ritual of checking for monsters under the bed, and in the closet, Heather assured the boys there were none, and kissed them each on the forehead, before leaving them to find dreams.

Back at the dinner table, a cross dresser, a Cuban and her husband were all discussing the politics of war. Alfonso could not escape his worries about the stories of violence on the north end of the Mississippi and could only think of how long it would take for the bloodshed to reach their doorsteps. Listening to the conversation, already in full swing, Heather, always the optimist, countered. "You boys are so silly! This will all settle down. Drew is nothing more than a loud mouth that the blacks are following just because they think he is going to get him out of paying that tax. The bigger problem is the Catholic Church getting control of the military and managing it."

"They're not gonna to get control of the military. The Northwest Command won't allow it. They've made NORAD their headquarters. Why else do you think Cheyenne is where they set up camp? They have control. More than you realize, dear." Edee said quietly, focusing on his glass of water, and knowing more secrets about the US Military than his Crypto Clearance would allow him to share.

"Well, Washington won't allow that. They'll take care of it. We have bases here on the east coast. Other countries will step in. *Hello!* Britain?" Heather argued naively, as the men exchanged pensive glances.

"Dear, other countries are just as concerned about the Command and Drew, as we are… but, they need to protect their own. They aren't going to come running to save us. They will let this play out. There's too much at stake." Edee said softly as Alfonso nodded in agreement. What no one at the table knew, and what Edee could not explain, was her vast knowledge of international politics and the plans she remained confident had already started to unfold. She already knew what to do should such events transpire inside US Borders.

"*Well, fine!* I will agree that the Command is a concern. That's why *we* are all *here*. But, Drew? Drew is just a loudmouth out to make a name for himself with the blacks. They follow him like sheep, even though most of what he says is bullshit!"

Almost as if he was waking up, Alfonso turned to Heather and said. "Don't you see, Heather? *That's* the whole problem. They *do* follow him."

The Art of War

Sun Tzu was brilliant.

It is amazing that his principles somehow escaped the mandatory readings for all American students, when so many other nations study his writings with such dedication and fervor. His teachings, applied both to military strategy and to business, have been proven effective and have been analyzed for over two thousand years. Perhaps a nation so young as America could not relate to such antiquated Eastern teachings and thought the age of the document would make the principles invalid in modern times.

Yet, the Bible is just as old.

The only difference between the books being: one tells us how to win a war, and the other has been the cause of so many. Still, Americans couldn't claim to be holy or united on religious lines. What they could not see, lacking a clear religious affiliation, was that it was that very lack of spirituality that made them targets for holy wars and attempts to convert, either willingly or by the sword.

But, the Middle East was not America's greatest threat.

So mistaken were Americans in their arrogance to not realize that the world map had been redrawn thousands of times over and that their own borders were subject to being rewritten by a cartographer's pen. For the United States though, throughout history, those lines only expanded out further and it can be presumed that most Americans were under the belief that the path of expansion would continue.

A dreadful mistake.

Had they bothered to pay attention to the lessons that other nations were studying, they would have seen the genius in Tzu's simplicity and maybe they would understand how America looked through the world's eyes: and why the enemy was content to wait at the gates. Certainly Americans were aware of the fact that around the world there were those who woke up every morning and continued to plot the fall and destruction of the United States of America. Certainly Americans knew that many of those that would harbor such intentions and hatreds were living right within US borders. Certainly Americans knew that the tragedy of September 11th, 2001 was nothing more than a test of their character and patriotism.

Surely, Americans knew they failed.

Were they blind to the enemies within?

They had to know that *they* were highly trained doctors that they brought their children to when they were sick with the flu and whose medical opinions seemed too profound to challenge when anti-depressants and behavior modifying drugs were prescribed.

They were respected professors that were allowed to mingle with America's intellectual elite, sponging up information that would quickly be shared with unfriendly nations on the internet: allowing them to know where the country stood.

They were the people that loaded their baggage as they boarded an airplane satisfied by the false sense of security that the TSA had provided them, never realizing that the Muslim loathing them through the window from the tarmac never passed through *any* security; and given the order, would have gladly taken the plane down.

The enemy was here.

And, *they* were patient.

But, Americans deemed no threat from their neighbors.

Political correctness had taught them it was wrong to judge and they were no longer allowed to do so without some sense of guilt. What they could not realize, though, was that other nations were focused on studying those reactions and emotions with intensity.

Law made no difference.

Man vs. Man is the oldest plot line that exists.

It was for this reason, America's enemies had no reason to attack. Had the United States listened to the Great Chinese Warrior's most basic lesson, "to win without fighting is best", maybe they would have looked around at themselves and understood.

America was weakening itself.

There was no need for an outside power to do that job when the US could exhaust their own resources and energies within their own borders. Civil war was inevitable: although, the history books would not describe the events of the year 2023, as such. America had let the overthrow happen. Older, more established nations had foreseen those inexorable days coming for decades, though: just as they had, so many times over, when they had to replace the globes on their desks to match up with modern times.

The difference between the United States and those other nations that had faltered, however, was the power and capability that was controlled by the once Great Superpower. Nations, desperate for nuclear capability, and willing to use it, were at the edge of their seats waiting to swoop in and take control. After all, why would they make the investment of casualities, if they could just take it in the spoils of war? American military dominance was unquestionable, but the American people were so disloyal to their own nation, the country was forced to bribe other countries with the promise of citizenship to get people to do even so much as to serve in their military.

It was all they had to offer, anymore.

It should have served as a red flag to them all.

And young men returned from service without arms, and without legs, but with hope for a better life; while there were so many of their peers, born unto America's soil, couldn't comprehend such nationalism. They couldn't see how very lucky they were in comparison to the way the rest of the world lived. And Vietnam had proven the draft was a disaster, so politicians were afraid to even present it as an option, although military service was mandatory in so many other countries.

Even though the English speaking population had been seemingly oblivious to the rise of the Derechos Party, almost every other nation on the planet was keenly aware of their existence and watched their every move. They knew it was the beginning of the end. The Hispanic population was growing so quickly, but America had allowed it, so they really couldn't blame the people they had taken advantage of for wanting to change the system.

They worked their farms and inhaled pesticides without as much as a warning of their potential effects.

They took low paying jobs in factories, losing fingers and so fearful of *la migra* that they never bothered to report the injury.

They took the jobs that Americans, when the economy was strong, had refused to work.

Now, they wanted their due and proper.

Black America had never gotten quite so organized, nor had their population reached the numbers required to win an election with their own party, but as other nations watched the rise of the Derechos they knew that white politics would not just bow down before them. Hispanics had a culture and white America didn't understand it.

Like children passing notes around a classroom, other nations exchanged strategies on how to divide the country when the final lines were drawn with America's population. Ideas, passed between close friends as they formed their alliances. America was completely unaware of what the world saw.

Sitting in the White House, even Gonzales was beginning to realize he and his party had been used, but what he couldn't tell was by what nation. *What country was it that could so intuitively sense the path that was destined for the nation he had so hoped to control?* What nation had such perfect foresight as to know every move a nation would make over the course of over twenty years? Those questions would keep him up at night, until the time when he would seemingly fade from history.

Just as Romulus Augustus.

The Northwest Command, however, was not troubled by such thoughts. They were certain that their own strategies were perfectly plotted they were and determined to take back the land they saw as their own. Happy to cleanse the country of anyone they saw unfit to live among them, they prepared the canvas for the future and prepared to re-enter the international stage, certain that they would be a stronger and more powerful force in the global arena than any other nation could have imagined.

And, they would be.

More so than any of their own could have imagined.

In the meantime, they viewed Drew, not as an enemy, but as a pawn destined for sacrifice. While they watched him, the violence he incited on a regular basis only served to help clear out members of the population they would otherwise have to deal with on their own, so it was easier to allow the fighting in the northeast to continue; knowing if the lesser forces remained stubborn they would eventually fall captive to the Northwest. They knew everything about Drew, though they would need to employ both orthodox and unorthodox methods to accomplish their goals.

The Northwest Command was not exactly what it seemed to Americans, but they did direct America's fate. Eventually, they would direct that of the world, but not in the way the world was expecting. Not even those living within the Territory's borders suspected the truth.

Most were happy and content with the world they saw around them.

Caroline was no different.

And, as most humans do, once the basic needs of food, shelter and security are met, she began to focus on more selfish goals. As the months passed, Caroline found herself contemplating tearing down some of the walls she had worked so hard, all of her life, to build around herself. Looking into Vladimir's eyes, she felt such a deep connection that pulled at her heart, pleading with her to let him in, despite what her mind was telling her. For so many years she believed that walls kept her safe.

In all of her relationships, her marriage, and even with her friends, she had never allowed anyone to breach the perimeter. Although, to many that had known her they were never left feeling as though they were so far on the outside. There were many people that would have sworn they knew everything about her. But, in truth, they were all wrong.

Caroline was good at this game. She had practiced it since she was a child. Guarding her heart like it was stored in some precious, secret little box somewhere inside the stony walls of the castle she had built for it, she kept the tiny unbroken pieces that were left, all to herself. She had never trusted anyone enough to even let them know they still existed.

In her quieter moments, she would visit with them. The little shreds she hoped one day would find their way back to where they once belonged. But, they had been away from that place for so long, she feared this box would be their coffin, even though her heart called out for her to free them from their prison and return them to their rightful place. Looking in on them, like beautiful little birds kept behind glass bars, she would run her finger along the edge of their cage, occasionally imagining what it would be like to allow them to fly and feel complete again. But, she really couldn't picture it, anymore. The tiny fractures that represented so much of her true self. The part she refused to let the world see. The part that let her cry, and feel pain. The part that had once let her truly love and experience joy.

She had such an incredible capacity for love.

And, she knew that.

She had just never found anyone that she felt could return such a deep and undying level of emotion. And, after marrying George, she had given up on the idea of ever finding true love, though she desperately wished to know what it might be like. The kind of fairytale love about which little girls dream, and which grown women pretend not to know they had once been taught to believe in.

In truth, she still had the heart of a child, and so, for Caroline, it was not that hard to make believe. She was sure if poets had written about it, and songs had been sung about it, surly it existed for some. And, looking in on herself, and knowing what she was capable of, she wondered why it had never existed for her before. She debated if it ever would.

Love.

All her life, she had dreamed of sharing this spectacular love with someone.

As she sat with her secrets, her mind wandered off to thoughts encompassing the range of emotions that she felt when she looked into his eyes. She was drawn in so deeply. He was the only man that had ever, truly, *made love* to her and she felt more physical and emotional sensation with him than she ever had with any other. It made every other experience that she had ever known in her bedroom seem meaningless by comparison. The very thought of him made her feel like her spirit was twirling with joy inside of her.

And that scared the hell out of her.

And she felt so guilty for her affair of emotion.

But, *every* conversation, *every* love letter, *every single moment* she had spent gazing into his eyes, only drew her in further. And, over time, she really began to feel he loved her, too. Looking beyond the crystal blue speckles that softly stared into her, she saw that Vladimir, too, was hiding some painful secret, but she never dared to question what it might have been. Instead, she simply told herself, that perhaps, if he too was hiding, they could freefall together to this unknown place and, hand in hand, with all of the little pieces shared, both of their hearts could begin to heal the other person's.

"Could this be that very love that she had longed for?" she wondered.

Unfortunately, every time her heart came close to convincing her that it was, her mind would remind her of the pain she would know if he ever hurt her, and she would throw her treasures back in their cell, slamming their door closed with fury, and angry that she had almost deceived herself into believing in such fantasies. Even though, she really did want to know love... just once... in *this* life.

Just once....

And then, one day, it must have been while she was lost in daydreams of him and not paying attention to anything else, she found her castle had fallen and her little box of splinters was exposed. Almost as though it had been left out in a field for all the world to see. Her panicked instinct was to run and hide it again before he saw, but it was too late.

Unable to contain such a sudden release of emotion, the tears flowed from her eyes like wine, as he walked over to dry them and offered to protect that which she held so dear. And the look of sincerity in his soulful eyes, gave her reason to believe that he would, as she nervously passed parts of herself into his hands, watching them leave her guard as carefully as a mother watches as she passes her newborn child into the arms of another for the first time. His every movement, every word, doing nothing, but convincing her more and more that she had made the right decision.

Walking hand in hand, along the shores of her dreams, she slowly began to relax and forget about her previous post, comforted by the knowledge that he would *never* do anything to damage the trust she had placed in him.

She felt so free, and happy, for the first time since she could remember.

Sailing over those deep, open, waters, she felt so at ease and unconcerned about the depths of the emotions she was allowing herself to feel. And despite the complications of her marital bonds, she allowed herself to believe that someday, she would find herself in Vladimir's arms. But, even with all her confidence and trust in him, there were times she would walk into that little room in her mind, and panic at the sight of the empty pedestal that once held her precious little pets, and she would angrily demand to see them, paranoid he had harmed them in some way.

But, each time she did that, *without fail*, he produced them, and gave her no reason to question how well he had been caring for them; and her love and trust for him grew just a little more.

No one had ever been inside the castle walls before. In truth, very few even knew they existed, and even for those that saw them, she would never talk about what she kept inside. It was her hiding place, to which she would retreat to block out the world. It was where she went to be with her own thoughts, and analyze the construction of her own walls. As she contemplated her nervous surrender the gremlins in her mind would, on occasion, taunt her with the notion that one day, Vladimir, too, would hurt her. And she knew, if that happened now, it would be impossible for her to ever be complete, because he would always have those little pieces of her with him. Inadvertently, she had made herself need him, when she let him inside.

There were a few people in her life that saw the great towers that stared back from her eyes, guarding some great unknown, and some had even questioned what was there. George never saw them. He was too focused on his own wants and needs to realize Caroline might have some, too.

As she sat, staring out at the rain as it fell over the city, her knees curled up under her chin, she smiled, remembering a conversation with her friend, Joey, from many years ago.

"You know, one day, you are going to have to let someone in."

She had rolled her eyes, smiling at him.

"Someone, Caroline... *Anyone*.... It *could* be *me*, if you *need* it to be."

Looking into this twenty something's eyes, that seemed to hold the wisdom and experience of a hundred lifetimes, she remembered she had smiled back at him as though he was a naïve child on when he spoke those words.

She knew, much like her virginity, this was something that she could only let go of once. And, if it went to no one, she would accept that fate.

"You have to admit, Caroline, in reality, it is an incredibly lonely existence... Isn't it?"

Caroline remembered how her eyes had started to well up with those words, and how she fought to swallow the tears that she refused to let fall. She still didn't understand how he could see past her barriers, but his words had cut her to the core. Afraid that she had somehow allowed him to see too much, already, she began adding stones to her already impossibly high walls.

But, now she had done it.

She had, after all this time, let *someone* inside.

She grinned to herself as she thought of what her friend's reaction to such information would have been, if she only knew where Joey was. In the middle of the country's chaos, she had lost touch. And, for a moment she wondered about her artistic friend with a seemingly limitless talent, regardless of medium, and what he was doing in that moment.

And, in a small café in Deming, New Mexico, a painter suddenly remembered a young woman he had once befriended as he worked on his desert scene over dessert and coffee with life partner, Fred, as the happy couple planned a new life in what was no longer "New" Mexico.

Caroline sat in the window, looking over the playground, feeling completely at peace and content with the world as it was until suddenly a tug at her sleeve brought her back from her daydreams. Looking into her daughter's young and hopeful eyes, she was paralyzed by the reality of the knowledge that she was no longer a child herself.

Nervously twisting the band on the third finger of her left hand, she looked around her unhappy home and was suddenly struck with the reality that this was her prison. And even more so than the miserable guard that provided for her meals and comfort each day she was bound by the little inmates that she, herself, had placed here for her own companionship. As thoughts of Vladimir now raced through her mind, she thought to herself, *"What have I done?"*

But, as she thought of her children, she slowly reached a conclusion. They were so young, and she couldn't make it on her own, nor interrupt the perfect romance that she shared with Vladimir, by adding the complication of children to a perfect portrait. Guilt swept over her and she began to wonder how the expression in Alli's eyes would change, if she knew what her mother had done. Worse even, was the fact that, although the love she shared with Vladimir was the exact love that she hoped her daughter would one day find, it would be impossible to explain such an affair to a child.

Caroline was suddenly overcome with an overwhelming feeling of self doubt, shame and selfishness, as another part of her heart slowly began to break. She realized, in wicked irony, her heart truly never would be complete, with or without Vladimir. She began to accept the idea that knowing true love, at least once, was all that she had ever really wished for, and, through Vladimir, she had done that.

And she was thankful for the dance.

She went over to Muriel's, making up a lie for an emergency errand, and decided that she needed to end things with Vladimir while she still had the courage. Heading out in the driving rain to find him, she arrived at a familiar doorstep and the scene of so many extramarital pleasures. The rain on her face did well to hide the tears that had fallen as she struggled to find the words. He welcomed her with open arms, but knew something was very wrong when he leaned to kiss her and she began to cry.

He searched deep for answers in her eyes, even though he already suspected what she was about to say. Bringing her a towel, and a glass of water, he gently wiped her tears with a tissue and tried to calm her so that she could speak.

And, for over an hour, he listened.

As Caroline was making her way through the third round of the same rambling and tearful arguments for ending their love affair, Vladimir began positioning for his next move.

"So you see, it isn't you, it really isn't! I do love you! I love you more than you can imagine, I'm not in love with George, but I *am* married, Vladimir, and I am so sorry that I have let things get this far with us! I know you think he is a terrible husband, but he is also the father of my children, and they love him, and I can't break that up! *They* need him! I know you can't possibly understand that bond, but you need to understand how incredibly strong it is and why we just can't go on seeing each other anymore!"

"I do understand, Caroline."

"No, Vladimir, you don't. It isn't even something I can explain, you would have to have children to understand."

"But, I do understand. Why do you think I cannot?"

"I can't keep doing this…"

Vladimir paused, looking deep into Caroline's eyes, knowing he was on the verge of losing her forever. "I do know."

Caroline looked curiously into him trying to understand his adamence, and saw, for the first time, that pain that she had seen so many times, hiding behind his irises, slowly rise to the surface, as Vladimir hesitated for a moment before speaking.

"I had daughter. Back in Russia. Her name was Nadia."

Stunned by the news that Vladimir would keep such information from her, Caroline took a moment to try to process it all and began to wonder about this girl and why Vladimir would keep her such a secret. Drying her eyes, she gently questioned, "What?"

Vladimir only smiled, remembering.

"Why would you not tell me?" Caroline pressed.

"Because… my daughter died, Caroline." Vladimir seemed to struggle with his own words.

Suddenly Caroline had none, but Vladimir continued. "You should not be so quick to assume things you do not know. Americans do this though."

For the first time since she had known him, Vladimir seemed almost irritated, but it was more his frustration with her attempt to leave him and his longing for her that was surfacing.

He was certain they were destined to be together.

"You assume friends. You assume enemies. You *assume* you are right. All are to be grave mistakes in world we live."

"No we don't." Caroline said, in an almost shy, and defensive tone.

Vladimir smirked, almost chuckling as he reflected on American society. "You do. I love you, Caroline. But, I promise you, you are not even able to see when real enemy is to be standing before you. Is true for whole country. Country is to be at war because you are not able to be seeing that the people most close to you are to be the ones that are to like to destroy your life as you would know it, to serve only what they want for themselves."

"I'm sorry."

"Is not your fault. All things in life happen with reason. And, meeting you is no different. I love you, Caroline. One day, you will see truth."

Caroline looked down: there was no doubt she was deeply in love with the man sitting across from her, but she had made up her mind and she was stubborn. She couldn't respond, though her heart wanted to.

Caroline held her head in her hand, searching herself for an answer. She looked up to Vladimir with a sincerity and compassion he had never seen in her eyes, and, although he desperately wanted her to stay, he instead decided, her last words being that which they were, that it was time for her to return home. He offered to drive her home, or rather, close enough to home that she would not have to get soaked, but far enough away that they would not be seen together. Her mind was too fragile to continue with conversation, and he was satisfied that, despite what she had come to his home to say, eventually, they would be together.

As he pulled over to let her out, she looked into his eyes in a way that told him the love between them just simply had to continue, and he decided, regardless the evening's turn of events, he would do whatever he could to keep her by his side. Leaning over, he kissed her deeply, and she looked at him with confused emotion. She was in love with him, and no matter how hard she might try, she couldn't fight herself on that point. Letting herself out, she thanked him for the ride, and began her two block walk home, and he watched her fade from sight, around the corner.

But, Vladimir now had his own plans.

He realized in that moment that, despite her argument to leave, Caroline wanted him. Circumstance was the only complication.

Reaching between the seats, he pulled out his cell phone and dialed the one person he knew that could help him with his current dilemma.

"Lieutenant Commander Zealey? Yes... yes... thank you... And you? Good, good! I am to speak with the General. He is there, no?... Yes, it is most urgent."

"Father? Мне нужна помощь"

Surrender Your King

Racing from the shower, with a towel over her hair and dripping water all over the living room as she hurried to put on her robe, Caroline flew to answer the incessant pounding on her front door. She opened it to find a tall, imposing young man standing in her threshold in what appeared to be a dress version of the Northwest Command Uniform. With a flawless salute and a click of his heels, he handed her a very official looking envelope, addressed to her husband, George.

As her eyes stared in disbelief at the words printed on the outside, words fell from her mouth at the same time as the thoughts ran through her head. "There must be some mistake, here? You must have the wrong George Anderson?"

And in true military, barking fashion, without any hint of interest in her emotions, the young man responded, "No, ma'am! No mistake, ma'am!"

"But, this can't be right! I don't understand?" she pleaded and wished he had never darkened their doorstep. She wished he would take this evil piece of paper back to where ever it had come from, and her hands began to tremble as she thought of the implications. Ignoring her reaction, just as he had ignored those of all of the wives that had come before her, he simply turned and walked away, leaving her to face the consequences of what lie inside the envelope in her hands.

Moments later, with Caroline still frozen from what she was reading, Muriel was making her way from her own door, on her way to the local market to buy food for the evening meal. Taken back by Caroline's appearance, Muriel brought her mind back, when she called out, "Caroline! My goodness, child! What's happened? Come on, let's go in, let's sit down and talk."

Caroline looked up from the paper and into the eyes of her friend, gravity finally forcing the tears that were just barely holding on, to fall to the paper. Her hands still shaking, she allowed Muriel to guide her to a chair, as though she was unable to perform any motor functions, on her own, and without assistance. Leading her to the table, Muriel then realized, when she had to push down on Caroline's shoulder to encourage her to sit, whatever it was that Caroline was holding, it had left her in a state of shock. Caroline stared into nothingness, and aside from her breathing, the only other sign of life were the tears that streamed silently down her cheeks.

Gently, Muriel reached over to remove the letter from Caroline's hand, then pulled her reading glasses to her face, from their usual position around her neck. As she put them on, careful not to tangle her hair in the pearly necklace that they dangled from, she cautiously watched for Caroline to snap out of it. Glancing down, the outside of the envelope told most of the story, but Muriel would have to read the letter inside to be sure her eyes were not deceiving her, and about half way through the document her fears were confirmed, and she reached out, taking Caroline's hand to comfort her. The sensation of Muriel's touch, must have awoken her, and Caroline snapped awake in anger.

"They can't do this! We never agreed to this, did we?! When did we sign anything that says they can do this! I didn't sign anything, I can tell you that much and I know George didn't either!"

"Honey, you didn't need to sign anything. That's the whole idea behind a draft notice." Muriel tried to explain in her gentlest voice.

"But, they can't do this! We have children! George has a job here! They can't do this!"

Muriel lowered her lenses, and sympathetically turned to her friend, "They can, honey. They can. We've been lucky out here, really, being so far west, this has been going on in the more eastern parts of the Territory for months. I suppose it was easier to take the men that were already closer to the action, first…"

"Action!? What type of 'action', exactly, are you referring to, Muriel?" Caroline looked to Muriel's eyes and wondered what she was hiding.

"The Mississippi, dear." Muriel seemed confused by the idea that Caroline seemed to know nothing about this, and tried to explain, "Well, from what Alfred has told me, since the Command took control of all of the barge and boat traffic on the Mississippi, there has been a bit of an… well, an… uprising… with some of the states on the eastern side. The Mississippi is a major artery for their supplies. They aren't happy."

"What do you mean by 'uprising'?" Caroline questioned in a tone that demanded the truth.

"An uprising, Caroline. They've been fighting."

"Fighting how?" she pressed.

"Well, according to Alfred, there has been a lot of gunfire. The eastern states, specifically the northeastern states, they're sending men by the thousands, to take back control. Thugs, really, I mean, they are not trained soldiers like the Command, Caroline, it won't last long."

"Gunfire! George isn't a trained soldier, Muriel. He's *no kind* of soldier. He hates guns! He's never even fired one! He'll be killed!"

"Don't say that… really, don't say that. They'll train him. Well, before you know it, he'll be able to take out the red eye of a target at three hundred yards!"

Caroline found her feet and looked at Muriel as though she wanted an explanation for exactly how she was supposed to find comfort in those words. Caroline began to pace the room and think out loud. "This makes no sense! George can't go, he needs to be here, with me and the kids, the kids need their father here! George has obligations, we have bills! He can't go! He can't fire a weapon, he wouldn't! He couldn't shoot someone! People aren't targets! Even if he shot a target, he would never shoot a person! *No, no, no!* There must be some way to appeal this, to get out of it! That's what we'll do! Where the hell did that damn thing come from?!" She gnawed the words with frustration, but it did not help to ease Caroline's burdon.

Made nervous by both her mother's tone and words, Alli slowly wandered out from her room and shyly inquired about where her Daddy was going, in a quivering voice.

"Back to your room, Alli! I don't want to see you or your brother out here until the adults are done talking, is that very clear, young lady?" Caroline snapped with ire.

Alli retreated, but would remain nervous about their home until she saw her father that evening. She sat in her room, compulsively brushing her doll's hair as she kept one ear on the conversation.

Muriel tried to sound comforting, but reality was no comfort as she read from the paper. "Honey, this letter is from Cheyenne. It's straight from Central Command. I can't really make out the signature, but it has been signed by a General, so I really don't think your going to have much luck. You are going to be fine, sweetheart, your bills will get paid, the kids will be fine, so will George! Look they list his pay and benefits rates, right here."

Determined to try to reverse destiny, Caroline snatched the paper from Muriel's hand and began searching for a phone number desperate to find a voice to yell at on the other side of the line. On the back of the letter, she found a number for the Cheyenne Draft Office and she immediately dialed. Concerned for the mental health of her friend, Muriel headed to the kitchen to boil some water for tea, as she prepared to settle in and wait this one out with Caroline. In the same moment, she decided that leftovers would be fine for dinner, tonight and decided to forego her ritual evening trip to market.

As Caroline tapped her foot, anxiously waiting to make it through to a human being, Muriel made her way to Alli's room with juice and cookies in an effort to bolster her small spirit. She tapped lightly and said Alli's name. The door flew open almost immediately, telling Muriel that the little girl had been eavesdropping for whatever information she could overhear. Making her way, purposefully, to the little desk on the far side of the room, Muriel put down the juice and sat down on the little chair that was certainly not designed for the girth of her hips. She then patted her thigh, asking the little girl to come to her with gentle eyes.

"What's going on, Miss Muriel?" Alli begged to know, holding back tears.

"Well, sweetheart, here, have a cookie and I will tell you." Muriel smiled as Alli began chewing through the chocolate chips like a child just back from fat camp. Then handing her the juice, she hoped she would come up for air, as she petted her sweet and worried little face.

"Well, Alli, first of all, you need to know that your mommy and your daddy both love you very much. You know that, right?"

Alli's expression showed that she did not at all feel ameliorated by the way this discussion had started, so Muriel changed her approach.

"Alli, dear. Your daddy is a very important man and he is getting called away for a little while by some people that really need him to be there to help them out with some things. Now, you see, your mommy doesn't want him to go, because she wants him to stay here with you, and she is a little upset. It is a little selfish of your mommy to be this way, but it is only because she knows that you and Georgie really like having your daddy, here. Do you understand?"

Alli nodded, tensely.

"Well, you see, your daddy will probably be away for a few months. It is not anything for you to worry about. Really."

"Do you promise, Miss Muriel?" Alli implored reassurance.

"I do, Alli." Muriel said, as she hoped that promise would hold and not break.

"No, you need to *say* it. Say you promise otherwise I won't believe you."

And, Muriel wondered for a split second how it was that she had been outsmarted so quickly by an eight year old. As she spoke the words, she was filled with apprehension that she may, one day, be held accountable for them. She knew the child would remember this moment, but Muriel spoke, anyway. "I promise, Alli."

And with that, Alli smiled, naïve in her trust that Muriel would never lie to her and now simply happy to have cookies and juice that did not need to be shared with Georgie, since he was still down for his nap. Muriel rose to leave, content to see Alli away from the door and now busying herself with her crayons, seemingly unconcerned about the door. With a sigh she closed it over, not shutting it completely and filled with a sense of guilt that made her wonder if she truly already knew she had deceived the child, and she then returned to find Caroline pointing at the phone, her eyes showing the focus she had on her task as she pointed to the receiver, indicating she had finally reached a human voice on the line.

"Yes! *Yes!* I need to speak to someone about a *draft notice* that was *obviously* mistakenly sent to my husband! So, I just need to find out *who* I need to send this back to and make sure we clear up this whole mix up between *this other* George Anderson and *my* husband…" But, Caroline's expression did not seem hopeful as she was listening to whatever the voice on the other end of the line was telling her.

"I *understand* that, Sir, but this is a mistake. It *has* to be…" She seemed almost confused at this point.

"He is."

Muriel poured out two cups of tea, and prepared for conversation, hearing imminent defeat was on the horizon in Caroline's voice.

"No… I see…"

As Muriel set the tea on the table, she was startled, just a little, by Caroline slamming the phone into its cradle. Understanding her frustration, Muriel immediately searched for words of solace, in an almost wistful tone. "Well, dear, you know you should look at the bright side of things, here…"

Cutting off her friend, not wanting to hear, Caroline fired back. "I am really not interested in any little nuggets of optimistic wisdom, right now, Muriel."

The two women sat silently at the small dining room table, as Muriel slowly sipped her tea and watched over Caroline as she obsessively read, and reread, the words printed on the paper in her hand. She could not understand why George had been targeted and she tried to convince herself that this couldn't be real, as she thought how her husband would react when he walked through their door. He would be devastated, she was certain, and she tried to think of think of how she could possibly break the news. Maybe George, himself, would have an answer that had escaped her in her panic. Perhaps he would be able to find a way out of this on his own. Surly he would. He'd have to.

It wasn't long after that George made his entrance in traditional fashion, through the front door. Dropping his things as he walked in and paying little attention to the look on Caroline's face that, to anyone that had really known her, would have indicated that something was terribly wrong. Chewing on a candy bar that he had picked up on his way home, he walked over and simply asked what she was holding before even saying hello.

She handed the paper to him, but was surprised by his reaction which left her even more at a loss for words than the document itself had.

"Wow! This is great! Did you see this Caroline? This is great news!"

Even Muriel seemed a little perplexed by his reaction.

"George, did you not read the letter? It's a draft notice. The Command is drafting you to go out east? Do you not understand what it says?" Caroline was certain he had misread. She momentarily wondered if he was illiterate or just stupid.

"Yeah, as an Officer! Do you see what the pay scale is, here, Caroline? Look! This is twice what I make! And Officers don't do shit in the military!" George pointed out the pay scale on the paper.

"George, I don't think you fully understand the implications here. You will be away from your family for God knows how long. They want to send you off to Cheyenne for training, and then who knows where you will be, or for how long!"

Muriel rose to clear the table, anticipating that a marital fight may be imminent between the two. She busied herself with slowly rinsing out her cup in the sink, but keeping one ear on the conversation and a watchful eye on the room.

"Yeah, well, Caroline, I could use the change of scenery, anyway. Epstein's cutting back on overtime and this is a lot of money! I know a couple of guys in the Command, it's no big deal." He crudely wiped some remnants of chocolate with the back of his hand and started back to towards the bedroom, unconcerned with her feelings or input and calling out for his traditional after work cocktail to be brought to him. As he passed Alli's room, she bounded out and threw herself around his thigh, hugging him and welcoming him home, hoping for her affection to be returned. "Not now, Alli, daddy's busy. Go play in your room. We'll talk later." George dismissed Alli as if she was an annoying housecat, getting underfoot, and proceeded back to the bedroom where he planted himself in front of the television and called out for Caroline to hurry up with his cocktail. Trained by routine, she dropped it off on the nightstand, but found she had nothing to say to him as he smiled at her and nodded a thank you.

She thought to herself that she shouldn't waste so much of her energy trying to hold things together with a man that seemed to care nothing for her or the life they had built, but she couldn't help it. As she walked back towards the kitchen she thought for a moment about Vladimir. Thinking to herself that a life with him would not have been one of such dismissal and servitude, but she reminded herself that she had made this bed a long time ago, and had already resigned herself to lying in it. She hadn't spoken to Vladimir in weeks, and more than she missed the romance, she missed his friendship. He listened to her, and made her feel needed on so many levels. She realized she was still, very much, in love with him.

She turned to Muriel in the kitchen. It did not take much for Muriel to read the sadness in her eyes. She understood how Caroline was feeling, even without an exchange of words, as Caroline simply tilted her head to one side and shrugged her shoulders slightly, accepting the defeat of her spirit. There was so little of her left, anymore, and she, herself, was reaching the point that she didn't even care. Though she hid it so well, from those around her, no one really understood the depths of her misery and depression.

Muriel tried to allay Caroline's fears by trying to convince her that everything was going to be fine, although nothing was really changing. She explained that she would still babysit for Georgie, that Alli would be back in school, Caroline could return to teaching in a few weeks, and that the extra money would come in handy for their household and savings. Although Caroline did not believe a word of it, she smiled and nodded as though Muriel had convinced her and announced that she needed to get dinner on the table.

Really, Caroline just needed to be alone.

Smiling back and now certain that her advice had helped her friend, Muriel made her way to the door, happy to know that all was well with Caroline. Calling out to George, Caroline asked if spaghetti would be alright for dinner.

"I don't care." Was his only response.

She thought to herself about how typical that was, as she set a pot of water on the stove to boil. As she worked to prepare their evening meal, her mind began to envision life without George, for a while. Really, things would not be much different. They rarely really even spoke, anymore, so she decided that the silence at night would not be much different from life as it already was. She wondered if George even knew who she was. He knew the schoolgirl, the dreamer, the young woman with big plans, that eventually gave up on them, but she questioned whether or not the man that had shared her bed knew the woman she had become. She doubted if he knew anything about that person's dreams, or hopes, or fears.

Her mind focused on the little things that so many married women obsess over and which cause them to grow angry without seeming cause: the flowers that never came, the cards, the letters, the calls... the absence in times that should have meant something.

Watching the water, and waiting for the perfect moment to drop in the pasta, she found herself seeing some positive aspects to George being away for a while. As Muriel said, she would be back teaching soon, and Caroline loved that more than anything. She thought to herself that with George gone, she would have so much extra time in the evenings, not worrying about keeping up with his mess or cocktails. She would have less laundry to do and she thought that life might not even be as stressful. So much of her time now was spent avoiding tension in the home and trying not to fight, when really all she wanted to do, sometimes, was scream.

They had no physical relationship, anymore. The last time they had made love, she had become pregnant with Georgie. It was an accident, and she recalled that instead of being happy about their new arrival, George seemed almost frustrated, at the time. His first comments being about how much this would cost him and blaming Caroline for 'letting this happen', as though she had done something wrong. After that, she found she had no desire to even kiss him, and eventually their relationship disintegrated into its current mundane routine. Not that it was really ever happy, before.

She remembered the dreams of a 17 year old version of herself and, looking around, she realized how far life had fallen short of them and she wished for so much more. George called out for a refill, as she wiped her hands off with a towel and smacked it on the counter. The water now bubbling, she dropped in the noodles and exchanged George's empty for a fresh glass, then headed back to the kitchen without comment.

As she waited for dinner to finish cooking, she thought about Vladimir and she began to realize how much she really did miss him and, more importantly, that she was still very much in love with him. She began to think that it was not worth it for her to fight herself and she began to almost welcome the idea of having some time and space to think, without George's demands interrupting her thoughts.

Two weeks later, George shipped off to Cheyenne leaving out on a bus from downtown Portland. Caroline and the children waved goodbye as George and about fifteen other men boarded on. Caroline thought to herself that it was strange that so few men were leaving on a bus that must have sat fifty and she questioned in her mind why George seemed so much older than many of the others that appeared to be waving goodbye to their parents and not to their wives and children. She decided the bus must be making several stops, and this was only the first one, since they were so far west.

As the bus pulled away, Caroline watched it drive off and was unsure why she had a feeling of almost relief that he was gone. And, for this, she felt a little guilty. She wouldn't sleep well that night, not that she missed George, per se, but she missed the sensation of having another person next to her at night. It was comforting, even if there was no love between them in the bed.

On the bus, George settled in and tried to make friends by passing around a bottle of liquor that he had hidden in his bag and regaling the others with tales of his heroic high school football days. No one seemed impressed, and whispers began in the back of the bus, among a few, that were trying to determine how someone with no college education was entering into the Northwest Command as an Officer. In the meantime, George was slowly allowing himself to become more and more intoxicated, and with that his voice grew louder, and he seemed completely unaware of the fact that a few of the men had began to mock him. Finally, when one of the young men sitting near him decided he was done being polite, and got up and changed seats, George gave up on story telling and settled in for some sleep, unmindful of how thankful the group around him was to see that his incessant chatter had been replaced by snoring.

As he slept, they gossiped.

But, George was oblivious.

He woke up in Cheyenne, the stale stench of liquor seeping through his perspiration, and with a pounding headache. Stepping off of the bus, into the sunlight, he could see the recruiter taking roll and noticed from the number of men that now surrounded him they had obviously made a couple of stops on the way. As the recruiter led them into a large marble building, he realized there would be no time for rest and that he would have to struggle through yet another day with an alcohol hazed mind, but he was used to this.

The men were put through a series of physicals and other exams, on none of which was George's performance stellar. Even the recruiter had, unbeknown to George, called Headquarters to verify that this disheveled excuse was really destined to be an Officer. Surprised by the confirmation, the recruiter simply shook his head and sent George through to Basic Training with the rest of the group certain that, despite what he had been told, someone up top had made a mistake. After the series of physicals George was next sent to the IT (Identity Tracking) Division to receive his GPS implant. The GPS implant was a small device, no larger than the head of a pin that the Command inserted in all of its members and eventually planned to use to track all residents inside the Territory. For now, they were working the kinks out of the system with those in the service. Initially, they had planned to insert the devices in the left hands of all members allowing Command Officers and Personnel to do all sorts of business with the wave of a palm, even though its main purpose was to track their moment to moment location and movement. Their software was so sophisticated that a Command Member could go to the store and simply wave their hand over a chip reader at the checkout and have the money for their purchases automatically deducted from their account. Of course, this also allowed the Command complete control of tracking purchases for alcohol, inhalants and other things that might give cause for concern among their Servicemen. However, the numbers of amputees returning from the front line would eventually make that a costly decision, so they resulted to implanting the device in the hairline, just above the forehead. The powerful tracking device was no bigger than the head of a pin and most did not even feel the device through their skin, though some complained of constant headaches after the chip had been inserted.

George was among those with no side effects and within a few weeks of having been denied alcohol of any kind, and after being put through rigorous morning and afternoon exercises, George's mind had cleared and he found himself truly enjoying his new lifestyle. Free from the burdens of married life, and all that goes with it, he had time to sit and think and actually enjoyed reading about military strategies and learning about the structure of The Command. He curled up for three nights straight devouring *The Art of War*, and when he was done with it, he reread it twice more, fascinated by its contents. Unlike High School, he was pleased with the mandatory reading he and his new classmates had been assigned.

He wrote to Caroline, every few days, telling her all about his experiences and, upon receiving his letters, she found herself remembering why she had married him in the first place. On paper, he was able to express far more than he ever did in conversation and his words were that of an endearing and loving husband. She was shocked by his eloquence. She began to feel hope, once again, for their marriage, for the first time in years.

By the time she had returned to teaching she was determined to work things out with George, and her own responses to his letters had grown more and more romantic. Even though she saw Vladimir throughout the day, and knowing the feelings she still harbored for him, she kept things very professional, although friendly. Vladimir noticed that George and the kids had become much more of a topic than they ever had been in past conversations, and he allowed her to go on without interruption or question, happy to have her in his life, even if they could only be friends for right now.

Vladimir listened and watched her hopeful expressions as she spoke about repairing her marriage. He was willing to wait this one out. His heart longed for them to be together, and despite her words of affection for her husband, every now and then their eyes would still meet in a way that told him she was still very deeply in love with him. The connection between them was undeniable, regardless of what she was trying to convince herself of in the moment.

Vladimir saw her struggles, but was not faltered.

Perhaps it was his Russian heritage, and notwithstanding Caroline's seeming belief that her marriage had finally turned around, Vladimir knew that everything in life was just a matter of time, or timing. He had convinced himself that her marriage was just a matter of time and that, eventually, the timing would be right for him to have her by his side. And he was going to make that happen, one way or the other.

But, for now, they would remain friends.

At least, he was content to allow Caroline to believe that was the extent of their relationship.

At no point did Vladimir ever feel jealous of George. The kinship he had with this other man's wife was like nothing else he had ever experienced. A complete trust in her and love for her that was almost unexplainable. If anything, George was simply an obstacle that would eventually work its way out of her life and he didn't concern himself with how the inevitable would come to pass. In the interim, Vladimir was just satisfied to see Caroline as happy as she was, even if she was fooling herself in many ways. In the halls of Meriwether Lewis, he always made a point to speak her, but only when she was surrounded by others.

"So, are you to reveal new play for this year or is such information to stay top secret among ladies only?" Her fellow female teachers giggled like teenagers in his presence, but she only smiled not allowing herself to reminisce of the times when their eyes had been only inches apart and he was kissing her deeply.

"We're considering *Charlie and the Chocolate Factory*. Mrs. Joseph Schavonie, one of the fourth grade math teachers suggested it. I think Ann Campbell is leaning towards just doing a talent show, though. I suppose it depends on the children's interest? Of course, Alli is hoping for *Charlie*. I think she has plans to play Veruca Salt or Violet Beauregaurde." Another teacher interjected, hoping to gain Vladimir's attentions and playing on rumors of a "very close off work, personal relationship."

The room waited for confirmation.

Vladimir never missed a step.

"I would have to vote for play, myself. With talent show, you don't know. Play is more interested, even though end is to be scripted." Vladimir smiled to her, hoping she would look up and ignoring the other women. Quickly realizing she was uncomfortable, he made his exit, encouraging the other ladies to vote for *Charlie*. The other teachers exchanged "knowing" glances.

As he walked away, Caroline thought to herself that she could only have wished they had met ten years sooner and certain, in another lifetime, they had been happy together. Her heart did not regret the time they had spent alone and in each other's arms, but her head kept reminding her of her children.

Caroline kept focused, and faithful, through George's letters.

At home, the dinner table was filled with conversation, and Georgie was finally reaching the age where he could contribute some things their evening dialogue. His off the topic interruptions amused Caroline, who was still amazed by how quickly a child develops, despite having already experienced this miracle through Alli. Still, his blurts were nothing more than a nuisance to his big sister who had become a master at rolling her eyes at him, when her mom wasn't looking. Equally, little brother had come up with a few ways of retaliating at her.

Alli had inadvertently taught her little brother well.

He smiled as he thought of where her favorite teddy bear was floating, that very moment, then dug into his dinner as he plotted an appropriate torture for her most cherished dolly.

Little did he know, his sister's mind was scheming equally sinister revenge on his own toys.

Typical sibling rivalry.

Caroline packed up a care package for her husband, filled with home baked treats and pictures that the children had drawn, and she asked Alli to help her little brother out with his counting to keep them both occupied. Aggravated that she had to spend time with this little booger eating creature, Alli had an idea, and became suddenly and inexplicably chipper.

"Sure, Mom! Why don't I teach him about money? After all, *that's* the kind of counting you use everyday?" Alli fired back in a gleeful voice, forcing her most innocent expression and Caroline bought into her deceptions immediately.

Pleased by her daughter's enthusiasm, Caroline agreed and pulled down the children's piggy banks, from the top of the refrigerator, handing each their own. Alli led Georgie back to her room, so she could work on her own turf.

The children spilled out their coins and Alli began with her lesson. Laying out one of each of her coins and explaining to Georgie what they each were, purposefully sorting them out by size. "Okay, this one here is a penny. It is a collector's item, 'cause they don't make them anymore, and it's mine, so don't touch it!" She snatched up the shiny little piece of copper colored metal and sat on it, hiding it from her brother's view, and protecting it as though it had the value of a Krugerrand, then continued. "Now this little one is a dime, they aren't worth much. And this is a nickel, which is a little bigger than a dime. And this big one, here, is a quarter." After reviewing the names of the coins, several times, Georgie finally had it, and Alli was proud of her student.

"That's great, Georgie! Now, let's go ahead and put all of your quarters in one pile, all of your nickels in another pile, and all of your dimes in a pile, too. I'll do the same with mine." And, like a little sheep, Georgie obeyed, happy that his sister seemed pleased with him for once.

"Good work, Georgie!" Alli eyed the large pile of dimes in front of her brother, and her own stack of nickels.

The trap was set.

"You know what, Georgie? You did *such* a good job, you've earned a *reward*! I'm going to trade you all of my nickels for all of your dimes. See, nickels are bigger, so that means they are worth more and you can buy more stuff." Georgie enthusiastically pushed his dimes into his sister's pile and reached out for her nickels, happy to make such a generous exchange.

The door flew open.

Alli suddenly jumped at her mother's voice. Caroline had been listening in on the children, and up until only a moment ago, was so proud that her daughter was demonstrating such patience and kindness to her younger sibling.

"Alli! How *could* you?! Do you have *any* idea what you have done? I am going to have to spend *hours* with your brother trying to undo what you have taught him! Now, since I don't know who started with what, give your brother ALL of your dimes AND all of your nickels!"

"But, Mom! You can't do that!" Alli exclaimed, angry that her investment scheme had failed.

"You heard me, young lady! ALL of them!"

Georgie's eyes grew as wide as Charlie's when he first glimpsed the Golden Ticket, as he watched the large pile of silver being pushed towards him, and Alli struggled to understand where her brilliant plan had gone wrong. Although Caroline had to act like the wrathful disciplinarian in front of Alli, she would later find herself chuckling about it as she recanted the story in a letter to George.

Unlike the exaggerated stories of running back a forty five yard touchdown when he was a senior in high school, the men in his barracks were actually amused when he told them about what Caroline had written. "Sounds like that little girl of yours is a really pistol, there, Anderson!" one of the men commented, laughing at the impish tale. Now sober since his arrival, George had actually managed to gain the respect of a few of the men in the barracks that had not been privy to his antics on the bus.

"Alli? Oh, yeah, she's that alright! She's smart! I mean, I know every parent thinks their kid is smart, but she's smart in that 'scary smart' kind of way... and she's so cute, too. It really is a frightening combination, speaking as her dad." George pulled out a picture of his kids, handing it over to the dark haired Private.

"Damn, Anderson! She is a cutie! You're like going to have your hands full in a few years!" The young man nodded approvingly as he passed the photo back to George.

"You think I don't know? Shit! Part of me wishes The Command would just keep me here until she turns twenty one. Then I won't have to deal with any of her high school boyfriends, and I can just return home to find her dating some nice college guy that Caroline has already approved of, you know?" George radiated with pride as he tucked Alli's photo back into its rightful place in his wallet.

The young Private smiled, unable to truly relate, but nonetheless amused. "So, you like head off for Officer's Training, tomorrow, huh? The rest of us are heading straight to the front line. It sucks." He continued with the task of polishing his boots, though part of him wondered what was the point, as they would certainly be dirty within 24 hours?

George looked around the room at all of the faces that were becoming familiar to him, "Yeah. It's going to seem really empty around here, without everyone else."

"Doubt it. They have another group arriving in the morning, like from what I have heard. Won't matter to you, anyway, you're moving to the Officer's Quarters."

"Yeah, I guess. Don't see it how that will be much different, though." George shrugged.

"Oh, it's different!" The young Private commented, as though he knew something, spitting on his shoes.

"How so?" George pressed for information based on his tone and a little surprised by the comment.

For a moment the young man with the deep brown eyes, and pale freckled skin, thought. Then, he responded, "Dunno. But, like my older brother is an Officer in the Command, and my mom says that he like changed after he went through that program. Kinda like fucked him up, somehow. He did tell her the food was better, but like, he just... I dunno... he changed." The young man continued buffing his shoes, and couldn't seem to come up with a better explanation.

George thought for a second, watching the young man, and wondering what this young man knew about the place where he was heading that had somehow escaped the rumor mill to date. "Um, it *'fucked him up'* how?"

Not bothering to look up, the young Private sort of bounced his head back and forth from shoulder to shoulder and said, "Well, my mom just says he was *'different'*. Like, he only came home once for Christmas, but it was like he was all dead inside. Like he didn't really know us, you know? He seemed really nervous, or something. My mom thinks maybe they like had him drugged or something, but the Command is like really against medication, so like I don't think that's it, ya' know? It was like he just wasn't there? But, who knows. He only came home once. That was last year. Ain't seen him since then. Maybe he's fine now."

George focused on the floor, as he pondered his next questions, but no matter how he phrased them, he realized the Private truly did not have any more answers, so he resigned himself to the fact that he would have to learn for himself in Officer's Training. George was looking forward to it, despite the seemingly ominous warning.

For the first couple of weeks, things seemed pretty normal. There were tons of classes, including studies on military strategies, traditions, beliefs of The Command, consequences of disloyalty, leadership and management of forces. It all seemed pretty boilerplate: lots of memorization and regurgitation.

But, Officer's School would bring many surprises.

On George's first day, he glanced across the room finding a face that seemed somewhat familiar. Noticing his stare, the other man nodded, fully recollecting their former acquaintance. He approached, reaching out his hand to shake George's.

"George Anderson, right?" The other man questioned, not in a completely friendly manner.

"Right." George still struggled to place him.

"Seems like a long time since Roswell High, doesn't it? I suppose I have not seen you since that day? How is Caroline?" the man that seemed to have familiar features questioned him.

Suddenly, George remembered. His name was Kenny Walls. Number fifty four on the football team and his rival for Caroline's attentions. He had often wondered, over the years, if Caroline had not become pregnant with Alli, would she have ended up with the man that stood before him. George had always wondered who she had loved more. After that fateful May afternoon, he never saw Kenny, again. He watched as his competition had been carried out the door on a stretcher, suffering from a gun shot wound to the leg.

One of many of the Unholy Trinity's Victims, that day.

Growing up, he had known the dark haired football star well and was often envious of his accomplishments. George had, at one time, worked for Kenny's father in the hardware store that Kenny's family owned. He resented it when Kenny would come in with his entourage and grab a hundred bucks from the register, then hit the town, while George found himself stuck mopping floors. That was a long time ago, though. Trying to make small talk, he asked the only question that came to mind and seemed polite, "How is your dad, Ken?"

The face of his one time adversary fell slowly, and the one time popular high school senior looked away, as he answered. "We lost dad, last spring. Heart failure."

Not knowing what else to say, he uttered the same words that anyone trying to be tactful would say. "I'm sorry. He was a good man."

Kenny nodded a thank you, and the one time NFL hopeful then returned to his previous group, George noticed he still walked with a limp. Upon further inspection though, he realized that a metal prosthesis now replaced what once was a shin and he knew why the young star's football career had come to such a sudden halt. Between the UT tragedy and the Iraq war, amputees were commonplace, yet George still found himself grateful that was as God made him. It was the only time he would converse with Kenny post Roswell Hornet Days and George would later decide not to tell Caroline about the encounter.

Years later, he was still a little jealous of the emerald eyed, chestnut haired Adonis that had once carried Caroline on his arm through the halls of Roswell High and he secretly wondered if Kenny would have treated her better than he, himself, had after taking her hand. In some ways, he knew his competitor would have done better by her than he had ever tried to. And, for this reason, he was afraid of opening the door for them to reunite: scared that she might realize that she could have so much more love in her life.

But, secretly, she had known such love in Vladimir.

If he had only known.

George assumed that Caroline just wasn't that type of woman, and her lack of complaint equated to satisfaction.

He was always so wrong when it came to emotion.

In the third week of training, they left the classroom. George assumed that they were heading to the firing range, much like they had in basic training. He was anxious to learn about all of the advanced techniques that they would surly teach him in his journey to leadership, but what he saw on the target range drew emotions that he had never felt before.

All of a sudden, it became clear, the fate of those unfortunates that had failed to leave the Territory. The homeless drunks that failed to realize the sweeps that were going on around them. The prisoners, unfortunate enough to be held captive behind bars, within the Territory's borders, now enclosed inside a larger penitentiary. And, those, simply of the wrong color, that chose to fight The Command and hold on to that which they had worked so hard for.

They were all there.

Naked and scared.

Scattered across the field before him.

There was no escape for them.

George became overwhelmed with the feeling that he was caught in some horrible time warp, finding himself in the middle of the Roman Coliseum at the height of Caligula's reign.

But, this was real.

George thought for a moment about his friend Ronald's cousin. He had disappeared inside these borders and George could only wonder if this was the horrible end that he had met. As he looked at the faces before him, he wondered if it was possible that somewhere out there, he was standing before him.

There must have been two hundred of them.

To attempt to flee was futile. Encircled by landmines and trained members of the Command, they were given no choice, but to accept the inevitable. Despite the odds, one man tried. He raced and, as pieces of him rained down on the others, a few more tried to follow his exact path thinking that he had already blown up the Command's perimeter, providing them with a route to safety. But, the Command knew better, and the second perimeter sprayed an even more powerful blast than the first.

George would spend the night debating if they were lucky or smart.

Death was a reward on this field, as some of the others would soon learn.

As George looked on in horror, he could hear his fellow, younger Officers laughing and making jokes. They were so desensitized, they didn't feel anything for the captive prey in front of them. They didn't even see them as human.

The Command began their show by announcing over a load speaker, to their soon to be victims, that the General would be sporting and spare one life. George could feel the terror radiating from the other side as each person contemplated their own odds of winning this twisted game.

The sound of an enthusiastic drum roll echoed through the sound system, followed by the voice of a young and sickeningly jovial announcer. "On the count of three, you will have an opportunity to spare your useless life. You will be freed, outside of our borders. You need only be the first to complete one simple task: kill a man on your field with your bare hands, and spare us the trouble!"

As the announcer's eerie laughter trailed off of the speaker, applause roared out from George's side, but he was not among the fans. He watched carefully as the fearful group on the other side began to search for weaker members of the pack. He felt for the elderly and the young among them. His heart raced as the announcer spoke and, on the word "three", he felt a shock hit his gut like he had never felt before as he watched the group beat and weaken one another in an attempt to draw first blood. Within less than a minute, a man was smiling, jumping up and down, dragging the dead body of a frail old woman in his grip, trying to catch the attention of the helicopter team above him.

She was only three days from her eighty ninth birthday.

Her braids, neatly groomed, hung from the sides of her head in two perfectly woven rows, and appeared as though a pound of powdered sugar had been gently sprinkled over her head: hints of a once ebony black color shining through.

She was the mother of nine.

The grandmother of thirty two.

The great grandmother of three and the great, great grandmother of one.

She was gentle and kind, and loved the earth.

She fed the stray wolves and coyotes with her scraps, in the hope her kindness would spare the lives of other animals that lived nearby. But, she never told her neighbors. She enjoyed weaving, conversation, long walks and a strong cup of coffee in the morning.

But, none of that mattered now.

A swift blow to the temple and a violent thrust of her neck had shattered her C-1 vertebra like a wishbone. She now lay in a small heap, a top the earth she once so treasured, as the young man jumped in celebration of her speedy demise.

As he ascended the rope ladder, the would be escapee hoped would lead him to safety, others swarmed to get on board, as well, only to feel the pain of a sharpshooter's bullet piercing them below the knee. Not enough to kill them, but enough to weaken their position as the real games were about to begin.

Games so cruel, they would change George's psyche forever.

George watched the helicopter pull off with the determination of a hornet returning to its nest and could only wonder about the ultimate fate of its dark passenger. But, the in flight members of the Command would keep their promise. They freed the bloodied young man on board just outside their borders.

They just didn't tell him they planned to free him at 3500 feet.

As Horatio Jacobs was falling to his death, an equally terrifying end had already come to many of his co-captors. George had watched in empathetic horror as the Command had dropped about seventy five guns on the field, telling the prisoners those that had the guns, would have a sporting chance. Those that had already been shot attempting to grab the ladder rope of the helicopter, struggled to get to the weapons pile, as others beat each other out of the way, forcing their way to the guns.

Command Members were ordered to pull up their scopes.

George's stomach was queasy the entire time he was taking aim at the faces, through the site, knowing he was being watched, but purposefully missing his targets. He would later explain his inaccuracy to his evaluators, by trying to write it off as simple nervousness. They countered, explaining that, on the front line, he would not be afforded the luxury of counseling.

And the next day, he went through the same exercise.

And the day after.

And the day after that.

Until, finally, he complied.

The Command never bothered to mention that the guns on the other side were loaded with blanks. They wanted the Officers to feel what it was like to experience the fear of being shot at, and never spoke of this small fact to anyone, even though George and several others had their own suspicions. They did, however, explain that refusal to comply with orders would place you on the other side of this field.

And that was plenty of motivation to convince them to fall in line.

After about a week, George found himself among the cheering fanatics, wanting to see the eyes of his victims through his scope as he planted the bullet. It was almost robotic.

They had stripped him of emotion.

They had forced loyalty through terror.

But, it was only the beginning.

A whole new level of horror would soon unfold.

He would learn soon, why the Command always reinforced the idea that only the lucky would die on that killing field. Now that he had satisfied the Command, by taking life, he could move on to the next level.

What to do with those lives that had something left to offer the Command?

While the US Military had adhered to certain diplomacies, the Command had rewritten policy. George, having successfully passed what would go on his record as 'Advanced Firearms Training', now found himself being instructed to attend, with several others, yet another training program.

He walked into the auditorium, of what had once obviously been a teaching hospital, and took his seat in the rafters. When the curtain opened he saw a man, with obvious injuries, strapped to a table below him. George thought to himself that the man had already passed, as he showed no real signs of life. That was until a grey haired man, with beady eyes, hiding behind a surgical mask, injected his IV awakening him to his nightmare. Another man, wearing a face shield and goggles, latex gloves and a gown, then began to speak, testing the mic as if it were a simple sound check and ignoring the body that writhed to be free, lying on the table behind him. With his every word, the man on the slab, gagged from vocal expression, and already fighting a gunshot wound to the leg, was pulled even further from his anesthetic state. And, with the horror of what was about to befall him screaming out, from his heart to the room, he struggled to fight the restraints that bound him to his deathbed.

"We are here today to discuss the various methods of effective tortures that you may need to envoke against your enemy." The man, dressed in full surgical gear, bellowed out from below. He pulled back a cloth, revealing an armory of portentous tools. Like animals used for science, for those that were captured, death was the only acceptable result. "You may choose to begin, with simple methods…" He opened, grabbing the man's hand and pulling his fingernails from their cuticle sockets, one by one, as the man fought agony.

Mercy was unwelcome in the room.

"And, you can add to this, your own variations. Rubbing alcohol, bleach or other chemicals may be poured over the exposed nail bed to increase the effect, if the information you seek is not readily divulged." The surgeon seemed to have no sympathy for the man that toiled to escape the leather wrist bands that held him down, seeing him more like a training tool than a human. As the rubbing alcohol drowned his fresh wounds, the poor human lab rat tried to jerk up, his eyes fighting their own sockets against the pain.

"Next, we move to digital amputation. This I have found is also quite effective."

Slowly, one by one, he removed all of the fingers on the right hand of his victim, watching as this man grew weak from blood loss and shock. But, his next words would startle him back to reality. The doctor then ordered blood and fluids to ensure his game could continue…

And then, the surgeon removed his eyes.

George fought not to vomit, despite the fact that several other Officers had already given into nature's response to the acts taking place in the room.

George watched as victim, after victim, was paraded in and out of the room subjected to one horrible end after the other. They were what was left of those unfortunate enough to only be injured, from the days before. And he found himself growing numb. By the third day of training, he, and his fellow students, now replaced the surgeon as the executioner.

And George felt nothing.

They had broken him.

Back in Portland, Caroline was confused as she struggled to understand how George's romantically sweet letters had now turned to rambling, almost non-sensible and incoherent babblings that she failed to comprehend. In her effort to salvage their marriage, she continued to respond with words of encouragement and love. The only thing she didn't know, was that George never read those words.

Eventually, she would seek the comfort of a friend that she had to begun to see on a more regular basis. Although platonic, their relationship had grown close and Caroline truly enjoyed his company and their conversations. Vladimir was extremely intelligent and insightful and Caroline needed him, now.

She needed someone.

"I am sorry, Caroline, you must not to understand such tragedies of war. Tragedies of my generation, and generation of my father. In Russia, we are to understand well. America, is young. She finds innocence in ways of war. You have toys world desires, but, you do not know how to use. Can you not see that eventually world will simply take if you do not defend? George is to defend, but soldiers fight many battles. The ones on field and the ones within. Wars are terrible. You must to understand what he has seen, he is not to get out of head for long time." Vladimir carefully tapped the letters that Caroline had allowed him to read on the edge of her desk, straightening them, then handed them back to her. Vladimir understood far more than he could explain to her and, to him, the letters did not seem as rambling.

"But, this is *not* a war, Vladimir! I don't even understand why he is there!"

Vladimir looked into her eyes with compassion, but with a deeper awareness she could not possibly understand, right now, he explained. "It *is* war, Caroline. *This*, you must accept." He pulled her in and allowed her to cry on his shoulder and release her fears into his shirt, but only for a few moments. Taking note of the time, he pulled her head gently from its comfortable resting place and instructed her to go wash up before her next class.

And she obeyed.

Although she could not know it, she would not even recognize her own husband if she had seen him now. George's eyes appeared, now, as stony granite orbs to the world, hardened by experience and sights better left unseen. All of those moments of horror, now, part of his own life experience which he would refuse to share, but could not help but be forced to remember in his nightmares.

No one could explain George's mental state to Caroline, although some thought it was worth trying. In an effort to understand and get the troubled thoughts from her mind, Caroline sought another opinion. She respected Vladimir's, but it just wasn't what she wanted to hear. After being allowed to read his letters, Muriel thought to herself that perhaps it was better to leave Caroline blind. She knew full well, from the stories her husband had shared, the dark path that George was walking. Furthermore, she knew explaining would only cause Caroline to worry more. Muriel would need her strength to counsel, soon enough, and she did not want to placate Caroline with lies that she would later regret. After reading the letters, she slowly removed her bifocals, and folded her hands in front of her, over the stack of papers. Looking to her friend, she half smiled. "Don't trouble yourself, Caroline. The world has enough troubles. Just let these go, for now. Just write back. Don't question this. Just write back and give him something positive to focus on."

Caroline struggled to respond. That was all she had done. Every letter she had written was nothing more than to cheer him and lift his spirits. Muriel knew that. Why she would give such vague advice was beyond Caroline, at that moment. Not knowing what to say, she simply nodded and rose to pour Muriel another cup of tea. Her mind wandering.

"Let me do this, Caroline. I will call Alfred and see if he can find out something for you. Maybe I can find out when George will be getting leave, or coming home? Then you can put that in your next letter and give him something to look forward to, okay?" Muriel knew that her husband had no such connections, but the offer filled Caroline's eyes with hope and, for the first time since his letters had gone dark, Caroline smiled wide and nodded.

"I'm going to write him, right now! Can you call Alfred?"

Muriel was on the spot, but she quickly made up a reason for a delay. "Um, well, dear... with the time difference and all... I won't get through until about seven this evening. But, as soon as I do I will let you know. It might be tomorrow before Alfred will get back to us."

The lie made sense to Caroline and she accepted her friend's words without question, giving Muriel time to make up some information. She knew whatever date she gave Caroline would have to be soon enough, as to put her mind at ease and far enough away in the future to allow for that which was to be expected. As they sat, sipping their Lady Grey from their cups, Muriel was pained by the truth she had known for sometime: George was not coming home. She remembered how her heart sank when she heard his Company Assignment. Company 318. They had been sent to the Mississippi and she knew from the stories she had heard that Company 318 had been assigned to a Terri Mission. For the Command, that meant they expected no survivors. Muriel remembered questioning how it could possibly be that her poor neighbor had been chosen for such unlucky duty. It was information that very few would have known, except for the highest ranking in the Command and Muriel dare not breathe a mention of it.

Alfred was not high ranking. Although he received his checks from the Command, he was nothing more than a simple printer at the Denver Mint charged with keeping the complex system of printing equipment running smoothly and the ink levels passable as greenbacks. Yet, almost fifty years of living with Muriel had caused him to develop a great talent that he saw as necessary for survival: he was wonderful at faking deafness. So good, in fact, most people assumed the quiet man that ran the presses was almost completely deaf. But, the truth was he had the hearing of a bat and equally impressive memory. As two of the Command's Lieutenant Commanders had come through the Mint for an inspection, Alfred had overheard their conversation about the fate of Company 318 and he remembered his neighbor's assignment and in a moment of weakness, he had confessed to his wife what he had overheard.

Muriel would be filled with nervous tension as she tried to determine an appropriate date for disclosure. Had Caroline known her better, she would have been able to tell she was lying when Muriel told her that Company 318 would be coming home on military leave in six to seven weeks. Muriel always rubbed her eyes when she was telling a lie, but only a few knew that small detail. Caroline was excited by the news and the next day she shared her excitement with Vladimir, who only seemed confused by her words. The Command never told anyone about plans for leave or return of any soldiers, but he simply listened to his friend as she rambled on about her letter and her aspirations that George would be inspired by the idea of coming home.

Although she could not know it, her letters would never find Caroline's hand.

The saddest part was that she excited the children…

Lunchroom Break

"He *is*, too! My mom told us last night after *she* spoke with someone that *knows* someone that's *real* high up in the Command in the Denver Mint." Alli was adamant as she sat across the lunch room table from her arch nemesis, little Becky Bagley, and encouraged her former co star, Nikki, to back her up. But, the raven haired boy only seemed confused by what Alli was trying to explain.

"*Nobody* at the *Mint* is high ranking! *Everybody* knows the Command is based in *Cheyenne, stupid*!" Becky remarked in her normally bratty tone, rolling her eyes, as she flipped her auburn hair from her face and rallied the other children to make fun of Alli's ignorance.

"*You* don't know that! *You're* the stupid face! *My daddy* is an *Officer*! Things are different for them!" Alli fired back, as little Nikki put his hand to his face, shielding it from the growing debate between the girls.

Shyly, the nine year old heart throb, tried to gently save Alli from making more of a fool of herself than she already had. All of the children of Command Families knew that there was never any notice about leave for anyone, except members of the Junior Heroes Squadron. Nikki cleared his throat and pushed his hair back, then turned his freckled face and big brown eyes to Alli, trying to speak to her as gently as he could. "Alli, I think Becky is right. None of us get notice when our Dad's are coming back. Maybe you just misunderstood what your mom said?"

"Did anyone *ask* for *your* opinion?!" Alli retorted before storming off to return her lunch tray and leaving the cafeteria. It would be Nikki's first encounter with the sudden mood swings of the opposite gender, but even as a man he would find himself as much at a loss for words at the odd behaviors of women as he was in that very moment.

As the children were returning to their classrooms in Portland, George found himself on the banks of the Mississippi, now a graduated Officer in the Command, leading a small group of young men towards the great brown river. As he stood there, looking down at an odd coagulation of thick jelly like matter that seemed to line parts of the broad, murky river's muddy edge and he wondered if this could be the source of the foul stench they had been unable to escape for the past day as they had been marching closer to the water. Turning to one of his subordinates, he questioned, "What *is* that goop?"

"Clotties, Sir." The young man responded, without hesitation.

George looked down, again, searching for a more positive response. "'Clotties' of *what?*"

Puzzled, the eighteen year old responded, "Well... clots of blood, Sir. And other stuff. From upstream."

"What *other* stuff? *Where* upstream?" George said as he looked at the thick piles that had collected and then noticed what looked to be an arm, floating down the river. Suddenly, he was filled with fear and thoughts of his children.

"Ya' know. *Stuff.* They say the fighting up north is pretty intense and ain't no time for burying a body, so they just toss it in the river. Body swells up and when they pop, you get clotties. I suspect a good many of us are gonna end up as fish food." The young soldier answered nonchalantly, as if the thought of death had no impact. Even for all he had seen, George felt a chill as he looked to the deep waters.

There was so much of it.

In that moment, he vowed... he swore... if he could only be delivered home he would be a better father, a better husband... a better man...

And, for the first time in years, he prayed...

And there was silence...

He wondered how many lives were represented there that were now reduced to nothing more than jell-o. *Thousands? Tens of thousands? More?* He couldn't imagine as he watched the currents carrying more and more red chunks that resembled parts of jellyfish to the muddy edge: the final resting places of those that had marched before them. George looked north over the seemingly endless river and wondered what dark red horse was thundering down its banks towards them.

Ink and Paper

"INK AND PAPER! It's just that simple!" he began. *"For all that America has accomplished over the centuries the final pursuits of the infidels would be for nothing more and ink and paper?!"* The boisterous old man, and one time accomplished cellist, with deep, almost ominous chestnut eyes smiled as he flipped through a pile of crisp $100.00 bills, smelling the sweet aroma.

"We've spent our whole lives pursuing *nothing more* than ink and paper! *Anything* of *significance* in *their* society is acknowledged by these *two things*. It is *recognized* in the form of *their* contracts! It is *recognized* in the form of *their* degrees that they would not let *you* obtain! It is *recognized* in the form of *their* meaningless marriage licenses! *And! most noticeably* my Muslim brothers, it is *recognized* in the form of *their money*. *The money* they would *keep for themselves*! *The money* they would *not let you* earn! But, in reality, *it is all nothing more* than ink and paper!"

The crowd cheered uncontrollably as Elijah set fire to a monstrous pile of brand new $100 bills.

*"THESE ARE NOTHING MORE THAN **SLAVE PAPERS**! I SAY WE **BURN THEM**!"*

The crowd grew frenzied.

Whatever the Islamic Nation was lacking, it certainly wasn't cash. No one really seemed to know where all of their funding came from, and no one bothered to question.

"That's where it started *and where it must end!"*

The old man smiled, his outward appearance as much teddy bear as he was tyrant. He controlled the Northeastern Corridor and everyone that hoped to survive in it… and he knew it. He was a powerful speaker that not only knew what to say, but he knew when to say nothing.

He fell silent for a moment allowing the group to excite themselves then waiting to speak once more.

"*Once again! The North* shall signify *independence* for *our* brothers and sisters! *We will be <u>united</u>! Not under their* religion, *but by our own! We shall have no contracts filled with empty promises with the infidels!* We shall *educate* our own in their *true* destiny! Where <u>are</u> your forty acres? Where <u>is</u> your mule? <u>They lied</u>! And we shall march west and fight those that would have us starve! AND **SPILL THE BLOOD** OF THE GRANDCHILDREN OF THOSE THAT **ENSLAVED** OUR FATHERS!"*

Fervor amongst the group reaches an almost panicked state of emotion.

In the crowd, Leticia leaned over to Ronald screaming just so she could be heard by him, although he was at her side.

"Ronnie, I think we should leave. I don't like this."

"'Tish, please. This is not a good time." He screamed back to her, though his words were barely audible to Leticia's ears over the crowd. Ronald took note of the armed guards that were scattered through the crowd.

"*If you are not **WITH US**! You are **AGAINST US**! **Sign** with the New Nation! Go west! Go south to Gonzales! **OUR MESSAGE WILL BE HEARD**! This is our <u>permanent</u> march on Washington!!!"*

Ronald and Leticia made their way through the cheering masses, trying to hold on to one another as not to be washed apart in the crowd. They finally made it home to their hotel where they were surprised to find Party Members signing up new Members to their cause, left and right. Glances said more than words as they entered the lobby and Leticia suddenly knew she would soon have to resign herself to the drab garbs and silence that most of the other Muslim women had seemingly become accustomed to here in this place. Ronald look sympathetically to her as he handed her the garb he would now see her in most of the daylight hours. He reluctantly signed on, but needed to secure the weekly rations of tea and rice along with the other basic staples that association with the Islamic Nation would guarantee them. Food was becoming more and more scarce in the open market and Elijah Drew's power base grew as he controlled the masses through their stomachs.

Once inside the hotel room, Leticia let loose.

"They're no better than the gangs in Atlanta that we were running from! They're turning over cars and setting buildings on fire! They have all the weapons and all of the food. They have *all* the power. What the hell is different here? I would say it's more controlled, but for God's Sake, Ronnie did you *see* that crowd? *They're crazy!* What!? A degree shouldn't *mean* anything?! *Money* doesn't *mean* anything?! Are these people *ignornant enough* to think Drew is going to support them?!"

"Please, 'Tish. You don't know who might be listening."

Leticia looked around the room as if she was searching for some unknown camera or recording device, then in a more hushed voice she quipped "I don't like this. I don't like Ty' being here and I don't like this *damned outfit!*" She threw the garb on the bed and sat down on the edge of the mattress, holding her head and rubbing her temples as though it might wake her up from this nightmare. Ty', a heavy sleeper, had fallen asleep earlier and had slumbered through his parent's absence.

Ronald looked out of the window at the street. He knew only two certainties as he stared down at the commotion that was gaining control of the streets. First, he knew Leticia was right. Secondly, he knew there was no turning back. They were too far north. They had willingly, but accidentally, entered a war zone.

At first, things in Harlem had seemed hopeful. Ronald landed a position with the Islamic Nation handing out propaganda and designing materials for distribution to its members, which were growing larger by the day. The job wasn't much, but it allowed them to stay free in the hotel room that was now their home and it provided for a small stipend which gave them enough to eat modestly. Leticia would spend her days in the hotel room and playing in a nearby park with Ty'.

She was content to avoid all contact with Elijah's henchmen.

However, as the Northwest Command was choking control of traffic on the Mississippi people in the Northeast were growing hungry and violent. Muslim influence was dominant and non-Muslims often attacked members of the Muslim community in an attempt to steal their modest weekly rations of rice, cous cous, dates and other basic foods that were imported from Middle Eastern countries that supported Elijah Drew and the Islamic Nation. Blacks converted to the Muslim faith by the droves, not out of a belief in Allah, but out of the basic need for survival.

In a matter of only a few weeks, the streets had become violent and rumors that starvation had started to drive some to cannibalism were spreading on the north end of the city. Leticia had stopped their visits to the parks weeks ago, in response to what she saw going on around them. She kept herself and her son Ty' imprisoned in the hotel room. There were a lot of families like theirs: people that had no religious affiliation, but that worked for the Islamic Nation and fed off of what they had to offer. Even though Ronald worked for the Islamic Nation, he saw the kufi and the robes that he donned on a daily basis as little more than a uniform: no different than a costume he would have to put on while working his nine to five. For weeks Leticia had flat out refused to wear the slate grey hijab and jilbab combination that the Islamic Nation issued to the faithful despite the negative attention her western clothing drew. The Islamic Nation was not giving anyone a choice now. They were tired of infidels taking advantage of their food supplies and saw such freeloading as a disgraceful affront to Allah, so now they were enforcing law. Religious Police began patrolling the streets and arresting women that had dressed in what the Islamic Nation viewed as an offensive manner and attending prayer was now mandatory and was enforced by Drew's religious Gestapo.

For those that showed interest and were more willingly compliant they did allow for a learning curve for those not yet familiar with customs and provided free classes to those that needed a primer on their new faith. Students learned proper prayer positions, traditional bathing and washing rituals, they learned which foods were forbidden and were taught to eat with their right hands. Eventually, Elijah planned to enforce all Muslim teachings by law.

Alcohol and drugs were strictly forbidden and anyone found with either was executed on sight and without trial.

Ronald pondered excuses that would allow their escape, but rumors of snipers placed on the interstates to shoot at cars on the southbound freeways below D.C.'s City Limits had been circulating for about a week and were confirmed amidst the hysteria they had just witnessed. Canada's borders were armed and he began to convince himself there was no way out. Even if some underground network existed here he wouldn't know whom to trust.

They were trapped.

He had heard the name Elijah Drew whispered in circles when they were living in Atlanta, Georgia. He was reputed as the next great civil rights leader, but Ronald was beginning to realize he was much more than just that. The entourage that surrounded this large man, that claimed to have been a direct descendent of the prophet Mohammed, armed and hooded, would show no mercy to anyone who stood in their way. Their weapons looked military, but there was something strange about them that Ronald had yet to put his finger on.

Before leaving Pennsylvania, he remembered a single warning put forth by Leticia's sister, Kenya. "You won't like it in Harlem. They don't follow the path of God, there. We call it the Valley of the Damned." Her words were haunting him, now.

Ronald tried to recall the conversation in detail, thinking it was nothing more than another attempt by Kenya to force them to join the church. He questioned how much she really knew about this place to which he had brought his family and quietly dismissed any thoughts that would make him believe she had knowingly allowed them to enter this hellish place. He remembered how his sister-in-law had begged to let Ty' stay, and now he wished he had obliged. In a way he hoped Kenya was praying for them now.

She had always been good at that.

Leticia's hands were now in front of her face, palms together, almost as though she had found herself in deep prayer, though Ronald knew better. Ronald stepped away from the window and knelt down in front of her, interlocking his fingers over her knee as though he wished to beg forgiveness.

But, this place was becoming beyond apologies.

"'Tish, we will get through this. We'll do it for Ty'. He's all we can think about now. He's our future."

Leticia's hands fell to her lap and, with a softer expression, she looked over at the sleeping bundle tucked snugly in the other bed. She stroked the side of her husband's face and nodded, holding back tears.

Ronald had an amazing ability to calm her in times of stress and to instantly turn her mood around, regardless of circumstance. After all of their years together, they were still truly in love with each other. Kissing his forehead, as if his presence was her only comfort, she retired to the shower, her eyes gesturing him to join her, but implying more than bathing. Later they would find their bed, after joking about all the water they wasted and mocking Kenya's penny pinching husband.

At 5:30 in the morning a siren rang out and fifteen minutes later was followed by a loud knocking at their door. Leticia walked over to answer and spoke through the keyhole to the man on the other side, loud enough to be heard, but trying to keep her voice down to avoid waking Ty'.

"We're fine, we didn't any room service."

"Yes. Is your husband there?" The stranger responded.

Leticia walked over to Ronald, with an almost fearful expression, Ronald was pulling on his shorts as he quickly made his way to the door and Leticia positioned herself shyly in the back of the room. She could barely make out the conversation, but she breathed a sigh of relief when she heard the door close and saw her husband standing there alone.

"We need to go, 'Tish. There's a meeting."

"At 5:30 in the morning?"

"There's a meeting. We'd better go. It's a few blocks away. Go ahead and get dressed, I'll get Ty' up."

"*This* is what we signed up for?" she sarcastically questioned under her breath as the now familiar disturbing wailing echoed in the background calling everyone to prayer. She had heard this obnoxious noise before, but assumed it was some issue with the weather alert system when they had first arrived.

Now there would be no escaping it.

Attending prayer was now mandatory.

Leticia reached for the garment she had fought so hard to avoid wearing and made her way into the bathroom. It took her a few minutes to get her headscarf to look like the other women's she had seen; and when she was done she stared in the mirror as though she was looking at a stranger. She was a strong woman, but for the first time, she saw defeat in her own eyes.

When she emerged from the bathroom, she found Ronald was already dressed and working on Ty's shoes.

"You look pretty, Mommy."

Leticia's eyes fell slowly as she looked over the loose fitting gown that did nothing for her figure and seemed to make her complexion look ashen. Ty' smiled as he kicked his little feet back and forth making the task of tying his shoes as difficult as possible as Leticia pulled at the side of her gown and tried to figure out where her waistline had gone.

"We'd better get going, 'Tish."

Leticia reached out for Ty''s little hand, as though it was all she had left of herself to cling to, and they made their way out to the hallway. A few blocks away they found themselves surrounded by a group of similarly caffeine deprived and sleepy eyed people, all which seemed to be from the same hotel, and Leticia suddenly realized they were entering into some form of 'training' as they were segregated from the more accustomed members of the group. They were instructed on positioning, and prayer. Ty' seemed to fall in line as though it was a child's game. He smiled as he mimicked the man in front of them once again surrounded by men with rifles.

In the crowd a young man stood up with a look of displeasure and resentment to his new authority. "Man, this is stupid! I ain't doin' this for no bag of rice and some shit ass tea!", he exclaimed and turned to leave the room.

He made it three feet.

A single shot fired from the front of the room changed the minds of anyone else in the room that may have had similar thoughts. Ty' laughed and clapped his hands not understanding the gravity of the situation, but only associating the sound of the gun shot with a video game he used to play.

He assumed it was part of some show.

Leticia grabbed Ty's arm with force pulling him to the ground, thrusting her hand over his mouth. Her heart sank to a bellows it had never entered before and she felt as though her mind and all rational thought would leave her. She was scared. She had never been so scared. So was everyone else in the room.

But, their instructors continued almost completely unphased.

At the end of the session the women and children were ordered out, stepping over the corpse, un-phased, as if such displays were routine. Women at the exit issued copies of the Qu'ran, prayer mats, and a list of things that would be expected from them in this new world to those that were not already properly equipped. No one seemed to make eye contact with each other as they accepted their gifts.

No one questioned why the men were staying behind.

Leticia walked back to the hotel, in an almost trance. Her mind raced with thoughts like some mad criminal trying to plan their escape from Alcatraz. Her steps were practically automatic, she said nothing, but she clung tightly to the hand of little Ty' who toddled beside her, occasionally looking up to his mother for comfort but feeling only her tension. They were approaching the hotel. She needed to rest.

Suddenly, a loud noise brought her back to the conscious world and she felt her right arm drop, almost pulling her to her knees.

She looked down in horror at her child and quickly scanned the streets for answers. She saw a group of young boys, armed with handguns and other weapons disappearing into the crowd; but, she recognized one face. It was the boy with the stone. He took a second to smile back at her as he faded into the group. Ty' was bleeding badly from his left shoulder, his eyes choked by the pain, implored his mother for help.

All of her angers and frustrations and pain manifested themselves in the form of an unearthly yell as she begged passersby for help; but no one answered.

She cradled Ty' in her arms and picked him off the ground, pushing his wound into her chest as she tried to control the bleeding with pressure, but the blood was quickly soaking through her garment.

Leaving the blood stained Q'ran and mats in the street, she ran at full pace to the hotel screaming at the front desk for an ambulance.

But there were no such services.

She begged the woman behind the counter to help her, but the woman's only accommodation was to hand over a few semi-clean towels. The light from Ty's eyes was fading quickly as hot tears streamed from Leticia's. Leticia ripped open his little shirt and frantically tried to convince Ty' to hang on, trying to assure him that mommy could fix his boo boo, as she pressed all of her weight against the wound.

But, it was too late.

Ty' was gone.

So, Leticia did the only thing a mother could do. She picked up his body, not seeing him as dead, and quietly sobbed as she made her way to the hotel room.

And she rocked the child to sleep, not realizing she was entrancing herself.

When Ronald found her she was soaked in the blood of her own child, sitting in the small hotel room chair, their dead son cradled in her arms as if he were an infant. She didn't look up or even acknowledge Ronald's presence.

She had nothing to say.

He feared she never would again.

Leticia had always been Ronald's strength. With the strongest member of the family this weak, the foundation could surely only crumble. Horrified, and unable to find his voice, Ronald knelt down beside her trying to comprehend the scene. His wife's tear stained face focused, not on Ty', but lost in some distance place where demons had confined her mind. The pale face of his son, eyes still open, but long gone from this world, still looking up towards his mother with a confused and frightful expression, frozen in the moment of his death.

Ronald began to scream for answers from Leticia, but there was no response. Demanding to know what had happened, yelling, he pulled Ty' from her arms and placed his limp body on the bed, then returned to her, shaking her more violently, and with more fury, than he had ever shown towards anyone.

But, she didn't even blink.

In a sudden panic, Ronald's next thought, as he stared at the blood soaked burqa Leticia was wearing, was that she, too, was injured. He lifted her in his arms and carried her into the tub, placing her body on the cold tile and fumbling to start the water for the shower. Ty''s blood flowed off of her as Ronald raced to removed the grey gown which had been glued to her skin by the dry, sticky fluid that had once flowed through their child. He scoured her left side, where she had been cradling Ty' so close, as bits of red flaked off of her skin, like paint chips. He desperately searched to find the wound on her.

But, there was nothing.

Despair flooded over him, as he pulled Leticia close, wishing she would show some reaction. Not even the ice cold water rushing over her did anything to rouse her from the place her thoughts had taken her to rest. He was certain she was just in shock and that she would eventually return to him. Looking into her eyes, he could not find where they were focused, no matter how he moved her face, and he knew, where ever she was, she did not see him. He wondered where her mind had been imprisoned and he blamed himself for her self-incarceration of being. Looking at her gentle face, that had so often been his own strength in his hours of need, he adjusted the water temperature, hoping the warmth would comfort her now, and he continued to gently bathe the violence from her skin, carefully washing her and making sure not to get soap in her eyes.

When he was done, he lifted her from the tub and carried her through to the bed, as Ty' dead lay on the other. For a moment he thought he saw her eyes move and look at their son, and he felt hope, but they faded back, almost immediately.

Perhaps, seeing her son in that state, she decided she was happier to wander from this earth, in her own way. So, she returned to the shadows of life.

He dried her off with a towel, and positioned her on the bed, talking to her, as a child would talk to a doll, hoping the sound of his voice would stir a reaction and bring her back. Lifting the covers he tucked her in, facing away from the little corpse in the room and Ronald now found he was uncertain what to do with his son's body.

He paced the room, cradling Ty' and trying to memorize every detail of his face and his little hands. His perfect little lips and nose. Ty''s tiny ears that stuck out just a bit too much when he was born. He laughed, as he cried, remembering how Leticia had made their son run around with pieces of duct tape holding them back, for the first year of his life. His little head was always covered with some type of hat or covering, shielding her perfectionism from the world. It had worked, though. They were flawless, now. He couldn't imagine parting with his greatest blessing, but he knew he couldn't go on pretending Ty' was still with them.

Next, he would then turn to his most difficult task.

Holding Ty', he cried uncontrollably, as the hot water raced from his eyes, falling onto Ty''s face, surreally making it appear as though the child was crying in death. He tried to hold him, just as Leticia had been when he found them, searching his little eyes and trying to interpret his final message and thoughts. He examined the small entrance wound that had exploded through the back of his shoulder and wondered what evil could take aim at a life so that was so pure and gentle. He wondered if they felt any remorse or guilt over what they had done but, at the same time, he knew that thousands of families had walked this same path with little reaction from the outside world.

All of the stories of tragedies he had seen.

Grieving families, put before cameras on the evening news, not because the media truly wanted to share their real grief, but only because the tears and suffering made for great five o'clock programming. Follow up stories, not telling of the emotion and hurt but, instead, focusing on vengeance for justice. Inside him, Ronald felt that same venom rising, but, with no one to focus it on, he turned it on the world. Hating the environment he was in and ashamed and enraged that he had brought his wife and child into this condemned and immoral place.

But, he had no choice.

The Territory was off limits and he was angry that the color of his skin had barred him from the one place that seemed secure. He hated that George was there. He coveted what he assumed was a happy and safe existence, unable to know the truth, his imagination wondered. His mind filled with jealous rage as he pictured George and Caroline, safe in some warm and happy home, sitting down to dinner and laughing as they enjoyed some 1950's style of loving existence. He hated Gonzales for winning the election and sending the country into this state of division. He hated the gangs, the violence, and everyone around him. He hated the entire country, for allowing things to fall so far out of control.

He blamed the world.

They were responsible for what he held in his arms.

He wanted vengeance.

He had seen the anger growing for years, but he had done nothing to stop it. No one had. He felt himself, as one man, he was unable to make a difference, but he was certain someone could have. And he hated that person for not trying to stop the avalanche, as looked at the cold flesh which was all that remained of what had once been his source of joy. With all of the hate of the world still pumping through him, he rose and carried Ty''s body through to the bathroom to prepare him for what would be his last bedtime.

He carefully dressed him in a little suit that Kenya had given him to attend church services in. He seemed so much smaller than he had, only hours before. Ronald fussed with perfecting his Windsor knot, determined to have his son standing tall at the gates of St. Peter, then contemplating what he would have to do next. He grabbed a clean hotel sheet from the top shelf of the closet and picked Ty' up in his arms. Then, Ronald tossed each of the child's cold arms over his shoulders, so he could feel the sensation of the boy's hug, one last time.

He turned back to Leticia. She still hadn't moved. Holding the sheet at Ty''s back, he walked out into the hallway, to find the streets of Harlem. No one seemed to notice the sadness that was cradled on his shoulders as he roamed from block to block, and searched for a place for Ty' to rest.

Ronald wandered into an old cemetery. Under an oak, that had fed itself off of the departed for what must have been a century, he found a monument marked by a beautiful angel, with welcoming arms. Brushing off the marble, reading the inscription, he decided this is where he would leave his son.

"Here lies Abigail Lynn McGee. An angel, that flew too soon from us. 1906-1913"

Staring at the marble monument, he was certain this grave belonged to a family of means and wealth. Beyond its aesthetic beauty and the quality of the carving, it had sustained, so perfectly, for over a century. He wondered for a moment about all of the tears that must have been shed over this ground, for the child buried below and he saddened himself with the thought that his son was not leaving this earth with equal ceremony. They were close in age, and Ronald comforted himself with the idea that Ty' would have a heavenly playmate. He excused his intrusion of Abigail's space certain that she, too, must be lonely in that cold ground.

And he began to dig.

His hands bloodied and cold from the hard earth below him, he cried as he pressed on, pushing through the dirt with a rock. He had only dug in about two feet, when suddenly the ground below him seemed to collapse another foot or so, and he realized what had happened. His disturbance having obviously collapsed the casket below him: but, he took that as a welcoming. In his mind, it was a sign that Abigail was through with this place, and was opening the door for Ty' to come into the space where she had found peace and rest.

So he gently wrapped his miraculous gift in the sheet, closing his eyes from the troubles of the world, and his own sadness. He kissed him, looking, one final time, for any sign of life, before pulling the sheet over his face, so he could not bear witness to what his father was about to do. Swiping the earth, and making sure there were no rocks that would cause discomfort, he laid the boy in a pile of soft earth and then buried him in the ground.

And for two hours Ronald cried, seemingly immune to the freezing weather.

When the cold finally woke him, and hoping Leticia had now recovered, he let himself feel the emotions that were fighting to surface. Ronald was certain he needed to release them before he returned to her side, and not caring about cameras, he punched a hole in the hotel wall on his way up to the room.

Certainly, things could only get better.

Ronald reached to open the door and prepared himself to mourn and cry with his wife, but he found her still in the same position. Too tired to attempt to engage her, he undressed and climbed next to her, pulling her close and gently sobbing into her shoulder. He prayed sleep would speed her recovery.

But, a new nightmare would be waiting in the morning.

The Sword and the Shield

Back in the village of Cambuslang, named after a little town in Scotland where Edee's mother had been born, Heather and her little family had found themselves quite at home. Now in charge of the canning project she stood with a new arrival and imparted her wisdom. The tall, bright eyed blonde, named Kim, watched as Heather demonstrated how to can corn while she readied a pot of tomatoes for their next project. Kim, a mother herself, suggested making the tomatoes into a sauce and canning the preparation to allow for quick spaghetti meals. Heather agreed and began searching her stockpiles for garlic and basil to add in, excited by the concept of having the occasional option of "quick fix" meals. She instructed Kim to go out into the small herb garden that Heather tended in her spare time and pull some fresh oregano and rosemary to add into the mix. Kim nodded enthusiastically and headed out to begin gathering spices.

On the Island of Misfit Toys, lacking the convenience of pre-prepped, store bought food women had to learn how to actually cook their dinners, and found they were spending more time in the kitchen than most would have liked. The two began to search their memory banks and began listing off some easy prep dinners that would allow them some relaxation time at the end of their days.

"We could can some soups? It's easy to make up big batches and I think there are plenty of women in the surrounding villages that would be happy to be able to dump out a jar and call that lunch for the kids! I sure would!"

Heather's eyes lit up at her new friend's suggestion and her own mind began to cycle back to her old life. As she searched for new ideas, it seemed their minds had joined forces, and simultaneously they exclaimed, "Baby food!"

Together they began to list off their ideas, planning out their cottage enterprise and salivating over the potential for trade that it would offer. As the two chatted on, a smaller, ringlet crowned version of Kim was becoming frustrated by her mother's inattention. Demanding to be in the center of the action, Kim's daughter Alex, began frequently interrupting with questions and demanding her own favorite foods move to the top of the recipe list. Smiling, Heather would respond to each request dotingly, seemingly not at all bothered by her inquisitive behavior. Kim simply shook her head at the child's impetuous nature, seeing herself and wondering how her own mother had managed to tolerate such behavior from her, when she was a girl.

Heather could see Kim's annoyance growing and decided to entertain little Alex by sending her off to play with the boys in the living room. Heather was so calm and at ease, Alex never even realized she was being sent off. The canning project had been a huge success and, as a result, Heather and her family had positioned themselves among the "political elite" of the small village. The village aristocracy basically consisting of; Edee, Alfonso and a couple of other families that participated in arranging for trade with nearby villages.

In addition to the canning, over the months Heather had perfected a recipe for making peach wine and that had served the entire village well in trade circles where her concoction was always in very high demand. Heather's family was the only one permitted to maintain their own dairy cow, on premises, exclusively for use by their own household. It was an immense privilege, and spoke to their status in the community. As the women continued with the lesson, happily discussing their plans to reinvent the Gerber Company, Heather reached for a jug stored in the back of her fridge, and pursing her lips while she held one finger in front of them, she poured two large glasses: one for herself, and one for her student turned business partner.

The women sat, learning about each other and enjoying the fruits of Heather's makeshift kitchen chateau as Alex busied herself by bossing around Heather's two young sons. Heather was amused, laughing at the child's sudden overthrow of the living room, and was happy to have someone to assist her in keeping the two boisterous little fellows in line. Over wine, Kim went on to explain her life's history and the women reveled in the fact that although they had lived States apart, their lives had once been so similar. Both of their husbands had been successful salesmen, they were both mothers, and they had, at one time, each enjoyed a certain amount of luxury.

"When Jud would travel, and was gone for a long time, I would purposefully go out and rack up our credit cards buying stuff for the kids!" Kim confessed with a gleam in her eye, as she admitted her guilty sin.

"I did the same thing!" Heather confessed with a grin.

"And when he really ticked me off with those long business trips, there was always the emergency room! That would get his ass on the next flight home! With three kids, you could guarantee that at least one of them would have the sniffles or an earache at any given time." Kim sipped her wine, raising her eyebrows, her grin indicating a slight hint of evil, as she admired her own talents for the occasional manipulation of her husband's travel schedule.

Heather laughed at her, nodding her head in agreement, then confessing, "Yeah, that was an effective one! If Blue Cross Blue Shield only knew! I would bet half the mothers in the waiting room had husbands away on business travel! My biggest problem with that one was that my kids never got sick!"

The women bonded over shared pleasures and their mutual capacity for straying from more virtuous paths. Heather reached over, topping off their glasses, enjoying the idea that she had finally met a real girlfriend in the small village. While most of the other women were nice, and she got along well with them all, she really had not met anyone to whom she felt she really related until now.

Laughing, they remembered a time when life in America was as ideal inside of the borders, as it appeared on the outside. Times when they could afford afternoons out with their "Mommies and Me" lunches to save them from boredom, and they reflected on how much things had changed since their childhoods. They remembered the times prior to September 11th, and long before the UT tragedy that would forever change the nation. They remembered the nights, when they were young girls, when their mother's had tucked them in at night, never fearing that a bomb would fall on the soil of the land they called home. And, as the conversation grew more somber, they realized that such blessed peace no longer existed in their own minds and were saddened by the thought that it may have *never* existed for their own children.

Half way through her second large glass, Kim posed a question, "Who do *you* blame for it all?"

Heather studied Kim's face, wanting to provide a simple and clear answer, but she couldn't. Swirling her glass, she shrugged her shoulders and then, with certainty, answered "Us."

"Us?" Kim seemed puzzled by the response.

"*Us.*" Heather affirmed. "We were so damn ignorant. We *were.* Do you realize how many Mexicans snuck back and forth across the borders just to exercise their right to *vote* in *Mexican* elections? They felt so privileged to vote, and they *did.* And, there *we* were. They controlled the politics of two nations, not one. And we were too freakin' lazy to make it to our own voting booths. *We* did this. All of it. We brought it upon ourselves."

"So, really, you blame the Mexicans?" Kim questioned, lifting her glass, for another sip.

"No. I don't. I blame *us.* We're the ones that let it get this far. We let the government disarm us. We let the gangs take over. We let them have our jobs, we outsourced the rest. We were so divided. We *still* are. Sometimes I wonder how it is, over all those years, not one damn politician ever had the balls to stand up and present an idea that wasn't controlled by the results of some CNN poll. Then again, even if they had, one wouldn't have made any difference. It would have a taken a movement. We were complacent and ignorant. We all were." Heather shook her head as she thought, momentarily, about her life in the present, then her mind wandered back to the comfort of her childhood, growing up in Coral Gables, Florida. Noticing her expression, and trying to offer counsel, Kim countered, "It wasn't us. It was The Initiative… Well… and the Command. And, maybe that Elijah Drew guy… It was all of that, too."

Heather's expression grew almost reflective and distant as she pushed the thick, strawberry blonde strands from her face. "It's sad, Kim. I remember growing up. Do you realize there was only one time I felt proud to be an American? There's only *one time*, in my memory, that I can remember this whole country uniting. Black… white… it didn't matter. One time we stopped all of our bickering and saw the big picture. We all had flags flying. We were, if only for that brief moment, all Americans."

Perplexed, Kim searched her own memories for the time that her new friend was referring to, and quickly realized her reference. Nodding slowly in agreement, she simply said, "It's a shame. It took the deaths of nearly three thousand people to make us all buy a flag."

"No. What's *sad* is how quickly we put them away." Heather raised her eyebrows, returning to the present, and as if she was trying to invoke a response, but Kim said nothing. Trying to change the subject to a lighter note, Heather, in her typical fashion, rose to her feet and exclaimed, "But here, we have the wonderful world of canned fruits and vegetables to return to!" Kim followed her over to the stove, stumbling a bit on her first step as the effects of the wine began to set in. Heather stirred their batch of stewed tomatoes and tasted the mix, then offered a spoonful to Kim as they debated adding in the garlic and basil. Just as she reached for a Mason jar, her front door flew open, startling the women to the point that Heather dropped the jar, shattering it on the floor.

It was Edee.

But, there was something different and purposeful about Edee's walk. Edee appeared strangely masculine and it was suddenly apparent that something was very wrong. It would seem, the man that liked to wear women's clothing, had decided it was no time to play dress up.

"Heather, get everyone out! We need to have a meeting! *Now!*" His voice bellowed loudly, unapologetic for the abrupt and forceful intrusion. Heather seemed stunned by his clean shaven and manly appearance and noticed that he was no longer walking with a sauntering gate, but like that of an Officer preparing to deploy his troops. The drastic change in his appearance was even unsettling for Kim, who immediately began to wonder what had brought on the sudden transformation.

Avoiding the broken glass, her nerves still shaken, Kim gathered her daughter, Alex, and prepared to leave. Right behind Edee, Heather's husband and Alfonso would follow in with two other men from the village: all rushing in at the same hurried pace and not bothering to break with their conversations to say a simple "hello". The men made their way to the kitchen table, and as Will passed by Heather whispered, "What is going on?" He shook his head, but his eyes gestured for her to follow as she saw Kim to the door. Raising her voice, Heather called out to warn the men, "Watch out for the glass on the floor! I'll come get it in a second!"

Once outside, Heather apologized for the unexpected end to their evening, telling her she would fill her in the next day. Kim nodded, wondering what had happened, but having no choice but to leave, she simply made her way down to another neighbor's house in an attempt to get an inside line on the gossip. Heather made her way inside, using the broken glass as a way to keep an ear on the conversation in the kitchen.

"But, I reckon iffin' it's gotten *that* out of hand, they *will* move south!" A tall, sandy haired redneck man named Jonathon asserted as he stroked his beard.

Trying to calm the group and his own mind, Edee paced and thought aloud. "He's right. We're far enough from reach, for now, but we do need to conserve, and more importantly *plan*. Otherwise, we are a target. They're on the move. It's just a matter of time, now."

"A target for *what*?" Heather interrupted.

Ignoring her, Alfonso interjected. "It has to look real, though, Edee. We can't just suddenly tell everyone, *'Get in the cellars, but don't worry about anything.'* No one will believe that! Besides, it's not just food they need! It's manpower!"

"Why are we going to the cellars? *Who* needs manpower?" Heather struggled to figure out their conversation.

Still not paying any attention to her, Edee nodded to Alfonso. "You're right. It has to look real. Even to our own people. We can't afford any leaks. From the outside... even from the inside... we can't appear as though we have anything. It has to be big. Big enough that they will leave us alone for a while. Right now it's just about survival. They'll need to think they've already gotten us all. This is going to have to be a serious KFB!"

"*Who* will leave us alone? What's a KFB?" Heather begged and Edee responded dryly, but did not take his eyes from Alfonso's. His expression was intense and it was obvious that his mind was spinning with strategy. "Ka-fuckin' boom, Heather. That's a KFB!"

Formulating a plan, Alfonso questioned, "Jonathon, you still got that stash of ANFO from those Opelika mines?"

"You know I do. A shit load of it!" The burly redneck replied.

"Okay. We don't have a choice. We'll blow up the coops. No one knows about the extra storage cellars, except the people in this room. We'll have to be tight with the rations and cut off trade. I would say, according to word I am getting, if they're in Chattanooga now, they'll reach us in a week or so at the rate they are moving. We'll have to burn out most of the crops and take out our own coops a couple of days ahead, to make it look real."

Edee agreed, with enthusiasm, "Yes! Yes! Let them think they have already burned us out... board everything up... we need to hide underground... *we can do this*...We'll take all of the animals out into the woods by the lake and just hope they survive. The cows, the horses, the pets... they all need to go. Try to salvage at least five cocks and about fifty chickens. That should give us enough to rebuild once they have passed through." His mind raced and the men hung on his every command.

Suddenly, Heather questioned the least important of the implications. "You can't blow up the coops! Think about all of those poor little chickens! The kids love those chickens! That's a major part of our trade! Why are you all talking like this? *What is going on?*" she demanded.

"There's a pretty big cemetery over yonder. It's not going to be a fun job, but we'll need to dig up about a half dozen bodies. Make sure you get a couple of kids, too. No one that's been gone more than a few years, they can't be too skeletal. The big thing is making them think we're all already dead. We'll douse a couple of the bodies with gasoline and burn them and leave them out close to the roads. The others we'll just kinda shoot up and leave out. We want to put them all towards Cambuslang's center and away from the cellars, in case these sick fucks decide to get up close with them. I don't want to give Drew's men any reason to start searching for people. I agree, the cellars are the only option, but if they find us we will be sitting ducks. *Oh!* And another thing, we'll have to change their clothing. Most will be in suits and nice outfits, we can't have that! It will look suspicious. Any jewelry that we find on them or in the caskets we'll collect and use for barter if we can ever get out of this hell hole." Edee affirmed with certainty.

Heather's jaw hung open in horror at Edee, shocked at the ideas presented. Will saw her expression and trying to catch her up quickly, Will explained. "Alfonso's friends up north have sent word that it's a blood bath. The Command has cut off all traffic on the Mississippi and up north they are getting hungry and running out of supplies. Drew's group is bringing in weapons from the Middle East and organizing against the Command. The Mississippi is infested with bodies. We can't head due west. Rumor has it the whole area is riddled with disease. Drew's men are pushing south, then west. They need men to fight against the Command. They're saying, you can smell the stench of death from twenty miles out if you are downwind. It's only a matter of time before they make their way down here and try to take over everyone's supplies. They're killing each other up north for a bag of rice. They're starving, so they are just taking everything they can down here. Some of the groups have gone against Drew and are just flat out taking everything and killing for sport. Others are trying to fight the Command and get them to free up the Mississippi's traffic. They need food. It's horrible, Heather. We don't have a choice, hon."

"What do they want? *We haven't got anything?*" Heather questioned.

The men exchanged glances, then Edee tried to gently, but plainly, break the news. "They need men to fight, Heather. They are killing *all* of the children... raping and murdering the women. The men that refuse to go, are being slaughtered. The harvested food supplies are being shipped north... they're burning the rest. They're burning the towns, the crops and everything of value and humanity that they find." His eyes looked to her with compassion as her face filled with fear.

"Why isn't Gonzales doing anything? How long has this been going on?" her voice held the innocence of a child.

Alfonso shook his head. "Apparently, for a few weeks. I can only assume my cousins up north are dead. They would have warned us sooner, if they could have. I just got word from a friend of mine in Dalton. The whole city's panicked, Chattanooga is just north of them. They're torching everything… even the forests… people have no where to go… It's all out jungle warfare."

Heather felt as if her spirit had left her body, sitting numb at the table and nervous about the coming week. The men continued their conversation without her and planned for the survival of the small community as best they could. Alfonso and Jonathon agreed to round up all of the horses and livestock and to work with the other men in the village to dump as much grain and hay in the woods, near the lake, as they could manage. Once the animals had been released, all they would be able to do would be to hope for the best. Family pets, chickens and roosters would go next. Their only prayer, that the cats would focus more on field mice than the village's poultry supply.

"Them animals gonna be fine out there! Hell, you ain't gotta teach no animal how to survive in the wild." Jonathon assured.

"Well, we're still going to need to put up some kind of fence. Those horses might be our only way out of here after Drew's men and the vigilantes tear through here and I don't want them getting spooked by all the gunshots and the ANFO blasts going off. We can use some cables and just fence off enough that the horses won't break through it.

The lake is big enough for them to have plenty of water, but small enough that we should be able to go all the way around it. We'll need to get about a dozen men and get started on that tonight. We'll move the animals in tomorrow morning and close it off. We should have enough rope and cable to go around about four times. That should be enough to hold them. Alfonso, how many horses have we got now?"

"Last count was nineteen, but Polly's knocked up and due any day. If the colt survives, that'll give us an even twenty."

"That'll be enough to at least cover us old farts and the kids and some supplies once this is over. We don't have any time to waste, we need to get moving now! Jonathon, help Alfonso gather the cable and use the vehicles to transport everything into the woods that we are going to need. I'll start breaking the news to the families. The cars are effectively going to be storage units, now: not that they haven't been, anyway. Have the families put basic, and I mean *basic*, supplies in them that they will need when we leave. We're all going to need to share so tell everyone not to bitch about it. We can't leave them out in open sight, so push them into the woods so they can't be seen and we'll camouflage them. After this, the cars won't be any use to us. We won't have any way to get gas for them, anyway."

Heather looked to Edee, nervously. "What are you going to tell the others, Edee?"

Edee sighed as he looked for the words. "I reckon I'm gonna tell them the truth, dear. We're going to the cellars to save our own asses. I suppose I'll leave out the part about burning down their homes and digging up graves, though. I'd imagine that would be a little harder for people to understand."

"Should I go with you and help convince them?"

"Honey, there ain't no convincin'! Get in or get killed seems about as basic as it gets to me! You just stay hear and look after the boys." Edee affirmed with a grin.

"They'll be fine. Really, I *want* to go and I know a lot of the women pretty well. Besides, people are going to be scared enough when they see you without your makeup." Heather tried to make light of the situation if to only make herself feel better.

"Well!" Edee pretended to be insulted. "What exactly are you tryin' to say, Heather? I'm not a good lookin' man? Listen, I know I'm a *damn* good lookin' woman, but I still clean up pretty good in a suit!" Edee winked and gestured for Heather to follow him out the door to go notify their neighbors.

Next, would come the hard part: to choreograph the destruction of what they had all worked so hard to build. Their small group made plans to burn the parts of their fields and orchards that were visible from the main roads and blow up the coops that could be seen, knowing their enemy was quickly advancing toward them. Unable to trust anyone, even those residing within the village, the townspeople were gathered, and each of them blindfolded. In small groups they were taken to a large root cellar, previously only known to Edee, Alfonso and a few others. Will and a couple of the other men had retrofitted the underground bunker to allow for sleeping arrangements.

Slowly, groups of five entered, secretly hoping that this underground haven would not become their grave. If discovered, their sanctuary would surely become a human abattoir. Once underground, the full story was explained. Kim's eyes turned to Heather, questioning why she had not said anything sooner, as she cradled Alex, crying, in her arms. Heather looked to her, with justification, hoping she would understand why she could not speak before this moment.

Having reverted to a more military train of thought, Edee, no longer donning his gowns or makeup, remained seated as Alfonso's less threatening personality appealed to the group. His wide brown eyes never giving hint of the true fear that lie behind them as he addressed the 48 people that remained and would share this underground shelter until the dark shadow had passed over them.

Clearing his throat, he stood up and searched the room, finding the eyes of the youngest members stood out the most to him. With their easily frightened little minds at the forefront of his thoughts, he opened speaking slowly as his mind tried to find words. "I know many of you are wondering why we are here… and I thank you for your cooperation…. And… with the littlest members of this room in mind, I hope you will understand if I am not incredibly blunt, or clear, in my explanations… I will be happy to clarify, privately, when the little ones sleep… For now, I just ask that you trust me… Trust *us*… We are here with very good reason…"

"There had better be a damn good reason! This is asinine!" declared one of the newer members of the village, and Alfonso took note of the heads that nodded in agreement.

Realizing he would need to quickly gain control, even if it was by fear, he decided he would need to be more direct than he would have liked in the presence of children, though his tone stayed calming. "I understand your frustration… and I share in it… Drew's men are moving south. Chattanooga is a total loss… Dalton, the carpet mills, they have all been destroyed… The fires were so intense, Atlanta was choked by them… The chemicals fueled the flames… And the same men responsible are pushing southward…

towards us… The battle for the Mississippi is getting intense… The Command has control and the Northeast is starving…"

"Screw the Northeast!" exclaimed another and the majority of the room agreed.

"Don't you people understand?!" Alfonso's voice suddenly challenged, angered by their inability to, even still, see beyond their doorsteps.

Suddenly, Beth Faust, a former attorney that had arrived alone in the village only a few months earlier rose and appealed to the crowd in a sarcastic tone. "I don't know who the *hell* you people think you are, but this is a *complete violation* of *our* Civil Rights to *imprison* us down here! What gives you the right to think you can put *yourselves* in charge of deciding what is safe for all of us when you never even *bothered* to ask for *anyone else's* input?! I know *I would've liked to have a little input*, maybe a little *warning*, that you planned to come to my house and *take my dog* and *toss him in the woods* and tell me that I need to go live *in some cave* for some *undetermined amount of time? Yeah, why don't you answer that one, Edee?* How long exactly were you planning to keep us here? *Or is that something else you've decided we don't have a right to know?*" Her performance, just as if she had been in a courtroom had the room's attention.

"Beth, you don't understand. There wasn't time for input or…" Alfonso pleaded, but she cut him off and continued her argument, her tone even more sarcastic than before.

"*Oh, there wasn't time?* I see. Did *everyone* hear that, because I want to make sure *I got that right? There wasn't time* to discuss these plans with us to stick us down here, but *there was time* for Edee and Alfonso and Jonathon and the little wine making princess' husband to fence in *a whole lake*? And *there was time* to move the livestock and, it seems to me, *there was time* to stock this little bunker with supplies? *Yes, I'm sure we all understand,* since you've been so very busy, how you wouldn't *have time* to hear *our* input? So tell me, Edee. *This little bunker?* How many *other* little secrets are you keeping from us? Were you and your little friends planning on sharing? Or was there just not enough *time* to tell us about this, either?" Beth raised her arms and gestured to the room, her eyes imploring an answer from Edee and Alfonso as if they were sitting on a witness bench. And Edee grew quickly frustrated with her show. More so, he was frustrated by the room's concurrence.

"Fuck this! We're leaving!" Suddenly, one man began to stand up and others began to join in his rebellion. Edee scanned the room, watching the mutiny form, and decided Alfonso had lost control of the room.

"Sit down!" He barked like drill sergeant and took the direct approach. "You have *nothing* to go home to! As we speak, we are blasting the village and burning the crops! And before you decide to take one more fucking step towards that door, you need to understand the only way you are going out is feet first, which is a much kinder homecoming than what Drew's men have planned for all of us! *Sit your fat ass down, Allen!*" Alfonso, Jonathon and Will revealed the guns that were strapped to their sides, from under their coats, as Edee continued to address the fearful eyes of the group in a powerful tone that no one had heard him use before. "*We had no choice!* Drew's men are converting the south by the sword! If you refuse to align, they will decapitate you and hang you feet first from any tree they find on their path as a warning to those that might think twice! If they can't find a knife, they'll tie you to the back of their bumper and drag your ass down I-75 until finally your brains find a home on the jersey walls! *They will rape your wives and your daughters! Then kill them dead! Your children?* Slaughtered!

This is no game! Our only chance is to make it look like they've already gotten to us! Believe me! We are in a far better position than most! *And as for you, Beth!* If I hear one more God damn word out of *your fucking mouth,* I'll strap your ass to one of the horses and send the fastest one running northbound. Maybe with a .45 crammed down your throat and some guy's dick up your ass, you'll finally learn when to *shut the fuck up!*"

Beth's neck began to feel hot and her lower lip began to quiver, but Edee showed no mercy. "This isn't a fucking court room and you ain't got no Civil Rights! *None of us do!* Damn lawyers were half the fucking problem when things were good in this country! Believe me, honey, I won't think twice about planting a bullet right between those two eyes if you as much as fucking *sneeze* the wrong way while we're down here! *Do you understand me?"* To prove a point, Edee, in one swift movement, pulled a gun from his hip and pushed it into Beth's temple forcing her to the ground as the room looked on nervously.

Beth nodded frantically, as she began to cry, but Edee was going to force her to speak and make an example of her in front of the group. He screamed so loudly it echoed off the walls, then he violently grabbed her hair, forcing her to look up at him. *"I said! Do you fucking understand me, you ignorant little bitch?"*

Her voice shaking and embarrassed as her eyes were straining to focus on the barrel she cried out. *"Yes! I'm sorry! Yes!"* Edee then tossed her aside and Beth went almost fetal as she choked on her tears.

Women began to cry hysterically as they watched the display and the children followed their reaction. Still adamant he would challenge, the second most vocal member of the group stood up and began walking towards the door, certain that Edee was bluffing. *"You ain't burnin' out my house, and you sure as shit ain't gonna talk to me like that! This is bullshit, I'm leavin'!"*

Alfonso and Will pulled their weapons, and the cocking of their triggers echoed through the room, as Edee spoke for his henchmen, in somber tone. "Don't make us do this, Allen. *Just sit down.*"

The room filled with tension and Edee wondered if three guns were enough to contain chaos in their underground cell. The cocking of the guns had made the man stop in his tracks, still facing the door. Edee softened his tone, appealing to reason, as he spoke to the man. "We do not want to shoot you, but we will, if you make us… But, before you move towards those steps, I want you to consider the terrible memory you will forever be implanting in the minds of the children in this group… in the mind of your own kid sitting over there. Sit down." Edee appealed to reason and watched as the man, arms raised, slowly turned to him.

It was clear that no one was leaving.

After the tension had settled and the man returned to his seat, Edee explained their plan, no longer concerned about the youth in the room. They had to understand, too. The threat above them was real and racing in their direction like Secretariat. There were only enough cots to accommodate twenty five, so the village slept in shifts. The worst part of the accommodations, for most, was the bathroom situation: five large jugs, concealed behind a curtain, but still offering little privacy. They were emptied by Alfonso under the cover of darkness, but the villagers were left to adjust to the odors they produced throughout the rest of the day.

On their third day of confinement, as he was carrying the jugs of discarded waste to the surface, Alfonso could hear Elijah Drew's men thundering through their once quiet village for the first time. Screaming from their vehicles as they raced through at a tremendous pace, Alfonso sat, nervous that the full moon would reveal his shadow, as he watched earth's lonely celestial companion illuminate the roadway ahead of him. From behind a small bush his thoughts turned to his cousins and his own place in the world. His confidence in his invisibility grew with each passing vehicle as did his fear and his sorrow for the people of Opelika.

There he found himself on his knees, praying for them in the moonlight, as he remembered the faces of those he had known through local trade. He wondered to himself if God had turned away from the Americas, or if it had been the other way around. As the soft light washed over him, he remembered his homeland and his father's anger and hatred for its leader: Alfonso's earliest memories having been his father's words, followed, not long after, by a ninety mile journey over water. Even after their arrival, his father had promoted the vast benefits of life in the United States, and Alfonso believed him, as he watched his father transform from a poor migrant worker to the successful owner of an Italian Restaurant with clientele that seemed to have been scripted directly from a mafia film and was rumored to have such ties.

Sheltering himself from Drew's thugs, he wondered, what his relatives in Cuba were wondering about his father's decision, now. Even though his family had been poor on that island, his only memories were happy ones, and he remembered being unable to understand his father's dissent for such a beautiful landscape. Sitting, in a destroyed field, after just having emptied the waste of close to fifty of his neighbors, he wondered if he would be so accepted, had he refused to do their dirty work: slaughtering the animals, disturbing gravesites and emptying their waste. It wasn't that he enjoyed his tasks, he was just the only one willing it seemed.

For a moment, he was overcome with thoughts of striking out on his own, as he began to feel used. He stared out at the caravan hurling down the road before him. Looking back at the pit that confined his neighbors, he wondered if Drew's group would reward him for his confession. But, the thought passed quickly, and his loyalties resumed.

Finding his sanity, in his mind the words to Ray Charles' *It's a Wonderful World*, began to play… and, for a few moments, he allowed himself to remember a happier version of life. His daydreaming was interrupted when Edee found his side. Alfonso was startled that he didn't hear his approach.

"How many are there?" Edee questioned softly, looking out to the road as they awaited passing vehicles, aware of Alfonso's pensive mindset.

Returning to reality, his eyes focused on the distant pavement, Alfonso responded quietly. "I don't know… a lot… first there were vans… then semis… then more vans… then the motorcycles… there are *so many* of them… I've just been sitting here, watching…"

Edee analyzed Alfonso's expression as he stared, blankly, towards the roadway that sat a good seven hundred and fifty feet from their position, watching the lights as they passed by them.

"What happened?" Alfonso interrupted his analysis.

Thinking for a moment, and reverting to his most fatherly tone, Edee smiled. "We messed up… but… we'll survive."

Suddenly, reverting to business, Alfonso reached in his pocket. "That reminds me. Here, this is what we got from the bodies. We had eleven of them. Three were kids, so there wasn't anything on them except one that had a gold cross. Couple of good wedding rings and earrings from the women… a gold man's watch, but I don't think it works… and this ring. It might be junk." Alfonso handed over the jewelry to Edee, happy to get rid of it. He was still disturbed by the memories that Will and Jonathon and he would forever share about how they came to be in possession of those pieces.

Edee held the one ring up and tried to catch its reflection in the moonlight as he analyzed the setting. "No, Alfonso, it's not junk. It's kind of hard tell if the setting is white gold or platinum in this light, but that is one of the prettiest star sapphire rings I ever have seen." Edee played with the ring, making a little white spider dance on the stone's surface in the moonlight, as he continued with his appraisal. "This is a good ring. Might be worth as much as $20,000. We might get $10,000 for it, if we're lucky? More likely $5,000. What else?"

"This ring. Looks like her wedding set. Came from the same woman as that one. Mrs. Ralston." Alfonso told Edee the unwitting donor's name, as if it mattered to him and Edee took note of his expression. He could see the events of the past few days had taken a toll on the normally chipper Cuban, but he went on to examine the ring.

"*Thank you, Mrs. Ralston!* This is a pretty one. Of course, diamonds make people nervous anymore. Too many lab created ones on the market, I think between that and the DeBeer's stockpiles people are afraid their value's gonna go belly up one day. These two side stones are yellow diamonds, though. They're the real deal. Couple of carats each, from the looks of them. We'll go through the rest later, but I think between this and the stones I've got stock piled, we might have enough for a couple of boats." Edee said softly, already having planned the next leg of their journey.

"Boats?"

"Yep! Boats." Edee said confidently.

"Where are we going on boats?" Alfonso seemed confused and wanted to know what was swirling around in Edee's mind that had them floating out over the ocean.

"Well, I don't know. First we'll have see if we can get one with what we've got and then we'll have to figure out the money situation from there. There's about fifty of us, Alfonso. That's a lot of life preservers!" Edee said as he searched the stars in the night sky and tried to make light of the situation.

"How much do you think we've got?" Alfonso asked.

"Well, let's see. All together, what you've handed me, might be worth about $50,000, but we'd be very, very lucky to even get $25,000. I've got about another $35,000 in loose stones and gold nuggets." Edee said unassumingly and Alfonso's eyes grew wide, surprised that Edee had never mentioned this before. Edee chuckled at his expression. "What? You didn't think I spent *all* my money on high heels, did you? I used to like to go mining in the mountains. Then, I'd cut the stones myself. Gave a lot of the good ones away to friends and family, but when things started to go down hill, I figured that there would come a day when the Dollar wasn't going to have much value so I started saving them up for a rainy day. So, we've got a good start. Of course, I'm more concerned about you and Heather and Will and Jonathon than most of them, down there.

Hell, I'd be half tempted to push that Beth Faust overboard…the little ones, though…
none of this is their fault. They need to get out of here. It's not fair to allow a child to
grow up in a place where they feel they have no security. That's not what this country
was supposed to be about."

Alfonso nodded and joined in Edee's search of the night stars as they both
allowed themselves to be distracted by fantasy. As he focused on the sky, he asked Edee.
"So, you think anything else is out there?"

"I do. I truly do. I truly, truly do." Edee quickly answered, nodding towards the
darkness above them, without a hint of doubt.

"You think?" Alfonso was undecided in his conclusion.

"Honey, don't ask someone that worked for NASA what their opinion is regardin'
life on other planets, if you don't want to hear it! But, look at it this way: how truly
arrogant does man have to be to assume, not only that the earth is only planet with any
forms of life, but also that we are the most intelligent creatures that the universe ever put
forth!? *Nah!*" Edee smiled, remembering what had once been seen through the eyes of a
man named Edward and tales that had been shared over cocktails with those that had
sailed the heavens above earth in machines Edee had helped engineer.

Alfonso pondered for a moment, then asked. "Well, if they're out there, why
haven't they contacted us?"

"Who says they *haven't?*" Edee winked and Alfonso's curiosity peeked.

"*Have* they?"

Edee's expression hinted that perhaps he knew more than he was willing or able
to tell, but rather than answer his question, he chose to have him answer it himself.

"Think about it, Alfonso. On this one planet, we have the amoeba… the jellyfish… the tiger… the bear… We have the gator… the elephant… the penguin… the bee… the butterfly… We've got trees… and flowers… and mountains… and oceans… and jungles… and rainforests…and deserts… and icecaps… and every one of them filled with life forms that can live harmoniously and share the same space and resources… *Hell, there's more creatures than you could list!* And, of all the creatures on this planet, the one that sits at the top of the food chain and that claims to be the most intelligent is the same one that can do nothing, but find quicker and more efficient ways to kill each other off. Who would *want* to contact us? We don't exactly come across as a species you would want to *befriend*. We're the universe's great mistake and every one of them out there knows it. So, this whole planet will stay under galactic quarantine until we either grow up or kill ourselves off. Personally, my bets would go to the latter."

"Yeah." Alfonso continued his exploration of the stars and wondered while Edee kept an eye on the road.

"Well, I'm gonna go and see if a cot has opened up. You plannin' to be up long? I can ask Will or Jonathon to come up and take over, so you can get some rest or to keep you company? *Oooh! I'm getting old!*." Edee's knees popped as he went to stand up, and he rubbed the right one frustrated that age was catching up with him.

"No, I'm fine. Honestly, I just think I need to be alone for a little while. The past couple of days just haven't set well with me. I just want some time to think." Alfonso glanced up, then turned away, afraid his expression would reveal too much about his true emotional state.

"I understand." Edee gave a half smile, then began walking away.

"She seemed like she was a nice old lady." Alfonso's comment seemed to come out of no where, but Edee knew immediately who he was referring to.

"Mrs. Ralston?"

"Yeah. Her first name was Beatrice. I made a point to put her down in the Murphy's rose garden. Jonathon tied a rope around her neck to make it look like she had been choked. She looked like the kind of old lady that would have had her own rose garden. I couldn't burn her like the others." Alfonso confessed his disobedience. Edee had been clear in his instructions and was somewhat disappointed, but didn't see reason to admit it.

Edee inhaled deeply, gathering his thoughts as he looked down at Alfonso's apologetic expression. "It's okay. I know you did what you thought was right in your heart. Sometimes we *all* have to, Alfonso, *despite* what we've been told. We'll talk tomorrow." Edee left Alfonso thinking there was more to discuss, but they both knew better.

Edee could see that Alfonso was getting ready to cry and, knowing he needed to, he turned his back and quietly returned to the group. Once he was certain that the large doors that sat flush with the earth had closed, Alfonso released the emotions that had been building inside him for the past few days. Staring over the barren landscape, there were only a couple of bushes to hide his image from the road. He cried hard as thoughts of what he had been forced to do over the past couple of days entered his mind, yet he knew it was all for the greater good. He looked to his left and the doors, concealed by a small mound that faced away from the road, protected the safety of his neighbors and blocked his profile from oncoming traffic on the country road that sat, in the distance, out before him. Behind him, a large patch of woods, with a small trail that eventually met up with another trail that led to where the animals were kept: a place where, so often, he sought sanctuary. Over the next few weeks, there, while Jonathon was on guard, he would crawl on his belly the entire 500 meters or so to the forest's edge, so as not to be seen from the road. Often times, he would find more comfort in sleeping with the horses and chickens than he would the villagers. Carefully, he would step through the woods and find the places the hens had chosen to nest and gently call over the cats and dogs to feast on the embryos of their unborn. Petting them and providing them with the love from human touch, that he was certain they were missing. Here, among the lowly little animals, he would find peace.

But, just for tonight: he would cry in the open field.

Wondering if somewhere out in the great unknown and blackness of space above him, anyone could see him? Wondering if they knew the kindness that was in his heart despite the species that claimed him as one of their own? Wondering if they would care?

His eyes cast to the heavens, he wished they would come and save him from the hell this world around him had become.

And, aside from his sobbing, there was nothing but the song of the bullfrogs and the crickets in the night.

It Takes a Village

Ronald had moved Leticia from Harlem and centered what was left of their family in White Plains, NY. Having no one to guide him, since Leticia had refused to speak in weeks, Ronald fell in line with a group of extremists loyal to Elijah Drew. With the growing violence in Harlem he felt they had to move, he reported each morning at 5:00 am, only to return in the early evening to find Leticia sitting in bed, slowly rocking back and forth, as though she was still holding their child. Her skin tone seemed almost completely deprived of its normal caramel hue now, and although Ronald tried to brush her hair, he could never get it to sit quite as she would have fixed it. He wouldn't even make an attempt at her makeup, but he still found her to be just as pretty without it.

He prayed for her to speak.

Although she never spoke a word to him, he would continue speaking and tell her about his day. She never looked up, always maintaining that same distant expression. If told, she would eat, but not much. Ronald cared for her and fed her. Every night he would gently bathe her and put her to bed. Her eyes were always fixed on some image she couldn't take them away from. Almost catatonic, he had resolved himself to the idea that although her body was still here and warm, Leticia was gone. Not wanting to accept that though, he still held her through each night and pretended: he refused to give up on hope.

After going through his day, and a brief run down on the weather, Ronald would turn on the television and comment to Leticia about the programs, as though she was there. He knew better, but the sound in the room, even if only the sound of his own voice, gave him some comfort. He had no time to grieve, himself. He could only care for her.

Suddenly, the phone rang as it had every night for the past two weeks since meeting his new protégé and pseudo adopted son: Rocky.

"Rocky! Hey, Rocky boy! Hey Leticia it's Rocky, Leticia says 'Hi'!" he lied to the young voice on the other end of the line. She hadn't moved, but, to Ronald, maintaining a fake sense of normalcy was all he had left.

"Oh, yeah, she's great, Rocky! Still pretty sick with that flu, though. You'll meet her, kiddo. Oh, she'll love you! *Huh?*... What's that?... You *did*!... That's great, son!"

Ronald pretended he was a father, again.

Rocky was a twelve year old somewhat troubled youth that had grown up in housing projects most of his life. Once a gang member in the Peoples Nation, just as his mother before him, he found himself now affiliated with a stronger power. Growing up in the city hadn't been easy. As people had been on the move, so were the gangs. Turf wars between Peoples and the Latin Kings took one of his best friends in the crossfire. His gang retaliated by killing five small children that were related to the shooters.

Rocky grew up in an environment where life was cheap. Even the deaths of innocent children meant nothing to his friends, who only rejoiced with the idea that they had made the evening news. They were even more pleased when the reporter announced that while the police believed the shootings were gang related, they had no suspects. Although Rocky was only eight at the time, he could remember being gathered round the television and mocking the pain of the parents and other family members that had cried for the cameras. To his friends the program was nothing more than a comedy that had been aired for their personal entertainment.

But, stories like this were happening everywhere.

With so many shootings, gangs knew they had to commit more and more offensive acts to make on the eleven o'clock news. Multiple victims were common as groups competed to see if they would make the top story that night. Rival gangs made bets between themselves as their sick games played out for cities around the nation.

It was the only form of attention many of these young people received.

Some groups even returned to the scenes of their crimes, so they could appear in the background, signing confessions in the camera with gang codes and laughing as the police tried to work the scene around them.

It was just life in the city.

In some ways, gangs were the only families many of these young people had. It was all they knew. At one point, a job application might as well have had a box for gang affiliations to check off on, since they were so prevalent, even amongst the adults. Not that any of them were interested in work. The crimes committed by the gangs helped to support its members and those involved felt nothing wrong with robbing and killing off a society they felt had wronged them. Still, they were aware of the threat of jail or the fact that they could end up victims themselves. Playing the odds, young women gave birth to multiple children, all by different fathers, in an attempt to secure that at least one would continue paying child support in the event that another was imprisoned or murdered.

Thug life was an accepted culture.

They were the children born to mothers, fathers and grandparents that all had the same illicit affiliations. They were quick to label themselves with tattoos, hairstyles and certain styles of dress that told the world where they stood in rank. For those who cared to know, the signs were obvious. Rocky sported a fresh teardrop tattoo just below his right eye, proudly: a sign that he was a killer. Ronald, having grown up in suburbia, never realized the implication and simply wrote it off to tactless fashion.

To Rocky and his peers, it was a badge of honor.

Rocky's mother, a former gang member turned crack addict, lost three other sons in the riots and shootouts that had taken place over the previous years. Having been a prostitute in her younger days, and high through most of her conceptions, she had no idea who the fathers of her children may be. Lying in the incubator, shaking and twitching through withdrawals, Rocky's introduction to the world was unkind. The overcrowded and understaffed hospital that he was born in would be his home for the first two months of his life. Living in a glass box, he rarely knew human touch, as the nurses were to busy to bother with him.

He was just another crack baby in the ghetto.

There were thousands of them.

Frustrated by the extra work they caused them, many of the nurses were angered by the thought of their existence. They knew whatever loneliness these little lives may have felt now, was only a mild introduction to their future. When possible, many would sneak other medications into their systems to shut up their incessant crying.

Although Rocky would never know, his mother's first words to the nurse when he was born were not about concern for her child. Her first thought was to enquire as to how much more money she would get on her welfare and food stamps and she demanded to know if she could start collecting the extra now, even though the hospital would be caring for the little baby for the next couple of months. The nurse had been asked the same question so many times, she was un-phased by the callous remark and simply tossed some forms at Rocky's mother and quipped, "Yeah. You'll get your check."

It would take the death of her oldest son, the third one she would lose, to make her attempt to turn her life around. When Rocky was ten, she joined the Islamic Nation and served Drew's cause loyally. Now a devout Muslim, she had encouraged Rocky, the last of her offspring, to fight against what she felt were the causes of his half-brother's deaths, never wanting to face any responsibility, herself.

She blamed the government.

She blamed white society.

She blamed America.

But, she never faced facts in the mirror.

Drew's message was one of hate and anger, but he spoke with such conviction that he almost hypnotized his crowds. A strong leader was all the black community needed. Even though his historical accounts of abuses towards blacks had almost no basis in fact, his supporters did not have the education to know better and Drew was a master at weaving lies with enough truth that even the most outrageous claims were easily swallowed up my his followers. When the white population, offended by Drew's lies, tried to counter his beliefs, he only used it as further evidence to sell his message. And, when he found himself cornered in the media, he would simply accuse the government of having destroyed the evidence of their own atrocities, demanding he knew the true story, and the black population would quickly buy into the conspiracy theory just as Rocky's mother had.

It was such an easy sell to a population that already felt beat down by a nation. The problem for the government and for Gonzales though, was that not all of Drew's arguments were so far out in left field. He demanded that the government explain why student visas and scholarships were given to foreigners from other countries above the black population that had been born and raised in the United States. He questioned why America would allow students from hostile nations to study nuclear physics in our nation's universities when their own nations did not have nuclear capabilities and demanded the government explain their stupidity for allowing such an obviously ludicrous practice to continue. Pointing to Russia's mail order bride market he wondered out loud to tens of thousands, in sold out stadiums that filled with his follows, how it was that an impoverished communist nation could afford to educate these women to the point of having M.B.A.'s and Doctorates only to lose them to United States soil and screamed for answers as to why black America was not able to even graduate from high school.

He insisted that schools and the hospitals in areas with dense black populations were purposefully overcrowded and under funded. From stages in sold out arenas, he would ask these questions before crowds of over 30,000 and then release them back to the streets. Angered and incited by his words, the crowds would flood the streets and take out their frustrations on whatever businesses or homes were unfortunate enough to be in their path. Law enforcement could not possibly control the riots, and when they failed to manage these crowds, Drew simply used it as another demonstration of how the government had turned their backs on black America.

It was a brilliant tactic.

He created mob scenes that were uncontrollable, then blamed the white population for failure to protect the attendees that came to his sold out events. The media did their part to show the path of destruction and the trampled bodies that were regularly associated with the Islamic Nation's *'Calls for Justice'* Seminars. The footage only served to anger the black population further and they were slowly brainwashed into believing Drew was the only leader that could take them to salvation.

But, whites saw it differently, at least behind closed doors. They would whisper their frustrations about the set up, but politicians were too afraid of being labeled "racist" in the media to say anything. The race card had been long overplayed, but no one was willing to strip it from the deck.

Black and white America had been too far apart for too long.

They were strangers, now.

Growing up in such a world, it is easy for a child to lose hope and sight of their own future. Rocky was among the forgotten, but when Ronald met him he didn't see him as the menace he truly was. There was something about the shape of his face, something about the shape of his ears, that reminded him of Ty'. Desperately lonely for a family, Ronald took Rocky under his wing, never questioning why this particular child approached him first.

Had he only known.

Strutting up, laughing under his breath, and accompanied by a boy that was dressed in very similar attire, Rocky's first words were, "How'd ya like Harlem?" Ronald could not possibly have known the true connection he had with the boy in front of him.

If he had known what action had put that fresh ink on Rocky's cheek, Ronald surely would have choked him dead right there, but Ronald didn't think a child was capable of such things and grief had made him oblivious to the obvious. Ronald just assumed the boys were being welcoming and smiled as he responded, "Well, we're hoping White Plains will be a good place. We weren't in Harlem very long." Ronald didn't want to talk about what had happened and, for whatever reason, never questioned how the boys had known he had been there.

The other boy laughed, commenting, "Long enough!" and walked away leaving Rocky with Ronald. Ronald didn't get it and simply continued conversation with Rocky. Rocky stayed engaged, unable to understand why this stranger in front of him was being so nice.

Not really ever having had a father, and the product of a miserable childhood, Rocky was drawn to Ronald's attention and, at this time in his life, Ronald really needed someone to dote on. Rocky reminded him a little of an older version of Ty' and he even caught himself once calling the young man that. When it was questioned, Ronald brushed it off never even mentioning that he had once had a son of his own.

The memory of the night Ty' was murdered was too much to confront. Leticia's now familiar posture had been so overwhelmingly disturbing that terrible evening, when he lifted their son from her arms without challenge and wrapped the boy in a used hotel bed sheet, leaving only his little face, and paling cheeks, exposed. He remembered how he had held Ty' so close as he walked the streets of Harlem until he found a cemetery.

He could still recall how the ground was hard and it was dark.

He remembered how he would occasionally look over to Ty', hoping by some miracle he would suddenly wake up.

But, there were no miracles in Harlem that night.

He thought about how he had placed his son inside the shallow grave he had dug out by hand, carefully wrapping his small face, as though shielding him from the dirt that was about to fall upon it.

As if that would make a difference, now.

Now, it was just easier to forget.

Ronald absorbed himself in the teachings of Elijah Drew's henchmen. Now, himself, much like the mob that Leticia had once been so critical of. To Rocky, though, he was becoming like the father Rocky never had, and Ronald happily accepted that role; although, like many youths, Rocky held secrets from Ronald that Ronald could never imagine. Rocky's secrets were as dark as the space Ty's remains now occupied.

Ronald had been a good father at one time. He had tried to do all of the right things, but now Ronald thought that God had betrayed him and his family. It wasn't his fault. He needed to focus on a new family and a new deity: Allah. Plus, the Islamic Nation had provided him with a new and much needed social network.

Rocky had called him that night to tell him he had been promoted. He thanked Ronald for all of his help in training and credited Ronald with his progress. To celebrate, Ronald had invited Rocky to come over and promised to take him out to dinner. Nothing fancy, but the boy reveled in the idea of a hot meal. Ronald resigned himself to the idea that it was time to introduce Rocky to Leticia, even though she had not progressed from the state she had been in since their son's death.

"Oh, yeah, 'Tish! Rocky's so proud of himself! Me, too! I mean, it takes most kids something like three months to get through this program and Rocky did it in two! In *two*! Aww, he's sweet to try to give me the credit, but *he* did it! You would so love him! He's such a good kid! I know you're still not feeling too good, but maybe I can bring you back some soup? Would you like that? Maybe some chicken noodle or vegetable? It won't be much, I'm sure, but it is a huge honor to even be allowed to go to this dinner! I mean The Nation puts on a pretty big spread at these things, considering the times! I so wish you would come. Will you? 'Tish, can you hear me? We're going to have rice and vegetables and soups and breads and there might even be some cheeses and maybe even some chicken, from what I heard? Well, I'm sure that whatever Elijah's got planned for us, it'll be good! I just hope they'll let me bring you a little something home. You must be getting sick of all the cous cous? Is that why you keep spitting it out? You don't like it? Oh, 'Tish I just wish you would eat, you look like you've lost fifteen pounds! You were *already* thin! I'm going to try to get you a nice bowl of soup. I really am. Okay?"

Talking to her, as he normally would, he tried his best to prepare her for his visit and himself for the inevitable introductions. A slight hint of lip gloss, to give some life to her face, was all he would attempt. He moved her to a chair in and threw a blanket over her lap and continued to talk to her as if he expected an answer. Soon there was a knock and he opened the door to let the young man inside. Upon entering, Rocky's first impression was that Leticia appeared to be a zombie. He whispered, almost confused, "Is she like that all the time?"

Ronald shook his head, remembering how she was, still not wanting to explain, "No. She's been sick for a few weeks, now. But, she's getting better." Ronald said with optimistic hope as Rocky grinned to himself and marveled at his creation. This was better than bloodshed. She looked nothing like the tall, shapely ebony princess he had remembered prancing down the street, always smiling, and so happy to be on his arm. She was broken and Rocky took some form of sick pleasure in knowing he had played a role. "C'mon, I'll introduce you." Ronald gestured to him to follow as the little beast crossed the threshold.

Kneeling beside her, trying to find that place where her eyes had focused that seemed to keep escaping him, he took her hand and spoke gently, "Honey, this is Rocky. He's the boy I have been telling you about." Turning to Rocky, quickly, he said, "I tell her about you all the time." He turned back to her, "Rocky and I are going to go out, now. I will bring you back some soup, if I can. Do you want to say hello?" He wished she would speak.

"She ain't got nothin' to say. C'mon, I'm hungry." Rocky said, disinterested.

But, suddenly Leticia's eyes moved: still out of focus, but they had changed. Ronald watched her intensely and begged Rocky to keep speaking. Rocky, suddenly felt nervous and wanted nothing more than to leave. He decided to make an excuse before it went any further. Rocky started to move towards the door, "Man, I gots to go. I forgot somethin' I gots to do." Ronald turned to him, and as much as he wanted to keep his commitment, he was certain Leticia was returning to him and he wanted her back even more than he wanted a hot meal. He didn't argue with Rocky's departure, as he watched his wife's hands begin to tense and tremble, hoping she was about to snap out of it. Rocky saw her reaction and rushed to the door. "I'll see you tomorrow!" Ronald called out with a beaming voice.

For the next hour he cradled her, talking to her and begging her to come back to him. Slowly, the tension and shaking in her hands faded to a soft tremble, and soon after she was right back where she had been.

And Ronald cried with frustration.

Within the next two weeks, orders from Drew would be handed down and Ronald was instructed to go west to fight to take back the Mississippi as the Northeast was slowly starving. With his mother's approval, Rocky insisted on going despite Ronald's pleas to keep him in New York. Ronald couldn't understand, as Rocky's mother told him how proud she was of him and how she hoped he would be a martyr for Drew, droning on about all of the fantastic rewards he would receive if he died on the field and how Drew would reward her for the life of her son.

Even after finding sobriety, this child was just a paycheck to her.

The Islamic Nation had promised $10,000 to the families of each person that had been confirmed dead. Of course, the catch was that no one was ever really "confirmed" to their standards and their status remained simply listed as "missing".

Ronald, after losing a child, looked at the woman that had already lost three with dismayed wonder and could not imagine how she could possibly believe her own words. But, Rocky believed them and was determined to go. Ronald feared that if he didn't take him with him, he would go on his own. At least, this way, he could keep an eye on him and protect him from the dangers that might lie ahead.

While he hated the idea of leaving Leticia behind, he couldn't help but imagine that when he returned she would be well again. He left her with Rocky's mother to care for her and ensured that the wives of a couple of his newfound associates would look in on her from time to time. Drew had explained the battles would only go on for a couple of weeks and that the Territory defenses were weak. In the morning, Rocky and Ronald headed to the mosque to pick up their weapons and instructions. He would make one last stop to explain Leticia's condition to Rocky's mother.

Everyone would soon learn that Drew had lied.

Rocky's mother followed him and walked over toward the bedroom, then slowly opened the door, noting the musty odor and smell of dandruff and death that lingered in the air. She looked in at the rocking figure and then back to Ronald.

"Her name is Leticia. I call her 'Tish. Most of her friends called her 'Tish. Someone needs to look after her..." Ronald rambled nervously.

The woman nodded in reply unable to take her eyes off of Leticia. Suddenly feeling a bit of the pain she remembered from the loss of her own children for the first time in years.

Ronald paused to regain composure for a moment.

"Don't give her aspirin... she's allergic... and she likes ice cream, but it makes her sick."

The woman nodded, closing the door over.

"... she likes jazz... I play some music for her every night when she has trouble sleeping.... and I... I... made her one... it's just me talking... but, I would like you to play it for her... just... just whenever you think about it... okay?"

Again, she nodded.

Passing by him, the woman reached out and took his hand. Looking down, she said, "I'm sorry.... about your son. Don't worry about her. I'll watch after her." In sobriety, the former crack addicted prostitute before him seemed kind and gentle. Ronald wondered how Rocky and her other children's lives might have been different had she found such clarity a couple of decades earlier.

Not wanting to make a scene, and certain he would return in a couple of weeks, Ronald lovingly kissed Leticia on the forehead, stroking her face once more as if he was trying to remember every detail, then he headed to the front with Rocky. As they came closer and closer, Ronald suddenly realized that Drew had seriously understated the gravity of the situation, but Rocky seemed unaffected by the chaos. Ronald wondered, in that moment, what he had dragged the child into; but, Rocky didn't seem afraid at all. In fact, he seemed amused by the death and violence that surrounded him. It was almost entertaining and enjoyable.

As he watched the boy's expressions, all he could ask himself was "Where had America failed this child?"

The Guff Is Empty

As she was sitting at the kitchen table, grading a stack of quizzes and enjoying a late afternoon cup of cocoa, while Georgie and Alli played in the little children's park in the center of the complex, Caroline was overcome with a sense of complete peace. They were safe here and Caroline never feared letting the children run out on their own. Neither did the mothers of any of the other children they had befriended in the neighborhood. She liked her clean and pretty little apartment. She had Muriel to watch the children, from time to time, when she needed a little space. She loved her work and was constantly helping out with every school play and bake sale event imaginable. She was comfortable with her life and thankful for those that were in it.

And, out of everyone, she was most thankful for Vladimir. He was, in her eyes, everything that she had ever wanted in friend, and in a lover, although she had kept her promise to herself that things between them would stay platonic. Her feelings for him had not changed, nor had his for her, but, even more than the passion that they shared, she simply enjoyed being in his company and, for now, that sufficed. The school lunch hour had turned into a regular afternoon date for them, for which Vladimir was always prompt. Behind her classroom door, they would joke and laugh and talk about the events of the day. He now knew her better than most anyone else, and certainly far better than George.

He could read her every expression and respond with the perfect words to comfort and calm her every concern and he possessed an uncanny ability to make her laugh for almost no reason. He could read her tone and instinctively know just how to ease her mind. Although they did not know it, the glances they exchanged had made them the subject of gossip in the teacher's lounge and the time they spent together did nothing more than fuel the rumors. Not that they ever flirted, or did anything even mildly inappropriate in their work environment, but something radiated between them that was obvious to even the most naïve observer. Sometimes it is easier for outsiders to see how perfectly two people can compliment one another.

Even Alli was beginning to see something there.

On occasion, Vladimir would come over for dinner at Caroline's home. Really, it shouldn't have seemed unusual as Caroline, in an attempt to fill an evening now and again with an hour or two of adult conversation, would host dinners with several of the teachers from the school. It was on those evenings, when Coach Stahl came over, though, that Alli would eat her dinner almost annoyingly slowly, trying to extend her time at the table, for as long as possible, so she could play detective to her mother's emotions. She watched their interactions and studied her mother's facial expressions. Focused with intensity, she would purposefully interrupt when Vladimir was speaking and inquire whether or not a letter from daddy had arrived that day, for no other reason than to watch her mother's reaction. It was at this point in the conversation, irritated by the reminder that she was still married, Caroline would politely tell her that no letters had arrived, then order her to stop playing with her food and tell her to clear the table. Alli would politely comply, but only so she could continue to eavesdrop from the kitchen.

When Vladimir was around George was almost never a topic of conversation at the table, and Caroline kept her worries about the disturbing contents of his letters to herself. As far as she would have the children know, their father was fine and serving proudly as an Officer in the Command. Despite Alli's pleas to read the letters herself,

Caroline would never oblige, afraid that their content would scare the child. So, instead she would make the children sit on the floor and read the letters aloud, making up superficial content as she went along. Still, Alli knew something was wrong, just as most children in unhappy and troubled homes do. It especially bothered her when she would ask her mother for re-reads of her father's letters and Alli would realize the words always changed. Though she never said a word and Caroline never suspected Alli knew she was lying.

There was never anything to confirm her suspicions about her mother's feelings for the boy's PE Coach, even though children at school had begun to whisper about them, just like the adults. Caroline had noticed Alli had become more withdrawn, but her grades were still good and so she wrote it off to the fact that Alli was beginning to grow up. Overall, for Caroline, things were better than they ever had been and she was determined to not allow preoccupations to control her mind.

Looking down at the marshmallows floating around in her half empty mug of hot chocolate Caroline debated indulging in a second cup and continued her task of grading, leaving a few words of encouragement on each child's paper, no matter their score. Suddenly, her peaceful afternoon was interrupted by a knock at the door. She thought to herself it was probably Muriel, stopping by to see if she needed anything from the store as she made her nightly pilgrimage to the market. In a single motion, she was off her chair and flinging open the door with a big smile.

But, her face would soon change, when she saw it was not Muriel standing before her.

There, before her, was a young, thin boy in full Command Uniform.

"I'm sorry, ma'am." After pressing a letter into her hand, he walked away.

Caroline suddenly felt a cold wave flush over her, beginning at her shoulders and working both down her spine and up her neck, at the same time, filling her with a sensation of empty numbness. Her throat, as if someone was slowly choking her, seemed to grow tighter with each breath, and she found herself unable to speak, although she wanted to scream, and her mind moved for immediate denial.

She felt weak.

Too weak to move.

Frozen.

And, there she stood, her mind lost, thinking nothing, for fear that allowing one thought through would release too large a herd of emotions, so she blocked them all out. Until finally, her body reacted to what she would not let herself feel on her own and an ungodly scream exploded towards the heavens, but Caroline was not even aware she was making a sound. Muriel ran out of her apartment, towards Caroline. Seeing the letter Caroline held in her hands, she hurriedly waved the other neighbors back to their doors, and pulling her arm around Caroline, she pushed her inside to a chair and threw a blanket over her shoulders. Wrapping the blanket around her as Muriel searched for her to say something, but there was only silence, as the shock took over.

Caroline just stared ahead.

Barely even blinking.

Then, the door flew open and Muriel was forced to face the apprehension in the little faces peering in from the doorway across the room. Alli stood in the threshold, not moving, Georgie hiding behind her leg and barely peeking in at his mother, while other children continued to race up the stairs, pushing each other, and trying to glimpse the reason for the commotion. Never taking her eyes from her mother, Alli reached for Georgie's hand and pulled him in with her, closing the door on the mass of little eyes behind them, knowing something was terribly wrong: the other children's curiosities muffled by the door, but still audible. Caroline, not even aware of the presence of her own children, could offer no answers.

Georgie ran over to Muriel, looking to her for explanation as Muriel tried to decide the gentlest way to break the news. She picked him up, in her arms and reached out for Alli's hand, leading them back to Alli's bedroom and fumbling for the right words in her mind as she led the children to their rooms.

Alli focused on her mother's silence.

For the next two hours, Muriel would sit at the side of Alli's bed, as she cried all of her fears and grief into her pillow, soaking it and trying hard to choke herself with her loss. There were no questions to answer: right now, she just needed to feel things, and Muriel understood this. So she sat there, her hand on Alli's back, offering what comfort she could, and occasionally brushing her tear dampened locks to one side, or forcing her to sit up and blow her nose, between fits of emotion. Georgie, too young to fully grasp what was happening, and uncomfortable with his sister's crying, had already headed to his room and was content to play by himself, as his big sister sobbed and Muriel's heart filled with dishonor certain that Alli remembered her earlier lie that promised her father's safe return.

For Muriel, Alli's emotions were exhausting, but finally she had cried herself to sleep. Muriel pulled a soft blanket over her and made her way back to Caroline who spoke to her as if she was coming out of anesthesia. "Are they alright?" she asked quietly, not making eye contact, and speaking as if she had not quite found her voice, yet.

"They're okay. They're asleep. How are *you*, Caroline?"

Caroline thought for a moment, everything seemed like it was flowing in slow motion to her, and, maintaining her focus on some empty block of air in the center of the room, she answered, almost whispering, and as if it was the first time in her life anyone had posed the question. "I don't know."

Determined to not let her friend fade back into the state she had entered when she first heard the news, Muriel brought her some water and reached for her hand, forcing her to look into her eyes, and, in Caroline's, all she could see was pain and confusion. "Drink this. It will be alright. I know that is hard to see, when you lose someone you love, but time heals. It does. Truly." Muriel counseled.

And Caroline's thoughts were back to reality. That was the problem. She didn't love George and in losing him, she realized it. She couldn't even cry for the man whose children were sleeping in the rooms behind her. And, for this, she felt guilty, but she wasn't mourning him, yet. She felt guilt, for all of the times she had wished he would walk out the door and never return. Guilt, for all of the times she had prayed their horrible marriage would be over. Guilt, for all of the times she wished she was free. She had meant it all. She just never expected that fate would grant her wishes in such a cruel way. She never thought that as she waved goodbye to George, as that bus took him away, she was really saying goodbye… for the last time.

But, she could tell Muriel none of this.

So, instead, she told her the thing that was next on the list of a thousand troubles on her mind. "I just can't help, but wonder how it happened... what he was doing... where he was... I just... I wish... I wish I could know. This says nothing." Caroline felt hollow as she allowed her hands to drape over her lap, still holding the paper loosely between her knees.

Muriel noticed the letter. It must not have contained much information. Such letters never do. "You'll drive yourself crazy, if you try to picture that... just remember the good times... don't think about the rest. Do yourself a favor. Don't ask those questions." Muriel tried to make her understand.

And there was more trouble: there weren't many good times to remember.

Most were so far back the memories had faded and were no longer clear to her. Despite the lack of love in their relationship, she still had affection for, and cared for George. She cringed at the idea he may have suffered and her heart ached when such thoughts flashed. She sipped her water and let her mind run through a series of possible ends, which was never good for her under these types of circumstances.

With the children safely tucked in, and deciding it was best to leave Caroline alone for the evening, Muriel stood up and announced her departure. "Get some rest, Caroline... I will be over in the morning to help out..."

"I'm alright, Muriel... there's no need for you..."

Muriel cut her off. "No, dear... you're not... I will be here at eight. In the meantime, I will call the school for you and explain that you will not be in for a few days."

Caroline nodded a thank you, giving Muriel a polite smile, even though she really didn't want the morning company. A few minutes later, Muriel would find the door and make the rounds with curious neighbors, explaining the loss in the Anderson home. Although Caroline didn't know it, as she sat in the darkened room, unable to sleep that night, the women around her, many that she did not even know, would be busy that evening cooking meals to bring to her door the next day.

Not that she would be up for eating.

The next morning, Caroline, still in her bathrobe and without any make up, graciously accepted the offerings, but never invited anyone in. She didn't want to drone on and on about George's death. Really, she didn't want to think about it at all, even though that was an impossible wish. For her, mourning was a private event, not a social one. She just wanted to be alone.

Her mind would not release her from the idea that she had the right to know what had happened. Knowing the Command would tell her nothing, her imagination wandered, playing out various scenarios, one more horrific than the next, until she would catch herself and try to ease her mind with the idea that George never knew what had happened. Of all of the scenes that had played in her mind it was, in fact, the last one that was closest to the truth: a single, but accurate, bullet that he could not have possibly seen coming as his eyes were too focused on things unrelated to warfare at the time God took him home. But, then her mind would cycle again.

In war, death finds no one gently.

And its shadow does well to darken many homes far beyond the battlefield.

Caroline paced the apartment, thinking.

The truth she knew she would never know would have been more than she would have been able to handle, though. Her only comfort would have been to know that George did not die in the presence of strangers.

As the fighting on the Mississippi had been growing increasingly violent to the north, Company 318 was sent upstream to help reinforce other members of the Command that were suffering severe losses. Before even being sent to the front, George was already dead. His spirit broken by the dreadful visions that still haunted him from Officer's Training, as his letters had already revealed, even though Caroline could not understand what he was trying to communicate. George Anderson was an alcoholic, a poor excuse for a husband and certainly no candidate for world's greatest dad, but he was, nonetheless, a gentle person. The kind of man that would catch spiders in the house, and rather than squashing them into his shoe, he would trap them and release them outside to the vegetation. It was his own unresolved issues with his own father that had molded him into the man, the husband, and the father he had become. When his father died in a head on collision when George was only nineteen, George's first thoughts were of the fight they had had earlier that morning. Unable to talk about his emotions, as many men are, he turned to suppress them with alcohol but his father's death taught him to respect the value of even the most seemingly insignificant life.

And, it is the small, almost unnoticed acts of kindness that buy passage to heaven.

And these were the things he did, routinely. It was the part of him that Caroline had fallen in love with him, when she was too young to see the rest. And, it was still the part of him she cherished. She could just never understand how a man that could be so gentle to an insect, could not see the love she would have returned if only he had showed her the same type of kindness.

Perhaps, the Command saw such weakness.

A good soldier could not be so benevolent.

They had to break that side of him: and they did.

As George tried to lead his men, he would never escape the images in his mind of the killings and the tortures that he not only witnessed, but participated in carrying out on those that the Command would choose to target. The dark skinned, the weak, the old, the troubled, the forgotten and all of the other members of society that the Command marked for death based on their beliefs or refusal to comply with the establishment's orders. Those that were judged as guilty, though they had no trial, and were subjected to being victims of the Command's most appalling cruelties.

George had struggled to understand his place in the world and what had led him to be caught up in such atrocities. Although, at the time, George knew his failure to comply with their orders to kill would have resulted in he, himself, becoming prey for the bloodthirsty that were serving beside him, he always wondered if he had would not have been better off to allow them to kill him, so he could leave this earth with his dignity and morality intact. As he took aim at the men and women across the field, he found himself searching through the scope for their eyes. He had to see them.

Really, he studied them intensely before pulling back on the trigger.

And if reflected there, beyond the fear and the terror of knowing that their lives were about to be taken for no other reason than the wish to see them dead, he glimpsed kindness: George's bullet would find a clear mark. In his mind, George was sparing them from untold agonies they would suffer, if only injury found them, and they awoke strapped to a table in the auditorium of anguish and suffering. He tormented himself with thoughts of the lives he had taken, wondering who they were before they had found themselves on that dreadful field. He could only hope, had he had the opportunity to explain, they would have thanked him for his mercy. On the killing fields, he purposefully sought out the elderly, the young, and the kind; planting his bullets accurately through their skulls, so they felt as little pain, as possible.

The eyes.

It was the one space, in all of us, that was the same. God's small reminder that no matter how different we may wish to be from one another, or how hard we try to separate ourselves, in reality, the windows to our very souls were all the same color. It was here we were made in His image. Not in the color of our skin, or of our hair, or even in the languages that we echoed with our voices.

No.

Black and distant, but somehow miraculously filled with light. A universal trait that man shares even with beasts. A tiny porthole through which can be seen both the radiance of heaven, and the darkest shadows of Hell, depending on the man.

The same dark void that exists in the nether regions of space leads to the very heart of every man.

Regardless of a man's outer shell, his true self could only be seen through those same onyx holes through which he viewed the world. Within that small space, he was always naked to those that cared to see him. It was here, and only here, that the very soul of a man could be exposed, for better or worse, to all who surrounded him.

George had wondered what he would see in his own reflection, if he ever really dared to look again, as he led his troops north into Iowa. Elijah Drew had been flooding troops into Illinois, and the entire border between the two states had become riddled with death and disease. Unable to bury the bodies that fell into the river, they floated downstream as if drifting on the Ganges. Swollen by death, they would eventually burst on their slow journey to the Gulf of Mexico and the odor along the lower banks was overpoweringly nauseating. The further north they pushed, the more George was able to understand the blood lined banks he had noticed on his first day on the front, as body after body burst from its paper thin cocoon releasing what once was the embodiment of life, into the murky waters.

The Command saw their move to cut off traffic on the Mississippi as military strategy, but the enemy they faced, traveling from the east, did not fight with any training or order making them even more difficult to conquer. Like dogs that had been raised hungry in a cage and beaten for no other reason that to make them violent, the forces on the east side of the bank were only interested in drawing blood for sport. Unlike the Command's forces, which had been ordered to their positions, Drew's people came willingly, attracted by bloodlust and the promise of great financial and spiritual rewards for their efforts. Money poured in from the Middle East to feed and arm the Islamic Nation's forces.

Crossing near bridges was the most dangerous point for Anderson's troops, taking a lesson from a confrontation that cost him four men, he pushed west, away from the great river, and decided they would circle back in when they reached their rendezvous point. As they pushed north, trying to come into Clinton, Iowa from the western side of the city, they were pushed forward by members of the Command coming in from the west, forcing them closer and closer to the Mississippi's waters. There, where a large bridge connected the Territory to the part of the US that Elijah Drew had claimed for himself, two islands sat in the middle of the river, calling to those on both sides that would hope to gain strategic position.

The battle for the islands began and George Anderson found himself in the middle of a bloodbath. No longer concerned with the location or positions of his own men, it was now just a matter of survival. George was determined to live, as between his apprehensions and terror, images of Alli and Georgie played in his mind. The scenery around him reminding him only of his high school days and he could not fathom how God had called upon him again to bear witness to such horrors of death.

But, before him was the nature of man.

Bloodletting was normal. It was their favorite pastime. Even the most peaceful of cultures had justified the sacrifice of lives of the young and the virtuous; if not to an enemy during times of war, then to some God they claimed would protect them from strife if only they would commit such heinous acts in His or Her name. It seemed, as George looked over the banks, he could find no reason to believe that mankind had any respect for life. It was overwhelming evident, though, that humans were fascinated and obsessed with death.

His rifle in hand, thoughts circling, he could not explain, nor remember, how he made it onto one of the small islands and found the momentary safety of an already established Unit of the Command, organized for battle with snipers positioned to take out those from the east that were attempting to cross the bridge. Hope for his own survival escalated as he joined in formation with more experienced Officers and troops, now completely oblivious to where his own men had run off to, or what fate had befallen them.

No longer claiming to be in charge, George took orders from a Captain that actually seemed to know what he was doing on the field, and followed his instruction to take position and start taking out those members from the east that had made it to the other island, separated from them by only a small canal. George pressed forward, crawling on his stomach, his elbows and knees being shredded by the broken beer bottles and debris that had been piling up for years, discarded from the bridge above. The ground was damp from recent rains and his head pounded from the unholy stench of gunpowder and rotting flesh that surrounded him. Following orders, he took position keeping his rifle at the ready. He first scoped the landscape, and seeing movement in the trees, he drew up his scope for a closer look. And looking across he found another man, rifle in hand, taking aim at him, in the same moment.

But, this was not just *any* man.

For a split second he was certain his eyes were surly deceiving him, as the man who *had* to see he was staring down George's barrel, lowered his weapon slightly, reducing the threat. He was too far away for George to see him clearly, but there was something familiar about the outline in the distance and his shadowed profile.

George stared through the trees and bushes for a second, then looked back through the scope.

It was no mistake.

But, George's mind had been so confused in all of this, he had to check his scope for a third time, before he could confirm he was looking into the eyes of a friend.

"How had fate been so cruel to put him here?" he questioned the heavens and whatever God may be there.

It was the man he once called his best friend: Ronald.

Or, at least, a broken, tired and much thinner version of him.

He thought back to the words he could not respond to the last time they spoke in the bar. He remembered having no answer and suddenly a thousand responses raced to his mind, but George had never imagined they would be in this place. Even if he screamed out, his words would be lost in the noise. So close to resolution and forgiveness, but still separated by the hatreds that surrounded them and the watery divide between them. In that moment he realized they were still friends and he saw Ronald's forgiveness and shared desire to communicate staring back at him. Either of them could have fired.

Although George couldn't know, more than anything, Ronald wished they could be close enough to hug and walk away from the field. With Leticia all but gone from him, he needed the comfort and understanding of the only other person on earth that he would feel comfortable crying in front of and he suddenly ached for Ty', again, as he stared across to his friend. George didn't even know his own Godson was dead and Ronald so wished to tell him and have someone to grieve his loss with him.

His tears blurred the magnified image of his friend's face.

Here, George would finally answer the last question Ronald had posed to him with his actions. The same question that had haunted them both since the day Ronald had stormed out of that small Atlanta bar that had once been like a second home for them. The question, they both thought, had ended their friendship.

A single shot rang out, finding its mark with deadly accuracy.

Right through the skull.

No remorse.

And, in that defining moment, as Ronald was taking another look through his own scope, just wanting to see his friend's face more closely, the only words reflected in George's eyes, were "I'm sorry" as his body fell to the ground. Blood gushed from the side of his head, as George fell forward on the lonely island that would be his final resting place.

Those few seconds, for Ronald, would feel like an eternity, as he watched his best friend die. He had lost so much already, and he searched to find the source of the little piece of lead that had stripped the last bit of hope from him.

He wouldn't look far.

Elated by his kill, Rocky celebrated, turning to Ronald for praise, not knowing the true significance of his actions, as if his conscious had escaped him. He rejoiced at the idea he had taken a life and, as he carried on, Ronald didn't hear a word. Instead, he just looked upon the young man, he had hoped would replace the emptiness that was left in his heart when Ty' was taken from him and he saw, not just one child, but an entire generation.

This child was not Ty' and this generation was damned.

None of the children and young men that surrounded him were anything like Ty'.

Rocky *was* what he had been raised to be. He was what his upbringing and society had made him. Ronald looked deep, but came to the conclusion that the Hall of Souls was filled only with echoes and that the monstrous animal in front of him was nothing more than a beastly shell. There was no light in his eyes. No innocence reflected. Whether it had been stolen from him, or never implanted, Ronald couldn't tell, but he knew what needed to be done.

In a glimpse, he heard Ty''s laughter above the gunshots and Rocky's rantings, as if it was a message from heaven: whether it was a call to duty or a reminder, Ronald would have to decide. In his own mind, he would struggle to define the difference between right and wrong.

Ty', for a moment Ronald thought, was the only thing that had been right in the world: a small, but truly complete, embodiment of innocence and truth. As for the creature before him, although he had eyes that gleamed back, there was no spirit within them. Ronald grasped, for the first time, the notion that the youth he had hoped could bring back some of what he had lost, was not even child. He questioned whether or not this thing in front of him was even human.

It was evil: that he could see, now.

So, with that, Ronald looked around him and began to scan the joy on the faces of those that surrounded him: joy for murder. He watched their antics and laughter as they hunted their own prey and he was suddenly overwhelmed by one thought: they had no *souls*.

The Guff, somehow, had been emptied.

But, as he watched those around him fall, succumbing to their mortal wounds, his only thought was to wonder what evil was rising to be reborn on earth. Somewhere, along the way, an entire generation had been born without conscious, nor morals, nor faith... in anything.

Then, his reflective state was interrupted by Rocky's thrilled elation.

"You see that! You see how I made that white devil infidel's head *explode*! How cool *that* be!? You see what I done *did* to that *mutha*! Bam! His brains done went flyin' to the other side of river! *Damn!*" Rocky danced around and bragged about his actions as if they deserved to be praised. Ronald stared out into the distance to the spot where his friend had fallen.

And he felt himself embracing his own rage.

Turning back to Rocky, he looked at him, seeing only a mortal version of the devil, himself. And, in that awakening, despite his recent conversion, he did the only thing a good Christian could do... the only thing his heart would allow... he followed his faith... and he shot young Rocky in the head.

Like a rabid dog.

And he fired again *and again and again* until the only sound he could hear was the clicking of the trigger pulling back on an empty chamber.

He watched Satan's prodigy grasp with death.

And Ronald would feel nothing.

Looking into Rocky's eyes, he could only focus on the fact that, in death, they were unchanged from how they appeared in life, and with that, he was certain in his decision as he looked down on the bloodied remains of his necessary release of frustration.

But, for George... and for Ty'...*and for himself*... Ronald would cry.

Staring across, to the point where George had fallen, Ronald fell to his knees as if he was praying to God for mercy to spare his friend. And, God turned away from that field.

And the battle continued...

After about an hour or so of staring across the waters that separated him from George's remains, Ronald had decided this was no longer his fight and he began to question how it was that he had found himself on this ground in the first place. Undaunted by the hail of bullets that sailed around him and the screams that filled the air, he dropped his gun and stood up, not even caring if he made himself a target.

And he began to walk.

And he walked.

And walked.

Until he found himself nearing the place where he hoped to find the one thing that he cared most about in this life, and the only thing that still mattered to him. He was exhausted and dirty, unshaven and emotionally spent. He had not had a bath in what seemed like weeks. After having lived off of foliage and berries for the entirety of his journey, he had lost so much weight that his clothes now hung off of him to the point his pants were loose at the tightest belt loop. Shuffling Illinois's dirt from his soles as he passed into Indiana his stomach felt as if his throat had been cut. He had tried to sustain on leaves and the occasional gulp of questionably healthy water, but Ronald could feel his body weakening and part of him would have welcomed the idea of simply falling asleep and not waking up, again. The soles of his shoes had worn down and his body had compensated by developing a large callous in the same spot where the leather had worn through to his right foot.

He decided to take rest in a small park, in an area he felt would shield him from sight. Ronald had nothing to steal, but had reached the point of being fearful of the possibility of any human interaction or contact. His faith was gone, his stomach was grumbling and his body had little left to give him. Finding an area that he felt would make a safe resting place for the evening, he noticed a dead bird lying on the ground about fifteen feet away. Ants had already begun to feast on its neck, but being able to put himself in the position of being king of this jungle, he brushed them off and smelled the carcass.

It was only slightly spoiled.

Relying on skills from his days in the Boy Scouts, he fumbled for some twigs and began the arduous process of trying to build a small fire without drawing attention. Guarding his kill, his stomach growled with anticipation for pigeon meat. Hurriedly, he striped off the bird's feathers, anxious to reach the protein below. Lacking proper kitchen tools, he ripped the animal open with his own hands and carefully scooped out the innards, then staked the meat and roasted it over the fire. The meat was slightly rancid, but on his tongue it tasted like buttered filet mignon.

And the little more than two ounces of meat the bird sacrificed to him was all he would have, but it was the most solid meal he had seen in months. As he passed through Ohio, he would find an unfortunate puppy that he convinced himself felt no pain as he twisted his neck, making it his evening meal. But, the guilt of that selfish act followed him the rest of his journey and he recommitted himself to a vegetarian diet, minus the occasional road kill that was still fresh enough to make a dinner out of.

When he found a familiar street, he suddenly felt like the richest man in the world. It was a small and dirty stretch of land in a place he had barely even known, but only a few blocks away was the apartment that held his motivation for traveling so far: Leticia.

He was almost home.

The End of Love

After George's death, Caroline would be left to wonder about her future without him. Although she was working, she did not earn enough money to continue supporting the children in their current home. But, Mort Epstein, George's former boss, was kind in allowing the little family to stay in place while Caroline tried to figure things out, even though they were in a corporate apartment owned by his company. In fact, on several occasions, Mort had come to visit her: his arms always loaded with toys and candy for the children. He paid her George's vacation and a few thousand extra to help her get by, since George had no life insurance policies either through his job or from the Command. In fact, the Command offered no help beyond his last month's salary.

Friends came to visit, but none more than Muriel and Vladimir. Muriel, lonely in her own right, with Alfred still away at the Denver Mint, spent hours enjoying Georgie as he played with the new acquisitions Mort Epstein had bestowed upon him. She tried to pull Alli out of the shell she had dove into, but that would be a far harder task than anyone could imagine. For hours the child would sit and stare out the window at the pool she once loved to play in, watching, with deep seeded anger, the other children that still found happiness in its sparkling clear waters. In her mind, she could only wonder if she had been laughing and joking with the others at that moment when Death found her father; and, in that thought, she found part of herself to hate.

And she focused on it with silent fury.

Sitting in the window she coveted the still perfectly intact lives of the little people she once called friends. She rarely even spoke to any of them, anymore. Alli was content to simply monitor their audacity and unable to understand how the world was not grieving with her. Even her mother had never cried in front of her, and she couldn't understand that.

And, for this, she hated Caroline.

And, even more, she hated Vladimir.

Hate was her only companion, now.

She was certain that somehow he was responsible for her father's death and she was even more enraged by her mother's happiness in his presence. Alli had wanted her mother to suffer just as she, herself, was suffering; but instead, Caroline's eyes would light up when Vladimir's sparkling blue eyes met hers and any sign of depression or grief that may have been lingering would immediately wash out. Alli convinced herself that the rumors of the love affair between her mother and this horrid man had all been true and she was determined to do everything in her power to keep him out of their lives. The fact that such misbehavior only served to make her mother miserable, and embarrassed, was an added bonus. Alli passioned to see that melancholy on her mother's face and so she provoked it at every opportunity.

But it always backfired and Alli couldn't learn the lesson.

Vladimir would only use Alli's weapons against her. He consoled her mother by explaining how Alli's behavior stemmed from her sadness, assuring Caroline that it was all a phase that would pass when her grief subsided. He was careful around the children: too careful, Alli thought. Her small mind wondered what devious scheme he was hatching. If her mother had only loved her father, she convinced herself, he would still be alive. *His* death was all *her* fault.

Alli's memory seemed to be wiped clean of all times her father had almost purposefully belittled her. The stench of bourbon that repulsed her on a daily basis was replaced in her mind only by the scent of the cologne he would wear on special occasions. When he died, she smuggled the remainder of the bottle into her room and, at night, she would go fetal in her bed, tears pouring off her cheeks in silence, as she uncapped the bottle and tried to remember the sound of his voice. It was fading and that upset her to no end. Not wanting the company of her mother, or anyone else, Alli had learned to cry without making out a sound. Had she allowed anyone to see her, it would have seemed almost freakishly disturbing for a child to exhibit such behavior.

But, she was like her mother.

When tears made way to the surface in front of anyone, it only served to make her angry at herself for displaying any weakness. Unless, of course, she was allowing them to fall for dramatic effect or to embarrass Caroline in public: that she would permit.

But, *that* was a tactic.

Curled up at her door, so she could hear in on their conversations, Alli listened hard to every word. But, Vladimir still treated Caroline only as a friend, allowing her time to grieve, in her own way, and helping her to sort out the financial burdens that had befallen her. He never even as much as held her hand in front of Alli or Georgie, and was especially on guard when the little girl was around.

He knew she was listening in. Their conversations were, for the most part, mundane, with the exception of the occasional gossip that they shared about one coworker or another. Caroline leaned over the table, her eyes hinting that she had something truly juicy to share.

"And, well, Ann told *me* that Mrs. Anderson told *her* that *she* saw Mr. Keahey and Mr. McDonnell *making out* after last period *in the science lab*! *Can you believe that? They're gay!* Mrs. Anderson *saw* them!"

"This is image I am not needing to have in head." Vladimir held up his hands, waving the information away and smiling as he laughed at her.

"*What?* You don't believe me? I don't see why Mrs. Anderson would make up a story *like that!*" Caroline pressed for a response.

"No, Caroline. Is *not* that I do not believe you! *Everybody* knows that Mr. Keahey and Mr. McDonnell have the gay for each other! *This is old news!* Is just image *I* work *very hard* to not have picture of in head! *And, here you go!* Making pictures in my head of science lab! *And, Caroline, you told me you were to be my friend?!* Now, I have pictures of chubby man with red cheeks kissing skinny man that wears lab coat!" Vladimir shivered as if a sudden chill had just run up his spine.

"How do you think *I* took the news?! I have Keahey's daughter for third period math! Try solving *that* as a word problem!" She laughed, wiping tears of joy from her eyes.

They both laughed so hard they almost cried and, for Caroline, it felt wonderful. It was the first time she had laughed that hard since George had gone missing.

"Oh, be serious! Not *everybody* knows! What about Keahey's *wife*? You know *she does not know that!*"

"I would be more concerned about boyfriend of McDonnell! He was good boxer at one time!" Vladimir's smile radiated at her and she could do nothing, but shake her head and laugh. "But, we are here to organize bills. I am to pour you some more coffee and we begin. You get box from drawer."

Vladimir rose and warmed up their mugs as Caroline pulled the familiar file box that Vladimir had been helping her to organize, since the news about George and the harsh reality set in that she needed to make ends meet on her own. And for three months this routine continued. Not once did Vladimir cross the line or give implication of his incredible desire to return to the place when he and Caroline had once felt so comfortable. His passion for her was deeper than anything he had ever known, but even more so he valued her friendship and their conversations. On occasion, he could tell from her expressions that she was still very deeply in love with him, but he never took advantage of those opportunities. Instead, he simply used the time to get to know her even better and smiled at the revelations and their shared opinions on so many things. It seemed almost impossible that they could ever have a cross word, although they did playfully debate on many topics. Each convinced they were right, but happy to see that it was okay to share differences without argument.

But, then one day the tone of their conversations began to change and Alli panicked. She threw a fit, then pretended to injure herself, when her mother announced that Muriel would be babysitting her and Georgie and, all of a sudden, Vladimir arrived to take her mother to a movie.

This was a date and Alli was disgusted.

As the happy couple prepared to leave, a scream let out from Alli's bedroom, instinctively causing her mother to go racing to the bedroom to see what had happened.

There, rolling on the floor, grasping her right arm and faking immense tears, Alli cried out in falsified agony. Through her hard, panting crying she told her mother she had fallen off a chair and that she was almost certain she had broken her arm. Vladimir, turned his back to the scene and rolled his eyes out of view of the group, then turned back, acting concerned about what he saw to be an obvious rouse. In truth, Alli had only thrown herself to the floor hoping enough of a bruise would rise to give her mother reason to suspect real injury. Kneeling down, Caroline gently examined her arm as Alli continued her performance. Her eyes occasionally catching Vladimir's as she wished for the power to strike him dead where he stood.

"Vladimir, I am afraid we're not going to make the show. Maybe she needs to see a doctor?" Caroline said in an anxious tone, worried for her daughter's welfare, as Muriel looked on, never suspecting deception, and nervously wringing her hands while praying for the child's wellbeing.

"Then we go. I am trained for medic, though. Let me to look at arm of Alli…" he said gently, and Caroline moved to get out of the way and allow him.

"NO!" Alli screamed so loudly it could be heard three units away, "KEEP *HIM* AWAY FROM ME!"

Confused by her reaction, Caroline suspiciously questioned, "Well, Alli, are you hurt *or not*? What difference does it make if Vladimir looks?"

"NO!" she exclaimed, breaking into hysterics and crying, "YOU DON'T LOVE ME! GO AHEAD! GO WITH HIM! YOU DON'T CARE ABOUT ME OR GEORGIE ANYMORE!" As she sobbed uncontrollably.

"Oh, Alli, you know better. Come on, we're going to the emergency room. I'm sorry Vladimir... Muriel, can you watch Georgie?" Caroline said in a dry tone, now accustomed to Alli's accusatory outbursts, as she helped Alli to her feet and Muriel nodded with approval, certain the little girl needed an X-ray.

"I am to go start car. Will wait downstairs."

"You are so sweet, thank you!" Caroline graciously and thankfully accepted.

Alli suddenly realized Vladimir's intention, as he called her bluff. *Her* intention had been to break up their date and make her mother spend the evening sitting alone and worrying about her. She wanted her mother to make a choice between her, and Vladimir, certain that she would win out over him, but she had never thought he would invite himself along.

Alli was pinned.

Having to keep up the act, she was now in too deep to admit it was plot to ruin their plans. Alli had no choice but to go to the hospital. Vladimir saw straight through her little show. After all, he had already seen her performance as Dorothy result in a standing ovation; he knew she was quite the little actress yet he had to go along with Caroline's concerns, if he was to secure his own position.

Sitting in the back seat, Alli watched with ferocity as Vladimir only continued to counsel her mother more, and her mother ate it up. When he reached for her hand, kissing it, as he had that first time, Caroline swooned and Alli's eyes grew wide with wrath. She was filled with a violent rage and wanted desperately to hit him causing him to wreck the car and kill them all.

She didn't care.

As they arrived at the doors to the emergency room, Vladimir let them out, allowing Alli and her mother to enter and Alli's eyes tried to tell him exactly how much hate she harbored for him. Vladimir only smiled, amused by the message, as he softly told her mother that he would return after parking the car and assured her that Alli would be fine.

He knew she wasn't hurt at all.

He had watched her in the rear view mirror as she had scooted herself into the corner with her 'bad' arm.

Alli entered the ER, seething, but still faking pain. She would find herself, within thirty minutes, behind closed doors in X-ray, unable to hear the conversation between her mother and Vladimir. Everything in the hospital seemed to take forever, and she began to resent the idea that she was out of earshot even more than she resented the wait.

With this, she decided she would become a difficult patient and make the staff want to get rid of her, as quickly as possible. The doctor would flag her chart as 'emotionally troubled', and would diagnosis her only with 'idiopathic pain to the right arm'.

When she emerged from behind the steely automatic doors that led to back to the waiting room, Alli found she had exhausted herself with emotion and rage. As her eyes opened to the room, she found her mother, sleeping comfortably, cradled in Vladimir's arms and adrenaline began to rush over her system.

"I want to go home." Alli said sternly, enunciating each syllable almost to the point of mocking him and looking Vladimir straight in the eyes.

"You are better now?" He countered, hoping to see her lie, but she said nothing, turning away, as he gently awoke her mother from peaceful dreams. Happy to see that Alli was alright, Caroline tucked her into the car, but Alli was inexplicably resistant to her mothering.

Her arm seemed fine, now, as Alli snatched the seatbelt and buckled up.

When they arrived home, Alli stormed passed Muriel, without a word, unconcerned about the adult conversations that would follow. She was determined to reach her bed and upset that her plans had been foiled.

Alli awoke at her usual time, wiping the sleep from her eyes, as she stepped out from her room. The smell of pancakes wafted from the kitchen, and she saw her mother in the kitchen and suddenly realized the water from the shower was running. Georgie was already at play in the living room.

"Well, good morning, Sleepy!" her mother said in an almost overly cheerful voice. Alli responded by glancing towards her mother as if she were looking at a whore, then turning around, without reaction, and returning to her room to get dressed. Alli hurried out the door, her backpack tossed over her shoulder, never bothering to make eye contact with Caroline or the unwelcome guest at the breakfast table.

"Alli, you need to eat someth..." the door slammed, as her mother's voice begged her attendance. Turning to Vladimir, with sadness and feeling like her soul had just escaped her, she remarked, "She never takes the bus... she always rides in with me."

Vladimir smiled empathetically, taking Caroline's hand: but, it seemed Georgie was content with their company and, for the moment, that was enough, as they shared the butter drenched, overcooked batter and syrup. They talked and it was there they decided to move forward with a few decisions.

"So have you decided or are you to keep me waiting?"

Caroline looked down at her plate and blushed, then smiled as she nodded to Vladimir and he reached for her hand, delighted.

"Then I am to have many plans to make. I have painters that come to house that are to take care of the guest rooms and I pick beautiful place to take you. Is lovely bed and breakfast on Nye Beach and with comes highest recommendation of close friend. A quaint place, with no disturbance and pretty room with fireplace that is to look over the ocean from deck. Pretty place, owned by family, and is to have lovely garden. I think you are to like very much."

"It sounds perfect, Vladimir." She smiled.

Muriel picked up Georgie, for their morning routine and Caroline told Muriel their good news. Forgetting her responsibility to baby sit, Muriel hugged them both then trampled off to the back bedroom, arm in arm with Caroline, giggling like a couple of teenagers. Vladimir laughed as he watched Caroline walking back, then looking down he reached for Georgie; picking him up and tossing him gently in the air a couple of times, making him chuckle, they walked back to join the ladies. Within a couple of months, Muriel would find herself being asked to watch the children for an entire weekend.

They would spend the night at the Sylvia Hotel, on the Oregon Coast, enjoying the warmth of the fireplace in the Mark Twain Room, contemplating the morning. At dawn's first light, they woke up in each other's arms, neither appearing to have stirred from the position they had fallen asleep in. Their eyes met, just as the light was beginning to softly float into the room, and Vladimir gently rolled over her and they enjoyed the same activities they had experienced the night before.

Three times.

The two would enjoy breakfast among strangers, mesmerized by the view and the magnificence of the sunrise as it poured in through the windows. At eleven thirty in the morning, with both hands of the clock rising, they walked down to the coast to meet a local minister; Caroline carrying a bouquet laced with ivy.

It was everything she had ever wanted.

It was simple, and pure.

There was no need for official witnesses, or pomp and circumstance; but the owners of the B&B attended, and watched the solidification of a love like no other they had seen pass through their doors

It was impossible to be in their presence and not feel the love they shared.

And now, she was his.

Completely.

Vladimir would bring her back to the room she had slept in as a widow, only the night before, and in the glow of the fire, with the doors to their deck that overlooked the coast flung open, he would look into her eyes, and slowly begin to undress her. With each button he slid free from its rope, her passion grew, and she could not take her eyes from his.

After undoing the final fastener, he pushed her gown down, revealing him to her in a way no man had ever seen her, truly, before...

She was wet with desire the moment his lips grazed her neck and they fell to the bed, becoming one. His touch was gentle, and there was no part of her that his hands could not wander without question. Her hips, rising off the bed to softly greet him, every time he moved to enter.

And she discovered the earthly form of heaven in his arms.

They returned home, a few days later, as one, united against what the world may present, her last name changed to his.

Immediately, Alli felt deceived when she saw them walk through the door. True, her mother had lied and said they were going away only to take care of some business. At the time, Caroline just didn't want to be bothered with the fight. Alli focused on the unfamiliar ring on her mother's finger as Vladimir stroked Caroline's shoulders, almost hugging her from behind. Then, Caroline braced herself for the reaction, as she passed a new ID card to Alli. Alli scowled at the words she read. "My last name is *Anderson*." She said firmly to her mother, holding the ID Card the Command required even children to carry; glaring with abhorrence at the man that would take her father's place.

"It is easier this way. There will be fewer questions." Her mother said, decided.

"NO!" she threw the ID, claiming her new identity as Alexis Stahl, at her mother.

But, Alli would not win.

Soon after they would move into Vladimir's larger home in the city. It was nice and he had truly made every effort to make space for them. He had even gone to the trouble of painting Alli's room her favorite shade of lavender, in an attempt to make peace, and he ensured that the room assigned to Georgie was adorned with baseball memorabilia: his favorite sport. And, in Caroline's mind, it was a perfect world, despite Alli's difficulties and silence.

But, Alli was finding it increasingly difficult to stay silent. As much as she wanted to hate Vladimir, she couldn't. The man did nothing but make her mother happy and, on some level, Alli was growing old enough to appreciate that. She still missed her father desperately, but could not help but to admit to herself that her mother, and even Georgie, seemed happy here. Both the breakfast and dinner tables were filled with laughter and conversation, and her mother smiled more than Alli had ever remembered.

Alli had tried being obstinate and unmanageable, but she only tired herself. She found that her mother had more patience than ever and Alli could not handle the kindness that Caroline tried to show her when she acted up. Even Vladimir was nice to her, giving her, materially, everything she wanted or needed.

Even still, she anxiously awaited the years to pass, allowing her escape, and focused on relationships with her friends from school. She passed hours sharing rumors with her best friends, Toni and Renee, and tried to spend as much time as possible at their homes and away from her own. When she did find herself, in her perfectly organized lavender room, she would stare at the ceiling wondering how it was that her father was not even mentioned in her presence anymore. Laughter from downstairs would reach its way to her ears and she would seal it off by closing the door and drowning out the happiness of the household with angry music. She would cry for George as she looked at his pictures, unable to remember the tension or anger that always lingered between her parents, and suspicious that Vladimir had stolen her mother long before they ran off to the Oregon shore together.

But, then she watched them interact. How Vladimir helped her mother clear the table and do the dishes, after each meal. Not because her mother needed the help, but simply because they were lost in conversation and wanted to spend more time together. She saw how he kissed her, how she looked at him. Her smile, her laugh and how light she seemed in his presence. No matter how hard she tried Alli couldn't help but wish that one day she would find that kind of love.

The kind of love little girls should believe still exists in the world.

"So, Alli. Your mother tells me of good grade you make on math test? Perhaps we should go shopping and by present for such good work?" Vladimir tried to engage his new tenant, but Alli was not interested and remained focused on playing with her food as she quietly responded.

"I always make good grades. I don't need anything from *you*."

Trying to get her to cooperate, Caroline made her own attempt. "But, Alli, that was a really hard quiz and you had one of the best scores in the whole school! Vladimir just wants to do something nice for you. *Isn't that nice?* You should say thank you." Caroline look to Vladimir, hoping that he noticed her own efforts.

Alli looked to her mother and with almost no emotion and dryness in her voice, and responded. "May I be excused?" Her mother nodded, disappointed that her daughter was so determined to segregate herself from the group.

Although, she could not deny that the people she cohabitated with were content with their blissful lives, Alli, at her young age, still began to focus on building a life of her own, away from this miserable room. Slowly, she grew to hate the color lavender, and dreamt of the day when she would find her own perfect love, run away and never turn back to this place. She would venture out, but not repeat her mother's mistakes by giving birth to little burdens she would later regret or feel anchored by. Alli's mind was always tormented by worries that children shouldn't know.

But, she would share these troubles with no one.

One Saturday afternoon, her feet brought her running down the stairs towards the ringing of the phone. Alli quickly grabbed for it, hoping it was Renee, calling to confirm some juicy gossip about another girl from school. If only she could confirm that Becky Bagley had gone to third base with a middle school boy, surely she could brand her reputation with a scarlet "A" through high school. She had been waiting for hours to get the full scoop. But, the voice on the other end was not her friend.

"Yes, may I speak with Commander Stahl?" The stern man, with a thick accent, requested and Alli seemed confused for a moment.

"I think you have the wrong number?" she responded, as her mother and Vladimir approached. "There is no Commander Stahl, here? Um…There's a *Coach* Stahl? Is that who you want?" Alli, still perplexed, told the cold voice frustrated that now she would have to wait for her archenemy to finish his conversation before she would get the dirt on her schoolmate. Vladimir demanded the phone from her and broke into angry Russian with the person on the other side.

Alli and her mother exchanged glances as they awaited the end of Vladimir's short conversation. When it was over, Caroline's mind was churning with the idea that he was holding a secret from her. They were married. Surly he wouldn't hide anything from her, now.

"*Commander* Stahl?"

Vladimir was forced to confront a moment he had never hoped to face, and simply nodded.

"You're in the Command? You never told me that? You're a Commander?"

Alli waited with anticipation as she watched her nemesis falling, quietly hoping whatever he would reveal would remove him from her life. But, he only stared at Caroline searching for words.

Even his native tongue would not have served him.

He was completely at a loss.

With his gentlest expression, he took her hands in his and begged her to understand, but he could see only confusion and pain. Vladimir knew he had to act quickly to calm her apprehensions, hoping she would never make the connection between how they ended up together and his great deception. Quickly glancing over, he worried that if Caroline didn't figure it out, Alli would. His English faltered, more than usual, as he tried to explain. "I am to be at charge of youth. I to make do their training. You not realize to boys school is only short time? Physical Education for Command? Boys all to serve older. Is requirement that boys are to serve for Junior Heroes Squadron. Is what the Command orders." Vladimir seemed frustrated by his own inability to communicate as his thoughts bounced back and forth from English to Russian.

Fearfully, Caroline looked quickly to Georgie, and immediately saw George's eyes in his. She thought about what it would feel like to lose her child and a chill ran up her spine. Spotting the weakness, and seeing an opportunity Vladimir begged an offer. "Georgie no Command. I arrange. Georgie never Command. I call my father."

"Who *was that* on the phone?" Vladimir could not answer, and she pressed, angrily. "Who *was that?*"

Pushing his hair back from his forehead as beads of sweat began to surface, he knew he would have to admit the truth. So he thought for a moment, before responding… "Father. He want from me, update."

Vladimir had never mentioned his father before, she couldn't imagine that Vladimir had kept this from her. Then her mind felt suddenly troubled as her intuition suddenly flared into action, "Who *is* your father, Vladimir?" she questioned begging herself to be wrong.

Alli looked on with equal curiosity, her arms crossed and smirking.

After a moment of silence, he answered. "He is head of Northwest Command. In Cheyenne."

Caroline needed only a minute to digest the implications, as the math slowly calculated in her mind. Alli didn't need so much time, and she ran back to her room, realizing the wickedness before her and she suddenly wanted to get away. Seeing Alli's reaction, and finishing the equation, she realized why George, of all the men they could have drafted from Portland, had met his fate on the banks of the Mississippi. She felt ill to her stomach, numbness running over her, as she stared at the man she once loved.

She had willingly chained herself to him by allowing him to place a golden band on her finger. In that moment, when he slipped it on, she could not have imagined wanting anything more, or feeling more completed, but she had no idea at what cost it had come. She had no idea that George had paid for the ring with his own blood.

Vladimir looked to her, seeking understanding in her eyes, believing he, himself, had done nothing wrong. He had only loved her.

But, the look in her eyes was changed forever.

The pieces of her heart that only he had held. The parts of her she had willingly passed over were now shattered to dust. Caroline would never again be able to return the love he felt for her, nor would she ever trust him again. She was as broken as George's spirit had been on his last day here on earth. In that moment, George was all Caroline could think about. She saw his face, in her mind, laughing, and his smile. She heard his voice calling her name and images of happy times randomly played. Vladimir's eyes begged her, knowing she now knew his great deception. Looking into her, he knew she now saw him as nothing less than a murderer.

He had raped her spirit.

With that realization, he knew things between them would never be the same. He watched as the stony towers reconstructed themselves in her eyes, as she climbed back behind her walls, closing the gates to him, and everyone else, forever. He ached, knowing how he had broken the most beautiful spirit he'd ever known and knowing that the love he had so desperately desired to have in his life was now as gone as if Caroline had died in that moment. He reached out to her, taking her left hand and cupping it in both of his, as if he was trying to hold her, as she slipped further and further away. The warmth, even in the feeling of holding her hand, had disappeared.

Caroline then turned to him, looking at him, as she would any other man in the world. Now firmly planted behind the walls, she acknowledged he would still be able to confine her and contain her to her obligation. She was saddled: unable to leave. He would keep her here, in his gilded cage, imprisoned. Her only power: her refusal to sing. She had no reason. She had given up on hope.

What was worse, it was not just Caroline's hopes that were ruined. Thinking of Alli, she remembered being a girl of the same age, and reflected on why she, herself, had learned to fear love and close off the world. Caroline knew her daughter would now be walking that same dark and lonely path. The little girl, for which she had changed her own life eternal, would never look at her the same. She had let go of the plans she had made for her own life to give one to Alli… and it was all for not.

Alli hated her.

And, for this, Caroline would always hate Vladimir.

Wormwood

Pacing nervously, Hector Gonzales tried to coordinate his plans for regaining control of the Northwest Territory, in the face of demands from the international community who sought to know exact accounts of America's weapons. Swirls of smoke from Cuban cigars filled the air in the Oval Office as Gonzales and his staff attempted to address the growing problems in the North and Northwest. Most of the United States' once vast military powers were now safely guarded within the Northwest Territory, and the nuclear capabilities they possessed were intimidating to Gonzales, although he had comforted himself with his own hopeful conclusion that they would never use such abilities on what the Northwest Territory still considered to be their own soil.

Rumors that Elijah Drew's group was being supplied with weapons from the Middle East were, at the moment, the most pressing concern; and with much of the technology, that otherwise would have been inherited by Gonzales, now disabled by hackers from the Northwest, he found his military powers were almost nil.

The Vatican worked hard on Gonzales' behalf to try to not only save their control of the United States, but also his image in the international arena. In the midst of international concerns, the Dollar's value against the Euro had reached a record low of only nineteen cents and the Vatican saw its dreams of a second Holy Roman Empire slowly slipping away as the Pope returned home to his City to pray for America's salvation. Meanwhile tempers flared amongst staff members that had been promised prestigious positions and unimaginable wealth.

Gonzales, knowing he would be unable to defend the land anyway, willingly gave back portions of the United States to Mexico that had been lost in the Mexican-American war. Those parts of California, Arizona, New Mexico, and Texas that the Northwest

Territory hadn't already guarded were now parts of the United Mexican States. Latinos

cheered throughout the Americas, and Mexico suddenly found other nations looking upon

them with green eyes. Ulysses S. Grant, who had in his memoirs recounted the injustices

associated with the United States' original acquisition of the once Mexican land, would

have approved of the gesture, if not the motives behind it. In truth, Mexico regained her

land for the same reasons she had lost it. No one was in a position to defend or manage it

any longer.

For Gonzales, it was more about propaganda, though. In his efforts to appear as a

great peace maker on the international stage, and ease international tensions regarding the

turmoil in the Northwest he used the 'The Great Balance', as it would be called, as one of

his first very first tactics designed to craft his image. The Vatican helped to promote him,

as the Pope himself, touted Gonzales' actions as proof that the new America would no

longer attempt to police other nations, but instead, under Gonzales, a New World Order

would be restored.

Talk of bloodshed on the Mississippi, and of bodies floating down the great

muddy divide were dismissed as gossip and lies, when addressed by other nations, and

Gonzales would next move to speak to the world promising that America was ready to

disarm. He hoped the promise of disarming all of America's weapons of mass

destruction would ease world fears and buy him some time. His first act would be to

announce the disbandment of USPACOM, and declare all military bases in Hawaii and in

the Pacific closed. Signing overly favorable trade agreements with China, he argued that as long as China was willing to keep the Koreans in check, there was no need for the US to maintain such considerable forces so close to friendly nations.

And many nations applauded, forgetting, momentarily, the real risks though some understood the real strategies behind the smokescreen.

Behind closed doors, leaders from China, Russia and several South American nations chuckled at Gonzales' naivety as they watched him parade himself around like a nervous poodle. Their own satellites had confirmed much of the activities he denied to less technologically equipped countries, and they had no reason to contradict him.

They just waited.

Seeing opportunity, Hawaii declared themselves an independent nation within weeks; never having forgiven the United States for what many native Hawaiians had viewed as a prolonged military occupation following the US role in the 1893 overthrow of Queen Lili'uokalani. Almost immediately, Hawaii passed some of the world's strictest environmental laws and restored Native Peoples to their governing bodies. All property, regardless of current ownership, or investment, was returned to the Republic and special taxes were imposed upon those that were not, not only Hawaiian, but not deemed to have "pure" Native Hawaiian heritage. Her ecological efforts would later earn Hawaii the nickname, the "Emerald of the Pacific".

While the world was focusing its attentions on other issues, Gonzales turned to the land of his forefathers for assistance. It had been Gonzales' hope that his previous maneuver would encourage the Mexican military to help defend against the Northwest, and they willingly offered assistance.

Excited to defend their newfound borders, Mexican Soldiers flooded north to assist, only to find themselves out-armed. And with whispers of Elijah Drew's alliance with the Middle East, they simply retreated most of their forces explaining to Gonzales that they did not have enough forces to defend that far north while still maintaining, and managing the new found resources within their new borders.

In truth, Mexico didn't really have to defend their borders and they knew it. America was all but a memory and The Northwest Territory was more interested in keeping people out than they were in trying to cross over, so it was a mutually agreeable situation for both parties. Still, in an effort to stay in the good graces of Gonzales, a light showing of Mexican soldiers would take full day siestas on the borders while the Junior Heroes Squadron heavily guarded the Territory and helped to maintain full control of the Mississippi River's traffic. In the few places where there were no natural divides, peddlers earned a living selling meals to both the Mexican Military and the Northwest Command: both groups content to sit and dine together as long as they each returned to their own side of the border by sundown. Not long after The Great Balance most Hispanics began their journey home attracted by the rapidly growing Mexican economy.

Then came tragedy unforeseen.

On the outskirts of Mexico City lies Popocatyl, known to locals as PoPo: a huge and ominous structure that the city had dealt with for years. The volcano was active, and the residents of the world's largest city knew that, but they had developed either a level of comfort or a lack of respect for its presence.

Since Mexico's new found economy was booming, Mexico City had been a thriving metropolis and it was growing by over 500,000 residents approximately every three months, as suburbs continued to spread around Mexico's Capitol. The problem being, that the same two antiquated highways which crossed the city were her only viable points of entry or escape.

When Popo blew unexpectedly and with ferocious might, in the middle of the night, the aftershocks were felt as far away as Texas.

It was estimated that approximately 6,000,000 people were wiped out in one singular natural disaster. Over 250,000 more would die in rescue attempts. The world mourned with the country so seemingly afflicted with such highs and lows. Some Mexicans took it as a sign from God. What was left of the Mexican military abandoned their posts in the vain hopes of finding survivors.

The Command's southern borders were left completely unchecked.

From Florida, a cry was heard from the Seminoles. They still remained the only Indian nation that never signed a peace treaty with the United States and they were proud of their oppositions. They called Indians from all parts of the United States to join them there to reestablish peace and Indian ways amongst themselves, as they prayed to the skies and elders and worried about the fate of their fellow Natives, still trapped in the Northwest Command's iron web.

The dam was bursting.

No matter where he looked Gonzales could not help but see the troubles building in this nation he had once so desperately desired to control, yet, even more, he desperately sought to hide his dirty little secrets from the world. All the while, the Northwest seemed to be gaining more and more control. They had struck a deal with

Canada to gain access to oil from the Alaskan pipeline, they had food, they had military power and they people to work.

And now, they were strong-arming control of the Mississippi.

His dreams were nothing like the new realities that existed before him and he needed to find a way to fulfill his promises not only to the Vatican, but to the drug cartels that had supported him for so long. He had to strike a deal somewhere. He just hadn't decided how. To tell the world the truth, would reveal his incompetence and that was unacceptable. But, the thought of his fate, should the Cartels deem him a failure, was an even worse horror.

"*Mira afuera!* You *don't* see a *problem?!*" Gonzales demanded of his incompetent staff as he gestured violently towards the window. "*Mira!* See them?! *THAT* is a problem!" Gonzales pointed angrily to the thousands of blacks that had taken over Washington, D.C. at Drew's request, shouting their demands for food and other basic provisions.

Gonzales rushed over to the window, as his men kept their seats, and anxiously looked over the dark crowd that was flooding his new neighborhood, certain he was their target and that the day was nearing when they would burst in and kill him. Picket signs held high and their screams echoing into his ears, he watched them, fearful of what they may do next.

"And, just what do you expect us to do, Hector?" His brother-in-law / Secretary of Defense, asked dryly as if he was putting off the expectation that he needed to get to work.

"Manuel! *You're the Secretary of Defense!* I expect you to get these goddamned niggers *off* my front lawn!" Gonzales screamed as he half crouched and gestured emphatically.

"Cuiiiiidaaaaadooooo…" Manuel almost sung the warning.

Fed up with his insubordination, Gonzales rushed to his relative and grabbed his shirt so hard it almost pulled him out of his seat. "Don't you fucking tell *me* to be careful! I am the fucking President of this fucking country and you will do what I fucking tell you to do! *NOW*! GET THESE GODDAMNED NIGGERS OFF MY FRONT LAWN!"

Gonzales released him, suddenly realizing the display and the lack of control he had shown in front of the group. Unconcerned and chuckling at Hector's lack of self control, Manual turned to them as he brushed his shirt back down. "I can see the headlines right now, 'President of the United States Demands Secretary of Defense Remove 'Niggers' From D.C.'" The men responded by laughing, but Gonzales was not amused as his mind fought to not go completely postal.

"You think this is a joke? *Chistes, no?* I've got thirty damn countries calling me on a daily basis wanting an account of our nuclear weapons and something called VX?! *What the fuck is that?!* Sarin gas, old CDC records?! And, where are *you?!* Where are ANY of you?!" Gonzales gestured wildly to his staff, his voice almost panicked, as he approached the point of insanity.

The joking continued as the men simply mocked Gonzales in response, which only served to cause a man on the edge to dive over. Hysterically, he ranted about the people outside, knowing the men in front of him were no more loyal than the group which he complained so emphatically about. He was certain that if Elijah Drew's group didn't get him, his own men would. He felt marked for death, but had reached the point of not caring.

For hours, late into the night, he argued with the group over how to go about rebuilding their powers, but they were more interested in getting drunk and most of them simply tuned him out. A room mixed with arrogance and ignorance spouted off self serving suggestions that couldn't possibly help the group as a whole. It was after one in the morning when Gonzales finally adjourned the meeting in total frustration, kicking everyone out and screaming like a maniac in a mix of language that could not be fully understood in Spanish or English.

Gonzales was slouched over his desk facing out the window, when his wife found her way to the door with a cup of coffee in hand.

"Que te preoccupes, mí amor?" Ana softly asked him.

He smiled at her gently and took the cup from her hand, "What's bothering me? What's *not* bothering me would be a better question, cariña."

"I can only imagine what troubles the mind of the President of the United States.", she said still beaming with pride and pretending to know less than she really did about his current problems, and he knew she was pacifying him.

"Ay, no se. The Cartels will have my head if Papa or Drew's men don't have it first. I'm a failure, Ana." He wanted his head to hang, but she would not allow it as she lifted his chin.

"*Digáme.* Tell me all of these troubles that worry my husband at this hour?"

Contrary to his cultural upbringing, Gonzales actually respected his wife's opinions, and being left with no one but God to talk to, he opened up to her despite the fact he knew he was placing some burdens on her shoulders as well. She listened patiently through the wee hours of the morning, not once interrupting, for fear it might silence him. When she was certain he was through, and thoroughly tired, she gave him a simple response.

"Go to the North. You can unite them with us."

He paused, reflecting for a moment on what he had heard about Elijah Drew's agenda, and not quite understanding why she would make such a suggestion. "How? They have their own agenda now." He thrust his chin in the direction of the window through which Elijah's growing forces could be seen.

"They still need food. There isn't enough agriculture there to support them for very long. And, what is there, they don't know how to farm. We can supply them food, they will supply us with weapons. We'll have an instant army. The south is ripe with agriculture. And, with the Mississippi gone, we can move goods by rail to them."

Gonzales chuckled, "You think that Elijah Drew is going to supply us with weapons in exchange for some apples and chickens, so that we can turn right around and fight them? I don't think so." He shook off the idea almost instantly, but she persisted.

It was true. With the Northwest Command controlling the flow of traffic on the Mississippi they had choked the northeast of many staple goods that would have normally flowed freely up and down her brown waters. Canada was no longer a resource, and much of the Northeast was beginning to feel the pangs of hunger as time wore on. Stories of food riots in major cities had already worked their way to his desk.

"You wouldn't be fighting *Drew*." she said firmly.

Gonzales looked confused for a moment, then suddenly grasping his wife's inference he began shaking his head with an expression that would have almost implied he thought she was crazy.

"Now, I *know* we have been up too late! If you think we can take on the Northwest, you must be dreaming. Besides, Drew is never going to side with us. They don't like us. Elijah Drew sees me as an enemy."

"They *don't have* to like us.", she paused for a moment, and looked deep into his cocoa brown eyes before making her most critical argument. "You don't unite nations because they *like* one another. Wars are not sided based on friendship. *They're sided by who you don't like*. You have already won this battle. Nations are bound together through common enemies, more than they *ever* would be through love for one another."

He held the title.

But, *she* was the politician.

Gonzales stayed up until daylight discussing plans with his wife. When they were through, he called an emergency meeting of his staff and explained to them *his* brilliant plan. He would tell them that God, himself, had spoken to him in the middle of a dream, that passed in the night. He called it a vision, making no mention, naturally, of his wife's input.

It was brilliant in its simplicity.

And his staff believed him.

They envisioned a return to power led by someone who had shaken hands with the Pope.

At the end of the meeting everyone left impressed with his brilliant scheme. A communication was sent to Elijah Drew's people requesting a meeting which would take place in Washington, D.C. Gonzales knew that Drew would not easily travel out of his safe haven, so a fabricated sense of urgency had to be created. The message said that intelligence agents working on the borders had discovered that the Northwest Territory was planning a nuclear attack on the North amidst rumors coming from Canadian forces that the North was building up their weapons arsenal. It offered assistance from Washington and any military aid that Mexico could provide.

Gonzales' lied and told them that Columbian and Nicaraguan forces were on board with the plan, as well, as he exaggerated his connections south of Mexico's borders. He then further claimed that Cubans in southern Florida had already begun heading north, promising to fight the Command on their southern front, as he alleged a strong alliance with the Cuban people, knowing Drew would be unable to confirm.

Drew accepted the offer to travel to D.C., under the condition that his bodyguards come with him, and remain armed at all times.

Mexico didn't know their services had been volunteered.

Although he did not know it at the time, Gonzales would go down in history as the last President of these United States. After only three and one half years in office, he would fade from existence, unaccounted for, from then on. However, for the moment, his role would change the world as it would be known from then on.

Sitting across the table from Elijah Drew, Gonzales felt as if he was facing Satan, himself, yet he could not release himself from the sensation that they shared a familiar bond. With two daunting dark and heavily armed figures at his back, and four more positioned around the room, Drew was almost arrogant in his approach to the man that would have, not so long ago, have been considered to hold the post of the most politically powerful man on the earth. But, as Elijah Drew watched his opponent apprehensively tapping his pen on the tablet before him, he knew he was in the power chair, despite seating arrangements.

"So, *you* have come to *me*, Gonzales. Seeking *what*, I can only wonder? So, tell me, *what exactly* do you want?" Drew opened with a slow, powerful and resounding tone, that practically bordered on sarcastic glee.

Gonzales thought for a moment, glancing around the room for guidance from those that had already sworn allegiance to him, but that even Gonzales knew they were for sale. Finding no immediate support, he ventured on his own, "We are seeking an alliance. The rest of the world cannot see the full extent of our problems, but the Northwest Command has become an issue to be dealt with, for both of us, and we are hoping you will join us in our fight against them."

Gonzales glanced up at each of the monumental men that guarded his adversary's shoulders, then, with an almost arrogant confidence, Drew began to examine his nails. With a soft laugh he countered, "*You* seek an alliance? With *me*? *You* think the world does not *see* your problems? They *do*. You are more naïve than I thought, Gonzales! The world *sees what I see and what I tell them*.... *Yes*... *I tell them*! The international media would just rather focus on your so called "humanitarian efforts" than admit the fact that you cannot account for your own military's weapons. Isn't *that* closer to the truth?" His eyes then met Gonzales with fierce expression.

Gonzales hesitated for a moment, then, in an attempt to save face in front of his men, countered. "That is *not* the truth! We are *fully* accounted for!"

With that Elijah Drew rose from his seat. "If you are going to lie to me, we are done here. I *know* the truth, Gonzales. The Command knocked out your ability to see what they were doing months ago. *Are you really stupid enough to believe that our own intelligence didn't figure that out just hours after it happened? We're done* here."

Gonzales and his staff began to watch as Elijah Drew and his bodyguards made their way to the door, when suddenly, Gonzales exclaimed, "*What do you want?!*" Gonzales' tone softened to a plea, and he repeated, "Please… Elijah… Tell me what you want?"

The words he had wanted to hear, ringing in his ears, Elijah Drew slowly returned to his seat. "*First*, you *will* call me *Mister* Drew. We are *not* friends. What do *I* want? It is not about what *I* want." Drew hesitated for a moment, thinking. "But, *I* can help you."

Gonzales nodded and Drew continued.

"*You're screwed, you know.* The Northwest is completely self sufficient. They have weapons, food, loyalty, power. Their people think they have money, although it has no value outside their own borders. They have oil. They feel safe. You need to disrupt that to win."

Gonzales listened, and enthusiastically nodded, along with his staff.

"*The infidels must be taken out*! *But how?*" Drew questioned the room as he slammed his large fist on the cherry wood conference table.

The room responded only with questioning expressions.

"Take out the pipeline." Drew answered for them.

It was so simple.

With the supply of oil gone, the Northwest would not be able to sustain, already having drained much of their resources prior to their arrangement with Canada. Their currency was no more valuable, outside the Territory, than Monopoly money. It would be like slicing their femoral artery with a scalpel.

Clean and quick.

A fast bleed.

Pondering the idea for a moment, and recognizing the Canadian alliance that was already in place, Gonzales questioned. "I see. But I don't see *how*?"

Drew smiled, with an almost wicked glint in his eye. "Leave that to me. Give me the resources and all I will tell you is that, when the day is done, the Northwest will be left feeling like the sun is rising in the west. My people will take care of it."

Gonzales consented and the men shook hands as Drew and his entourage made their way to the door. As he left, he cleared the lawn of the voices that had been keeping Gonzales awake at night and instructed his sheep to the west, to fight the Command's unjust and unlawful takeover of the Mississippi River. With a wave of his hand, they disappeared into the night.

For the first night in weeks, Gonzales found peaceful rest.

A few weeks later, New Jersey Harbor accepted a most important and delicate delivery from Pakistan. Consequences of her release, yet unforeseen, Elijah Drew greeted her arrival as if she was his young trophy bride in some arranged marriage. Anxious to see the full power behind the veil of this siren of destruction, they coordinated with Gonzales' team to set her assail, almost immediately.

In ceremony, they would name this beautiful beast "Wormwood."

And three days later, she sailed the heavens.

Her light lit up the night sky, falling on target and setting the pipeline ablaze in ways that no one could have imagined. As members of the Command, stationed on the Canadian border, sought to interpret what they were experiencing, Cheyenne called an emergency meeting.

They needed to retaliate.

But, they would realize their true enemy later.

It was not Gonzales, nor Drew, nor the country that provided this great weapon.

Their true enemy was close.

Very close.

When Iron Birds Fly

For nearly two weeks Edee, Alfonso, Jonathon and Will had kept a careful night watch of the roadway that stretched out in front of the dank underground pit that they, and the rest of the villagers, had called home. All of them taking careful position behind the bush that served to camouflage them from the hoards of thugs that were racing through the southeast on their mission of destruction. It seemed to all the men that each group that passed became more and more violent and out of control. Automatic weapons fired off into the night encouraging those down below to stay there, as their watchful guardians looked on at their enemy.

"They really are a bunch of sick bastards!" Jonathon whispered angrily as he watched the latest vehicle pass; trailing behind it the bodies of three people that were presumably alive when they were forcibly strapped to the bumper. The back seat passengers hung out of the windows, amused by the corpses bouncing off the roadway and screaming obscenities at them. Alfonso, his expression almost completely blank, nodded in agreement, but found it impossible to look away. "I've seen at least a hundred of them." He whispered and Edee took note of his face.

Edee placed his hand on Alfonso's back and tried to comfort him with science. "They didn't feel much, Alfonso. They would've been knocked out quickly. They didn't feel much."

Alfonso turned to Edee, cynically, as he ranted in an angry tone. "They would have *felt it* when their legs were strapped to the back of the car. They would have *felt it* when the car started moving and ripped the skin from their backs and their asses as they tried to hold their head up and get their legs free. They felt *fear*. They felt *trapped*. They knew they were about to die. So, don't tell me they didn't feel it, Edee! They felt enough pain to finally give up and let their head smack the pavement so they could stop feeling *anything* is more like it!" His voice was dry and filled with contempt. Alfonso was almost annoyed by Edee's pathetic attempt to pacify his mind.

Jonathon bowed his head and concentrated on the road. The vehicles were traveling through at a much slower pace, now than they were only a few days before and he wondered to himself how much longer they were destined to spend in their crowded pit. Suddenly, a new set of headlights approaching on the road caught the attention of the men.

The lights seemed to be moving southward at a much slower pace and were accompanied by an unmistakable and repeating *"thu-thump"*. The men all held their breath as the car came to a stop in a most unfortunate place and four young men exited the vehicle and began arguing over who would change the flat.

"I been drivin' you bitches since Kentucky an' I sure as shit ain't changin' no mutha fuckin' tire!" The driver exclaimed as he slammed the van door and Edee, Alfonso and Jonathon huddled together as tightly as possible. Through the leaves and the branches, only Edee now had a clear view of the enemy as he raised his index finger to his lips instructing the men to be quiet. Jonathon nodded, gently tapping the .45 on his hip then pointing to his ankle indicating he had a backup weapon. Edee gestured for Jonathon to hand him the second gun as he carefully watched the vehicle. Holding up four fingers, warning his comrades, he then positioned himself to take aim, if necessary.

"Stay quiet!" Edee mouthed the words to the others and they nodded, as Alfonso and Jonathon were secretly frustrated by their inability to see the road. Then, two of Drew's followers began to approach the bush.

"I gots to piss! That mutha fucka can change that tire his damn self! I been sayin' I need to piss fo' the last hour! *He* the one drivin'! *He* the one that done fucked up the tire! Let his bitch ass get dirty an' change it!" One said to the other as their voices grew clearer and they both continued to approach the bush. Alfonso's heart raced as he reached for his own piece of American craftsmanship.

Jonathon, an expert hunter and sharp shooter, slowly unlatched his holster and pointed towards himself, then held up two fingers and pointed towards the road signaling to Edee and Alfonso that he would take out the two men at the roadway. Edee and Alfonso nodded and Edee pointed to himself indicating he would take care of the man in front of him. He pointed to his eyes, then pointed through the bush at an angle, telling Alfonso where the fourth man stood as the two men approached, unaware of the presence on the other side.

When they heard the zippers of their pants coming down, the three stood up and attacked so quickly that the two men at the roadside never knew what hit them. The adrenaline raced through them as Alfonso continued to scan the bodies for signs of life and Jonathon, just in case, emptied the rest of his rounds in their skulls. Satisfied they were all dead, he felt over the corpses for weapons and found three guns on the two men that had come so close to discovering them, then dragged the bodies to the other side of the bush, so they could not be seen from the road. Jonathon and Edee moved to gather the other two and stacked them with the others after recovering a few more weapons from the van.

"I can't believe one human could do this to another. They're not human. These people are Goddamn animals." Jonathon said disgusted as he moved to untie the legs of one of the battered bodies that was trailing behind the van.

"Leave it!" Edee said firmly and Jonathon responded with a confused expression that questioned where Edee's humanity had gone.

"Leave it. We're not safe here, anymore. We need to get out of here. Traveling with the bodies behind us, if we run into any of Drew's thugs they'll just think we are one of their own. The windows are tinted, they won't be able to tell what we look like. We'll give them a proper burial when we get to safety." Edee affirmed as he looked sympathetically at the torn and battered people that hung from the bumper.

"Where's that? If this place ain't safe, where do we go? An' this van ain't gonna hold fifty people?" Jonathon could see the gears turning in Edee's mind, but was unable to see where her train of thought was going.

"I have a plan." Edee asserted.

Edee and Jonathon drug the bodies of the other two black men they had just executed for suffering the misfortune of a blown tire too close to their underground sanctuary back towards the bush then the three men approached to inspect the contents of the van. Inside, they found a few automatic weapons, two full five gallon gasoline containers, a little food, and a bag of weed. Alfonso immediately reached for the herb and smelled the contents. With a look of disappointment, he simply turned to Edee and said, "Schwag!"

Edee smiled, then returned to his planning. "I heard stories from a couple of the men in Opelika that used to come up here and trade with us, that the Seminoles gathered a bunch of the Indians in Northern Florida. Hopi, Cherokee, Navajo… you name it. If we can make it there, maybe we can find a way out. Drew's men would not have made it that far."

"How can you be so sure?" Alfonso had heard the rumors too, but couldn't understand how Edee could be certain that the Indians would be safe or how they could help them. More importantly, he wondered *why* they would help them.

"My great grandmother, Ahyoka, was Cherokee. She lived on the reservation in North Carolina on the Qualla Boundary. I never knew much about that part of my heritage, but I do know a couple things and I know how Indians fight. They chose Northern Florida for a reason: they can defend that position. They would have a way out, either to the Atlantic or the Gulf. It is strategically ideal. It makes sense. I'm sure that's why they are there." Edee was confident.

"You saw these bastards yourself, Edee? Nothing was going to stop them. Northern Florida will be just as bad off as we are, here." Jonathon didn't follow the logic, but Edee pressed on with his explanation.

"You have to trust me. Drew's men wanted control of the *Mississippi*. They have no reason to go that far south. We will have to stick to the back roads, they would have taken out all the main roads by now." Edee planned out the route in his mind.

"Drew's men would have?" Jonathon questioned.

"No, the Indians. To protect themselves. I promise you, I-95 is gone, so are I-75 and I-10 and any other major road that leads in to Florida. Drew's men may be violent and insane, but they are also weak and hungry. They aren't going to go to the effort to find an alternate route. They would just turn west. Besides, these southern roads are too hard to navigate if you don't know where you're going. If they tried, the Indians would have them trapped with no escape and just take them out. We have to stick to the back roads, but there will be ways in." Edee assured.

What Alfonso and Jonathon could not know at that moment was how accurate their friend was. The Seminoles had gathered and put out a call across the nation for all Native Americans to join them in Northern Florida. Strategically, it was a perfect location. They could defend the land to the north by blowing up the interstates, which they had done successfully at several points with explosives brought in through the Port of Miami. Still, there were well guarded access points that led into the Indian controlled land. Anyone that tried to approach was well known to the Indians far before they reached the checkpoints as carefully positioned scouts communicated the movements of any groups that attempted to enter.

To the south, the Cubans were no trouble and were eager for the business in the north. Cattle farming, a major industry in northern Florida, thrived and the Indians were able to sustain quite nicely off the beef and boating industries. Families that had reached Edee's same conclusion traded their remaining worldly goods for boats that allowed for escape from the ever growing violence in the country and in Florida there was no shortage of them. Unsure of their destinies, they took to the waters and wandered out into the sea, often in groups, finding safety in numbers.

"We don't have much time. We'll have to go soon. If the pace continues, more of Drew's men will be coming through in a couple of hours. We need to go." Edee spoke with determination.

"We can't just leave the others, here?" Alfonso emplored.

Edee scratched his head as he looked towards the van, then back to the cellar. "Go get Heather's family and a couple of other people. The van should hold eight or nine. Her kids won't take much space. We'll send for the others once we are certain it will be safe. They'll have to come on horseback, assuming the horses have survived and are strong enough to travel."

"I checked on them the other night. They are fine. A little restless, but fine." Alfonso confirmed, exchanging an odd glance with Jonathon as he continued, "But, Edee, most of these people won't be able to make it. They've never ridden. And, well, we can't exactly trot down the roadways like it's the freaking Macy's Thanksgiving Day Parade, we'll have to cut through the woods and the orchards. They'll never get through with Drew's men still out there. I can't go with you. I'll stay behind and help them." Alfonso looked out towards the road, unaware of where the enemy was, but certain that Drew's men were somewhere in the night.

"Me, too!" Jonathon asserted. "I know these parts like the back of my hand. Ain't no hill or valley or track of land I ain't been through at some point or another."

Edee looked to the two men he had grown to be friends with and half smiled at their courage and compassion for the rest of their companions below, knowing that goodbyes would soon be at hand. They quickly finalized their plans and went below to explain what was happening to the group. They found everyone had been awakened by the gunshots and were anxiously pacing and staring towards the large wooden doors that opened from the ground, revealing the pit they depended on for any sense of security. Several of the women crowded in a corner, protecting the children and unsure if it would be friends or enemies approaching as the huge wooden doors creaked open.

"It's alright! It's just us! No one is hurt!" Alfonso called down to the room as a collective sigh of relief echoed off the walls and the women released the children from their overly tight and shielding grasps. Edee gestured for Will and Heather to come to a corner of the room by looking in that direction, then slowly walking towards the wall, as Alfonso and Jonathon distracted the room by informing them of the plans. The three had decided not to tell the rest of the group about the van, and instead simply told the room that Drew's men had approached and come close to discovering them, so they had to kill them. They hoped their lie of omission would help to create a sense of urgency and avoid any fighting over who would travel in the van. As they spoke, Edee told Heather and Will the truth.

"But, if Alfonso and Jonathon are staying here, there's room for at least a couple more, right?" Heather whispered as she thought of her friend, Kim, and began to feel nervous about the journey.

"We can't take any more risks than we need to Heather. I can trust you and Will, but I don't know *them*. Besides, neither way is going to be easy or safe. I don't even know for certain if we will get through. If we run into Drew's men, we're dead. You have to understand that." Edee said tensely, not wanting more company than necessary.

"I know her! I can't leave Kim, she's my friend. *Please, Edee!* Please let them go, too!" Heather begged in her softest and quietest voice.

343

Edee looked over to Kim and her family and reluctantly nodded to Heather, a little frustrated by the notion. "Alright. But, don't say anything about the van or the guns! Alfonso has plenty for the rest of the group to take when they travel through with him and Jonathon. There is no time. We have to go now."

"Okay, okay!" Heather hurriedly waved for Kim and her family to come over

Kim walked over and Heather began to explain as the others in the room wondered about what kind of secret conversations were taking place in the corner of the room. Jonathon noticed the stares and decided to dump a pre-emptive strike on their curiosities.

"Edee and a few others have volunteered to be the first to go. It ain't gonna be easy and it ain't safe. If they make it through, they will be waiting for us on the eastern coast of Nothern Florida. Rest of us gonna follow starting tomorrow night. Gonna take that long to get packed up. Alfonso and I are fixin' to go saddle up the horses and get 'em ready. Ya'll need to pack up what you can carry. Food, mostly. We ain't got but twenty horses, so the young'ins gonna have to ride two or three to a horse. Some of us are gonna have to walk." The heavy set redneck fussed with his scarlet beard. Had anyone in the room played poker with him, they would have known he was lying and that gesture was his tell, but the confidence in his voice seemed to reassure the room. Besides, although Edee was respected, he was still misunderstood by most of the group and the majority felt more comfortable traveling with Alfonso and Jonathon as their escorts.

Edee and Alfonso grabbed a modest food supply from the stock and loaded it in the vehicle, as Jonathon kept everyone else below ground. Quickly, they all then said goodbye. Heather's eyes turned to Alfonso, welling up with tears, as she focused on the journeys they both had before them and she hugged him.

"I think I'm going to miss you most of all! If I never told you before, thanks for everything you did for us." She whispered in his ear as he embraced her.

"You'll be fine. Really. Edee knows what he's doing. We'll meet you there." He looked straight at her and nodded with a confidence and that set Heather's mind at rest.

"Let's go!" Edee called out, conscious of their time table and still frustrated by the idea of having additional travel companions.

Heather, Will, their two sons, Kim, little Alex and her husband all followed Edee up the old cellar steps that led to an outside world that most of them had not seen in weeks. As they approached the top, Edee warned them to not look to the right, fearing the children may be disturbed by the bodies piled by the bush. Heather's sons, Tony and Perry, were both too sleepy to glance over. Unsure of what they might see, Kim's husband pushed his daughter's head gently under his chin, making sure her eyes stayed focused away.

Stepping outside into the fresh air, Kim suddenly realized how dank and musty it had smelled below. For the first time in years, she truly appreciated the sweet smell of the country air and the peaceful hum of the cicadas. Kim tagged along after Heather, as Edee hurriedly led the way to the van listening hard for the sound of approaching vehicles and looking out for any sign of headlights. Alfonso and Jonathon had already changed the tire for them when they were loading up the food and the group was ready to set out. Suddenly, the moonlight began to bring into focus what was trailing behind them and Kim cowered back in horror, *"Oh, dear God! What is that!?"* She exclaimed as she began walking backwards, shielding her eyes as though the bodies were putting off some tremendous and unsightly light and she screamed at the top of her lungs.

Edee ran after her, grabbing the back of her neck, covering her mouth, and pushing her towards the van like she was a dog whose face she was about to rub in a pile of feces. Kim struggled against his grip, crying and begging for him to stop. "*That* is what will happen to you if you stay here! *Do you understand me?!* Get in the damn vehicle!" Edee shoved her to the floorboards, as Heather helped her up, shocked by Edee's actions. Heather was not used to this side of him. Kim cried uncontrollably, unable to get the images of death out of her mind and petrified by what trailed behind them, as Heather tried to comfort her by placing her arm around her and attempting to wipe away the tears that would not stop falling.

Edee wasted no time in starting the engine and looked to Heather in the rear view mirror, angrily. "I *told* you extra company was a bad idea! *Those bodies are our ticket out of here!* Drew's people will think we are one of their own! We only have a few hours before daybreak. *If we don't make it by then we are all as good as dead!*"

Their true situation was now apparent and tension filled the van and they all fell silent. As they pulled away, the bouncing of the carcasses behind them immediately disturbed everyone in the vehicle, but no one more than Kim. Less than fifty feet into the journey Kim, almost panicked, exclaimed, "Well, can't you put some music on or something! My God, are we going to have to listen to that awful sound all the way to Florida!?"

Will, equally disturbed but not willing to speak about it, fumbled around with the digital player hoping he could find some music to cover up the noise coming from the back, as Edee navigated, turning off of the main road at their first opportunity, and began their back road journey to Florida. Nothing stored on the player was much to anyone's liking, but the thumping of the bass served well to conceal the less pleasurable sounds that surrounded them. Still, every once in a while, one of the bodies would catch the road in a way that would send it aloft, casting its shadow through the rear window reminding everyone of their less fortunate travel companions. Driving as quickly as possible, without headlights, for fear of being seen from a distance, Edee pushed forward in silence, his full concentration on the road before them and lost in his own thoughts.

Kim watched the outside landscape, cradling Alex in her arms as she slept, and occasionally playing with her daughter's little mousey blonde curls to help relieve some of her own nervous energy. There had been no sign of destruction or burning for miles and after about thirty minutes of seemingly undamaged landscape, Kim softly questioned. "We are going to do the right thing and bury them, aren't we?"

No one spoke.

The other passengers waited for Edee to answer as he looked back through the mirror at them and took note of what Kim was observing, somewhat confident that they had reached a safer place. Not wanting to seem uncompassionate, he looked at their faces which implored that none of them were comfortable with the idea of doing any less, and he nodded, answering in stern and somber tone. "Let's get a little further out. If everything still looks safe, I'll stop in about twenty minutes."

In truth, the group still didn't know exactly where they were. Coming in on the back roads, through small town Alabama and Georgia, there were no large signs welcoming them to the Sunshine State. They had been across State lines for over forty minutes, though. Finally, comfortable they were safe, Edee pulled off the road. Still concerned about their security, he pulled behind a building that sat next to a large grassy area that he felt would be appropriate. The three men exited the vehicle, leaving the women and children inside.

As they walked behind the vehicle, the stench was overpowering. While the van had been in motion it had done well to keep them upwind from the odors, but now there was no escape. The unfortunate trio now lay on the ground, most of their clothing and flesh stripped away by the road. Kim's husband, Judd, bowed his head and looked away for a moment before reaching in his pocket for a knife and finally cutting the ropes free at the bumper. "How are we going to do this?" He questioned.

"I guess we just take them out there and bury them? Should we say a prayer or something? I mean, we don't even know their names?" Will answered.

"No... I mean... sure... we can say a prayer. But, *how* are we going to do this? We don't have a shovel and, honestly, I am not sure I want to carry them out there by hand?" Judd clarified as the thought of actually touching them made him want to cringe.

For a moment the three men looked around surveying the landscape for tools and trying to figure out exactly how they would manage the task at hand as the flies, attracted by death's perfume, began to find their way to the corpses. Ever the engineer, Edee asked Judd for his pocket knife, then bent down and popped off one of their hub caps. "The ground in Florida is pretty soft, we can dig with this. I say we use the ropes to drag them over there and we just do it." Edee pointed in the direction of the field as Will and Judd grabbed the ropes of the two larger men and began to drag what was left of their earthly shells towards what the group had determined would be their final resting place.

Softly, Will turned back to Edee, "That last one looks like he's just a kid. Can you handle it yourself or do you need help?"

"I got it." Edee's tone was melancholy as he looked down at the bloodied flesh before him. They were right. He couldn't have been more than ten and Edee wondered what this boy had done to deserve such a terribly frightening end to such a short life. As Edee grabbed the rope and began to drag the remains towards the field, Heather cracked open the van door. "Save the ropes and bring them back to me."

Perplexed, Edee questioned. "Why do you want the ropes?"

"We just do." Heather's eyes asked him not to question and Edee nodded, returning to fulfill her request just a few moments later.

Kim could not stand the sight of death. In reality, she couldn't even handle the concept. The thought of her own mortality sent her mind reeling to places she did not like for it to venture, so she worked hard to block out such thoughts any time they would try to slip into her conscious mind. With the images of their ill-fated passengers now burned in her mind though, she had to refocus herself and turned to ceremony. Heather had noticed how quiet her friend had been and wondered what was passing through her mind when she had requested that she ask Edee for the bloodied cords that had trailed behind them. Ropes in hand, Kim exited the van, careful to walk in the opposite direction of where the bodies had been taken. With the children all sleeping, Heather followed her friend to the edge of a patch of woods near where they had parked and watched her curious behavior.

"This one looks pretty good, don't you think?" The tall blonde sought Heather's approval, but Heather was unsure how to judge the three foot long branch that Kim was holding.

"I guess, if you think so?" Heather responded.

"I need to find another, about this thick, but not so long. Help me look." Kim's eyes squinted trying to see in the little bit of morning light they had as best as possible as she searched for the perfect companion to the piece of wood in her hand.

Heather obliged with the search, but as she looked over to Kim, finally her curiosity forced her to question. "Um, Kim, what are doing exactly?"

Surprised, Kim turned back to her as if it should be obvious. "We're making crosses. You can't bury someone and *not* mark the grave?"

Heather seemed confused. "Why not?" Then, handing over a small limb that seemed suitable, she asked. "Here, is this one good?"

"Perfect!" Kim checked Heather's limb against her own and decided they were a an ideal match for her project. "What do you mean, *'why not?'*, it's what you do. Now, we need to make two more. They don't have to all be the same size, but they need to look close." Kim searched the ground with determination, unable to understand why Heather was not equally anxious.

"Why? I don't see how it matters, Kim? *They* won't know the difference."

"*I* will. I want God to know where to find them, alright?" Kim said, almost irritated that Heather was not engaged.

"I am sure God has found them already, Kim. This won't make any diff…"

Kim cut her off, with tears falling from her face and the fragility of her mental state beginning to surface. "Listen, this is important to *me*. Between the Command and Elijah Drew I have lost my home, my friends, family members and most of my sanity, but they're not getting my sense of decency or my morality. *That's* mine." Kim dropped the two pieces of wood and pulled her hands to her face, sobbing into them, no longer able to hold back emotion.

Heather reached out for her and for a moment the two women held each other and cried, then Kim broke out into laughter, without warning, as women that have allowed themselves to become emotional, often do: uncertain of whether or not their tears are seen by those around them as justified, or simply some exaggerated response to a temporary hormonal imbalance. "You must think I'm an idiot. I'm sorry." Kim wiped her face, embarrassed by her own display.

Heather pacified her.

"Not at all. C'mon, we still need to find two more." Heather smiled shyly at Kim and the two women searched for the pieces of wood, in the shadows, as the men worked to bury the corpses that had served to camouflage them as members of Drew's following. About thirty minutes later, with the first beams of light truly beginning to glow, Edee approached and found the women carefully criss crossing the selected branches, using the blooded rope to secure the two pieces of wood together, forming what would be the first of the markers for the graves. Heather glanced over, noticing how carefully Kim was working, ensuring that the marker was as perfect as it could be. Heather then glanced up at Edee, furling her eyes with an expression that told Edee to say something nice, considering they hadn't gotten off exactly on the right foot, at the beginning of their trip.

Watching Kim, then rolling his eyes at Heather, Edee conceded and knelt down. "That's a nice touch. I'm sure they would have appreciated this."

Kim nodded, not taking her eyes from her project and Edee continued. "Just bring them over, when you're done. We'll all say a few words, but then we need to get back on the road."

Again, Kim nodded, as she was finishing up the final marker. Edee's eyes flashed to Heather's as if to sarcastically question "*Happy?*" and Heather responded with a quick nod in the affirmative and a smirking grin that disappeared in less than a second, before Kim had a chance to notice their nonverbal exchange. Edee walked back over and soon Heather and Kim followed. Will and Judd used the hub cap to hammer the makeshift headstones into the ground and the group then recited a short prayer for the nameless people below them, before filing back into the dust covered Ford.

Only forty minutes further into their travels they hit their first road block: literally. They slowed for the flashing lights and barricades and Edee quietly warned the group to let him do the talking. Will turned around to the rest of the group and commented. "I think this dude's the biggest fucker I've ever seen!" As he stared ahead at the man guarding the barricade.

Covering little Tony's ears, Heather chastised him. "Will! *Language?*"

Shrugging his shoulders and rolling his eyes at her, "Well, he *is!*" Will turned his attention to the large Native American that was approaching the vehicle. He must have stood over seven feet tall with thick, broad shoulders and chiseled features that made his face appear like it had been carved from a rich piece of mahogany. Edee rolled down the window and the imposing figure stuck his head in, inspecting the group and the van's contents. Heather waved, but he ignored the gesture, then turned his attentions to Edee. "What's your business, here?"

"I was told that all of the tribes are gathering here? Is that the case?" Edee questioned, trying to seem as confident as possible.

"And?" The large man questioned.

"Well, I'm Cherokee. Well, part Cherokee. My great grandmother was full blooded." The tall figure searched Edee's features for his heritage, then questioned. "And the rest of *them*?"

Determined that they had come this far and that she and her children were going to get through, Heather blurted out. "And I'm one sixteenth... Apache..." she threw out the first tribe that came to mind.

Suspicious, the Native looked at her firey strawberry blonde hair and freckles and asked, "Really?" Edee whipped around, telling Heather to shut up with his eyes, certain she was going to get them in trouble, but the Indian just brushed off her attempt and turned his attentions back to Edee. "You all with the Command? Defecting from the Command? What's your story?"

"No, no, no! We're all from just a little ways north. You've heard what happened up there, I am sure. We're not with the Command." Edee asserted.

"You're lucky. We were expecting more of you. Not that many made it out. I've maybe seen just a few thousand, but we've heard the stories." His hard features seemed to soften as a somber expression came over his face and he nodded towards the group.

"Well, there should be more of us coming through. Close to fifty more. They'll be on horseback and it will probably take them a few days." Edee tried to feel out whether or not the guard would let them pass through or not.

"None of them with the Command? Mind if I scan you?"

"No, no. We all lived together in a small town just up from Opelika. No one's with the Command. Scan us? Scan us for *what?*" Edee seemed confused.

"The Command started micro-chipping everyone in their borders about three weeks ago. At first, it was just their military, but now it's everybody. We just can't take the chance of letting anyone that has been in the Territory that long get in here."

Concerned that other friends or family members might be trapped inside the borders, Kim questioned. "So, if they were in the Territory you won't let them in? What happens to them? Don't you understand what its like up there?"

Shaking his head and reaching for the wand designed to detect the micro-chip implant that would have been placed by the Command, he began passing the detecting device over each of their foreheads and explained. "No, we just send them west towards the panhandle. They can get out through the Gulf of Mexico, or they can stay near the coast and enter into Mexico, if they like. We just won't let them go east. Too much of a risk, since the pipeline was nuked."

"What?" The car questioned in unison. Having been shut off from contact with the outside world for so long, word that the Alaskan Pipeline had been bombed had not made it to their ears, but the Guard was not surprised by their ignorance.

"Yep. Drew brought it in from the Middle East and cut off their oil. Should of cut off all of their damn nuts, far as I'm concerned. All the bastards should be shot. We expect all hell to break lose soon. That's why we need to be so careful. And, I am going to have to confiscate your weapons." He was nonchalant about the whole ordeal, not realizing how concerned he had just made the group. After he had made his way around to everyone and checked them for any signs of the chip, he then unloaded the firearms from the vehicle. Speaking into a radio pinned to his chest, he called ahead to the next post. "I've got eight; three men, two women, two young boys and a little girl. They're clean and heading in your direction. All are traveling in a white Ford van. Over." Turning his attention back to Edee, he then gave instructions on where to go next. "Just follow the road about a mile down. You'll pass through about ten of these posts, depending on how far into the State you are traveling, but I wouldn't recommend going any further than Orlando, unless you know what you're doing. If you really are part Cherokee, when you get to the third post, let that guy know, his name is Tate, he'll let you know where to go. But, hey, I'm warning you, his name means 'he who talks too much' and, believe me, it is fitting! If you aren't careful you'll be there all day!" Tapping his goodbye on the hood, he lifted the barricade, waving them through and allowing the van to pass. Normally, Edee would have chuckled at his remark, but his mind was lost in thought about the news they had just received. In his mind, Edee tried to strategize what the most logical next move for the Command might be as he took his own mental inventory of the weapons he knew they had access to within their borders.

None of the scenarios were comforting.

It would have seemed they should all have been happy, now having passed into a seemingly peaceful place that offered hope of escape, but there was an uneasy tension that encircled them. None of them knew where they were going, or what they were going to do when they got there. They didn't have much money to establish fifty people or any real plans, and now they were left to contemplate the idea that a nuclear weapon had landed on American soil. They couldn't be further away from Alaska, but secretly they all worried about where the next bomb would fall.

The group made it to the third checkpoint where, as promised, was a chatterbox named Tate. He detained them with his ramblings for almost half an hour, but eventually they were able to gather enough information from him that told them they would need to continue west onto the Port of Jacksonville if they were looking for a way out. He instructed them to find the Marriott Hotel there and told him about how they had combined and converted a couple of the ballrooms into message centers and encouraged them to check there first to find out where some of their friends or family may have ended up. But, in the same conversation he had also told them all about his girlfriend, his new baby girl, his lactose intolerance, his cousin's bad haircut and about fifteen other things that the group had simply tuned out.

Everyone in the group was relieved when they arrived in Jacksonville and found a City that seemed to be bustling with peace and some sense of order. There was plenty of signage directing those that would make this their final stop before a long journey over water to check in with the Marriott Hotel and leave a note on their Message Board, so the group made the hotel their first stop. In truth, they were all curious to see if any of their friends or family had left notes telling them where they had gone and why and, since they had not figured out where they would be heading to, there was no reason not to be open to a little advice. However, when they entered the ballroom, they were all a little stunned by what they saw. At the top of the high walls were large signs bearing the names of various islands and tons of locations south of US Borders. From floor to ceiling, the walls were covered with notes and photos and it seemed impossible that anyone could actually find any valid information in such a chaotic collection of postings.

Standing underneath the sign marked St. Croix, a well dressed older woman was scanning the notes, as the group entered in and fanned out, but when Kim noticed the woman reaching to remove one and shaking her head at the words she was reading, she made her way over near where she was standing, as she fussed with Alex to be quiet.

Dorothy.

She had gentle eyes that were complimented by a heavy gathering of wrinkles that surrounded them, though the years had not seemed to affect the rest of her, otherwise far younger looking, face. Her skin tone was supple for a woman in her eighties and she had the grace and posture of a woman of half her years. Curious about the piece of paper in her hand, Kim interrupted her thoughts as she shuffled Alex to her other hip. "Do you mean to tell me you actually found something in all this mess?"

Dorothy nodded, then quietly remarked in a southernly debutante voice. "Yes. But, it was not the news I was hoping for."

"Oh?" Kim questioned, sympathetically and then asked Alex to behave once more, as the child continued to get more and more fussy. Apologizing, she went on. "I'm sorry, she's normally not this bad, she's just been in the car too long and her schedule got all turned around, so she's being fussy. Why is it not what you were hoping for? You found your family, no?"

Smiling, Dorothy looked to the little girl with compassion, and to her mother with sympathy. "Well, some of them. My sons. I just wish they had not gone so far as St.

Lucia. It's not one of the more popular destinations for people heading out of here, for whatever reason. It's a pretty place, but it is a little hard to find others that are going that far down. Looks like I missed my youngest, David, by a couple of months. He says here that my oldest, Peter, has been down there for quite a while. Then he just mentions the whereabouts of a few others that we knew. I suppose I'll just have to wait it out." Dorothy pointed to some scribbled writing, then neatly folded the little scrap of paper and placed it in a handbag that she held close to her and adjusted her eyeglasses back into the little groove on her nose which had obviously been home to her corrective lenses for years. The small reddened indent on the bridge of her nose looked as though it might be painful, but she pushed them into the small home that her body had created for them and smiled with a hint a disappointment lingering in her expression.

Confused, as she looked up at the sign under which they were standing, Kim questioned. "But, the sign up there says St.Croix?"

Dorothy slowly nodded. "I know. I am sure David knew I would look here. We have friends on St. Croix. Well, I should say we that we used to years back. I know why they chose St. Lucia. Peter knows a man that owns a resort down there. It's just hard to get down there in most of the boats they have for sale, here. They're too small for the journey and the last thing you want is to be caught at the mercy of the sea with nowhere to refuel. Well, at least it is good to have some word from them. It's been hard for everyone, I would say." Dorothy almost resigned herself to the fact that this might be the last she would hear from her children, though, as any mother would, she found peace in the idea that they were safe.

As Kim shuffled Alex, yet again, it was obvious she was beginning to lose her patience as she chastised her daughter in a tone that revealed more annoyance than she would normally display in front of someone that she had just met. For a moment, Kim reflected on what Dorothy had just said as her apprehensions grew.

The boats they had *for sale?*

With no money or real resources she wondered how they would pay.

Had they come this far only to be trapped on the beach?

Kim knew nothing of the jewelry that Alfonso and Jonathon had stockpiled for the group, nor of Edee's stash of gems, but even if she had it would have offered little comfort when she thought of the others that would be arriving on their heels. Then, she suddenly remembered her fear of water and the fact she couldn't swim. Her children couldn't swim. Every imaginable complication flooded her mind to the point she felt almost paralyzed by her own fears, then Alex made the mistake of pulling on her mother's hair in an attempt to get her attention.

"Alex, enough!!!" Kim exclaimed, drawing the attention of a few other families around her. The outburst startled Dorothy a bit, but she quickly remembered those days and simply turned her own attentions to the child. "Are you hungry, sweetie? I might have some crackers in my purse?"

"No. I'm bored!" Alex said in her most pouting tone as Heather approached with her own brood, attracted by Kim's sudden flare up.

"Bored, eh? Well, we could go play a game outside if you like? Do you know how to play hopscotch?"

"No…" Alex whined.

"Would you let me teach you, then?" The one time educator appealed to the little girl. After almost thirty two years working as a teacher, she had mastered the tones of voice that would gain compliance from even the most difficult of children.

"Okay." Alex, still pouting, was quickly comforted by being the center of attention, but she still hid her face in her mother's shoulder as Dorothy reached over to stroke the back of her hair, gently pulling it away from her eyes.

The women made their way outside to a small garden with a sidewalk, at the side of the hotel. The courtyard showed evidence that it had once been proudly manicured, and even though it was overgrown, now, it was still quite pretty. Heather, Perry and Tony were now engaging in conversation with an elderly woman that carried herself with an inexpressible quality of grace. Dorothy held on to Alex's small hand, as they made their way to the sunny spot where Dorothy would draw mark out the children's new playing field. Reaching into her purse, she pulled out a small bottle of fruit flavored antacids and marked out the board, explaining the rules of hop-scotch. The children, having spent the past several weeks cooped up in a cellar, seemed anxious to burn off their stored up energy and, as usual, Alex immediately took control.

Smiling at the children as they enjoyed her pharmaceutical artwork, bouncing back and forth between the squares, Dorothy sat down next to the other two mothers, brushing her skirt and crossing her ankles as if she knew she was being judged by her old charm school matrons. Heather smiled watching the children play, happy to see the children enjoying themselves for the first time in what seemed like forever and Kim was simply happy to not have to carry Alex on her hip. The three watched the children for a moment, each lost in their separate set of thoughts, then Dorothy asked. "So, newcomers, are you?"

Heather nodded and Kim commented. "I still can't believe you found that note from your sons in that mess! There must have been a million pieces of paper in that room!" Kim recalled the walls, covered from ceiling to floorboard and could not imagine the luck of finding any real information amidst the messy handwritten scribbles.

"One point two million and counting, from what I have been told. Most of those papers represent entire families that have been separated. The staff has been really good about logging everything, though. All of the older notes have been transferred into a database that can be searched, but in the past few months they have gotten so many that it has become a little much for them to handle. A lot of the newcomers help, when they can. Entering in the information they find and then archiving the originals. They leave up most of the ones with photos a little longer. I suppose it is easier to recognize the pictures than the handwriting. Who did you all come here to meet?"

Heather turned to Kim and shrugged a little, then answered for them both. Hours of conversations between them had drawn out that neither of them really expected to find any more family that was either alive or not in the Northwest Territory. "No one really, I guess. We were Misfits. We just got here today." Heather said shyly not wanting to recant the details of their morning.

"Really?" Dorothy seemed surprised. "From what we had heard things had been pretty horrible for the past few weeks. The flow of cars really seemed slow down, here of late."

Heather did not seem surprised by her words. "So, where are your families heading?" Dorothy asked and Kim looked to Heather with and expression that told Dorothy that they had not come that far in their thought process or planning. Remembering some of the stories she had recently heard, she chose not to pry into their minds and instead simply offered some advice from her own experience in her short time in Jacksonville. "Well, there are a few things you need to know while you are here that might help you out. Like most, I would imagine that you have arrived with the clothes on your back and not much else and the hotel runs a clothing closet for free. A lot of clothes for children and old ladies, but not very much you would find fashionable. Still, the girls that work here are kind enough to wash everything so at least they are clean. There are two pawn shops in the area that will pay fair prices so you can put a few Euro in your pockets and get by. And, when I say fair prices, you'll get about half of what you think anything you have may be worth, but it's better than you will do in most places outside of the city."

Kim suddenly found herself subconsciously tugging at the half carat diamond studs that Judd had given to her on their first wedding anniversary. She almost never took them out and, until that moment, she had practically forgotten they were there. Still, she imagined at the rates that were being offered they would not provide for much more than a couple of nights in the hotel and she hated the idea of parting with them. Heather's thoughts were in a similar place as she tried to think of what items of value they would have between them to provide them with enough to survive until the others arrived, but even if they sold the van, she assumed, an old Ford would not provide for more than a few hundred Euro at best. How she wished they could have driven their Mercedes. Surely, that would have fetched a far higher price.

And, now they had to wait.

Heather knew about the jewelry from the bodies that Alfonso and Jonathon had unearthed to provide for everyone's survival, but she assumed he was traveling with the jewels. Now, more than ever, and for more selfish reasons, she prayed the rest of the group would get their safely and quickly. Coming on horseback, though, she knew it would take them quite a while: maybe a couple of weeks.

They didn't have enough to survive that long and she knew it.

Her mind then turned to the value of the weapons that had been confiscated at the border and the ones Alfonso would lose when he crossed. Those, alone, could have let the whole group eat for at least a week even if they did have to sleep on the beach. Everything between them now had a value. Anything they could scrimp together to make it until the others arrived.

But, what if the others didn't make it?

What then?

And how long did they need to wait?

Would it be respectable to just leave a note on the wall, like all the others before them and save themselves if an opportunity presented?

As the women were mentally debating their stay in Jacksonville, Edee, Will and Kim's husband, Jud, were off on a mission. In a city where they could trust no one, Edee taken it upon himself to find another honest man. He had carefully selected a single, beautifully cut, high quality emerald stone from his collection. What no one could see was that he was carrying close to two hundred stones, all of varying values and he had memorized each of them. The stones, carefully sewn into a variety of secret pockets that each of his outfits, all of his outfits, were outfitted with before he put them on for the first time. This particular stone, he knew for a fact, had an exact wholesale value of €3000. He would accept €1500 in this buyer's market.

The first dealer offered €450.

The second, €900.

After haggling for a few minutes with the third, they settled on a selling price of €1200 and even the buyer knew he had gotten a bargain. Satisfied with their sale, the men made their way back to the hotel and Edee plunked down €450 for two rooms with two double beds and one with a queen. Feeling somewhat guilty, even as he made the purchase, he turned back to Will and Jonathon and explained. "I'm near seventy years old and I've spent the last three years of it in hell, fellows. Damn it! Tonight, I'm gonna enjoy shuttin' out the world and havin', what I believe, is a much deserved bubble bath. Hell, ain't like I'm wastin' the money on make up and shoes!"

Will and Judd grinned, but still felt beholden to Edee's generosity. There was nothing they could say even if they wanted to, in the moment. Then, after paying for their rooms, unexpectedly, Edee handed them each €200. "Go out and get something to eat. We could all use a decent meal away from each other. Just don't go hog wild. This money needs to last us several days."

Looking down at the money, neither of them knew what to say, but Edee responded as if he had done no more than hand them a Kleen-ex. Not wanting, nor needing, to hear them say thank you, he swooped up his room key and paced off towards the elevator calling back. "We'll catch up at breakfast! It's from 6:30 to 9:00 in the lobby! I plan to sleep in, so I'll be down 'round 8:30!"

It was almost as if the elevator knew to open the moment he walked to the doors. And, with that, Edee made his exit.

After searching the lobby and the pool and the playground, Will and Jud had finally exhausted all of the typical haunts where they might expect to find their wives and their children. Growing nervous, they had described their families to a few staff members and finally were directed around the corner. Jud, who stood almost a full foot shorter than the blue eyed, one time model he had married, immediately exclaimed. "We were worried sick! What are you doing out here?"

Kim looked to the hopscotch board that was entertaining Alex and the other children, as though it should be obvious, and commented mordantly, "Uh, *hopscotch? Duh!?*"

After getting over his public emasculation, Jud told Kim the news about their room and Edee's kindness and their breakfast plans. Even Heather reveled in the idea of a bed, having been certain they would be all either be sleeping in the van or on the beach. In that moment, Kim whispered in Heather's ear and Heather's eyes grew wide with enthusiasm as she turned to Will holding out her hand. "We need money!"

"What?" Will asked, but the men were not completely surprised by the idea that as soon as a Dollar found their hands their wives would want a share.

"We'll tell you later!" Heather blurted, then turned to the new friend they had been so rude to not introduce to their husbands and placed her hand over both of hers, which were neatly crossed over her knees and eagerly pleaded an invitation. "Oh, Dorothy! Won't you join us for breakfast so we can continue chatting? *Please!*"

"I couldn't impose." Dorothy excused herself.

"Impose? *Impose?* Are you kidding? The stories you have shared! You have no idea the things we have seen today, alone! Anyone that can take our minds off of... well, off of everything... please... join us!" Heather implored, then turned to her husband. "What time, again, Will?"

"8:30 in the lobby." Will said, not at all bothered by the company and handing her €20. Jud, taking note of the amount, handed his wife the same, but wished his counterpart had only given away €10."

Dorothy smiled. The invitation was nice, but she really didn't want to accept. She had become accustomed to being alone. Still, although they hadn't spoken in detail, she could tell the young women had been through more than most could handle and she wasn't willing to disappoint Heather in the moment.

"Alright." Dorothy agreed to attend, with hesitation.

"*Okay!* Then it's settled! We'll meet you downstairs and grab a bite in the morning! I don't think I have ever looked forward to the free breakfast bagels at a hotel so much!" Heather beamed.

"Okay, Kimmie! Let's go!" Heather seemed excited by the normalcy of her schedule and the two said their goodbyes and rushed off to take care of the plotting they had done in the men's absence. Now, with a little money, able to elaborate even more than they had originally planned. With their own room keys in hand, they left the children in the care of their fathers and, predictably, headed straight for the free community clothing closet that Dorothy had told them about.

Catching a glimpse of herself in one of the hallway mirrors, Kim exclaimed. "I look like *crap!*" As she gestured for Heather to follow her into the bathroom before they made their way upstairs to search among the donations for a change of clothing. As she washed her face, she took note of how filthy her clothing was and imagined the group must have appeared terrible in Dorothy's eyes. Dorothy had been so kind, yet they were dressed like homeless gypsies and surely, she thought to herself, they must have all stunk after living underground in the same set of clothing for weeks. As she washed her face, the warm water felt so good that it drew more and more of her in, and soon she found her entire head submerged in the flow. Using the hand soap, she started washing the dirt from her hair as Heather looked on and finally commented. "There's going to be a shower in your room? Can't you wait?"

"Oh God, no, Heather! *Oh my, God!* Oh, this feels *sooooo gooooood!*" Kim moaned and Heather worried that anyone standing on the other side of the door might get the wrong idea as she watched the dark water filling the sink and wondered if there was that much dirt in her own hair. They looked like street urchins, but had been come so used to seeing each other that what it almost didn't seem noticeable. "Well, at least don't make a mess!" Heather noticed the blackish grey liquid overflowing to the counter and grabbed a stack of paper towels for Kim and herself, then followed the routine. She had to admit that once she, too, felt the hot water on her scalp it seemed as if her neck was unable to lift her head up any longer. For the next fifteen minutes, they washed themselves up then blew their hair half dry with the hand dryers and cleaned up the mess they had left. When they emerged from the restroom, they felt like new women and headed back to their original mission.

As Dorothy had promised, there was a large clothing closet filled with other people's cast offs, that was just there for the taking. A lone, but very friendly, attendant was there to assist them in making order out of chaos as they tried to find clothing for themselves and their families. All in all, the children made out best but they did find some sweats and blue jeans and a few shirts that would be appropriate. There was also quite a selection of ladies suits and a few blouses that they made away with in addition to a few modest pairs of shoes and a couple of pairs of heels. Holding up one of the suits, Kim asked, "What do you think?"

"I think it'll work." Heather agreed then held up one of the tackiest shirts she had found and started laughing as she imagined her husband's face if she were to come back with it. As she went to put it back on the rack, Kim stopped her. "No, I want that!"

"You have to be joking!" All of Heather's faith in Kim's fashion sense just went out the window as she looked at the extra large men's silk atrocity. One sleeve was brown and the other was orange. The front vest panel on one side was white and the other was yellow; and the back panels were black and the other an almost neon green.

"It's perfect!" Kim affirmed as an idea popped into her head that Heather would not understand until later.

"Suit yourself! But, don't ever feel the need to buy me clothing for any special occasions. Really! Birthday, Christmas, I'm good!" Heather looked at her own selections, then turned to the attendant. "Is there anywhere around here where we might be able to find some makeup?" The attendant directed them to a drug store near by where they made a few quick selections of the basics, spending a total of €19.87 of the money they had between them. They then used the remainder to buy a couple of small items at another store, which took up all of their remaining money minus less than enough to buy a soda.

The women then returned to the hotel and Kim made a quick stop at the front desk. "You don't by any chance have any of those little hotel sewing kits, would you?"

The young women with thick glasses behind the front desk began to rummage through the items stocked behind the counter. "I know I've seen a box of them around here somewhere, unless someone moved them? Oh! Wait! Here they are!" Kim asked for five of them and the woman at first hesitated, but when Kim explained she would need to do some altering to the clothing from the community closet the woman's expression grew softer with understanding. Kim and Heather returned to the room that would be Kim and Jud's, later in the evening and immediately got to work. As soon as they walked in, Kim tossed her own bags on the bed and immediately dug for the impulse 'purchase' that had so surprised Heather. Ripping into the sewing kit, she grabbed the little pair of scissors and immediately began cutting along the seam in the back, exclaiming. "Isn't this perfect?"

"Well, I suppose, but burning it might be more effective." Heather looked on.

"No, you moron! This is perfect! I am going to make some scarves for Edee! This brown is an almost perfect match for that one dress you picked out, and the orange will go with that yellow suit, and black and white, well, they go with anything, but it will be great with the hounds tooth!" Kim smiled and Heather was suddenly eager to help.

Breaking into their little sewing kits, they fashioned four perfect scarves in only and hour then called the front desk to find out in which room their friend was staying.

"Edee's in room 710. Do you have everything?" Kim called out to Heather as she used a leftover scrap of fabric to tie up the scarves in a bow so they would appear more like a gift.

"Yup!" Heather called back happily, wishing she would hurry but giving no indication in her tone.

The two headed down the hallway and Kim quietly asked. "So how do we do this?"

Heather simply winked and responded confidently as she knocked on Edee's room door. "Just follow my lead."

Edee answered, appearing as if they had woken him from a nap that he had fallen into immediately after taking a long shower. The scruffy beard that had grown in within their first week underground was now gone from his face. He stood there, wrapped only in a towel that hung from his hips, looking more masculine than even they could have imagined after having known him for the time they had. And, of this version of Edee, they had both had enough. Heather, bags in hand, paid no mind to their interruption and marched straight passed him, announcing. "Edee. This is an intervention!"

"What?" Edee, who barely drank and who had never done a drug stronger than aspirin in his life, seemed puzzled by Heather's words as he fought to wipe the sleep from his eyes.

"You heard me!" Kim nodded in agreement. "Now, we know how women get when their surroundings are depressing... We stop doing our hair!" Heather whipped a short haired, woman's auburn wig from the bag. "We stop doing our makeup!" She dumped out a small bag containing some cheap foundation, mascara, blush, two shades of lipstick and two sets of eye shadows. "And, Lord knows we forget how to dress!" Kim handed Edee the bag of clothes and another that contained three pairs of shoes and one pair of panty hose. She then handed her the little pack of scarves that were tied with a bow and said. "We made these for you. We didn't see any scarves at the clothing closet and, well... you know... well, we know you like to cover up... you know." Kim grinned as she motioned across her neck in the place that an Adam's apple would be and Edee blushed at their gesture. Then, as quickly as she had made her entrance, Heather marched back towards the door, calling back. "Breakfast at 8:30! Don't make us come up here and do an ambush makeover at 8:45! Sweet dreams!"

And they were gone.

For almost thirty seconds, Edee stared at the wooden barrier between himself and the world trying to reconcile what had just occurred while still half asleep. But, whatever it was it made him feel wonderful to know he had found a few true friends in the middle of these tumultuous and final days of the nation once known as the United States of America. Sitting down on the edge of the bed, he gingerly pulled each of the carefully chosen hand me down outfits from the bag. They were all his size. They would be perfect fits. Then turning to the shoes, he thought they must have chosen the highest ones they could find, and he grinned. Though the soles were scuffed up and they showed signs of having been worn a good few times, he treasured them all as if they were fresh from his favorite shoe boutique.

One by one, he hung up each of the three new additions to his wardrobe and neatly lined the heels up below them in pairs, in the closet. He then moved to neatly arrange his makeup on the bathroom counter that he knew would be a very temporary home and then walked back to the bed. Standing before the desk, with a large mirror behind it, he slicked back his own hair and exchanged it for the hairstyle the girls had picked out for him. The short, pixie style cut was exactly the look he would have picked for himself, though the shade of auburn was just a little lighter than he was used to wearing. Still, it would go well with the shades that Kim and Heather had chose for him to adorn his face in. Then, he slowly untied the bow in which the scarves had been wrapped and sat down in front of the mirror. Taking out the white one, he wrapped his neck with the same ease he would have tied a Windsor Knot and gave a slight smile to his reflection.

Miss Edee was back.

She sat down at the desk and pulled the dirty pants that had been clinging to her flesh for a couple of fort nights from the chair's back. Turning them inside out, she felt for the left pocket and, using the tip of the pen from her desk drawer, she broke open the threads one by one unzipping the bottom of the secret little safe she had sewn into them. Holding the cloth close to the surface of the wood, she allowed a small pile of stones to slide out onto the surface cautious to not let as much as one chip to land on the floor. Edee knew the value of each and every one of those little beauties before her. She had even named them all; Ivana was a small quarter carat Alexandrite chip that was worth $350, Rex was a perfect Red Star Ruby weighing in at about two and a half carats and worth more than $23,000 and Maria was an Emerald, just like her sister stone Mara that had sold earlier that day, but she was worth about half the other stone's value. In total there were twenty three precious and semi precious stones, most of which she had mined, polished and cut herself over the years: each holding not only a Dollar value, but memories from Edee's life and journeys. Meticulously, she sorted through the stones and worked out different scenarios of how long they would be able to stay, and eat, depending on how long it might take Alfonso and the rest to reach them.

And what would then be leftover.

"If they get here in five days…" She thought to herself, then quickly dismissed that as too soon a time frame, given the little ones that were traveling with them. So she rearranged the stones. One pile representing the cost to keep the current eight in food and shelter, and the other representing the money that the group would have to share to buy passage and transportation out of Jacksonville and to another country.

"If they get here in ten days…" She moved a few stones over, then a few back, calculating the cost with them all sharing two rooms.

The numbers were already not looking good.

"If they get here in fifteen days… and we buy some food at the grocery store, instead of eating at restaurants…" She moved the stones back and forth, debating.

"If we all share a room, and we go to the grocery store… and they get here in eighteen days…"

Edee sighed as she looked at the piles and could only hope that Alfonso would make it through safely and with the other half of the village's shared finances, though they were the only two that really knew the whole sum of their accounts. There wasn't much left for transport, and certainly not enough for a boat that would carry fifty people safely.

Her mind then wandered to thoughts of what the others might do, if they ran into trouble. She certainly couldn't blame Alfonso for keeping the money to try to help support the others, but the question then became: how long should they wait? As she looked down at the small piles, she wondered how long they *could* wait. Selfishly, her mind flashed with the hope that some terrible tragedy would befall the others and allow the current group their own escape. But, as quickly as the thought entered her mind, Edee forced it out, mentally chastising herself for entertaining such a notion, even if was only for a brief moment.

Her spirit was too kind to wish any harm to anyone.

Edee selected three stones, that she hoped would provide for the basic necessities until the others arrived then, using the scrap of cloth that Kim had used to make the bows to tie her bundle of scarves, Edee carefully sewed a small satchel to hold them and proceeded to tightly sew the small bundle of stones into the one accessory she knew she would not be without: her wig.

In the morning, Miss Edee would make her triumphant return to the breakfast table, wearing a sun yellow blended suit, her orange scarf and a four inch pair of gold sling backs. She looked like a walking sunrise. Her wig, neatly styled, and her face made up to perfectly coordinate with the bright outfit. As she walked through the lobby, her outfit drew a few glances, but she quickly found the sway was back in her hips leaving several to mistake her for a natural woman. And, as any good woman should be: she was fashionably late, but only by ten minutes.

She approached the table of familiar faces and was introduced to a new one. Dorothy extended her hand with the grace of lady and shook Edee's with the strength of a man. Edee was impressed. Edee noticed her firm maintenance of eye contact with hers, almost as if she was sizing him up: she was. She smiled, already having surmised her real gender and simply commented, "You know, sling backs really were a poor choice for that outfit. What size do you wear? I may have something more suitable in my stash if you are interested?"

Edee smirked, pretending to ignore her comment, but finding it humorous. "Heather said it was *Dorothy*? Well, if you're offering shoes, are you willing to part with the ruby slippers?"

"Oh, now dear, *that* I could never do. But, my best friend used to work in fashion and I have more pairs of Dolce and Gabbana's than you can shake a fist at!" Dorothy grinned and all of the women felt a quick pang of jealously wondering what glorious footwear might be wasted in the collection of a woman far too old to truly get the best use out of them. Heather casually leaned over the table, trying not to be obvious about the fact that she was checking out Dorothy's shoe size and thought to herself *"Damn!"* as she realized there was no way they would be close. Dorothy noticed Heather's investigating, but didn't say a word as she smiled to herself and, almost ritualistically, spread a small bit of butter over her bagel, took a bite, dabbed her mouth with a napkin, then, returning the napkin to her lap, took a sip of coffee.

"Well, I have not even had my morning java, but I just may have had a small orgasm! I never had friends like that! Closest I ever came to knowing someone that worked in fashion was the friend of a neighbor that was a Greeter at Wal-Mart!" Edee joked and the table chuckled at her. "Some people have all the luck!"

Suddenly their attentions were distracted by a mass of people that seemed to be moving towards, and gathering around, a television in the commons area that was broadcasting a Spanish news program out of Miami. The table rose to join in the commotion and made their way over to little sitting area and the screen that appeared to be broadcasting satellite images of the earth.

But, something was terribly wrong.

Even from outer space the fires and smoke seemed impossible to fight, pulled high into the atmosphere and drug around the continent by the earth's own spin. The small parts that were not covered with smoke, reflected a light so bright it was like a huge patch of ice was reflecting the sun, in a part of the world where no such creation should have existed.

Edee didn't need a map, or to see the borders of nations, to immediately know both what and where she was looking, nor how many countries had been affected. A chill ran up her spine as she thought of the implications and she could only hope that Alfonso and his group would make it there soon. Yet, at the same time she knew they were probably safer than ever. He walked ahead of the group focused on the locations and the plumes that were rising steadily towards the heavens. Not even realizing Heather had followed, or that the words fell from her lips. With a look of astonishment, Edee simply uttered a single word: "Siloviki."

"Who?" Heather immediately broke Edee's trance.

"Nothing, dear." Edee caught herself speaking words she was not allowed to and turned the conversation in a different direction. "My God, I can only imagine the suffering." Edee's head filled with images of the consequences of misguided science, yet she found herself unable to turn away from the screen. Her mind focused on each of the smoke stacks, she calculated the day's casualties in silence and predicted the deaths that would follow within the next few weeks.

Those within a fifty mile radius.

Within one hundred.

Within five hundred.

The global implications and the effects on the ozone.

She was the only one in the room that really could really see the big picture.

"We're at war, *aren't we*? I mean, *really* at war?" Heather said apprehensively hoping for guidance on what to do next. Edee had brought them this far and she could only hope that she would now know what to do in such dire times. Bouncing her focus from the screen to Edee's seemingly calm expression, Heather was confused when she answered. "No, dear, we're not. They just *ended* it."

While the room around her filled with panic and unease, Edee was overcome with a sensation of calm. She felt, in this moment, they were in one of the safest places on earth, but only because she was far too familiar with the enemy's tactics and the politics of the world. She walked away and returned to the table where they had been eating breakfast and calmly enjoyed her coffee while the others remained chained to the television. About half a cup into her thinking, Dorothy joined Edee at the table.

"You know, I'll be eighty six years old in three days and I never thought I'd see it." Dorothy shook her head, reflecting on her life, from childhood to now. "In the forties we celebrated it, in the sixties it scared the piss out of me and in the eighties it gave my boys nightmares: somehow I thought I'd escaped it. I was getting out of here with having to witness it, again. *Now*, look at us."

Edee agreed and looking for something nice to say, that would stray away from the conversations going on in the room behind them, she commented. "Eighty six? I can't believe that. Funny, you don't look eighty six." And Edee smiled, thinking she had made the old lady's day.

Unexpectedly, Dorothy fired back. "Yeah well, that's funny, because *you* don't look *straight*!" Dorothy winked as she smiled and gestured to Edee's outfit, then took a sip of her own coffee and Edee nodded a touché as she pointed to Dorothy in jest. "*Heather* told me. Well, no, that's not *quite* right. It was more like Heather gave me the old *'don't judge our friend by her pink pantsuit'* speech that went on for about twenty minutes, and both apparently, and mistakenly, she thought I needed." Edee smiled out of half of her mouth as she pretended her coffee needed more stirring. "They *really* think a lot of you, Edee. You have *no idea*. I can only imagine what you all have been through after what little they have told me. I know there is a larger story there."

"There is. But, I imagine everyone that comes through here has a story." Edee said softly, still looking down at her cup.

"You're their hero, you know. You saved them." Dorothy tried to pry a reaction, but Edee only shook her head.

"No." Edee pushed the praise back to the other side of the table, still unwilling to look up.

"Well, you can go on believing that. Or, you can believe the truth. There's a very nice group of people over there that single handedly credit you for their lives and the lives of their children." Dorothy waited a moment for a response, but there was none. She politely sipped her coffee, keeping one eye on the crowd and the television across the room, then warmed up both of their coffees from the pot that had been sitting on the table.

"Creamer?" She offered to pass, and Edee declined. Not wanting to seem rude, Edee asked, almost innocently. "So, it seems you know part of our story. What's yours?"

Dorothy thought for a second, then laughed at herself. "Love, I have no story. Just that of a stubborn old woman that was too obstinate to move out of her comfortable home on Amelia Island when her own two sons were begging her to do so. That's all. So, here I am. Alone."

"Did your sons head into The Territory?" Edee questioned almost sympathetically.

"Oh Heaven's, no! Peter, at least, would *never* move anywhere that there might be a risk of the temperature falling below 60 degrees on a *cold* day! They both headed to St. Lucia." Dorothy tried to make light of their separation though, inside she was afraid she would never see them again.

Edee tried to reassure her of their decision with what she knew of the island. "Not a bad choice. Independent nation. Warm. Pretty good golfing, from what I hear."

"Yes, well, still. It's a long ways down and I'm a little too old to get a cutter from Jacksonville Port to St. Lucia, anymore."

Noticing Dorothy's mannerisms and designer suit, Edee assessed that, at least at one time, she had been a woman of means and he questioned why she hadn't just flown down to meet them. "*Oh, Heaven's, no!* I *cannot* fly! *Deathly* afraid of it! Always *have been*. Besides, for the past few years you can't be sure who's at the controls. Some young Top Gun that's had his license a full week and stolen a plane in an attempt to make a few extra bucks off of those desperate to escape? Do you know how many of them have gone down in the ocean, down here? Oh! It has been a big problem for the past few years. *No, no!* I couldn't even imagine! At least, the ocean, I understand. Besides, I'd sooner drown at the surface of the waters than be counting my seconds left to live as the fuselage plunges towards the ocean floor."

"Well, I suppose I can understand that." Edee, having once been a pilot herself, couldn't fully relate, but was compassionate about the fears of others.

For a few more moments, the two sat in silence, sipping their coffee and listening to the humming of the people around them. And then, almost out of no where, Edee felt the yearning to ask a question that she had not ever felt a need or desire to ask ever before in her life: always feeling that she assume the answer. "So, Dorothy. When Heather told you about me... when she told you what to expect... the whole 'pantsuit comment'... *Did* you?"

"What? Did I *judge* you?" Dorothy seemed a little surprised by the candor of her question and she paused for a moment to search Edee's eyes for expectation.

"Yes." Edee responded, all of a sudden not sure if she wanted to know the answer.

"*Of course!* Love, I was raised in Miami! We don't do *anything* better than shop and judge each other, down there! *And,* I gave you my *honest* opinion when we were *introduced.* Sling backs were *really* a poor choice!" Dorothy toasted her coffee cup to Edee and smiled, wondering where such a wonderful group of people had been at a far more confusing time in her life. Satisfied that she had them surrounding her now, she began moving around little piles of stones in her mind, adding one more to her list of orphaned souls and planning to reunite a soon to be eighty six year old woman with her sons.

Somehow.

On the third day, concerned about their resources, Edee consolidated the group down to one room with two double beds. Dorothy had been joining them for breakfast, each morning and, upon hearing the news, invited Edee to come stay in her room and take the other double bed allow Kim, Jud, Heather, Will and the children to share the other room with two doubles and a couple of fold away beds. It was common, at the one time luxury hotel that had now turned to accommodate those that passed through their doors and treated the establishment more like a youth hostile. Each day that passed, they waited for the others and Edee was anxious for the sunset each night, knowing that would be drawing Alfonso and the rest closer to them. Still, she knew she could not expect them any sooner than twelve days after their own arrival at the pace they would be keeping and considering the roads they would have to take.

But, after fifteen days she began to get eager. Edee watched, as each night drained more and more Euro from their pockets and she began to worry about whether or not they would be able to buy a boat. Dorothy and she had spent several evenings talking about boats. Dorothy had all but convinced her that the only safe way to travel would be on a sailboat, lest they be at the mercy of the sea and those that might choose to take what was left of their kitty to pay for the simple cost of fuel. Still, sailing required knowledge and talent and Edee had none in that arena. Lying awake at night, she imagined she could figure it out, though. She was an engineer that had mastered the intricacies of flight and of satellite technologies, so she assumed that sailing, like the rest, would boil down to math and simple equation. Still, most sailboats on the market would only carry about a dozen people safely and she worried about how to divide the rest of their money. But, given the skill required to operate them, cutters were cheap when compared to their cigarette companions and that did give them some advantage in the market place.

Anticipation of the group was eating Edee's nerves and wallet.

On the seventeenth day, a tired and wary group arrived at the Marriott Hotel in Jacksonville, Florida on horseback. From the original group of eight that had arrived, one was almost waiting in the lobby, hopeful that their friends would find safe passage. The one time valet parking area of the Marriott looked like it was caught in a time warp as the horses, more suitable for a western saloon scene, were tied up to the pillars of what would have once been a vacation destination hotel.

And, in walked Alfonso and Jonathon.

Jonathon looked like a light haired version of Grizzly Adams and Alfonso had lost fifteen pounds, if he had lost one. They looked exhausted, but Alfonso's eyes immediately lit up with life when he saw Miss Edee, perfectly coordinated in her hounds tooth suit accented by a black scarf and a pair of 5 inch patent leather pumps. Edee rushed over to the pair that looked like they would be more suited to marching towards the line of a soup kitchen than into the lobby of a hotel. Edee embraced them, not caring what dirt or odors might seep into her suit. Following behind were about twenty three others that had completed the journey with them. At first, Edee's mind raced with the thought that they had encountered some unspeakable horror on their way down.

"Dear God! What happened! Only *half* of you made it?" She questioned, afraid to hear the answer as Dorothy, her lunchtime companion, looked on saddened by the expression on Edee's face.

"No, Edee... We're good. When we got about as far as Moultrie, there were several of them that wanted to branch off and head west. The Murphy's used to live in Dallas and, even though Texas pretty much all belongs to Mexico, now, they felt safer doing so. That scientist guy, Michael Cole, he convinced a few others and we lost about half of them that night. It's okay. It's what they wanted to do. We split the horses fifty fifty between us, but gave them about seventy five percent of the food, seeing as how they had further to travel. And, you should know, I gave Cole that one ring you said might be worth something. We've got the rest of it. It only seemed fair." Alfonso explained, his voice weak and cracking from dehydration.

Edee looked to the ceiling, wishing that of all of the pieces that had been stripped from their collection, that one ring had remained. Still, she couldn't argue without feeling self-centered. "I'm sure you did the right thing. Michael's a good guy. He'll look out for them." Still, she was a little disappointed in the decision.

Slowly, a small and dirtied crowd began to appear behind Jonathon and Michael with little, sullied faces poking out from behind their parent's knees. Dorothy looked on and offered up the one thing she knew she could easily provide to them all.

"Well, if you all feel anything like your friends here did when they first arrived, I am sure that nothing would sound better to you right now than a hot shower and a hotter cup of coffee." She smiled with understanding as she imagined the incredible dirt ring that would be left in the tub and the group smiled back shyly, but enthusiastically, at the kind stranger's offer.

"Okay, the ladies and children can follow me. Edee can track down Will or Jud and loan you use of their shower, then. I suppose the front desk is about to have an incredible run on soap and shampoo." Dorothy smiled and waved for the group to follow her as Edee dealt with the task of getting the men cleaned up and shaven.

Later that evening they all reconvened in the entertainment area in the lobby. The children, fascinated by the cartoons that were playing from a DVD that one of the Lobby Attendants had been kind enough to pop in for their entertainment.

And they tried to plan.

The group was shocked by the news that was conveyed about the events that had transpired over two weeks ago. Traveling on horseback, on the back trails of South Georgia and into Florida, they had no idea of the world-changing events that had taken place nor the incredible loss. Immediately, most began to feel ever more thankful for their decision to avoid ever stepping foot inside the Northwest Territory. As they sat and debated and argued plans for the future, they began to realize that now that they were free from the confines of the Island of Misfit Toys. They all had their own ideas for their own futures as independent thought returned. They had been prisoners, in a sense, together. They were no different than hostages that found comfort in waking up each morning to find that each of them was still alive, yet now they began to seek not reasons to stay together, but reasons to separate.

Beth Faust, as usual, was one of the first to speak. Her tone, however was gentle and empathetic and kind. She had found the ballroom of notes and, amazingly, she found a note from her mother and it had made her cry. Passing the note to Edee, she said. "I will never be able to thank you enough for what you have done for us. There were parts of this trip that I am afraid I will have nightmares about for the rest of my life, but we made it and I wish you all the best. I just can't go where you are heading."

Edee unfolded the scrap of paper and read the handwritten words that had been left for the girl that he had, at one time, regretted allowing to stay in Cambuslang.

My Dearest, and Only Child, Beth:

My heart aches as your father and I are leaving and we have no idea where you are. We pray nightly that you are safe. Please know we made every effort to find you before leaving and that we have left this note in the sincere hope that it will somehow get to you. Know that we are okay. We are. I know you will be worried, too. We met a lovely couple that has offered to bring us to St. Thomas and help us get situated. That is where we will be waiting. If these words only reach the eyes of others that may know you, I just hope they know what an incredible woman you have become and how very proud we are to be your Mom and Dad. Wiley is safe and still loves a treat after a walk. We make a point to walk him three times a day, just as you would have wanted. He misses you, too.

Love Eternally,

Adrianna Faust (8-14-1967) Born in Rye, New York

James Faust (8-17-1964) Born in Deming, New Mexico

Will be residing in St. Thomas, US Virgin Islands as of approximately 5-15-2022
until we see our loving daughter, again. Should anyone have word of our only child's
whereabouts, please send word to any port. We will be checking them all regularly.
Shalom!

Edee, neatly folded the paper back and handed it back to Beth and nodded, her eyes questioning how Beth planned to make the journey.

Almost laughing and showing her good side, Beth responded. "Well, I didn't say I had figured it *all* out! It's just good to know my folks are safe. This letter is over a year old. Do you think they've waited?" She asked, afraid to have the fears in her own mind confirmed.

"I'm sure they did… I'm sure they *are*. You just need to get out of here. We *all* do." Edee assured as the one time attorney carefully placed the scrap of paper in her pocket, as if it were the only connection she had left to her youth.

Later, without anyone knowing, and after having sold off a few more gems, Edee would give €250 to Beth in the hope that it would be enough to buy her passage to hitchhike a ride with the other group. St. Thomas was fairly easy, compared to other destinations, but Beth gave Edee such a hug that she thought it would choke her there where she stood.

By the morning, Beth was gone.

She found passage with three families that were sharing a boat that was heading in the same direction. In a few days, her mother and father had a tearful reunion with their darling daughter and a very happy, but *very* old dog named Wiley, was reunited with his master. Wiley would be content to pass away in his sleep, curled up at her side in bed, only three weeks later.

Little Wiley had waited, too.

His little body had begun to give out months earlier, but in his small mind he still held onto the images of the kind human that had once brushed his fur, daily and spoiled him as though he had been the product of her own womb. Upon seeing Beth again, he fought the clock to buy himself hours in her company but, finally, he passed: dreaming of chasing squirrels through a park, as she called for him.

Within the next twenty four hours, between the database that the hotel had kept and the notes pinned to the walls, four more families had decided to break from the group and travel in different directions.

Winfred, his two daughters and his wife Julie, found a note from Julie's cousin praying that anyone from the family would join them in Phoenix and they took three of the horses and headed west. Not before Edee saw fit to sneak a stone worth about €1000 Euro in their pockets, for which Winfred was immensely grateful. Uncertain of the finances on the other side of the panhandle, Edee explained that they would be better off to take the stone than cash and was adamant about its value. He had allowed for the depreciation in the market and was hopeful that they might even get a little more, once they made their way across the new border.

Lipson King and his long time companion, Dick, found a troubling note from Dick's son, begging them to join him in Bermuda and apologizing for the behavior he had displayed upon learning about his father's new lifestyle. It rambled on, but concluded with the basic message that he desperately wanted his father, and his life partner, to join them on the island and shared the news of the birth of a new grandson. Upon reading it, Lipson's eyes welled with tears and despondence and an immediate desire to speak to the son that had turned his back on him nineteen years earlier.

The date on the letter was only a week old.

They had just missed each other.

Lipson and Dick explained to Edee and the others that they would be taking off with a group in the next couple of days and would work in servitude to pay off their debts, once on the island. Dick, willing to do anything to wipe the anguish from the eyes of the man he loved so dearly. The fourteen page letter that had been tacked to the wall brought tears to Edee's eyes, and she handed the couple enough Euro to buy their way to Bermuda.

No strings attached.

They would arrive there safely and find Lipson's namesake only a few days later. And, a few hours later, they met Lipson King III.

Former heroine addict turned preacher, Terrell Chastain, quickly found a group of missionaries that were determined to head to Mexico City to provide what comfort they could in the wake of Popo's eruption. Having been shut off from the world for so long, Terrell had not fully understood the destruction of the one time metropolis that now rivaled that of Pompei and he was certain that God had put him in touch with this group for a reason. He told Alfonso that he was being called to the boat that would be leaving in a few hours. The destruction he would witness would leave him scarred for life, but a few months later, a young Mexican girl named Zuheiry, would take his hand and renew his faith. They would have three children and resign to live a modest life in Mexico.

Gillian Street, her husband Jim and their four children, would decide to take a similar path, heading towards the Gulf. Her skills as a nurse were in high demand in the more industrialized parts of Mexico and throughout South America. Over the years, she would learn the Spanish language and by the year 2027 her family would make their way to Brazil, where the economy was beginning to thrive. Her husband would find work as a mechanic and they would live well until 2049, when a bomb would unfortunately find its way through the roof of their suburban home, killing everyone inside as they celebrated a grandchild's birthday.

The one time extended family began to dwindle and splinter off.

And, Edee was fine with it all.

She understood the need for those she had called both friends and neighbors, for what had seemed like a lifetime, to set their own course in life and find their own paths. In truth, it was a relief for her: a final exchange of kindness and the wish that they would all be well. But, there was one departure that would be exceedingly difficult for the man that had accustomed himself, once again, to high heels and makeup: one she would not see coming.

Sitting in the lobby, fully engaged in conversation, Edee adjusted her skirt as Dorothy attempted to understand the intricacies of the mind before her as they enjoyed a light round of cocktails that Dorothy insisted would be billed to her room. Sipping on her Rob Roy, as Edee enjoyed a tempered rum and coke, Dorothy argued. "So you would have the world live in a Police State?" Dorothy delicately returned her cocktail to its coaster as she awaited Edee's response.

Stirring her own, Edee responded. "It's safe. That's why the Territory was such a success. People felt safe." In truth, they had been duped by a false sense of security.

"It's not free. It goes against everything this country stood for. Freedom: it was what we were all about." Dorothy countered.

"I guess at some point America should have asked which one we valued more: security or freedom. Seems to me, we've proven you can't have both." Edee sipped her cocktail wondering how Dorothy, an intellectual equal whose opinions she had grown to value, might respond.

Suddenly, their debate was interrupted by Alfonso and Jonathon. Alfonso, clean shaven, and his head shining from a fresh coat of moisturizer, was carrying a large knapsack. He sat down next to Edee, placing his hand on her knee as if he was about to break difficult news to his own mother. "I just wanted to say goodbye."

Edee turned to Jonathon for confirmation, unable, at the time, to understand what Alfonso's words meant, but Jonathon's own expression only served to confirm that Alfonso was not joking.

"What do you mean, 'goodbye'? We're a team! We're all getting out of here, together!" Edee pleaded like a parent not quite ready to see their child venture out into the unknown world, aware of the traps and dangers and afraid that she had not taken enough time to explain them to her child. Alfonso was not hers, but they had grown close and Edee thought of Alfonso as a son.

And, in that moment, she realized it.

"Some guys told me about a ferry to Cuba. It leaves out of Miami every afternoon. The fare is pretty cheap. I can take one of the horses and head down the coastline. I am pretty sure I *can't* miss *Miami*." Alfonso smiled, trying to break the tension with a joke, but Edee was not ready for this.

"But, *you* can't go! You can't *just* go! The others *need* you! You brought them this far? How can you leave *now*?"

Alfonso searched for words, then placing his backpack on the sofa, he took Edee's hand and turned over a small bag of jewelry. "They are all going to be fine. You were always the leader, Edee. I was just there. You took care of me, too." Alfonso explained recalling his first encounter with a kind man in a dress that gave him a meal when Alfonso felt his own ribs were ready to be broken by his own flesh. "This is everything, minus the one ring that I gave to Cole and his group. You'll look after them, Edee. You looked after *me*, that's for sure!"

"And, *exactly* how do you expect to get by? How do you *expect* to get on that ferry?" Edee tried to talk him out of his decision in an argumentative tone that parents normally reserve for teenagers.

"I dunno. But, I'll be figure it out. I can build a fire and I can fish and I am sure I can sweet talk some hot chick into letting me tag along and meet her parents in Cienfuegos." He grinned with the impetuous nature of a seventeen year old, though his eyes told the story of a thirty something that had witnessed more than he had cared to have seen and , now, simply needed a change of scenary.

"*What, Edee?* Did you *really* think we would all stay together? Did you *really* believe that? We all came together because things were... well... they were *bad*... is it *not* a good thing that we would part this way? *We made it!* That's a *good* thing! You seemed happy to let Lipson and Dick go and see *their* family? Terrell? The Street's?

Winfred and his family? I'd mention Beth, but I know you wouldn't fight *her* to *stay!*"
Alfonso smiled and looked for Edee to return one, but she only looked concerned. "This
is what I need to do. I still have aunts and uncles and God knows how many cousins in
Cuba. I'm gonna be fine." Alfonso was decided, and Edee knew it, so she did the only
thing she could.

She hugged him and offered to see him off.

Dorothy and Jonathon followed as Alfonso freed his riding companion, but Edee
wanted time alone on the shore and would ask them both to stand down when it came to
goodbyes. Well hydrated from drinking from the fountain outside, Charlie the Horse
seemed anxious for the journey. Knowing that without the ring that Alfonso had given
to the others the bag Alfonso had handed was only worth a couple thousand, Edee stuffed
the remaining jewels that Alfonso had turned over to her into his saddle bag, when
neither Alfonso nor Jonathon wasn't looking. It was more than she should have given
away, but Alfonso had earned it in every sense. Edee watched as his would be son took
to the saddle and walked out with him to the beach to say their final farewells. As
Alfonso rode south, along the shore, Edee watched the young man fade into nothing more
than a shadow on the sand and he realized it was the last time he would ever see the
Cuban man that had served as Second in Command in Cambuslang.

Firmly planted, where the water met the sand, Edee watched as Charlie's
footprints were softly washed away by the tide that was coming in, erasing any evidence
that either the stallion, or the man on his back, had ever occupied space on the shore. His
mind tried to record every detail, knowing this moment was significant in his life, as

Alfonso's silhouette slowly blended with the ocean mist and faded into a grayish blue haze.

Soon, Alfonso had completely disappeared and Edee felt a little empty.

Alfonso never even looked back.

And a few months later, stories of a heroic drag queen impersonator, that saved the lives of what would be told as hundreds of people, were spreading on the Cuban Island.

Over the years Alfonso would, from time to time, think of Edee and wonder about where she was and what she might be doing. But, ultimately he would be content to finally settle down into the normalcy of married life and raise a family while managing one of his uncle's chain of Italian restaurants that had sprung up throughout Cuba. His wife, Christiana, would, on occasion, try to get him to speak about the path that led him home, but he always declined.

And, as an old man, he would die with most of his stories from Cambuslang never having reached the ears of those that loved him.

Never once sharing his troubles, but only fond memories.

Although a large portion of the original villagers had decided to take different directions, Edee had more trouble in dealing with Alfonso's departure than any of them. He was the closest thing he had known to a son since her own had made their way into the Northwest Territory or to parts unknown of the world and Dorothy could see the worry in Edee's eyes as she nursed a fresh rum and coke and Jonathon found comfort in a draft beer.

Sipping on her Rob Roy, Dorothy found the courage to break the silence, but found her question would be quickly answered, as Edee had been working the plans out in her mind since they had arrived. "So what will you do next?"

"Everyone is fine for the night. We'll sleep... eat... then move to the docks and see what we can buy with what we have left... then... I suppose... we hope for the best."

Jonathon nodded along in agreement as Dorothy continued to question. "Where will you go?"

"Well... I don't know that the group agrees. We are pretty much stuck. Although, I am not against the idea of making a few stops. I'm thinking that we can take what we have and see what we can buy and get out of here, before the powers that be spread to this side of the country. The land we are sitting on is pretty much up for grabs and, quite frankly, I'm too old to start learning other languages, now. Jonathon told the others to be ready in the morning, if they're going. We'll figure it out from there. Every night we spend here is just taking away from the funds we can spend on a boat." Edee said dryly with almost no inflection in her voice.

Dorothy smiled. "So at what time are you heading to the docks? Can I accompany you? I know the fair values of boats, around here. I might be able to help you all pick one out."

Almost feeling guilty, as if she had left Dorothy out of their plans, Edee turned to her. "Of course, Dorothy. We had planned for you to *join* us. Did you not realize that? I guess I just figured you would have assumed. I'm sorry. It might be some rough going, but we'll get you to St. Lucia. A few others have told Jonathon they want us to make some pit stops on the way. St. Bart's, St. Eustatius, I think… St. Lucia's just a hop, skip and a jump from there."

Jonathon nodded, showing Dorothy that she had indeed been discussed in their plans, although Edee had neglected to recant the conversations with her, simply assuming she wanted to get to where her sons were and that she would surely join them.

That night, Jonathon and his remaining group of nine, made plans with Edee's group of seven plus one: they returned to their separate quarters and agreed to meet at eight in the morning, prepared to set sail… hopefully. No one was really decided on a final destination, but Dorothy. They met for a quick breakfast and headed to the docks: several of the women, stuffing extra bagels and bread into their bags in case they might need the food on their journey.

At the docks, the group that mostly came owning only what they had worn or had taken from the community clothing closet, found themselves gathered by on a pier as Edee tried to wheel and deal with an Indian man whose appearance seemed more like that of a used car salesman. He woefully under appraised the value of the stones before them and offered up a small speed boat and some directions for facilities where they could refuel along the way and Edee was infuriated.

"You *expect* me to take seventeen lives, *several* of which are *children* and take try to make it to *St. Lucia* in *that*?!" Edee exclaimed, angered by the proposal.

"I don't care where you go, I'm just telling you what this will buy you." The heavyset Indian man looked down at the small pile of leftover stones before him. "This isn't much. Really, *I'm* doing *you* a favor by offering up what I am." He assured as he chewed on his cigar and spied the pier for his next victim.

"A favor? *A favor!* You want me to put eighteen people on a boat designed to hold *four* with the hope, the *very faint hope,* that we will have enough fuel to make it to the next so-called fueling destination?" Edee's angry side was starting to show.

"Hey, I just sell 'em… I'm not advising on how to take 'em out… We've got plenty of life preservers, though… fifty Euro a piece." The vein on Edee's forehead seemed as though it was ready to burst and Dorothy had seen enough.

"We'll take the cutter down there." Dorothy stated firmly, as Edee turned to her, almost shocked why she would make such a silly request considering the rusty bucket offer before them. The salesman found her offer equally amusing as he laughed at her. Unaffected, Dorothy, her designer luggage in tow, was determined to make it to St. Lucia and she was doing it with this crew. Reaching into her pocket, she casually tossed a ring in the direction of the salesman, confident in the spin she had put on it as it flipped end over end and found its way to his hand.

Sparkling and twinkling, until he snatched it from the air.

There she stood, in a face off with the boat dealer, as her escape awaited at the end of the dock. Not giving him time to respond, she snipped. "Now, both of us know that ring is worth far than that cutter was in her *good* days, but I'll take your boat in trade." The Indian examined the four carat stone before him and glanced over at the once glorious three masted vessel, that now sat in his harbor with a broken motor and fresh sails that had never felt the sea air. Looking up at Dorothy's adamant stare, he affirmed they had a deal and moved to push the other stones to his drawer.

"The deal was for the ring. Give my friend back his stones." Dorothy said in a tone that demonstrated she had once spent time dealing with difficult children and that she intended on taking no crap from the little man in front of her. Almost regrettably, he handed Edee's memories back to her and Edee turned to Dorothy not knowing what to say. Dorothy did not want thanks, though.

The hardest part of their journey was just ahead.

The tall wooden ship would hold them all, but would require some skill to sail if they were to make it safely across the waters. Thankful for the deal, but fearful that some "unexpected catch" might arise if they stayed at dock too long, they pushed back and drifted a bit out before raising the sails. Kim and Heather and the other mothers aboard kept the children entertained as Dorothy, in Drill Sergeant form, instructed the men on how to sail *her* boat.

It had nothing to do with the purchase, she just wanted everyone to arrive safely and she knew the sea better than any of the others so it was necessary to take control. There was no questioning that Dorothy was the Captain of the ship that a previous owner had given the name *The Aquaholic*. Edee smiled and was the first to fall in line at her demands, amused to see the very controlling and in charge side of this seemingly unassuming and demure woman he had known for only a couple of weeks. By the time they had reached open waters, Dorothy had ensured that all of the men learn the basics of sailing and by the time that the group had parted ways with the North American Continent, both Dorothy and the group were comfortable enough to feel somewhat at ease on the vessel. The women, not quite as relaxed, insisted the children wear life vests, even in bed, as the sixty foot well traveled hull made its way over waters.

They had all found peace in the desolation and the Atlantic was unusually cooperative as they passed over her surface.

On the first night, after everyone had gone to bed, Dorothy found herself unable to sleep and wandered up on deck to the bow of the ship where she found Edee enjoying the night air and the sound of the waves as they crashed against the side of the boat they would all call home, for the next several days. Knowing his mind was racing with a million thoughts, she steered the conversation in a different direction as she looked up at the night sky.

Away from the light pollution, the heavens appeared black as coal and the moon glowed with an eerie blood red haze, softened only by the twinkling of the pink stars that surrounded it. Taking in the sight of the unfamiliar celestial landscape Dorothy commented to the scientist at her side, as she leaned over the rails taking in a deep breath of the sea air and with her eyes on the luminous display. "Isn't it amazing how man's own destruction can create such beauty in the heavens? Amazing to think a few little bombs could impact the whole world like this."

Edee nodded. Her mind filled with more understanding of the universe and man's place in it that anyone on board could ever even hope to imagine. Perhaps she could have found fair and intellectual debate with Stephan Hawkings, but lacking such companionship she simply resorted to smirking at Dorothy's simple observations and smiling to her old friends, Orion and Sirius. There was something about constellations that were comforting to Edee, beyond the fact that she had studied the bodies that surrounded them and the workings of the universe: they were a constant. For centuries and through civilizations they had been there. They bore witness to man's progress and self-destruction.

They were real: if only in mythology.

She stared out into space, contemplating both the expansion of the universe and the light that was racing to meet her eyes, hoping that a newcomer would begin to appear to her naked eye.

Dorothy looked on as Edee's pensively gazed towards the twinkling lights above them and wrung her hands. Satisfied that Edee would have companionship with her own thoughts, Dorothy saw no reason to fight her need for sleep. Her arthritis paining her, but too proud to admit that is what had kept her awake: she turned, announcing her departure.

"Well, I suppose I will give the Sandman another chance to find me. Jonathon knows to keep a southern heading and steer clear of anything that looks solid on radar. Otherwise, he can wake me." Dorothy hoped for a response, thankful for those that would see her safely home to her sons. "You coming, Edee?"

Edee, only barely aware that she still had company, simply responded. "No, I'm good. I'll come down when I'm tired. Might be a while." She turned back, smiling politely in a way that told Dorothy she was happy to be alone. Though they were a long way from their final destination, the sea looked kind and Dorothy was confident in their ability to make all of their stops. She knew the waters far better than she had led on and was her confidence was growing in the notion they would make landfall with ease.

And they would.

First to the Bahamas, to drop off the Walsh family who would meet up with a long lost uncle that had been hopefully been expecting their arrival, saddened only by the fact that his wife had passed just month's earlier and would not have the opportunity to meet their ten year old nephew.

Then, on to find Puerto Rico, and Anguilla, then St. Barts and a few other stops along the way. In each port of call finding hospitality and thanks for the safe return of the one life or another that meant so much to some other person standing waiting on the shore. In between their trips, there would be feasts and goodbyes. Someone that had touched their own life to the point they were willing to wait hours on a lonely shore for the hope that a ship would find them.

Eventually, they would safely find St. Lucia and the remaining nine people on the boat would come to have a full understanding of Dorothy's wealth and Edee would remember the conversation that first cued her into Dorothy's background, as they had taken to the waters and let *The Aquaholic* find her legs for the first time in six years. Standing over the port side, looking out into the open waters of the Atlantic, Edee had questioned, jokingly. "So, Dorothy, what's on the other side of that rainbow, dear? Do tell." She said jokingly as they both stared out into the great unknown.

"Nothing, but a bunch of funny colored horses and overextended egos. Wasn't much different than Miami in her hay day." Dorothy winked and smirked as she watched the sun reflecting off of the waves, never one to brag about her true experiences.

Looking to her, Edee could not help but chuckle. She was witty, humble and smart. Edee could not help but to engage her in banter.

"Never found that pot of gold on the other side though, did you?"

"Oh, honey! *I more than found the pot!* I found the whole mine! But, you know, it's not the gold that counts in the end… it really is the rainbow. It's the ability to see the beauty of the sun through the rainstorms that life brings to all of us really is what gets us through. It's not the money." It took a moment for Edee to really understand she was serious.

"That really was quite a gesture. That ring bought safety for a lot of people. How do we repay you?" She questioned, feeling a little beholden and very thankful for the good fortune of having met her new traveling companion.

Dorothy smiled, but looked away, not wanting gratitude, as she unnecessarily fussed with a few of the ropes. "You sail this boat to St. Lucia and take me home to my boys. That is all the thanks I need, Edee. All the thanks in the world. I am too old to do it on my own, anymore." And in her sudden shyness, Edee saw a younger and more vulnerable girl before him. So, he reassured her: "And *we* are too ignorant to do it without *you*." Edee said firmly as he inspected the mast. "So what did you do before you found yourself here, Dorothy?" Edee gently questioned, curious about what she might reveal.

"I *lived*." She smiled and winked.

Edee studied her for a moment, hoping she would clarify the very meaning of existence, then asked "What do you mean? We *all* live?"

Looking away, as though she had the key to some secret society, and now knowing that Edee was unaware, she glanced over empathetically, but still smiling. "No, dear. I *lived*. I *enjoyed* it. What *else* can you do? *Life* is what you make of it. It is. You make your misery and you make your destiny. *You* craft it. It *is* in your hands, but is not my job to make you see that…. What about you?"

And Edee told her the short version of a long and interesting life that could not possibly be summed up in a single night. What the other passengers on *The Aquaholic* could not know in that moment was they were sailing off to a much better life than any of them could imagine. Dorothy's sons, Peter and David, had worked as developers for several chains of Tribal Indian Casinos. In the late nineties, when the Indian Tribes began converting all of their assets away from the Dollar, and investing it all in gold and platinum, her sons followed suit with their own money and over the years the price of gold would spike so high, they would eventually become two of the wealthiest men in what once was the United States.

Dorothy's former home was a little $10,000,000.00 birthday gift, they gave her back in 2007 to celebrate her 70th. It was a drop in the bucket for them: and, for getting their beloved mother to them safely, Dorothy's sons would ensure that everyone on that boat would be able to comfortably live out their lives on St. Lucia without a care.

Heather would open up a small bar and restaurant that quickly became a favorite local island hot spot, mostly due to the popularity of her homemade wines. Eventually, it would be taken over by her sons, leaving her with more time to socialize with her customers and friends. When she passed away, at ripe old age of 93, it seemed as though the whole island turned out for her services and to comfort her sons and the six grandchildren, and two great-grandchildren they had given her.

Kim became an interior designer, noted for her upholstery skills, and eventually opened a women's clothing store that exclusively carried her own designs. Every year, for Christmas, Edee received a new package of fresh scarves, handmade from Kim's favorite fabric selections. And, twice a year, she had a new custom made dress or suit to show off.

As for Edee, she spent the rest of her days strolling the shores, often seen accompanied by Dorothy who enjoyed sharing stories and debating science with such a brilliant mind. Eventually, using a modified application of a Tessler design, Edee created a motor that almost completely eliminated St. Lucia's dependence on oil. It would become the small country's largest export by the year 2038 and earned Edee King, international notoriety in scientific circles.

Although Dorothy knew all of this would be in store, she would never hint at her secrets while they were on their journey and simply smiled at the group's surprise when they arrived on the beautiful island in the Caribbean. As the small group was slowly making their way to safety, and far from the nightmare they had just escaped, Elijah Drew was meeting with his own final destiny. With no food supplies and with all support cut off from his Middle Eastern Allies, his followers turned their rage against him. Breaking into his compound, and with little resistance from even his most trusted guards, the mob decapitated him and drug Drew's body through the streets. The remaining food supplies from the compound were stripped, but still many would die of starvation over the next few months.

But, all of those troubles were far behind, now.

Stargazing, and with the troubles of a failed nation behind them, Edee took in the night air and enjoyed the way the waves gently rocked them from side to side. Confident they would see sunrise with Jonathon at the helm.

They were all safe.

In the silence, only interrupted by the splashing of the waves against the hull, Edee looked for Sirius: Orion's loyal companion. She marveled at the constellations, and the wonderfully complicated universe that surrounded them understanding more about the skies above them than any of her shipmates could possibly comprehend. Even with all that she understood, the stars still amazed her. They had looked over the earth, constant and unchanged and at peace in the heavens; each one associated with folklore and myth that had been woven by man's tongue and past down through the centuries in all languages.

But, tonight, they all looked just a little bit different.

And. as the last of America's Misfits floated over the unseasonably calm Atlantic waters, Edee was comforted by the fact that, on this first night of their journey, they were being watched over by Orion: a warrior that had *finally* found the courage, and confidence, to don a sparkling pink gown.

And, if ever there was a perfect society, it was floating in a place that had no borders.

The Trail of Tears

Ronald was completely unaware of the international chain of events that were unfolding around him as he wandered, broken, back to the little hovel in White Plains that he had called his most recent home. The only motivation for him to follow one step with another had been the dim hope that Leticia would have returned to him and been whole by the time he came back. His calves ached and his once muscular frame now seemed almost skeletal. Having lost his keys somewhere along his way, he knocked on the door hoping his prayers would be answered when it opened.

But there was nothing but the echo of his fist rapping on the other side.

He waited for a moment, frustrated, but not yet to the point of concern.

He knocked again.

Nothing.

Suddenly a small, high voice interrupted his one sided conversation with the metal door before him. "Ain't nobody live there no more."

Ronald turned and found a young girl in the hallway, no more than four, draped in tattered rags and clinging tightly to a small doll that appeared to have been discarded, more than once, into the trash. It was missing half of its hair and one eye, and was riddled with ink stains from where another child had obviously marked it, but the way that this young girl cradled it, Ronald could tell she was certainly not the abuser. He looked down at her unkempt appearance, nappied hair and the bruising on her tiny arms that could not have been any more wide around than two of his own fingers put together. Her wide brown eyes stared up at him, trying to see past his dirtied appearance and wondering where he had come from. Ronald simply stared at her in response, confused by her words, and she repeated. "Ain't nobody live there no more. Spirit Lady gone. She done been gone. Long time!" The child questioned his presence.

Ronald took a moment to contemplate her words, before kneeling down and asking her with interest. "*Spirit Lady?* Who is Spirit Lady?"

The child's eyes grew wide, almost as if she was about to speak the words "Bloody Mary" for the third time as she looked into a mirror and afraid that her voice would surely invoke some demon spirit to her side. So, she just shook her head, pushing the hair of her doll over to the other side in the attempt to give her a bad comb over and make her presentable for company.

Ronald's heart was racing. The child *had* to tell him, but forceful words would only make her run, he knew. Kneeling down, he could see the faded outline of a blackened eye that had almost healed and wondered if her missing front tooth was the result of simple aging or the product of the same angry hand that had also managed to bruise her small lower lip. Her eyes were sweet, but saddened, and part of him wanted nothing more than to pick her up and take her in his arms and run as far away from whatever she was suffering through as he could take her.

But, she wasn't his child to take.

He knew that.

At the same time he wondered if she would be missed for more than a punching bag at the end of a bad day.

Desperate to know where his wife had gone, or been taken, he softened his tone and smiled at her. He fumbled to find words. Little boys, Ronald understood. He had been one. He had one. Little girls were an anomaly.

So were women.

Despite his appearances, his outward good looks and strong features, Ronald had always been shy around women. All his life, it seemed as if only his mother and Leticia understood him. His mother, having passed long ago, he needed that understanding from the one person on earth that still knew him. He thought back to his interactions with George's daughter, Alli, and thought for a moment before speaking, choosing his words carefully and remembering that women, even as girls, responded well to flattery. "Your doll is really pretty. What is her name?"

The small girl looked down at her doll, still fussing with its hair and half smiled as her eyes focused on the broken toy as though it was her greatest gift. "I calls her Cyn-tee-ah." The girl struggled to pronounce the name.

Ronald watched as her small hands gently caressed the dolls forehead before she gave it a kiss. "Cynthia? That's a beautiful name."

She nodded in agreement.

"I'd bet that Cynthia is your best friend?" he questioned and the child nodded before blurting out a question of her own and providing him with the perfect in road. "Who your best friend be?" She asked innocently.

Ronald paused. Anxious to know where Leticia had gone, but cautious about his words, he tried to solicit her help. "Well, see… That's the problem. I can't find my best friend. I don't know where she is."

"Your best friend ain't no *girl?*" Her small face queried as if such an idea was preposterous and he nodded his response.

"Who your best friend be?"

Ronald had seen the fear in the child's eyes, just a moment before, so he approached the topic gently. "Well, you see… my best friend… my best friend in the *whole* world… she saw some pretty terrible things and now she won't speak…. not even to me. Have *you* ever been so scared that you couldn't speak?"

He was saddened by the fact that when she nodded, he knew she was telling the truth, but he continued. "See… it would mean a whole lot to me if you could tell me where the people in that apartment went. Maybe I could find my best friend, again?"

The young girl seemed confused as she glanced over to the vacant apartment door and then back to Ronald. "Spirit Lady ain't got no friends? She done gone. I told mama I ain't been bad 'cuz Spirit Lady would done got me if I was. Spirit Lady get all bad kids and she make 'em like her and kids goes away forever *and ever!* I *told* mama I ain't been bad 'cuz Spirit Lady done leaved me alone!" The child clung tight to her doll as if she was trying to protect it from something and she shook her head as she recounted recent the urban legend that had been told to all the children in the building. As she crossed her arms in front of her, cradling her doll, a series of burn marks were revealed and Ronald felt almost sick to his stomach as he examined them with his eyes. He couldn't imagine why someone could have such rage for something so small and innocent in the ways of the world.

"Where is your mama?" Ronald inquired partially out of concern for the little girl and partially with the desire teach her mother how to properly land a right uppercut to the jaw, but the child only shrugged her shoulders.

"How about your daddy?" Ronald asked.

The child shook her head and looked up into his eyes as Ronald struggled to cope with his own culture. "Ain't got no daddy."

In only a few seconds, Ronald's mind had processed a million thoughts. He wasn't certain if he would ever see Leticia, again, and the idea left his chest feeling as though there was a gapping hollow hole inside of it that had taken all that was left of warmth and love in his body, yet at the same time he looked at this small girl, her body scarred and broken from abuse, but with such a sweet and gentle demeanor. He recalled the horrors of his own life. The things he had witnessed. The memories he wished he could force from his mind. All of the evil that crept into his dreams when he was most vulnerable and least expecting of it. Then, he looked into her small sunken cheeks, and into his own heart, and for the first time in his life he had a truly criminal thought.

So he plotted a lie.

"What did you say your name was?" He asked her as he searched her face for any similarities, but finding none, he was already one step ahead of her regardless of what her response may be.

"Savannah." She almost whispered as her eyes fell to the floor.

"What did you say?" Ronald faked surprise.

"Savannah." She repeated shyly.

"Okay, now *wait* a minute! Did you say *Savannah*? I don't believe you! What is your *mother's* name?" Ronald continued his act, adding a slight tone of excitement.

"Peoples calls her Tiny."

Ronald stood up, smiling wide, and did an almost pirouette as he ran his hand over his head then returned kneeling down before her and using the marks on her diminutive little frame to aid with the details. "Okay, now! Wait! *You're* Savannah? And your mama is *Tiny*? She smokes, right? And, *if I remember right* she has a *really* bad temper when she drinks! *Right?* Wow! It's been so long since I have seen her! *Gee!* I don't believe this!" He used the cigarette burns on her arms to aid in his deception.

Savannah looked to Ronald almost confused, but certain that he must know her mother and she nodded.

"Don't you see, *sweetheart*? *I'm* your daddy! Oh, it's been so long! You're so grown up! The last time I saw you, you were just a little baby! The *cutest* little baby you were!" Ronald reached his arms out to her hoping for a hug, the back of his mind wondering if his performance had been convincing.

Her eyes grew wide as tears rose almost immediately to the surface and she thrust herself into Ronald's arms so desperately wanting to believe him that she almost immediately convinced herself it was the truth. "I love you daddy! Where you been? Don't you ever go away, again! It been so bad here! Mama's always so angry! I ain't been bad, daddy! You gots to tell her I ain't bad!" She cried into his shoulder.

And Ronald panicked.

Sweeping her up into his arms, he promised he would never leave her side, as her teeny arms clung so tightly around his neck that he felt almost choked by them. Having made his decision, he quickly convinced her that they needed to go and that she had other family members that she needed to meet. "I will *always* protect you, Savannah. No one is *ever* going to hurt you, again, *okay*?" He promised to the one possible connection to Leticia that he had on this earth, as her eyes turned to him with hope that his words were meaningful and that her days of being beaten for sport were over. He cradled the back of her head into his shoulder, hiding her face as he made a quick break from the building, hoping that no one would recognize her as belonging to another, and he made his way down the streets that were close to her building.

Nervous about his take, he had only one thought: he had just kidnapped a four year girl. In less confusing times he would be serving twenty five to life for his compassion, but in *this* place he just might get away with it. He walked with her in his arms for what seemed like miles and the child never broke her embrace. Ronald could feel the small doll bouncing against his back with every hurried step and finally logic set in and he thought about what to do with her. He had already promised to keep her safe, but in truth, he couldn't think of anyplace that was safe for a child. His feet seemed to carry him, almost automatically, to a set of railroad tracks. Gently he sat her down in the grass and told her not to move as he foraged for some edible berries for them to eat. She was obedient, sitting on the little knoll and playing with her doll, but never letting her new found daddy wander from her eyesight. She looked to him as though he was some wonderful celebrity or superhero and Ronald felt humbled every time he caught her gaze.

He turned up his shirt, using it like a basket as he gathered enough wild blackberries to qualify as a meal, and then made his way back to her side. He placed over half of his findings in her small lap, and she immediately pressed one of the berries to her doll's lips. "Cyn-tee-ah likes it!" She smiled before taking her own meal. "Them's real good!" She exclaimed at the first bite.

Ronald smiled back, nodding. "And see, the darker they are, the sweeter they are." He commented, winking to her, as he stroked her small ebony cheek and kissed her forehead making her blush as though it was the first compliment she had ever been paid in her little life.

They finished their meal, and Ronald put his arm around her, tucking her to his side like a mother bird. As she leaned in, her little skirt rose up, just enough to reveal a large fresh bruise on her thigh that Ronald thought must have been incredibly painful as his eyes turned from the yellowed and purpled mass that had been previously hidden and he felt the back of his neck growing hot with anger. He then loosened his grip on her, wondering what other painful marks might be hiding under her clothing and not wanting to cause her any pain. Softly, she asked him "Where we goin', daddy?"

Looking out towards the tracks in front of him, Ronald could think of only one place to take her. The last place he had remembered feeling safe, although he, himself, had been miserable there.

Kenya's.

He was decided.

He had no other options.

Ronald stood up and then reached his hand to help young Savannah from the ground. Using the excuse of brushing off her clothing, he examined the back of her calves for any bruising, then told her to climb on his back, certain that the long journey would be far more comfortable for her if she was riding piggy back and without pressure on the large bruise he had just observed only moments before. Savannah and her dolly climbed aboard and she nestled her small head onto the back of his shoulder. Momentarily, Ronald was reminded of Ty' and how much he had missed that sensation.

And they walked.

And walked.

And walked.

Surviving on berries and edible leaves and the occasional nuts they found along their way, they slowly made it into Pennsylvania and finally to a familiar brownstone house. Ronald looked up at the threshold, remembering the last time he had been there and wishing that he had left Ty' inside. He felt guilty and broken as he stared up to the doorstep and wondered to himself how life might have been different had he never left. From the sidewalk, he let his mind wander until suddenly the door flew open and he saw his sister in law standing before him. Thrusting her arms into the air, as if she was testifying in church, Kenya exclaimed *"Praise Jesus! Praise the Lord! Clyve! Our prayers have been answered! Dear child, you get in this house!"* Kenya began to cry as she then motioned for Ronald to come forward and he found himself unable to control his own tears. Putting Savannah down, he reached for her hand and walked her up the stoop allowing Kenya to throw her arms around him and, for the first time, he felt comforted by her smothering.

And for a moment they cried as the family began to gather behind them, smiling.

"And who is this young traveler?" Kenya questioned enthusiastically as she looked down at Savannah and Savannah responded, smiling wide. "Aunt Kenya?"

Ronald turned to Kenya, his eyes asking her to not ask questions, as he reached for Savannah's arm, discretely revealing the burn scars, as he simply stated. "It's a long story, Aunt Kenya. I just couldn't leave *my* little girl where she was. Savannah was in a really *bad* place. You *understand*?"

Kenya was a little confused by the proclamation, but she simply nodded and smiled down at the sweet, small face before her. "Well, child! You are in luck! I am baking some of the most delicious cookies in the world, and it just so happens I need someone to lick all my spoons! You think you can handle that!"

Savannah nodded, excitedly.

Placing her arm around Ronald she herded him in.

One by one, his extended family gathered around reaching out for hugs and seemingly not bothered by his overwhelming stench and dirty clothing. As soon as the initial hugs were over, however, Kenya immediately commented. "Honey, we need to get you a bath and into some clean clothes. Clyve! Go get him some decent clothing, these are too dirty to even bother washing and you, Ronald, you throw out that egg timer in the bathroom and just stay in that shower water until you feel clean! Four minutes ain't even gonna take off the first layer of the dirt you been carrying!"

Ronald nodded a thank you, anxious at the idea of feeling clean, when suddenly, one last familiar face appeared in the hallway and his heart swelled, hoping his imagination was not playing tricks on him. Her voice was cracked and almost whispering, as if her vocal cords had not quite regained their strength, but her eyes were unmistakable, as he watched the tears fall from them with disbelief.

"Ronnie?"

Kenya's hands flew to her face in prayer position, smiling, as she watched him walk to her and take her in his arms. "Tish? *Tish?* Is it *really* you! *Oh God!* Please tell me *it's really you! Please tell me it's you! Oh, Tish! I love you so much! I never thought I could ever love someone so much!"*

Ronald's eyes flew to Kenya's shocked and unable to let go of his wife. He had been so certain she was gone, but now he had her back. Still his mind would not allow him to move forward without asking a simple question. Ronald's voice begged Kenya, *"How?"*

Kenya walked over to the two, placing one hand on the back of each of them and smiling to her baby sister as she shook her head wondering how either of them could possibly question that a higher power was at work as they held one another. "Was one of our church members that recognized her up there. Damn *Valley of the Damned."* Kenya looked down shaking her head. "I *warned him* not to go, but The Lord works in mysterious ways. He found my baby sister walkin' in a park. She wouldn't speak, but he knew her precious face and he said in that moment that Jesus spoke to him and he knew he done needed to bring her home to where she belonged." She reached down, clasping tightly to each of their hands then pensively she turned to Ronald, warning him. "It was a long road and a lot of prayer. But, now that you're here, she's gonna be fine."

Ronald nodded, wanting to believe her as he then turned his attentions to the eyes of the woman that meant more than anyone else in the world to him. Kenya walked away, taking small Savannah to the kitchen and happy to have another young person to entertain and amuse as she had once with her nephew. Her face seemed plain without makeup and her hair was combed down in a manageable, but unfashionable, manner. Leticia looked to Ronald as if she was breaking news to him gently. It was as if she had no recollection of his presence at the time their baby boy had been taken from them. "Ty''s gone. He was killed. In Harlem, I think. I tried to help him, but there was so much blood." Her voice was barely audible.

Ronald wrapped his arms around her tighter than he ever had before, and he cried pressing his dirtied cheek to hers. "I know."

And, there they stood.

Until they both felt secure in the notion that once they let go, the other would still be standing there. Suddenly aware of his appearance, and still enchanted by his wife's beauty, he wanted nothing more than to take a long shower and shave his face. Grabbing a towel for him, still not quite herself, Leticia followed him into the bathroom.

After thirty minutes under steaming hot water, Ronald felt like a new man. Not wanting to be away from each other, Leticia had waited in the bathroom, sitting down on the toilet seat and holding the same towel that she would eventually use to dry him off when he was finished. He took the opportunity to explain Savannah's presence to her and Leticia shook her head wondering how someone could have been so cruel to a child. Along their journey, Savannah had revealed many secrets: one more terrible than the next and all of them only convincing him more that his decision, although beyond the law, was justified. Leticia, still not in full command of her own voice, didn't say much, but she heard every word that he spoke and her heart ached for the little girl in the other room.

"She thinks I'm her dad, Tish. I hope you are okay with that?" Ronald peeked out from behind the curtain, worried about her reaction, but Leticia only nodded and looked to him with an understanding expression. He smiled, looking to her and their eyes communicated in a way that only true soul mates could. Nodding, he returned to his bathing, and called out, in a more teasing tone hoping to invoke a smile. "She *also* thinks you're some kinda 'boogie woman', so I hope you're okay with that, too!"

And for the first time, in what felt like ages, Leticia let out a small laugh.

And it felt so good.

As she heard the water turning off, Leticia rose, fanning out the towel she had been holding in her lap and as the curtain slid open and she pointed her finger downward, swirling it in a gesture telling him to turn around. She dried his back, as she had so many times before, but still unable to comprehend the idea that they had been reunited. As he turned around again, she dried his chest and thighs, then his calves, and he watched as she stood up and lovingly pushed her toweled cover hands to either side of his face, drying his neck, his cheeks and his ears. Reaching out for her, he kissed her, holding her tight and sharing her same thoughts. It wasn't sexual. They were just happy to be near one another, again. As Ronald made his way to the bedroom to change, Leticia wandered into the kitchen to investigate the newest little adoption into the family. As she entered, she found Kenya pulling a fresh batch of sugar cookies from the oven and watched as little Savannah clapped, applauding their safe return from the oven.

Kenya rinsed her hands in the sink and turned to her sister asking if Ronald was through with the tub. Leticia nodded and Kenya then turned to Savannah, tapping her nose and smiling at the pasty line of batter that was drying around her lips on top of the layers of dirt. "Then, child! I know someone else that has a date with Mr. Bubbles!" Kenya smiled, but was taken back by the little girl's reaction and the expression of fear that suddenly took over her face. Savannah pushed herself into a corner, shielding her doll and shaking like a trapped animal. Having heard Ronald retell her stories for the past thirty minutes, Leticia came to the logical conclusion that even something as simple as a bath gave the child reason to be overwhelmed with fear and anticipation of torture as she watched her pull her dolly close and look around the room for Ronald to save her. Leticia's heart sank and she wanted nothing more than to reach out to the small girl and comfort her, but it was clear she would have only panicked her more if she had stepped closer.

Just then Ronald walked in, now dressed in some of Clyve's sweats, that he had to adjust tight at the waistline to keep them from slipping off. His eyes immediately caught Savannah's and she ran past Leticia to him, hoping he would protect her. Ronald looked to the women confused by her display as she cried begging him, "No tub! *Please! No water!* I ain't been bad!"

Ronald held her, uncertain for a moment as to what to say and looking to Kenya and Leticia as if he expected their help, but even they were at a loss. So he turned to psychology. "Savannah, sweetheart. I just had a bath. I haven't been bad either? Baths feel good. They get you all clean."

"*No! Please!*" Savannah's eyes pressed with the fear of some horrid memory that had surfaced with the idea of being submerged in water and the three adults could only imagine what she had suffered. One of Leticia's oldest daughters walked over witnessing the scene. Disturbed she could only cover her mouth and shake her head, walking away again.

Thinking on his feet, and knowing a little more about her history than the others, Ronald suggested a plan. "How about this, sweetheart? What if I go and run a bath for Cynthia? Not a *bad* bath, a *good* bath. And we'll have Miss Kenya and Miss Leticia watch and you can tell me what to do and then, once they *know* how to give a *good* bath, they can give one to you?"

Savannah looked to Ronald with fear and hesitation. Still, in the child's mind, he was the only person that had always been honest with her and she trusted him enough to believe he would not hurt her. After thinking for a minute, she handed her precious Cynthia to him and made him promise not to hurt her, repeatedly informing him that she had been good. Ronald took the doll and patted Savannah on the head as he realized for the first time the incredible trust the child had placed in him.

It was the first time she had separated herself from the doll.

"You stay here and eat some cookies. I'm going to clean out the tub and run a nice warm bath for Cynthia, then you can come help, okay?"

"Not too hot! She been good!" Savannah called out as she watched Ronald carry her toy away to the bathroom. "Not real cold, neither!" The child cried. She fidgeted nervously as he walked into the hall, then Leticia knelt down, in a soft but breaking voice, reassuring her. "It won't be too hot or too cold. It'll be just like Goldilock's porridge. *Just right!*" Leticia smiled.

"Who Goldilocks?" Savannah questioned.

"*Goldilocks and The Three Bears*?" Leticia seemed stunned that a child would not know the story, so she searched for another analogy. "Um, Cinderella?"

Savannah shook her head.

Now, just curious, she simply started naming Fairy Tales hoping at least one would have a familiar ring. To each Savannah only shook her head not understanding what Leticia's cracking voice was trying to communicate. Walking over with a warm cookie, Kenya then questioned, "Why child, did *no one* ever read you a bedtime story?" Savannah's tear stained face fell to the floor and she softly responded, "I don't think so?"

"Well, that changes *today!*" Kenya shoved one of her most recent baked creations into the little girl's tiny hands and, a few cookies later, Ronald called out for Savannah. Cautiously he led her to the bubble filled tub, feeling her resistance grow stronger with each step that drew closer to the bathroom, as the two women stood in the doorway pretending to take careful note on how to wash a doll. He could tell she would be panicked if the door closed, so they left it open, allowing her an escape if needed. After checking the water temperature and smiling at Ronald the two began bathing the vinyl skin of Savannah's most prized possession and, eventually, he convinced the young girl to jump in the water, herself. Leaving the room, but promising Savannah that he would be just outside he exited and went to help out with the evening meal by setting the table, as he had so many other times during his previous stay. From the hallway he could hear the echoes of Kenya's voice as she recanted the tale of three little bears and Goldilocks. Of course, in *her* version the three little bears had been away at church and Goldilocks was a thieving heathen that had strayed from the path, but that was turned around by the bear's pastor. Shaking his head he smiled at Savannah's laughter and the modified version of what just might have been her first bedtime story.

When Leticia and Kenya emerged, they were toting a towel draped and smiling Savannah, who still held on to her doll's arm. What was left of Cynthia's hair was dripping water onto the floor, but nobody seemed to mind as Ronald made his way over to her beaming face. "Why are you telling me that under all of that dirt was *this* pretty little girl?"

Savannah blushed, but nodded, now having changed her mind about bath time.

"Why I had no idea I was traveling with a *supermodel*?" He continued to feed her small ego and she hid her smiling face in Leticia's neck, then bounced back grinning at the room. Even Clyve, who was normally a crumudgen, broke with his traditional frown and complimented her. "Why all she needs is a crown and we could call her Miss America."

Still there was the issue of clothing. Hers were too dirty to wear and all of Kenya and Clyve's children were too big to provide hand me downs. Snapping her fingers, as an idea suddenly burst to mind, Kenya pulled Leticia and Savannah into the bedroom that Leticia and Ronald had once called their temporary home. Reaching to the back of the closet, she pulled out a small child's choir robe that had accidentally been sent with an order a few years back.

"I knew there's a reason I kept this!" Kenya exclaimed as she removed the plastic wrap from the small gown.

Savannah's eyes gleamed with amazement as she ran her tiny fingers over the soft material unable to believe something so pretty was now hers. Zipping up the gown, she looked at herself in the mirror, twirling around and admiring the seemingly almost perfect fit. "Well, it'll do for pajamas until we can get her some more clothes from the church coat closet." Kenya nodded with satisfaction and Leticia agreed.

Excited, Savannah raced into the living room, still dragging Cynthia behind. "Daddy! Daddy *look!*" She ran into Ronald's arms and he immediately picked her up and spun her around. "You're just gorgeous! Did you *thank* Aunt Kenya for that lovely robe?"

"Tank you, Aunt Kenya!" Savannah called out with a big grin, still having trouble with her 'th's'.

About an hour later, the families sat down to dinner. In the meantime, Savannah had been entertained by Kenya's oldest daughter, Shuvonda, who carefully took the time to gently comb out her hair and braid it into neat cornrows. As Shuvonda braided away, Ronald and Leticia helped out in the kitchen, not wanting to be far from one another. Their conversations kept light by the desire to forget their own recent pasts and the need to return to a sense of normalcy in their relationship. Meats had become scarce, so most of the meal was an assortment of vegetables grown and shared by members of the church. Still there was plenty for the family to enjoy and Kenya's homemade biscuits did well to fill the voids in anyone's stomachs.

Savannah could not believe the bounty before her as she watched one dish after another make its way to the table: a little portion of each being scooped onto her own plate, by Leticia. There were mashed potatoes and collards and carrots and peas and even some stewed tomatoes: and, of course, plenty of biscuits and cornbread.

After supper, Kenya and Leticia cleared the table and began cleaning up the kitchen, but only a few minutes into their cleaning, Kenya shooed Leticia into the living room to go spend time with Ronald. "You go on an' get, baby girl. *I* got this. Go see your husband." Leticia smiled appreciatively, laying her dish towel on the counter neatly and making her way to Ronald's side. Ronald and Clyve had been chatting, actually having a *real* conversation, as Leticia entered the living room. Kenya's children had all made their way to their respective rooms, but little Savannah was curled up in Ronald's arms, fighting to stay awake. Leticia sat down next to him, and gently caressed Savannah's calf, rousing her just slightly and she smiled.

"Ronnie, I'm going to go get ready for bed. Are you tired?"

"Tired? I passed tired three hours before we got here, Tish. And, I am pretty sure this little one could use a decent night's sleep in a bed instead of on the floor of some abandoned railcar. She was a trooper. The whole way. She never complained once." Clyve smiled, watching his in laws reconnect through the girl.

Leticia rose to wash her face and Ronald soon followed behind. As he slipped under the covers of the queen size bed they had once shared so many nights in, he thought to himself that he had never felt a mattress so comfortable. Placing little Savannah between them, Leticia crawled in on the other side and carefully moved Cynthia up under Savannah's arm. Almost instinctively, Savannah rolled over pulling her plastic companion close and nuzzling into the warm bed, as she whispered, half asleep. "I love you, daddy. I love it here." Ronald smiled, empathetically, to Leticia as he leaned over and kissed Savannah's forehead, making her smile just before falling asleep. Leticia looked down at the daughter her husband had adopted in her absence, and running one finger over her small hand, not wanting to wake her, she said in her softest voice, "Goodnight, angel." Then slowly turned to Ronald, still unable to believe he was back at her side.

From her expression, Ronald was unable to tell if she was really saying goodnight to the child between them, or to the one they had conceived together and lost, as he watched a single tear fall silently from her right eye. He pushed her hair to the side, and carefully wiped it away, then explored her face for answers. Even without make up, her high cheekbones and perfect features made her beautiful in the moonlight. Leaning over he kissed her gently, not wanting to rush things between them, and, in that moment, he decided it didn't matter to which child she was speaking. A rush of calmness and serenity washed over him as he laid there, under the comforter that now seemed so soft and cozy, and he felt completely at ease with the world. Savannah's small frame was tucked safely between them and seemed so relaxed and at ease as she let out a small sigh and welcomed peaceful dreams. Leticia snuggled her head into the pillow and reached over Savannah, placing her hand on Ronald's shoulder, not wanting to close her eyes for fear she would lose him as she dreamt; and, for the first time in her short life, Savannah understood what it was like to fall asleep feeling safe and loved.

They were a family, again.

Mate In Three

With the Alaskan pipeline ablaze, General Ivan Stahl spent several of the hours that would follow pretending to explain how it was that the Northwest Command did not see such an attack coming to the world? How did they not pick up the missile as it traveled across Canadian air space before finding its mark? After several hours of conversation, he had finally convinced Canada's Prime Minister that his nation was safe, excusing the singular incident as a massive and unforeseen breach of security.

It was a lie.

In truth, this was the moment Stahl had been waiting for; hoping for, even. *Of course he saw the missile launch!* He even knew its destination. Intelligence from another nation had informed him the moment it left Pakistan, but he told nothing of this to his men. He would fake shock and horror with them when the news of the blast made it to Cheyenne.

He paced the war room, as his men debated strategies and wondered about the consequence of their recent loss. Mathematicians calculated how long the Territory could sustain without a crude oil supply and crunched various series of numbers, projecting them on a screen. Even with conservation efforts, the Territory would be doomed within nine months, and no other countries would sell to them fearful that might make them targets for similar attacks by the unpredictable Islamic Nation. The money printed at the Denver mint and circulated around the Territory had no value outside of its borders. As much as they had tried to choke the Northeast into submission, by cutting off their food supplies and other goods, through control of traffic on the Mississippi, members of the Command, themselves, were feeling the noose as it tightened around their neck.

Patiently, Stahl listened to the fears of the room before addressing them. Quietly, his second in command, a seasoned Officer by the name of Rick Thomas, pondered the calculations that seemed to be taking place behind the General's eyes and tried to decipher the reading. Thomas watched the General's body language closely and suddenly was overcome with a feeling of uneasiness.

"Enough!" He belted, and the room was called to attention.

Stahl's presence dominated the room, as he purposefully made eye contact with each of his men, trying to determine if there would be any defectors in the group, before he presented his plan. Thomas worked to hide his suspicions. Stahl either ignored them, or failed to see them.

"You would be submissive to demands of enemies? Are you *fools*?!" He demanded, then paused as the room searched for answers from his comrades. "No! Enemies do not control fate of this Territory! *We* control fate! *We* control enemies! Da!?" His thick Russian accent, seemed to add emphasis to his every word.

The room nodded, but was left feeling uncertain of their direction, given their recent losses. After a few moments of silence, one brave Commander Thomas would question the General, softly and respectfully. "Permission to speak, Sir?"

The General nodded, seeming almost impressed by his candor.

"We agree, Sir. The safety and preservation of the Territory is our most paramount concern. However, in light of the situation… in light of intelligence which indicates Middle Eastern involvement … How can we proceed? We don't even know who the *real* enemy *is*? We cannot 'control' what is unknown to us. There are rumors the missile came from Afganistan, but Pakistan is also being rumored. Iran has nukes, as well. For all we know, at this point, it may have been one of our own?"

The General purposefully waited a moment, before responding, allowing the room to fill with enough tension to make for perfect timing. "So, you take out *all* enemies... at same time."

Glances were exchanged, and it was clear that the room thought the concept was preposterous. The men seemed confused by the General's path. It was impossible to eliminate the entire Middle East without massive international fallout and retribution. It couldn't be done, they were certain. Maybe they had misunderstood Stahl, some thought. Besides, they didn't know who was foe or friend, and the silent concensus was to attack Elijah Drew's group and be done with it, but Stahl saw the bigger picture.

He just needed to get his men to agree.

He allowed the room to think him ignorant, for a moment. Then, like a magician pulling the impossible from thin air, he reached behind a cabinet and produced a dust covered cardboard tube, that appeared to have been in storage for sometime. Although the Cyrillic writing was unfamiliar to most in the room, the date 1988 was clear. The large yellowed blueprints contained within seemed to be a Middle Eastern map, of some sort, with a large red square clearly marked out spanning the borders of several nations. The document had been produced by Russia's Komitet Gosudarstvenoi Bezopasnosti; more commonly known to Americans as the KGB. Naively, no one would question how it was that General Ivan Stahl came to have it in his possession.

As the men stood around the aged papers, trying to decipher the writings, Stahl continued with his pitch. "You take out all enemies. At same time. Gentlemen, is here, is document from old KGB Plan. Plan, to destroy enemies, if needed, in most effective manner. They had one for you, too." The General winked and chuckled and the men joined in light laughter, momentarily breaking the tension in the room.

"KGB plans never fail. This you must know."

Focusing on the drawings and what appeared to be four specifically placed targets, one of the men questioned, "I don't understand what we are looking at here? A map of the oil fields?"

"Niet. Not fields. Not exactly. Russia was to friends making with countries America could not understand us to be so much friends with. But, is knowledge that we must have from them. So we play games of friendship. Yes, map shows oil. Map shows size, location of reserves. And, depth."

"But, Sir, what are we looking at here? What are these four marks? Targets?" Commander Thomas, now curious, began to examine the paper more closely.

"Da. In KGB, in Russian, you translate this as 'The Magic Square.'" The General scrolled his finger along the wording at the top of the map that would seem to be the document's title.

"The Magic Square? I don't see how this works? If we bomb four different targets, affecting all of these countries, the whole world would blast us out of existence! We *can't* do that!"

"Yes we *will*! Is *only* method for survival!" Stahl demanded, sure of himself and unwilling to accept criticism from the room. "Not bomb, nuclear warhead! We launch four, all at same time. The oil here is underground. These networks, much like underground river that is to connect these four points, destroy for us that we need not to target." Intensely focused on the plans before him, he ran his fingers between the points as if he was delicately petting some exotic woman and becoming aroused with anticipation of the events to come.

"You can't possibly be suggesting that the United States of America launch four simultaneous nukes, in an attempt to bomb the entire Mid-East off this planet? Think of the collateral damage! International reaction! My God, Sir, some of these areas are highly populated! There are hospitals... schools... innocent victims! Aren't you forgetting we *don't know* for certain who the enemy is?" The Commander demanded, garnering agreeable nods from the room.

Stahl, however, was unphased. Seeing that the hard sell approach was not working with the room, he softened his tone, and placed his hand on Commander Thomas' shoulder, in a fatherly gesture. "Commander Thomas, your opinion I respect much, but your logic is not correct... This we *must* do. Is only matter of time, before attack is to be closer than pipeline of Alaska. Is only matter of time, before Elijah Drew, fed and made to be fat by money of these countries, is to come to battle on west side of Mississippi. Is only matter of time, before we lose this war. Before whole world is to lose this war. To destroy Middle East is to save future of all nations."

Shaking his head, the Commander could see a glimmer of reason in Stahl's approach, although he also could find strong argument against him. "Think of the casualties, Sir. And why nukes? We can't."

Still certain, Stahl explained. "No, we must. And must to be nuclear weapons…
These areas, you are happy to be knowing, are not with many people. Casualities are to
be not so many that you think. But, with nuclear weapon, the fire is made impossible to
fight. Deserts burn without control. All wealth and power for Middle East is oil. Drew is
to be cut at knees. No more to be threat to us. Gonzales, is not to be threat. Power is lost
from both hands. He gives to Mexico much land, and with land, people follow. The south
is empty of Latinos. The Northeast will be made easy to take back."

"We'll never make target. As soon as we launch, every nation will be after us to
blow those weapons out of the sky. Britain, China, Isreal, Pakistan… they'll all know the
moment our silos open. Everyone is going to know!" Commander Thomas tried to
reason.

Stahl, then turned to the one member of the group that had always been allowed to
attend such meetings out of uniform. His sloppy attire was an irritation, as he sat feeding
himself snacks and slugging caffeine, but Stahl needed this obnoxious little genius,
known only as "Tommy" to the group. To anyone that didn't know him, they would think
he had been oblivious to the conversation around him, but Stahl knew better, although the
young man seemed deeply focused on some complicated math problem that he was
scribbling rapidly to solve on a pad in front of him. His shirt, sporting a large coffee stain
and crumbs, was almost a distraction to the obsessively organized General. "Tommy,
you are to buy me two hours of blindness with nations that would see? Do not worry of
Isreal, I am to deal with her, myself."

Without looking up, seemingly not paying attention, and while stuffing yet
another ding dong in his mouth, the young man known as the world's most brilliant

hacker, simply nodded, almost anxiously, and responded through his cupcake lined teeth, as he spat bits of cake to the floor. "Yep! No problem." He then rose from his seat and headed over to a computer to begin work on things that others could not possibly understand.

"Why are you going to leave Israel on line?" The Commander gently questioned.

Grinning, out one side of his mouth, with an almost evil, but knowing glint, the General responded, "I am to think Israel is to enjoy to watch very moment that all of her enemies are to be destroyed… and, I am to be thinking they must know where to send thank you card."

The Commander sighed as he looked at the map and ran through all of the potential disasters that could befall the Territory in the wake of such an action, but he knew one thing was true, the strike on the pipeline was a warning shot. Things could only get worse as Drew's power and influence grew stronger. If the Territory faltered, the fate of America would be lost. He debated the need for such strong action, though, but was unable to come up with a better solution to present. As the Commander's mind raced, General Stahl continued to explain their position, and soon he had convinced the vast majority of the room.

"So, we agree?" He asked firmly, returning to his more military style barking, knowing his timing was perfect.

The men in the room prepared for a task that they had drilled thousands of times, but had never actually put into action: the launch of a nuclear warhead. Only this time, they would have the complication of timing this launch in coordination with the efforts of knocking out satellite capabilities which would allow other nations to see what they were up to. As the group tried to decide where to launch from, Tommy went to work, trying to breach the highest levels of other nation's security.

"China's a *bitch*!" The talented computer whiz exclaimed to no one, at one point, as his fingers flew at MOCK 5 speed across the keyboard.

Finally, he screamed, *"GOT EM!"*

" Who's your daddy, you little kung pao bitches! THAT'S RIGHT! I'M YOUR DADDY!" Tommy performed a little celebratory dance, cabbage patching in front of his keyboard, as the rest of the room prepared for the real task at hand. Proud of himself, a fresh donut now in hand and sprinkling powder across the keys, Tommy nodded with satisfaction to the General. Forcing a smile, the General nodded a thank you.

The room fell silent.

All eyes turned to the large screens before them.

The Territory took aim.

Tension filled the room, as phone calls began pouring in from concerned nations, one after the other, demanding to speak with Stahl. Stahl, in his typical fashion, tried to blame Gonzales and Drew, claiming, he too, had just recently lost communication and could not understand what was happening. His arguments so convincing, he was able to quickly coax other nations into choosing to wear blindfolds and not see the big picture before them. Exaggerating that the Northwest Command's systems had been compromised, and that he was certain that Drew and Gonzales were behind such an act, he told the world he was making every effort to get his weapons systems up and running as quickly as possible, encouraging other nations to be on guard, but assuring them that the Territory was the only logical target.

For show, Israel opened several of her silos, positioning aim at Washington D.C., and other targets that had been dictated to her by Stahl. When Britain and China called to confirm Israel's move, Israel readily backed Stahl up, verifying she had moved to retaliate, furthering international suspicions that either Drew or Gonzales were behind this act. The idea of Middle Eastern annihilation was almost enough to bring Israel's Prime Minister and his staff to the point of masturbation, as they watched the satellite images of the bombs approaching their marks.

And the world waited.

And as if they were four wild horses, running full gallop through the night sky, the last of America's hopes sped towards their targets. Gonzales and Drew, still trying to comprehend the flood of recent calls and the obvious anxieties expressed by leaders both of Allys and enemies, feared for their own safety and cast their eyes to the west, as they wondered what horrible payback was en route to their doorsteps on the heels of the pipeline attack. Neither could have ever imagined the events that had already been set in motion or what was soon to be the fate of America.

No one could have imagined America's fate.

The war room, in Cheyenne, was silent. All members of the Command awaiting the inevitable transformation of the world, that knew was about to take place. Stahl, perhaps the calmest member of the group, occasionally glanced up at the screens to monitor his angels of death as they flew across the hemisphere, but was otherwise focused on how to explain what would become of the Territory, once they had landed. He poured a glass of Merlot, sipping it slowly as he watched, and fielded the intermittent phone call or two, pretending to share the exact same trepidations that were expressed by whatever party was on the other line, with the skill of an Academy Award winning actor.

And then the moment came.

And, as Stahl had promised, the deserts burned with unimaginable fury.

It was destruction on the level that not even the KGB could have imagined.

The bombs set into motion, a chain reaction throughout the Middle East. Just as the brilliant strategist members of the Komitet Gosudarstvenoi Bezopasnosti had predicted, the underground rivers that connected various fields, set off one underground explosion…after another… after another… as firey spears of oil shot thousands of feet in the air, raining down on areas not meant to be targets for destruction. From the satellites, the Middle East looked like a huge, smoke filled land of volcanic activity. Millions were set into states of panic, looking for refuge and unable to comprehend what had just happened. Schools and homes were overcome, as bodies, consumed by flames, seemed to melt into the sands. Huge rivers of oil poured out from the earth, some finding its way into the Persian Gulf, setting the sea ablaze and catching fire to harbors, that were loaded with plenty of combustibles to continue feeding the inferno. More explosions were set off, and the bodies of workers were flung effortlessly to the sky. In an instant, once wealthy nations were left with nothing to do, but watch their futures literally go up in smoke.

It worked.

The KGB's plans, as the General had promised, were always successful.

Back in Cheyenne, the phone rang, and with General Stahl engaged in other conversation, Commander Thomas answered. On the other end of the phone was a man with a thick accent, much like the General's, but it was not the General's son. The Commander knew Vladimir's voice, and was surprised when the General, almost seeming to expect the call, immediately broke into Russian.

He rarely spoke Russian, on the phone, not even with Vladimir.

Watching, curiously, the Commander thought that the General's tone of voice and body language seemed to indicate he was somehow being thanked or praised for something he had done as he watched him gesticulate with joyous embarrassment. Suddenly, as he watched the man that he had for so long now respected and appreciated as an exceptional military strategist he was overcome with a feeling of uneasiness and Thomas could only pray that his instincts were betraying him.

But, his instincts were never wrong.

Stahl called the men to gather in their seats, and in front of them, he stood and explained that which the Commander had feared. Some were stunned, others numb and in shock, but they all left the room when the General stopped speaking. Save one: Rick Thomas.

Still sitting in his chair, trying to digest what he had just learned, his eyes almost welled with loss, as he realized what had just happened. "So it was *all* a lie? All these years?" he begged a response from the General.

"You are not to worry, Thomas. You serve well. There will be place for you. High rank. I will see to this, myself."

The Commander's expression was distant; as if he had just woken from a dream, and was momentarily confused by his surroundings. "I am not worried about rank, Sir... You lied to a whole nation? Your country lied to the whole world...for years... for decades... *How?*... Even before the break... before Gonzales... before... before all of it... before the Command... How could Russia have known this would happen? How could you see?"

The General smiled knowingly, and somewhat sympathetic to the Commander's loss. "I know, for you, is hard to understand truth."

"The end of the cold war? The disbandment of the KGB? The food riots? The fall of the Iron Curtain? They were all lies?" The thoughts inside the Commanders head fell from his mouth as he tried to pull his mind from the shock.

The General nodded, and tried to explain. "Not all lies. The riots... the hunger was real. The pain was real... this you must know. But, for the rest, yes, were lies."

Commander Thomas could do nothing more than shake his head, "How? Why? We were at peace? *Your country* ended the Cold War? Gorbechav ended it. We made peace."

Placing his hand on the Commander's shoulder, the General tried to comfort him. "No, Commander. *We* only make different strategy. Always enemies, were we... Russia and the US...For young America, was easier to believe lies... America is like child... still to believe in fairy tales and Santa Claus... And, much like child, America is to be impetuous and unpredictable in war... So, we make new plan...Even then, your country was failure... You are just too blind to see what world sees..."

Commander Thomas looked deep to the General. Realizing, his genius and heartbroken for the loss of the nation he once had called home, as the General continued on. "...but, for all wars you make, you never see the one you make here... with each other... And, for Russia, was easier *this* way... We let you make war... and grow weak."

As the Commander sat and tried to contemplate the implications of Soviet world dominance, the General began to gather his things. With the Middle East still ablaze, her oil fields no longer a resource, Russia was now left with the world's largest supply of oil, and with total control of all of the wealth and vast military power of the former United States. The international community would have no choice, but to bow before her and obey her every command.

The Imperial Soviet Union announced their existence to the globe. Their first action was to reclaim the land given to Mexico, and Latinos fled deep into Mexico's borders and far from what was now Soviet land.

There was no argument.

Like Romulus Augustus, Hector Gonzales faded from history, never to be heard or seen again.

The General made his way to the door, content to leave the Commander with his thoughts, understanding how such defeat must bother him as a military man. Just then, the Commander found he had one final question. Softly, "General Stahl, Sir... What do we do now?"

Looking into the Commander's eyes, with more compassion than he had openly shown to anyone in years, he simply replied. "Young Commander... may I suggest you learn to speak Russian."

Thomas knew it was over. His mind reverting to military tactics, and the General's nature, he also knew that the majority of his fellow Officers, and most likely he, would be executed at sunrise. The General would not tolerate the chance for dissention in the ranks.

Knowing that word of the Soviet overthrow had not made its way to the lower ranks, Commander Thomas gathered his things and headed quickly to the Command's closest airbase. He was suddenly overcome with a sensation of fear and was certain that America's new leaders would have no place for him, or the other formerly American men, in their new military. Most of them had already proved their disloyalty by organizing a movement that intended to have a large section of the United State secede from the Union and Thomas knew the Russians would sooner execute men, like himself, than risk another mutiny. Plus, they couldn't take the chance of allowing the world to know the truth.

The Soviet Government had plotted this moment carefully and they had patiently waited almost forty years for their plans to reach fruition. The story they would tell would argue that the attack of the Alaskan pipeline had fallen too close to their own borders, forcing them to mobilize troops, and they successfully convinced other nations that they only had taken over the United States forces to prevent further violence. They publicly condemned the use of nuclear weapons, and assured the international community that the world was safe so long as they were guarding all of the former United States' little red buttons. They had been a Judas to Israel, first convincing them they would eliminate their enemies, under the cover of a US Flag, and now telling the world that Israel was to blame. They convinced other nations that the Jews had plotted with the United States for mutual revenge and the lie was easy for other nations to swallow as both nations seemingly had motive to hate the Middle East. Israel's Prime Minister tried to argue the truth, now able to see what had happened, but no one would listen.

It had been the greatest military deception in modern history.

The Russians had planned far more than a mere military occupation of United States' soil. This was the end of a forty year war and the Russians had won. The victors had no intention of sharing their spoils and Commander Thomas knew it.

He was a pilot and he saw a small window of opportunity for his own escape.

He made his way to the airbase. The young men charged with its guard found nothing unusual when the Commander approached and signed out one of their fully fueled, smaller planes. With no money, or food, and only the clothes on his back, Thomas took to the air, flying dangerously low to avoid detection, but he would not feel safe until his wheels found ground in another nation.

As the sun rose over the western hemisphere, Thomas stepped out onto the abandoned airstrip where he had landed. Looking around, he now could only wonder if he would be accepted in this new land where he would be considered an immigrant: and, having no other choice, he set out to find the lost American dream.

THE END

Epilogue

Towards the end of the second Cold War, the Soviet Union was coming to the dark realization that they were positioned for defeat. Although their communist ideology was still strong, financially they could see that they were losing the battle they so very desperately desired to win against the United States. As the Soviets moved to form alliances with the Middle East and similarly minded nations throughout Southeast Asia, politicians and military strategists in Washington grew nervous as they reflected on the Soviet Union's prior coalition with Cuba. Those old enough to remember those days when the world teetered on the edge of nuclear conflict began to feel as though the Communists were slowly beginning to encircle them like a pack of hungry wolves, positioning for attack.

And the arms race continued.

Attacking the Soviets was not an option for the United States. A military conflict with the Superpower would surly only serve to destroy them both. From behind the Iron Curtain, Russian sentiments were similar. There was one great difference between the nations, however and the KGB's intelligence argued, to the highest levels, a concept which at the time, was almost absurd: end the Cold War. Soviet intelligence was brilliant and there was no argument in international circles that the KGB knew more about American politics and military strategy than the United States did itself. Even four decades before their eventual overthrow of the United States, the KGB saw an incredible weakness in America, one that even Americans refused to admit: division.

As "political correctness" found center stage in America's culture, other nations chuckled about how such a seemingly strong country would allow themselves to be controlled by such a novelty. The United States struggled to maintain dignity in international circles as Russian strategists searched the board for their next move.

It was so simple.

In 1983, a young General Stahl, then known as Mikel Andropov, a rising star in the highly secretive KGB, was given a new identity. Labeled as a defector, and given all of the paperwork that would define him in the eyes of the US Government as a mild mannered history teacher that had angered the Soviet Union's Government by teaching positive aspects of Capitalism, he was sent, by his Comrades, on a mission. He left behind a wife and nine year old son, without remorse.

The following year, Ivan Stahl would enter the United States claiming political asylum, and touting a loyalty to his new nation that even those born on American soil would not claim. Not long after, he would enlist in the US Army. He quickly rose through the ranks, seemingly the perfect patriot, as he excelled in every course of military study and strategy presented to him. In Operation Desert Storm, his acts of bravery earned him, not only medals and commendations, but the undying loyalty of those that served alongside him. He was a model soldier. He was, by all accounts, a model American.

In reality, though, he was a Trojan Horse.

And he wasn't alone.

There were thousands of them engrained in American society: living among them, working among them and secretly plotting the end of the United States.

The KGB was not as interested in the military knowledge Stahl could provide, as their own intelligence had provided them more than what they needed, at the time. They were more interested in the political climate in the United States than their weaponry. Their eyes were focused on much bigger prizes. So, they waited.

Everything in life is just a matter of time… or timing.

Many nations had observed, with so many internal problems in the US, that the clock on America's survival was ticking; but none saw this so keenly as the Soviets. Stahl, or Andropov, as he was still known to them, was their deepest plant. Although his communications with his Soviet partners would be limited for the next several decades, he never lost sight of his mission.

America's position as the ultimate world power was watched carefully by Red Eyes.

Waiting, for the right timing was in Stahl's command.

Stahl was chosen for this reason: his timing was *impeccable*.

On the Soviet side, they appeared to the world to be financially crumbling under Gorbachev's perestroika, but they weren't. Their plan was easy: *lie*. Lie to America and the world. They used America's most powerful weapon to their own advantage: the American media.

It was such a simple tactic.

Convince America that the Soviet Union was a threat no more. As much as Samantha Smith had once greeted Soviet school children with open arms, over the years, rising generations in the United States would soon forget the threat that those before them once saw looming over a large portion of the European Continent, and younger Americans would accept Russians as their friends. The real threat hiding under the well preserved, although now hidden, Iron Curtain.

It was as hard and steely as ever. It was just tucked out of sight.

It became a vault.

With help from the world's most influential family on the diamond market, the Soviets slowly started funneling money and hiding it in pretty shiny stones, well guarded within their own borders. Their economy appeared to be faltering on the world market. The Russian mafia would use diamonds as currency and deals continued to be struck with other nations that shared their hatred for the United States. As Russia allowed the world to think the KGB had been disbanded, she cried poverty and played ignorant when nations began to question what had become of her nuclear weapons supply.

In reality, the KGB knew the location of each and every missile.

Wars are expensive, both in terms of casualties and monies expended.

Americans would have revolted against Soviet imperialism, and that would have drained even more and complicated plans for unification and complete domination of resources. So, instead, they took a lesson from Capitalism. Soviets gave themselves a new identity. Just as Valu-Jet changed names to Air Tran, hoping America would forget prior disasters, the Soviet Union became Russia, and appeared to the world as a more gentler nation than history had ever previously presented.

It was sheer brilliance.

Taking studious notes on Sun Tzu's teachings, Russia let America wear itself down, tear itself apart, and take out Russia's enemies and competitors. And now, Russia could reap the spoils.

Not even Stahl's highest ranking men in the Command ever questioned his motives, up until the moment he announced, at that fateful meeting, that the Command was now under Russian control. Word announced, to make official statements to the Northwest Command's team, by Russia's President, himself, who had phoned to thank Stahl for his loyal service to the KGB and his homeland. The world, however, would hear a different story and never know of Russia's deceptions, although conspiracy theorists would tell tales for decades to follow.

Stunned by the news, Stahl's men, some that had served under him in Desert Storm, could do little, but file out of the room and try to come to terms with the words that had just been spoken. They would struggle with the idea that their greatest hero was a traitor.

Only Commander Thomas would remain and question. And, to a large degree, Stahl respected that.

But, none had reason to fear, they had been loyal to Stahl.

Although, flashes of the atrocities committed on their own killing fields would flash in the minds of every man, which had unknowingly been serving at Lucifer's throne. *How could he have deceived them all, they would wonder?* How could one nation, so perfectly delude another and walk away with everything they had worked for, for so many years?

It seemed too easy.

The Russians were nothing, if they were not patient and strategic in matters of war. They, unlike America, had learned from the mistakes of their forefathers, and would now take their rightfully earned place of power.

They were now, unquestionably, the world's most dominant financial and military power. Now, sitting with the world's largest oil supply, and a military force that literally encircled the earth, they would make the world dependent upon them. They now had the world's largest stockpile of nuclear weapons, and they had proved, unlike America, the Soviets were not afraid to use them. The implications to global politics were frightening. They would give other nations no choice, but to align, or meet the fate of the Middle East. They made no apologies.

Stahl prepared himself to take his place at the table of the Imperial Soviet Union, as many of his once trusted servants found their bodies discarded on the same fields on which they once took aim. The new empire born, they quickly began taking back control of a country that had willingly allowed itself to be torn apart. As nations applauded, the Russians were already planning their next move. Although they had seemingly taken the world's queen from the board, there were other pieces to be won.

For the new Imperial Soviet Union, this was just the beginning...

.

www.ingramcontent.com/pod-product-compliance
Lightning Source LLC
Chambersburg PA
CBHW020925020726
47495CB00002B/345